Veil of Dawn's Promise

AI-Watched City - Quiet Rebel
A CYRONIS NOVEL

Joe Sarkic

I dedicate this to my wife, whose unwavering patience and boundless support became the guiding light that illuminated my path through countless days and nights, transforming a mere concept into a living, breathing narrative.

Contents

Chapter 1 - The Edge of Night

As dusk unfurled its velvet cloak over the expansive cityscape of Cyronis, the world transitioned into a spectacle of golden radiance. The setting sun cast a fiery glow over the city, painting the sky with a tapestry of burnt orange and magenta hues, which slowly gave way to the moon's emerging silver luminescence, like a master artist handing over the canvas to the night's cool whispers.

During this enchanting transition, the towering skyscrapers cast long dancing shadows across the metropolis, each one a silent rhythm syncing with the heartbeat of Cyronis itself, blurring lines between the animate and inanimate. These shadows, stretching from the city's heart to the distant horizon, blurred the boundaries between the urban expanse and the darkening sky, creating a dynamic interplay of light and shadow as the sunlight played its final encore.

Below these giants lay an ancient cobblestone street, smooth from the passage of countless travelers over an ageless span. This charming path, with its old-world allure, wound toward a bustling marketplace, echoing with the soft whispers of footsteps and distant conversations.

Leaning against a cool, rough-hewn stone of an age-old wall, a lone figure stood enveloped in the market's shadowed embrace, where the ancient heartbeats of the city whispered tales to the moonlit skies. This observer bore witness to the vibrant tapestry of life unfurling along the marketplace streets.

Each stall, draped in vermilion, azure, emerald, and gold, brought vibrant life to the marketplace. The colors stood out vividly against the backdrop of the city, gleaming under the light. Lanterns, in a myriad of shapes and colors, floated overhead, suspended by unseen forces, their luminance casting a radiant ballet of light and shadow across the stalls and ancient cobblestones below.

Merchants, a spectrum of ambition and hope personified, heralded their wares with voices rich in eagerness and sincerity. Their gestures, as if choreographed, beckoned the onlookers to pause, to gaze, to yearn. Amid this symphony of commerce, the future made its presence known through the gleam of holodisplays. These luminous beacons oscillated between the enticement of goods and the stern countenance of governmental edicts.

"For Your Safety, Always Comply," they intoned, a mantra echoing the cost of peace within Cyronis. "Cyronis Thrives Under Watchful Eyes," they proclaimed, painting a portrait of surveillance as the bastion of prosperity. "The Watchers Protect," they vowed, the promise—or perhaps the threat—left hanging in the air like the unspoken end of a conversation. These proclamations, nestled amidst the allure of commerce, spun a narrative of benevolence intertwined with control, illustrating the city's inherent duality.

Above this bustling tableau, the dominion of the Watchers was omnipresent. Their silent vigil was marked not only by drones—quiet yet pervasive—but also by the constant watch of cameras. These devices recorded every moment, capturing the rhythm of the streets, archiving every transaction, every whispered secret, within their digital annals. The Watchers, standing vigilant across various blocks of the market, had dual roles as the overt and the covert guardians of order. While some adorned the stark uniforms that heralded their authority, others dissolved into the throng, their true intentions masked by the guise of the mundane, be they merchant or passerby.

To this lone observer, a figure ensconced in the depths of their own darkness yet illuminated by an acute perceptiveness, Cyronis was laid bare: a city of stark contrasts and intricate contradictions, where the echoes of the past mingled with the whispers of the future, where the dance of freedom and surveillance was performed with a delicate, if uneasy, grace. This silent sentinel, an observer in their own right, absorbed not merely the sights and sounds but the very essence of Cyronis, understanding its complex narrative not with judgment but with a profound, silent acknowledgment of the beauty and the burdens that define its existence.

Having seen enough, the lone figure drifted away from the wall's embrace, weaving through the throng with a presence that whispered of epochs seamlessly folded into the fabric of the present. As they passed by a vendor's nook nestled amidst the vibrant chaos of the marketplace, they gave only a fleeting glance at a display of technological marvels, which starkly contrasted with their timeless aura. Among these marvels was a device that defied gravity: an orb whose core emitted a brilliance that painted the surrounding air with an aurora of light. Adjacent to it, a slender, crystalline rod pulsed with an inner light, casting dynamic shadows that seemed to narrate their own story. Not far from this, a compact cube hovered silently, its surfaces intermittently becoming transparent to reveal a miniature, luminous galaxy swirling within. Despite the boundless imagination of Cyronis's denizens manifested in these devices, the figure showed no more than a fleeting interest.

A beam from one of the devices momentarily illuminated the side of the figure's face, revealing her blue eyes and a mark to the side of an eye, in the shape of a crescent moon. The rest of her face was hidden by a dark covering. As quickly as the light had caressed her visage, it dissipated. She was once again enveloped in the anonymity of the shadows, continuing her passage through the marketplace as an enigma amidst the tapestry of life and innovation.

As two women talking approached her, she did not alter her path. Instead, she forced them to part as her movements carried her between them. One of the women looked over her shoulder, annoyed, and appeared to swear under her breath.

The lone figure moved purposefully, navigating the crowd with ease. To onlookers, she seemed to be just another person making her way through the market, blending into the evening's activities. But those with discerning eyes caught subtle hints that betrayed her concealed intent: the nearly imperceptible pauses beside certain stalls, the furtive piercing glances from beneath her hood, and the nimble gloved fingers that lingered, ever-present yet never making contact.

At a defining moment, a striking procession of city Watchers makes its way through the bustling marketplace. These enforcers, clad in sleek military gear that catches the flickering lights, present an imposing sight. Their tactical vests and uniforms, made from cutting-edge materials, reflect the vivid hues of the marketplace, creating a captivating effect. Adorning their gear are patches and insignias of deep crimson, adding a dramatic touch to their appearance. These details, swaying gently with each movement, offer a vivid contrast to the utilitarian, dark fabric of their military attire.

The Watchers move in unison, their boots striking the cobblestone with a rhythmic, authoritative cadence that reverberates through the air. Each step appears calculated, exuding an air of disciplined power and control. Their presence is not just physical but also a tangible force, emanating the essence of law and order.

As they march, the throng of market-goers instinctively part, creating a clear path for the procession. Faces in the crowd display expressions mixed with respect and a touch of apprehension. Eyes follow the Watchers' every move, some with admiration for their unwavering duty, others with a hint of caution regarding what their presence signifies.

In stark contrast to the crowd's reaction, the hooded figure in the vicinity exhibits a different demeanor. She moves with a fluid grace that allows her to seamlessly blend into the background. As the Watchers advance, she becomes just another shadow in the evening's tapestry, her presence unnoticed, her intentions concealed. Her cloak, unassuming and nondescript, serves as the perfect camouflage against the backdrop of the market's vibrant activity.

The hooded figure re-emerged once the procession of Watchers had passed, their echoing steps gradually fading into the distance. Her emergence was subtle, almost like a specter materializing from the shadows. Undeterred by the Watchers' intimidating display, she continued on her path with purposeful movements that carried an air of mystery toward a grand fountain located at a bustling crossroads. Carved from polished marble and glistening onyx, the fountain featured a majestic sea dragon spiraling upwards, its mouth releasing cascades of water. It usually attracted a lively crowd; but this evening, as the twilight deepened, the area around the fountain was relatively calm.

With careful, calculated movements, she drew a small cube from within her cloak, cradling its cool, smooth obsidian surface in her palm. Its appearance gave no hint of its intended purpose. Leaning over the fountain, she deftly placed it into a hidden recess at the base of the water. To any casual observer, this artifact appeared to integrate seamlessly with its surroundings, now hidden yet poised.

She continued onwards through the marketplace's heart, her movements fluid as she navigated the maze of stalls overflowing with electronic artifacts and curious wares, her path lit by the soft glow of lanterns that hung like stars in the night sky. Around her, the air was alive with the murmur of voices and the scent of spices and sweet perfumes. Ahead, a bench worn by time lay hidden in the shadow of a towering clock, its face a silent guardian of the square. With a glance that barely disturbed the air, she slid a second cube into the darkness beneath the bench, its presence as discreet as a whisper. Lifting her eyes to the ancient clock, she noted the time: 8:48, a silent witness to her secret rendezvous.

Moving to a quieter section of the market where old-time merchants had set up permanent stalls, there stood a venerable oak tree, a living relic from a bygone era that the city's residents named Whisperingwood. Its expansive canopy offered solace by day and transformed into a serene sanctuary as night fell. The ground around it was blanketed with fallen leaves, their scent rich with the essence of fertile soil. Behind the tree, hidden from the casual gaze of passersby, the cloaked figure discovered a natural hollow. It was a secret pocket within the tree's aged bark, perfectly sized and secluded. Carefully, a third cube found a home in the hollow, its presence almost merging with the ancient wood.

After completing all tasks, she spent a moment surveying the area. Feeling content, she then blended with the meandering crowd and vanished into obscurity.

Nearby, a towering figure with silver hair and a meticulously groomed beard emerged from the crowd, his presence commanding attention. His deliberate and authoritative movements hinted at a man accustomed to being in charge. A mix of inquisitiveness and wariness in his eyes further underscored his commanding presence. Automatically, the crowd gave way, sensing the significance of this towering man. Purposefully, he surveyed the surroundings, his gaze sweeping through the crowd as though in search of something or someone.

He paused at a jeweler's booth, where gemstones shone brilliantly. However, the gleaming treasures didn't captivate him. Instead, a discreet head shake from the jeweler—a balding man with a dark military mustache—signaled a quiet understanding.

Advancing further, he approached a stall filled with the intoxicating scent of exotic fragrances. The vendor, a young woman with raven-black hair and piercing green eyes, didn't tout her aromatic wares. Instead, she subtly handed him a tiny vial, its contents shrouded in mystery, their fleeting exchange against the backdrop of the bustling street easily missed by the casual observer.

As he continued deeper into the market, he took notice of every person, each whisper of cloth against stone, scrutinized and dissected under the weight of his attention. His eyes, twin orbs of piercing judgment, missed nothing—every presence absorbed, cataloged in the vast library of his mind.

Amidst the flow of life that continued to part from his path, two Watchers, poles apart in the journey of years—one in the spring of youth, the other in the winter of age—found themselves ensnared by his scrutiny. As if touched by the hand of fate, they straightened, spines aligning with the sudden tension that his gaze wrought upon them. The elder, with a wisdom honed by the passage of countless moons, conveyed a silent edict with a mere shake of his head, a gesture echoing the jeweler's earlier message.

Undeterred, the towering man's search continued.

Meanwhile, at the fountain, where water danced playfully in the lantern's glow, a subtle shift occurred. Alongside the calming sound of flowing water, a faint hum emerged, causing gentle ripples across the fountain's surface. An observant eye might notice a soft, pulsating glow emanating from within the water—a mesmerizing dance of eerie green light reflecting in the water's undulations amidst the golden rays of the lanterns.

Murmurs wove through the thinning crowd in the market. "Did you catch that sound?" a vendor paused his tidying to ask. Another quipped back, "What sound?" her voice quivering with barely masked nervousness.

Beside the aged wooden bench that rested in the shadow of the majestic clock tower, passersby experienced an unusual sensation: a subtle vibration originating from the soles of their feet, which sent a faint, tingling thrill coursing up their legs. A few observant souls noticed a delicate glimmer of green light, almost ethereal in its quality, spilling out across the ground at the base of the bench, casting an otherworldly glow that hinted at hidden mysteries beneath.

The most unsettling transformation occurred at the base of the ancient oak tree. Unlike the other two locales, no distinct light or sound manifested here. Instead, an intangible change wafted through the air. The tree's customary fresh scent, mingled with the earthiness of the soil, now bore a metallic tang, evoking the charged aftermath of a lightning storm. The leaves, which typically whispered in the nocturnal breeze, appeared eerily still, as if in suspended breath, awaiting an indeterminate event.

As the silver crescent moon rose higher in the sky, casting a luminous glow on the city, the once lively and cheerful marketplace transitioned into an arena of suspense. The three inconspicuously placed, yet purposeful cubes began a silent symphony of humming and glowing. Most of the market remained largely unaware, except for a select few who perceived an eerie undertone.

The air, previously fragrant with roasted meats and floral perfumes, took on an unsettling aroma—charged, metallic, and electrifying. This scent tingled the nostrils and created an uncanny static sensation on the skin, reminiscent of the tension before a storm. As this electric atmosphere intensified, the city's mechanical guardians showed signs of malfunction.

Surveillance drones, previously hovering with effortless precision, began to waver. Their lights blinked erratically, and they descended from the sky, crashing onto the cobblestones below. As each drone fell, gasps and screams erupted. Amidst the chaos, the Watchers, usually the epitome of calm and control, showed the first signs of panic. Their usual stoic expressions were replaced with furrowed brows and hurried whispers, a clear testament to their uncertainty. Glances were exchanged, filled with questions none could answer, as they grappled with the sudden loss of their aerial allies.

Many of the floating devices in the market stalls followed the drones' example and dropped, some shattering as they bounced against the stalls and fell to the hard stone roadway. Vendors and visitors scattered in panic; their evening's tranquility disrupted by sudden turmoil. The Watchers, now amidst the disarray, struggled to maintain order. Their attempts to communicate were hampered as their own devices flickered and failed, leaving them visibly unsettled and momentarily directionless.

The array of ever-watchful wall-mounted cameras, strategically positioned for both the market's safety and surveillance, ceased their vigilant watch. This cessation of the all-encompassing electronic gaze resulted in a brief lapse in the city's encompassing fabric of security.

As the surveillance fell silent, the clock tower heralded the arrival of 9 o'clock with a robust clang. The first bell's resounding toll pierced the quiet, its deep vibrations spreading across the cobblestone streets, filling the pause left by the silenced monitors with a resonant declaration of the hour.

From the network of alleyways, shadowy figures began to emerge. Previously mere extensions of the darkness, they had been there all along, unseen and unnoticed, their presence as imperceptible as the night air. These figures moved with an elegance that was both mesmerizing and terrifying. Their fluid movements in the shadows resembled specters, rendering them nearly invisible to the untrained eye.

The clock's chimes rang out, marking the hour with a resonant echo that cut through the market's lively noise. At the sound of the bell striking two, shadows began to emerge, cloaked figures blending into the panicked hustle of the crowd. With each subsequent chime, more joined, moving unseen until the ninth toll, at which they sprang forth. One Watcher found himself tragically unprepared as he was the first to fall victim to an assailant's naked blade—a stark and gleaming weapon that seemed almost to materialize from the shadows themselves. In a swift, merciless arc, the blade found its mark, leaving the Watcher crumpled on the cobblestones.

The attackers, previously mere murmurs hidden in the darkness, emerged as harbingers of chaos, their assault sharply reminding everyone of the thin line between order and anarchy in Cyronis.

In the ensuing chaos, two Watchers, one bearing the weight of many years and the other considerably younger, found themselves oblivious to the peril that stalked them. Camouflaged within the commotion, two assailants closed in with deadly intent. They moved with a silent, predatory efficiency, weaving through the dispersing crowd, inching ever nearer to their targets without raising any alarm, before striking swiftly. The younger guardian's face registered utter shock the instant a weapon struck him down with fatal accuracy.

The elder Watcher, suddenly grasping the full gravity of his predicament, reached for his weapon in a desperate bid for defense, but his reaction came too late. Another assailant emerged, executing a swift, forceful action that silenced him before he could even react.

Near the central fountain's cascading waters, a Watcher found himself deep in discourse with a jeweler. Unbeknownst to the engrossed pair, two enigmatic shadows crept closer, their approach masked by the din of the marketplace. A glint of menace reflected in a polished bauble caught the jeweler's eye, yet the moment to act passed in a whisper. With swift and fatal grace, the intruders extinguished the lives of both the vendor and the Watcher, leaving silence in their wake.

As the grim scene unfolded, the stark reality became inescapable: the Watchers, the bastions of surveillance and peace, were marked for death. This grim fate also extended to certain civilians, known for their keen observations and their affiliations with these guardians. The air, once filled with the mundane murmurs of daily commerce, now thrummed with a palpable sense of dread.

Despite the shock that gripped their ranks, the remaining Watchers mustered their resolve. In the heart of chaos, they sought order; against the tide of fear, a semblance of defiance. Barricades emerged from the cobblestones and overturned stalls, commands cut through the air, and within the whirlwind of turmoil, they fashioned fragile havens. Yet, despite all their efforts, they were continually outmaneuvered, their strategies undone by adversaries with almost preternatural foresight.

Standing in the center of the cobblestone street, not far from the ancient tree, the towering man with hair like moonlit silver watched the chaos unfold, his expression a blend of concern and contemplation. Before him, a panicked crowd burst into a frenzy, parting to reveal the grim scene of a Watcher, lifeless and painted crimson against the pale stone. Nearby, another guardian stood on the precipice of doom as a shadowy presence crept closer. The silver-haired man tensed, prepared to intervene, but his attention was captured by a fleeting movement at the edge of his vision. A shadowy silhouette, quick as a ghost, vanished into the night, slipping into an alley. With the silent grace of a predator, he left the imperiled Watcher to his fate and darted after the elusive shadow.

Rounding the corner of a building, the silver-haired man came to an abrupt halt, facing a short dead-end where his quarry was ensnared. Against the cold, stark wall stood an elder, fear widening his eyes, revealing the grim acceptance of his fate. Shadows from his hood deepened the lines of age and dread on his face, yet failed to hide his once formidable, now diminished, stature or the wisdom etched into his gaze.

The towering adversary, exuding an overwhelming presence, narrowed the distance with intent and purpose. His focus, sharp and predatory, never strayed from the elder, making the alleyway seem to constrict around them. Yet, in the elder's stance was a defiance, a silent refusal to bow to the impending doom. Their gazes locked, and with a calm borne of acceptance, the elder yielded to his fate with quiet dignity. "Good evening, Commander," he said with some familiarity.

The Commander, in stark contrast to the old man's silence, responded with a smile and retrieved a vial from his attire, given by a female vendor. Activating it with an embedded switch, the vial erupted into a vibrant glow, illuminating the dim alley with an otherworldly light. Its eerie green luminescence and the dramatic shadows it cast transformed the scene into a haunting spectacle, with the Commander looming over his quarry, the mundane vial now a source of ghostly light.

With a deliberate gesture, he aimed the vial at the old man, who was frozen in terror. Under the Commander's control, the vial drew out shimmering, spectral streams from the elder. These luminous tendrils, aglow with vibrant energy, flowed from the man into the vial, shimmering as if the very essence of life itself was being inexorably siphoned away.

The old man's visage, etched by time, now bore even deeper marks of distress. His once lively complexion faded to an ashen pallor, a stark backdrop to the vibrant energy funneling into the vial. His eyes, previously alight with terror, now seemed to dim, their inner light waning.

His legs, potential instruments of a futile escape, now quivered, barely supporting his weakening frame. It appeared as if the vitality that once propelled him was being siphoned away, leaving behind nothing but a shell.

The alley, a silent observer to this unsettling act, had transformed from an ordinary passageway into the backdrop for a macabre drama. Here, the line between the tangible and the mystical blurred, with the old man's once fervent life force reduced to a mere extract, drawn forth by the ominous luminescence of the vial.

In this moment of heightened suspense, fate, both capricious and untamed, played its hand. From the shroud of night, a figure emerged — not imposing in stature but commanding in essence. A woman, the architect behind the trio of cubes, stepped forth. Her arrival was sudden, her movements a tapestry of precision and grace. The Commander, caught in the snare of surprise, watched helplessly as the vial slipped from his grasp, struck by her decisive blow from a high arching kick. The vial met the cobblestones with a fatal kiss, shattering, its secrets spilling into the night air like a whispered curse.

In a fluid motion, she gracefully dropped, sidestepping his advance with the elegance of a shadow. Swiftly stepping behind him, she found her mark with lethal precision. A sharp, targeted blow to one of his kidneys unleashed a burst of excruciating pain, causing him to instinctively twist to the side, his hand flying to the afflicted area. The sudden agony disrupted his stance, forcing a stagger as he fought to maintain his composure, momentarily overwhelmed by the precision and potency of her strike.

The battle reached a fever pitch as the Commander, with a sudden burst of determination, unsheathed his charged weapon, signaling his intent to finish the duel. But she, with the agility of a panther, conjured a dagger from the shadows, its edge a silver flash in the night. With a precise and fluid motion, she struck his arm, the blade slicing through the air and disarming him with a clatter that echoed off the stone walls.

He barely flinched at the sting of the cut, his warrior's resolve allowing him to shrug off the pain. With a swift reaction, he seized her wrist in an iron grip, a move born of desperation and the instinct to dominate. Yet, contrary to his expectations, the dagger did not fall from her hand.

Undaunted by his grip, she executed a twist with the elegance of a dancer, her body moving with a flexibility that defied the solid hold he had on her. This movement, as unpredictable as a gust of wind through the narrow alley, allowed her to slip from his grasp with her weapon still in hand, and she launched a kick, as rapid and forceful as lightning, propelling him into the scattered remnants at the alley's edge. When he staggered to his feet, the alley was deserted - no adversary, no elder - leaving behind only the lingering echoes of their fierce engagement as proof of the intense encounter. Frustration and resolve mingled in his gaze as he surveyed the emptiness before him, leaving him to stew in a storm of wrath and determination. His eyes, alight with an almost otherworldly intensity, betrayed a tempest of emotions: anger, regret, and above all, an unwavering resolve to pursue his quest.

As he departed, his steps echoed against the cobblestones, each resonating with his determined mission. His form, gradually fading into the distance, left the tumultuous marketplace behind, now a scene of sorrow intertwined with the aftermath of violence. Lanterns that once illuminated joy now cast light on a landscape transformed by fear. The assailants, their departure as methodical as their attack, left chaos in their wake. In their absence, the Watchers, outmaneuvered and disoriented, scrambled to regroup amid the ruins of tranquility. The once-lively stalls, now silent, and the marketplace's heart, once vibrant, stood desolate under the night sky, a stark reminder of the night's harrowing events.

The final act in the marketplace centered on the enigmatic cubes as each commenced to radiate a verdant luminescence, intensifying to such brilliance that all who were present, found themselves compelled to avert their gaze, their hands rising in unison to shield their eyes from the searing emerald inferno.

Accompanying this blinding display, a trio of screeching cacophonies rent the air, a sonic assault so piercing that it drove all who were present to press their palms against their ears in a futile attempt to block out the harrowing din. The marketplace, once abuzz with the tranquil hum of evening commerce, was abruptly ensnared in this tumultuous tempest.

And then, as swiftly as it had erupted, the chaos receded into darkness and silence. The once vibrant scene now lay shrouded in an oppressive quietude, the sudden absence of sound and light as jarring as the spectacle that preceded it. Some Watchers amongst the sparse crowd, their senses returning, cast wary glances around the marketplace, seeking the source of the upheaval. Eyes darted between stalls, and the spots once occupied by the mysterious cubes.

But the cubes were gone, vanished as though they had never existed. In their place, dark patches marred where they lay, each a mute witness to the intense energy that had once coursed through the artifacts. These marks, reminiscent of scorch marks left by some unfathomable heat, still pulsed with a residual glow, except for the one in the fountain, which had now dimmed to nearly black within the steaming water.

Chapter 2 - City of Shadows

Dawn was more a concept than a daily reality within Cyronis. The city's horizon was forever masked by a veil of neon and steel. Sunlight struggled to penetrate the forest of skyscrapers, which seemed to compete with each other in their quest to touch the heavens. These structures were more than just buildings; they were titans of glass and metal, shimmering with the vibrant hues of neon lights that cut through the perpetual twilight.

Dominating the city's skyline stood the Nexus Tower, an awe-inspiring edifice that reached a staggering 285 floors, rising to an astonishing 1253 meters. More than an architectural marvel, it was Cyronis' lifeblood. This tower was the epicenter of city governance, the neural hub for The Watchers, and catered to the essential needs of the city's residents. Towering over adjacent structures, its peak audaciously pierced the heavens, grazing clouds of its own creation. Indeed, those clouds were the handiwork of the Nexus Tower and the advanced artificial intelligence many called Orion.

At its zenith, beneath a star-studded sky, the tower's peak emitted a faint glimmer of energy, the city's lifeblood. This luminescence gracefully ascended, unfurling above the clouds like a celestial tapestry, then spread outward, forming a protective dome over the metropolis. The dome, a marvel of technology, captured violet energy threads from the heavens. These delicate strands, interacting with the planet's weakened magnetic field, created a spectacle akin to an aurora borealis. The violet hues danced against the barrier, painting a surreal scene that shimmered in the night's embrace.

This display was more than a natural wonder; it symbolized the city's resilience and ingenuity. The dome, energized by the Nexus Tower, shielded Cyronis from external threats while transforming cosmic forces into the city's source of infinite energy.

Against the darkness of space and the stillness of the night, this aurora-like display was a vivid testament to the city's harmonious coexistence with nature, blending technology with cosmic beauty. Yet, on this day, even the formidable Nexus Tower seemed muted. The events from the previous night had sent shockwaves through its influential corridors. Despite its vast surveillance and seemingly omnipresent gaze, The Watchers had been blindsided. A challenge was posed, and the city held its collective breath, awaiting the unfolding drama.

As the city awakened to a new day, it did so with its usual vibrancy tempered by newfound apprehension. Beneath the neon lights, behind the holographic spectacles, and beyond the watchful eyes, there was a stirring of fear, a whisper of change, and the promise of a story yet to unfold.

The people below the Nexus dome had adapted to a life of continuous observation. Their behaviors spoke of a subtle, internalized choreography performed for the ever-present audience of lenses and sensors. Conversations in public spaces were conducted in moderated tones, punctuated with polite laughter and measured gestures. A mother might scold her child, but her voice never rose too high. Friends could debate, but they ensured their disagreements never got too heated. Subtle glances upwards often preceded certain topics, a non-verbal acknowledgment of the omnipresent listener above.

The Watchers' reach extended to every citizen's Personal Data Device, which continuously synced with Orion's ever watchful systems. These devices offered news updates, weather forecasts, personal schedules, and more. However, they also served as personal identification, tracking movements, transactions, interactions, and payments. To misplace one's personal device was not just an inconvenience; it was a grave offense.

Despite their control, The Watchers were not merely brute force tyrants. In many ways, they acted as guardians. When accidents occurred, response units were dispatched with astonishing speed, with drones deploying first aid even before emergency crews could arrive. Lost children were located promptly, thanks to personal implants embedded at the backs of their necks at birth. Moreover, the efficiency under The Watchers extended to the city's very framework: its infrastructure. The floating trains and public utilities operated with a precision that was nothing short of miraculous, a clear demonstration of an omnipresence that was about more than just surveillance. It embodied a commitment to efficiency, safety, and responsiveness that permeated every aspect of urban life.

Yet, amidst its vast influence, whispers of defiance could be felt, indicating that the spirit of some citizens hadn't entirely bowed. Shadows in the form of graffiti artists left behind murals that, superficially, seemed benign. But to those in the know, they bore encrypted messages visible only from just the right perspective. These rebellious strokes were fleeting, their creators vanishing into the ether before drones or enforcers could converge, leaving behind only their silent protests.

It was against this backdrop of subtle rebellion and omnipresent surveillance that a particular apartment, high above the bustling streets within one of the city's gleaming towers, stood out as an anomaly. This modest dwelling, an oasis seemingly untouched by the city's relentless neon glow, represented a stark departure from the external world. Stepping inside, one felt as if they had crossed into another realm, a sanctuary of tranquility amidst the perpetual momentum of the ever-watchful metropolis.

Inside, the contrast was immediately palpable. While the city's exterior was a synthesis of metal, glass, and ever-present neon, this dwelling celebrated the organic and tactile. Warm wooden panels embraced the walls, soft textiles covered the furniture, and living plants — a rarity in these modern times — adorned the space, injecting vitality. The gentle aroma of earth and blossoming flowers lingered in the air, a design choice that echoed a nostalgia for bygone eras.

Yet, in stark contrast to this homage to yesteryears, a technological wonder claimed its space. A single wall was transformed by a workstation that seemed plucked from the realms of tomorrow. Amidst the echoes of the past, this niche pulsed with the lifeblood of cutting-edge tech: holograms floated in the air, weaving through data streams, cryptographic sequences, and pulsating urban vistas. Nestled beneath, a console, bedecked with responsive touch panels and holographic displays, stood ready to spring to life at the slightest touch.

The bedroom within the apartment was a study in opulence, with a massive window that framed the sprawling metropolis and the towering Nexus, whose peak vanished into the clouds. Yet, this haven was occasionally breached by the fleeting shadows of drones, a subtle reminder of the world beyond its walls.

At the heart of this sanctuary, a grand bed stood as a focal point, its dark wood forming a stark contrast against the backdrop of lavish bedding. Plush pillows enveloped the room's sole occupant, a woman enshrouded in sheets that whispered luxury. From a distance, she appeared ethereal, her form bathed in the reflections from the towering city buildings, weaving a tapestry of light and shadow across her peaceful visage.

Up close, however, her peace was disrupted by visible signs of distress: brows furrowed in concern, soft gasps breaking the silence, and her hands tightly clutching the sheets as she navigated the tumult of her dreams.

Trapped within a nightmare's grip, she shifted restlessly, her movements a silent plea for release from the clutches of her unconscious fears. Wrapped in satin sheets, her body twisted in agitation. Her fingers clenched the fabric, desperately seeking comfort in the midst of her mental storm. Her muted cries, "Mom! ... Dad!" laden with vulnerability, pierced the room's modern tranquility.

As her dreaming reached a fevered pitch, her form stirred with increasing fervor.

Suddenly, she sat upright, gasping for air as if surfacing from the ocean's depths, with sweat beading her forehead in the room's dim light. As she took deep breaths to dispel the nightmare's remnants, her disoriented gaze swept across the room, the familiarity of her surroundings gradually calming her racing heart and bringing a fleeting relief, despite the dream's intensity lingering like an echo.

Her dreams, a mélange of fragmented images and emotions—longing, fear, sadness—unfolded like an incomplete puzzle, its pieces seemingly dredged from her subconscious. These recurring visions, increasingly frequent and unsettling, blurred the lines between dreams and reality, seeding her mind with unanswered questions.

Particularly haunting were the voices—affectionately dubbing her "little poet" and her own childlike cries for her parents—elements so foreign yet emotionally charged that she questioned their origin and whether they were echoes of lost memories surfacing unexpectedly.

Awakening from these visions in a cold sweat, she wrestled with their vividness and the reality of a potentially forgotten life and family before her current existence, a revelation that plunged her identity and known reality into chaos.

Caught in the liminal space between memory and imagination, these dreams suggested fragments of a lost childhood, forcing her to navigate a maze of uncertainty about her past and its impact on her identity.

Clad in nightwear designed for comfort and thermal regulation, she moved to the bed's edge, where the cool floor beneath her feet served as a tangible anchor to the present, offering a semblance of stability amid the turmoil of her unraveling dreams.

Leaning forward, elbows resting on her knees, she let her fingertips graze her neckline, finding solace in the familiar touch as it anchored her amidst the dream's disorienting aftermath.

Her gaze then shifted to the expansive window, where dawn's early light fought the city's haze, reflecting off steel and glass towers, with the Nexus Tower standing tall as both her workplace and a symbol of order. This view of Cyronis, with the tower's dominance, tethered her to the city's pulse, readying her for the day.

Elysa Jane Hawthorne rose, her movements blending control and elegance as she navigated her space, her gown encapsulating her form's harmony with the environment. Each step was a measured ballet of strength and grace, embodying her life's delicate balance between vulnerability and resilience.

Elysa walked toward her home office, a space carefully organized to meet her work demands and her desire for order amid chaos. The design blended seamlessly from her living area, where soft curves contrasted with sharp lines, rich textures complemented sleek surfaces, and calm shades were enlivened by bold accents, defining the character of her workspace.

As she neared her desk, a familiar voice punctuated the room's stillness. "Good morning, Elysa."

"Good morning, Orion," she responded, a tinge of fatigue evident in her voice. This exchange was a staple in her daily ritual, but today, the aftermath of her restless night pressed down upon her. Remarkably humanistic for an artificial voice, its masculine timbre conveyed a calm that contrasted starkly with typical digital inflections.

"I need a coffee and two strong headache pills," she uttered, seeking solace from the echoes of her disrupted sleep.

Without delay, a concealed panel to the right of her desk slid open. Within the alcove, a freshly brewed cup of coffee emitted tendrils of steam, its rich scent promising both warmth and rejuvenation. Next to the cup lay two distinctive blue pills, engineered for swift alleviation of pain.

Elysa paused to marvel at the wonder that was Orion. Far surpassing any ordinary household AI, Orion functioned as the very neural network of Cyronis, weaving itself into every technological strand of the expansive city. At the core of this urban sprawl, it transitioned effortlessly from overseeing vast infrastructures—like transport grids, power systems, and security frameworks—to aiding in day-to-day household tasks. Orion's reach was boundless, its sensors blanketing every crevice, capturing both sights and sounds to ensure Cyronis flourished under its vigilant gaze.

However, despite its computational prowess and its ability to ingest immense data streams, Orion had its confines. It lacked true consciousness. It could discern patterns, forecast scenarios, and even replicate empathy to an extent. Yet, it was bereft of genuine emotions, incapable of mulling over those profound existential queries that occasionally plagued Elysa's nights. While Orion stood as an emblem of technological marvel, it was not, and could never become, truly sentient. It functioned as both protector and mentor, but it couldn't grasp the profound depths of human emotion or appreciate the subtleties that rendered life in Cyronis both enchanting and, at moments, deeply challenging.

Orion's surveillance was unyielding. Its knowledge was expansive, adeptly anticipating Elysa's needs even before they were articulated. She never had to detail her coffee preference, specify her required medication, or determine their timing. Orion observed, learned, and adapted, rendering her demanding mornings slightly more bearable.

Reaching into the panel, Elysa cradled the cup, letting its warmth envelop her hands. This tangible sensation anchored her. She procured the pills and swiftly consumed them, using a mouthful of the steaming beverage to assist their descent, slightly scorching her esophagus as the pills slid down her throat. The coffee's inherent bitterness was a solace, a consistent anchor in her ever-fluid world.

With her immediate needs attended to, she settled into her chair, allowing its advanced ergonomic design to contour around her physique. With Orion interwoven into her surroundings, she felt fortified and primed to tackle whatever challenges the day might present. Strengthened by technology and propelled by her indomitable spirit, Elysa felt a sense of readiness.

As she relished her rich aromatic coffee, Orion's voice gently broke the morning's stillness. "Elysa, you should be apprised of an incident that transpired last evening. It has made the headlines."

Elysa's expression shifted to one of piqued curiosity, her morning routine momentarily forgotten. She placed her coffee cup down, her movements deliberate, signaling her focus shifting to the unknown news. "Play the news on my desk display," she requested, her tone laced with intrigue. As the holographic screen sprang to life, revealing the stern face of a government spokesperson, Elysa leaned forward, her eyes sharp with anticipation.

The spokesperson began detailing a malevolent act by The Veil of Dawn. Elysa's curiosity slowly morphed into concern as the gravity of the situation began to dawn on her. The previous tranquility of her morning was replaced by an eager attentiveness, ready to absorb and understand the unfolding events.

The holographic projection vividly depicted the marketplace, a place Elysa knew intimately—its vitality and vibrancy now cruelly snuffed out. Images transitioned from joyous families and animated vendors, to the harrowing aftermath of the attack. The desolation of the once-thriving market square, now a mournful expanse, struck a chord deep within her. Among the debris lay the chilling emblem of The Veil of Dawn: a crescent moon painted against a building wall. These haunting images, combined with the news presenter's somber tone, bore down on Elysa with overwhelming force. Grief for the lost innocence of a place she held dear welled up inside her, mingling with the melancholy cast by her unsettling dreams. Her fleeting tranquility was shattered, replaced by a deep, acute awareness of the tragedy that had unfolded disturbingly close to her own world.

"The search for the culprits is underway," continued the spokesperson, his resolute tone unwavering amidst such bleak revelations. He gazed intently into the camera, forging a connection with the myriad unseen spectators. "The government is committed to ensuring thorough retribution," he said, pausing briefly to let the weight of his declaration permeate the airwaves. "A significant reward awaits those who can offer leads resulting in arrests." His voice, tinged with urgency, underscored the significance of his statement. His unwavering gaze penetrated the camera, almost as though he was beseeching each individual viewer to heed the call.

"Any information, however inconspicuous, might be the key to apprehending these offenders." His pronouncement lingered in the quietude of Elysa's space, a poignant appeal amidst a metropolis grappling with trauma and sorrow.

The room, once a tranquil sanctuary, now felt like a prison, amplifying her growing fears. The constant hum of data streams and the broadcast's echoes created a tumultuous noise, reflecting her inner chaos. The screen's glow cast unsettling shadows, embodying the terror that had seeped into her city. Elysa's view of The Veil of Dawn, previously regarded as freedom fighters against tyranny, was now marred by their actions that starkly contrasted with her beliefs, causing a deep sense of betrayal and confusion. This contradiction seeded doubts and fears, as she struggled to reconcile these violent acts with the group's stated aim of challenging Cyronis's oppressive regime without resorting to chaos.

Her unique access to a rich mosaic of clandestine tales, fragmented data, and covert channels enables her to grasp the complex essence of the faction. In the data-driven operations of Orion, Data Miners like her are crucial, blending sophisticated data analysis with the indispensable human elements of intuition and soul, akin to digital archaeologists who mine the present for hidden narratives rather than the past, revealing the veiled truths of a society shrouded in surveillance.

Elysa and her peers represent the vital human touch amidst impersonal datasets, adept at uncovering stories and secrets that transcend mere numbers. Their keen perception of data's subtle shifts — a skill that eludes even advanced algorithms — melds logic with a deep empathy for human motives, making them indispensable in an era overshadowed by artificial intelligence. Their work breathes life into entities like The Veil, portraying them as vibrant beings with goals and fears, thereby highlighting the profound gap between mere data analysis and genuine understanding.

Daily, Elysa engages with her state-of-the-art console, interpreting the data streams that capture Cyronis's essence, from whispered conversations to the city's heartbeat of actions and transactions. Her task is to sift through this data deluge for signs of discord or hidden dangers, a vital role in maintaining the city's fragile peace. As she tracks the faint digital footprints of resistance groups and potential rebels, she embodies the city's watchful guardian, alert to the faintest hints of unrest.

Yet, the role of a Data Miner in Cyronis is fraught with moral dilemmas, straddling the line between public safety and privacy invasion. Despite her reservations about the intrusive nature of her work, the prevailing dystopian ethos deems such surveillance necessary for the city's stability. Elysa's expertise not only uncovers threats but also places her at the heart of a perpetual ethical quandary, emblematic of the city's struggle between order and freedom.

Today, within the Nexus Tower and the corridors of the Centralized Data Mining and Surveillance Agency (CDMSA) where Elysa worked, she anticipated heightened activity. The aftermath of the previous night's horrific attack would undoubtedly echo through its expansive halls. She could vividly imagine her fellow Data Miners, now primed to dissect the vast influx of information related to the grim event. A palpable sense of urgency would permeate the environment, with each analyst deeply engrossed in the monumental task ahead. Elysa felt the weight of the day pressing down on her. A growing sense of unease overshadowed her typically upbeat disposition.3 The significance of her role as a Data Miner felt amplified, and she sensed the coming challenges would test her mettle.

Lost in contemplation over the bleak update about The Veil of Dawn, Elysa momentarily lost track of time. A swift glance at her digital clock snapped her back to reality, the luminescent digits warning her of the morning's rapid advance. Realizing she was dangerously close to being late, a wave of urgency washed over her.

The clock's relentless march echoed in Elysa's pulse as she sprang from the levitating embrace of her chair, holograms winking out like the last stars of dawn. Fabric whispered against her skin as she slipped into her professional attire, each movement honed by a life of necessity. With a glance at the unyielding digits of the clock, she dashed past her apartment door, her heart racing with the tempo of the city awakening beyond.

♦♦♦

As the front doors of the apartment building automatically slid aside, she stepped out into the muted hues of a city freshly kissed by rain. Her coat, echoing the overcast ambiance, was cinched snugly around her waist, its hem whispering against the tops of her knee-high boots. Beneath a deep gray cloche hat, her auburn hair stayed dry, shielded from the drizzle. Droplets clung to the hat's brim, sparkling mysteriously in the fading light, as she navigated the rain-slicked streets towards the day's uncertainties.

A gentle drizzle wrapped the city in a cloak of silvery mist, raindrops gently kissing her shoulders to leave glistening patches on her coat, which shimmered with the city's otherworldly lights. Her steps, encased in suede boots, danced across the puddles, sending ripples outwards in fleeting displays of ephemeral art. These boots, dark as the rain-soaked streets, blended with the pavement, enhancing the urban landscape's radiant glow.

Nearby, a sleek vehicle stood as a marvel of modern elegance fused with practicality. As Elysa neared, its gullwing doors unfolded skyward with a grace that mimicked an ethereal bird taking flight—a silent dance of engineering amidst the soft patter of rain. She glided into the seat with a fluidity that spoke of countless such entries, enveloping herself in a haven far removed from the damp chaos outside. The seat, upholstered in deep blue leather, enveloped her in its plush embrace, while the doors closed with a hush, sealing her away in an almost otherworldly tranquility.

She gently brushed the residual dampness from her coat and settled her hands on her lap, turning her attention to the holographic screen that illuminated before her. The dashboard, minimalist in design yet brimming with functionality, mirrored her own reflection amidst the soft luminescence of the on-screen commands. "Nexus Tower," she intoned, more as a ritual than an instruction, knowing full well that the AI anticipated her daily trajectory. "Of course, Elysa," replied Orion's soothing voice, tinged with a warmth and familiarity that belied its digital origin. The console illuminated, showcasing a 3D map plotting the optimal course to their destination. "Estimated arrival at the Nexus Tower is approximately 15 minutes."

Though physically solitary, Elysa never felt alone with Orion. The AI, ever-present but never invasive, anchored her days. Through the car's panoramic windshield, the rain-drenched city sprawled before her, each droplet narrating a vignette of Cyronis' heartbeat. Sensing her readiness, Orion elegantly commenced their journey. The vehicle hummed a gentle celestial tune, harmonizing with the rhythmic rain outside. Elysa relaxed, trusting Orion to expertly traverse the rain-swept avenues, finding solace in his familiar digital embrace.

As the aerocar glided gracefully through the city, Elysa's thoughts drifted. The rain's gentle tap on the windowpane became distant echoes of yesteryears, each droplet symbolizing a haunting shard of memory. Her reflection in the windowpane looked spectral, eyes shrouded in the phantoms of persistent nightmares. Just as the cityscape outside blurred into a wash of lights and shadows, the boundaries between the present and past began to dissolve.

In the quietude of the journey, as the world outside softened into a hazy dreamscape, Elysa's eyelids grew heavy with the weight of unspoken stories. The steady thrum of the aerocar's engines morphed into the comforting yet disquieting sounds of her childhood home. Muted conversations emanated from the kitchen below, her mother's fearful voice piercing the oppressive silence. Subtle sounds filled the void—her father's anxious pacing, the muted echo of his steps juxtaposed against the rhythm of her young, racing heart. The present moment faded, as if the aerocar had traversed not just space, but time, immersing Elysa in the vivid recollection of a distant fateful night.

In the dim shelter of the staircase, a twelve-year-old Elysa sought refuge. Peering through the banister's ornate filigree, she caught fleeting glimpses of a past too weighty for her young mind: her mother's face, veiled in shadows and concern, and her father, reduced to a ghostly silhouette under the weight of a grave secret. In the half-light of her fragmented memory, echoes of hushed, urgent whispers darted like elusive shadows. "It's suicidal," echoed with chilling resonance, the words tinged with a foreboding that sent shivers down her spine. They were her mother's words, steeped in a fear so visceral that it seemed to reverberate through the very fabric of her recollection. "He'll never let you back in."

Her father's presence was a constant, pacing back and forth, a silhouette of determination against the backdrop of despair. "I must find a way," he countered, his voice a determined whisper that cut through the mounting tension. Each step he took manifested the turmoil writhing within him, a relentless search for a glimmer of hope in the encroaching gloom.

As their dialogue dwindled to whispers too soft and fragmented to discern, the emotional turmoil etched on their faces spoke volumes. The candlelight flickered, casting an erratic glow that played upon their features, deepening the furrows of worry and painting their despair in stark relief against the darkness. Their words might have been lost, but the profound anguish and fear of impending doom were as palpable as if they had shouted.

Then, in a moment that pierced the somber stillness, her father's voice rose in a whisper that carried the weight of a thousand normal tones. "The future will be made by my little..." His words were cut off as darkness engulfed everything—a void that consumed all but the sharp, disjointed memories of chaos. Faceless figures, agents of a terrifying unknown, burst through the doors. Their movements, stark and efficient against the night, were a violent ballet. They came wielding threats made of steel and dread; their intentions as malevolent as the shadows that danced at their feet. In mere moments, Elysa's world was shattered. The shocked gasp of her mother and the muffled outcry of her father lingered in the air like chilling epitaphs of that fateful night.

A vast void of emptiness remained. Young Elysa, isolated on the staircase, felt the engulfing desolation. In the pitch-black, she remained seated, gripping the rail, weighed down by a heavy silence. That very silence now enveloped the aerocar, drawing her out from her memories and back to the present moment, a constant quest to decipher the enigma of her haunting visions.

Staring distantly, her voice barely audible, she whispered, "What are these memories? What do they signify?"

"We have arrived," Orion's voice intoned, jolting Elysa from her introspection. With her focus reestablished on her immediate surroundings, she observed the aerocar's graceful descent towards a vast arrival area, teeming with vehicles in various stages of embarkation.

Looming close, the monolithic Nexus Tower stood supreme amongst the structures of Cyronis. An architectural titan, it dramatically contrasted with the city's skyline—a potent emblem of the surveillance state's omnipresence. The tower's sheer size, symbolic of dominance and oversight, cast an imposing silhouette over the landing area, serving as an ever-present sentinel.

As the vehicle gently alighted on the wet concrete, Elysa watched its approach, accompanied by a subtle hum. The rain-drenched exterior of the Nexus Tower, its surfaces awash with water, combined with the haunting remnants of her memories, painted a somber picture of her current circumstances. The muted voice of the AI, resonating within the car's confines, underscored her arrival at the nerve center of Cyronis' surveillance apparatus.

Chapter 3 - Into the Unknown

Draped in a sleek, rain-deflecting trench coat, Elysa approached the main entrance of the Nexus Tower, a majestic archway flanked by guards reminiscent of metallic sentinels. Encased in gleaming carbon-fiber attire, their inscrutable visors glowed with unwavering vigilance beneath the ambient neon lights. Adjacent access points boasted high-resolution cameras, their ruby-red indicators gleaming ominously in the subdued light, monitoring every nuance with inexorable precision.

Beside these stoic guardians, towering full-body scanners hummed softly, the resonance of cutting-edge technology. For all who entered Nexus Tower, passage through these devices was mandatory, ensuring a meticulous sweep for concealed items or illicit materials. The machines pulsed with subtle energy, their interfaces bathed in a sterile green light, as they examined, processed, and classified each entrant.

Within the expansive confines of the tower, the atmosphere of stringent security persisted. From corridor to cubicle, from data chambers to strategic overlooks, guards stood sentinel. Their gazes constantly roamed; hands ever ready near holstered weapons. An inescapable aura of surveillance permeated the air, the pulse of unceasing watchfulness echoing throughout the vast edifice.

Wherever Elysa looked, the omnipotent reach of Cyronis's regime confronted her—the armed guardians, the ceaseless vigil of the cameras, and the daunting silhouette of the scanning equipment. Nexus Tower wasn't just an epicenter of information; it tangibly manifested the city's unyielding control, its vigilant oversight, and its relentless pursuit of stability and order. Nexus Tower was both a bastion in the literal sense and an emblematic fortress, guarding the intelligence and serving as the bulwark against threats to Cyronis's intricate governance framework.

Within its vast confines lay a labyrinth of specialized divisions, each claiming several floors. Strategically layered, these sectors collectively formed a dynamic hub of information and surveillance, buzzing incessantly with activity. The structure's design was intentional: the loftier the floor, the more critical its operations, underscoring the building's intrinsic hierarchy.

Spanning floors 271 to 278, an enclave accessible only to a select few, was the heart of the metropolis: Cyronis's primary AI data center. This was the city's digital nerve center, humming with a vast array of servers, processors, and storage mechanisms, processing immense volumes of data in mere moments. The ceaseless surge within this space echoed like the consistent rhythm of the city's AI, its sophisticated algorithms and calculations orchestrating every beat of Cyronis.

Above the 278th floor, at the apex of this architectural marvel, lay the enigmatic sanctum of the Chancellor and his select coterie. This innermost fortress, a citadel within a citadel, witnessed the birth of Cyronis's most pivotal decisions, the chiseling of strategies, and the issuance of sweeping directives. Shrouded in an aura of secrecy, its inner workings remained shielded, the knowledge of its affairs known only to an elite few.

Directly beneath the primary data center spread eleven floors, the nerve center of data mining operations — the Centralized Data Mining and Surveillance Agency. Here, within the intricate synapses of Cyronis's surveillance matrix, the ceaseless deluge of raw data was meticulously sifted, dissected, and deciphered. From these chambers, Data Miners like Elysa distilled insights, unearthed patterns, and spotlighted anomalies amidst the constant torrent of intelligence. Their discernments informed and influenced policies crafted in the highest corridors of power.

Elysa's journey through the expansive main floor was both deliberate and poised. Her strides carried her seamlessly towards the elevators, their gleaming chrome facades capturing the soft luminescence permeating the atrium. As she approached, a subtle chime heralded her presence, and the elevator doors glided apart, as if in silent recognition of her arrival.

Stepping into the enclosure, Elysa found herself enveloped in an ambiance that seemed to mirror her very essence. Bathed in the soft glow of discreetly recessed lighting, the compartment was a harmonious blend of brushed metal and smart glass, elements converging to fashion a contemporary sanctuary reflecting her solitary visage back at her.

As her foot alighted across the threshold, the elevator hummed to life. "Nice to see you again, Elysa," intoned Orion with soothing equanimity. The panels slid closed with a hushed sibilance, and Orion continued, "Destination set: Data Mining, 269th floor." A gentle lurch reverberated through the floor, signifying the commencement of their vertical journey. Within this seemingly mundane voyage between strata lay a microcosm of Cyronis's grand vision—a future harmonized through the symbiosis of technology and human exigency.

Sequestered within the ascending capsule, her ears sensitive to the rapid ascent's pressure change, Elysa was accompanied only by the low drone of the elevator, and the omnipresent, yet invisible, vigilance of Orion. Her reflection gazed back at her from the lustrous surfaces, a silent witness to her solitude. Yet, she felt anything but alone. She was enveloped in the rhythmic pulse of the Tower, cradled by the sonorous hum of its intricate machinery, and lifted within a vertical channel that linked the myriad layers of this sprawling building.

As the elevator's panels retracted, Elysa faced an imposing figure. The man stood at the entrance, arms folded defensively, his face marked by commanding authority. His voice, sharp and commanding, sliced through the hallway like a keen-edged blade. "You're late!" he thundered; his words imbued with a power that seemed to echo off the walls. The chastisement hung heavily in the air, amplified by the intensity of his piercing stare and the stoic calm that enveloped him like armor.

Elysa's response was swift, her defiance veiled in a whisper of steel. "Marek, I was not late," she declared, her voice firm, a bastion against his critique. "And surely, you've got more pressing matters than to linger here awaiting my arrival," she added, her words a subtle challenge as she brushed past him, her gaze briefly catching the newly minted nameplate by his office door, "Marek Ján Wójcik, CDMSA Director," it proclaimed.

Crossing the threshold of the now-open sliding doors, she remarked, "A new nameplate, I see." The words floated back to him; light yet heavy with silent observations.

Marek, momentarily rooted to the spot near the elevator, watched her enter his domain. A sigh escaped him, a mix of frustration and amusement, as he shook his head, a begrudging smile breaking through his usually unyielding façade. Collecting himself, he followed her into the sanctum of his office, the interaction leaving a subtle shift in the air, like the passing of a storm.

Just as Marek crossed the office threshold, a communication notification buzzed on his Personal Data Device wrapped around his left wrist. Stopping in his tracks, he touched his index finger to the skin below his right ear, activating the implanted ear-piece nestled beneath. He listened intently, his gaze lowering to the carpeted floor beneath him, his left hand brushing across his thinning hair. A shadow of concern darkened his face, etching deeper lines into his weary expression. With a subtle touch to his neck again, he turned off the device and proceeded to sit at his desk, which was cluttered with holographic displays flickering with unattended reports. Across from him, Elysa watched him intently, her sharp eyes missing nothing of the silent drama unfolding.

"What's wrong?" she inquired, the concern evident in her eyes as they cut through the heavy silence that enveloped the room.

Ignoring her question, Marek's response was strained, his voice barely above a whisper. "I assume Orion has already filled you in on what happened last night?" He avoided her gaze, the air between them charged with an unspoken tension.

"He played the news reports for me. I learned The Veil were responsible—they left their calling card on a wall—and that many innocent lives were lost." Her voice faltered slightly, betraying her inner turmoil. "Was no one apprehended?"

"Not one person."

"And what do the surveillance cameras show?"

"Not a single thing," Marek admitted, watching as surprise flickered across Elysa's features. "Something disabled all the drones and cameras before the assault began..."

"You mean slaughter," Elysa interjected, her tone sharpening at his euphemism. "And how could they disable all the surveillance?"

Marek offered a brief, apologetic look. "Yes, of course—slaughter. Sorry," he sighed deeply, the weight of the night's events pressing down on him. "It's been a long night." His gaze finally met hers, earnest and searching. "They managed to jam the drones in flight and shorted out the camera circuitry, all of The Watcher devices, and even some random electronics being sold at the market."

"Did The Watchers recognize anyone, see any faces?"

"They were all shrouded behind strange cloaks with hoods that seemed to repel the light from within, keeping each assailant wrapped in shadows."

"Why did you not call me right away?" Her voice was a blend of concern and mild reproach.

"There was nothing for you to analyze. Orion is still compiling the data." A soft chuckle escaped him. "And you are at your best when you are not tired."

"I am always at my best," she countered, undeterred.

"Of course," he conceded with a smile, then his expression sobered, the previous lightness fading. He hesitated, as if searching for the right words. "Elysa," he began, his tone heavy with significance, "you've been chosen to sift through the chaos, to unearth the truth hidden within this aftermath. The entire investigation now rests in your hands." The gravity of his words hung in the air, emphasizing the enormity of the task before her.

She suddenly stood up, her eyebrows arching upward, lips parting slightly in astonishment as she absorbed the implication of Marek's statement. Her surprise was palpable, mirrored not only in the widening of her eyes but also in the subtly heightened pitch of her voice. "You want me on this?" she questioned, her words imbued with a blend of astonishment and disbelief. Though her exterior remained poised, she could not wholly mask the surprise at his assignment—a task that clearly bore immense significance.

"Given the severity of the situation, I would have presumed senior members would be the ones commissioned for this task," Elysa elaborated, her voice regaining its steadiness as her brows furrowed in contemplation.

Rising from his chair, Marek responded with succinct clarity, a hint of rigidity returning to his tone. "This isn't my decision," he declared, elevating his right index finger in a skyward gesture. The motion served dual purposes—it directed Elysa's gaze toward the higher tiers of the building, where high-stakes decisions were made, and symbolically invoked the upper echelons of authority. "This directive comes from the top," Marek clarified, his eyes unflinchingly locked onto hers, reinforcing the importance and gravity of their mission. "That was the communication I received as we entered this room."

"But why me?" Her words lingered, heavy and haunting, in the charged air between them. It was more than a question; it was an echo of her disbelief, a silent plea for an explanation that might shed light on the unexpected directive that had singled her out. She stood motionless, her gaze fixed on Marek, her face a canvas of anticipation and trepidation.

Advancing towards her with an air of urgency that rippled through the dimly lit chamber, he extended his right hand in a silent command, gesturing for her to accompany him to the door. With a solemn nod, she complied, and they moved together to stand once again before the elevators.

Drawing a deep breath, Marek finally spoke, his voice tinged with a mix of confusion and concern. "Elysa, I'm as blindsided as you are." He spread his hands in a gesture of vulnerability. He paused, allowing the implications of his words to sink in. "One doesn't question the Chancellor's decisions."

Elysa whispered, her voice barely audible, "I wish they hadn't placed this burden on me."

Marek sighed, "I share that sentiment. If it were up to me, I would've shielded you from this. But it wasn't my decision to make."

A palpable silence enveloped them, emphasizing the seriousness of their shared predicament.

Elysa raised her eyes to Marek, the weight of the challenge ahead evident in her gaze. "Where should I even begin?" There was a rare vulnerability in her voice, a departure from her usual assertiveness.

Marek cleared his throat, the levity of their previous conversation dissipating, replaced by the seriousness of their current predicament. "Orion is collating all pertinent data as we speak," he began, his tone deliberate and laden with urgency. "Orion's reach is extending beyond just the marketplace. Every surveillance point within a five-kilometer radius is being tapped into."

The scope of the task took Elysa aback. "That's a vast expanse of data, " she remarked, momentarily overwhelmed by the sheer volume of information they would have to comb through. But her resilience quickly surfaced. "I assume it will take some time for Orion to analyze the data first?"

"Under normal circumstances, yes. But much of the data from within the marketplace that Orion could find appears to be corrupted. Orion's algorithms are drawing erroneous conclusions from it. This mission requires a human touch, a discerning eye, especially given its sensitivity," Marek responded.

He paused briefly before continuing, "Orion has been in overdrive for hours. By the time you return, the data will be ready for your inspection."

Elysa's eyes narrowed in confusion. "Return from where?"

Marek took a brief moment, choosing his words with care. "The marketplace—the very epicenter of the incident," he elucidated. "It's vital you witness it firsthand, discern any nuances that may elude Orion's advanced sensors. There are subtleties that human intuition perceives, which even the most sophisticated cameras might overlook." His statement underscored the unique value of a human perspective in the midst of technological prowess.

A flicker of astonishment crossed Elysa's face. "They expect me to be onsite? In the midst of the actual event?"

Marek, maintaining a calm facade, affirmed with a nod. "There's transportation arranged for you downstairs. They seem to want a holistic grasp of your insights," he remarked, stressing the word 'holistic' as if it bore deeper implications.

The elevator doors seamlessly slid open behind Elysa, unveiling a serene, luminous interior.

Gently guiding her towards the elevator, Marek's hand rested briefly on Elysa's back—a gesture of camaraderie and silent encouragement. It was a minuscule touch, but it conveyed a world of unspoken understanding between them.

Elysa hesitated for a heartbeat before stepping into the elevator's embrace. As the doors began to close, she glanced over her shoulder at Marek, lips parting to voice some final thought. But the closing doors interrupted her, sealing her within and muffling the words she'd intended to share. It symbolized a transition—from the comfort of the known to the uncertainty of what lay ahead.

Chapter 4 - With Fresh Eyes

Just as Marek had mentioned, a shining beacon of modern engineering awaited Elysa at the entrance. Its polished exterior mirrored the urban sprawl around her. Hesitantly, she stepped inside the vehicle, enveloped by its cool, state-of-the-art embrace. As the door sealed with a muted hiss, the aerocar gracefully ascended, charting a course to the marketplace—the heart of the enigma.

Soft illumination emanated from the dashboard, confirming her destination, and showcasing the route coordinates. An enveloping silence pervaded the cabin, allowing Elysa's thoughts to spiral amidst a tempest of emotions.

Suddenly, a compartment slid open, revealing a compact, yet sophisticated case. Orion's voice, smooth and unobtrusive, intoned, "An investigative kit is at your disposal, Elysa. Touch the case, and a multi-tiered biometric scan will grant access."

Gone were the days of the unwieldy cases of yesteryears. This kit was a paragon of modern aesthetics and efficiency—a matte black case, deceptively simple in appearance. Standard for field investigators, the case's lid unfolded gracefully, reminiscent of intricate origami. Soft, ambient lights illuminated the interior, briefly bathing the contents in sterilizing UV radiation before allowing access. This ensured the utmost purity of the tools within.

The case's interior was an ode to meticulous organization. Precision-cut foam cradles held shatter-resistant vials with smart caps, which communicated real-time chemical analysis data to Elysa's wearable tech. Adjacent to these, a cutting-edge pipette rested, its presence signifying the precision required in Elysa's work. Far from mundane, the case also housed an analysis scanner. This scanner, equipped with a digital interface, boasted unparalleled accuracy and featured a self-sustaining battery that demanded minimal recharging, streamlining Elysa's research without interruption.

Another section of the case unveiled an assortment of gloves—pristine latex for routine tasks, nitrile tailored for resisting chemicals, and a unique pair infused with antibacterial nanofibers, reserved for the most delicate of operations. Each was vacuum-sealed, ensuring they remained untainted until use.

Further exploration revealed even more cutting-edge tools: nimble drones designed for overhead reconnaissance, swabs embedded with nanotechnology capable of capturing the minutest of particles, and a collapsible microscope empowered with AI-driven imaging. Nestled alongside these was a compartment with essential first aid supplies—a nod to the unpredictability of fieldwork.

However, the crown jewel of this kit was its embedded AI framework. This virtual assistant meticulously tracked the status and inventory of each item, autonomously placing orders for replacements as needed, and even providing insightful usage pointers and safety protocols. Its secure cloud connection enabled Elysa to analyze her findings instantaneously with the main processing laboratory.

The kit's adaptability was another marvel. It could be hand-carried like a contemporary briefcase or donned as a backpack. The ergonomically designed straps ensured weight was evenly distributed, offering comfort during extended outings. And when placed on uneven surfaces, automatic stabilizers ensured its steadfast balance.

To Elysa, this state-of-the-art case felt like an extension of herself—a harmonious amalgamation of design and function, forged for the pioneers of investigative science.

Yet, as she sealed the case, a whirlwind of emotions surged within. Apprehension tightened its grip, intertwining with burgeoning doubt and a simmering resentment for her disrupted routine. Was this an unparalleled chance at excellence, or an unjust penance for an unknown transgression?

Fear's icy tendrils snaked through her, the gravity of her mission weighing heavily. The sprawling data, the omnipresent surveillance of Cyronis, and the myriad unknowns ahead only intensified her unease.

But beneath this tempest of emotions, a spark of anticipation ignited. The prospect of venturing into uncharted territory, of pushing her limits, stirred a fervent excitement deep within.

The incessant query, "Why me?" reverberated in her mind, an unyielding refrain lacking clarity. It was a riddle unto itself, one that danced at the edges of her consciousness, vying for attention alongside the enigma of the marketplace. With the city's silhouette streaming past, her gaze remained anchored to the distant horizon, her thoughts ensnared in introspection.

Time felt both elastic and fleeting. Lost in contemplation, her destination materialized sooner than anticipated. The tangible enormity of her mission became undeniable, casting an unmistakable shadow over her resolve.

Above, Elysa discerned the marketplace's transformation. Watchers stood like silent sentinels, cordoning off the area with an aura of strict vigilance. The market, once a tapestry of life and color, now lay dormant, most likely prepped for her arrival under Marek's directive. A chill coursed through her as she reckoned with the magnitude of the challenge ahead.

Descending towards this sanctified ground, Elysa's pulse quickened. The marketplace, traditionally alive with cacophony and movement, was now shrouded in an unsettling hush. Echoes of the tragedy permeated the air, with strips of yellow tape dancing mournfully in the breeze, testifying to the market's stark metamorphosis.

Stepping out, the cobblestones whispered beneath her feet. Surveying the ghostly scene, every nuance beckoned her closer. Taking a steadying breath, she delved into the epicenter of the conundrum, every fiber of her being attuned to the hidden truths enveloping her.

Her eyes, sweeping over the haunting stillness, were drawn to an anomaly—a distinct mark sprayed onto a wall. Set against the backdrop of muted stone, the emblem gleamed subtly beneath the filtered sunlight, a lone symbol amidst the desolation. It bore the signature of the "Veil of Dawn"—an emblem of deceptive simplicity. The unembellished crescent moon, etched with stark lines, exuded an aura of enigma and allure.

Elysa's gaze lingered on the emblem, a flicker of familiarity awakening within her. This wasn't her inaugural encounter with The Veil of Dawn's distinctive insignia. On previous occasions, tied to the group's less hostile activities, she had come across this very symbol. Her innate curiosity had propelled her to delve into its origins. Historically, the crescent moon epitomized hope and the promise of rebirth, mirroring the waxing phase of the moon. Its associations with Artemis, the Greek goddess renowned for hunting, wilderness, and safeguarding, added layers to its significance. Particularly poignant was Artemis's affiliation with dawn, as she rose preceding the sun in her hunting pursuits, further tying the emblem to The Veil of Dawn.

Drawing her gaze away from the emblem, the somber desolation of the marketplace stretched out before her. In the lingering hush that followed the turmoil, Elysa wandered between the various stalls, her footfalls echoing back in haunting resonance. A sudden rustling momentarily heightened her alertness—a Watcher lurked in the penumbra, his posture unwavering, his visage masked by an inscrutable expression. As her vision acclimated to the dimness, she discerned multiple guardians stationed discreetly, their unwavering vigil underscoring the incident's seriousness. A shiver of apprehension coursed through her, suggesting layers of undisclosed truths, hinting perhaps at Marek's intentional omissions.

Navigating deeper, Elysa traversed past deserted stalls. Once draped in vivid textiles, they now bore tattered remnants that billowed softly with the wind's caress. Merchandise, previously arranged to allure, lay strewn in a chaotic display upon the stones. Some shattered remnants caught stray sunbeams filtering through the towering edifices, while others lay displaced, testifying to a frantic exodus.

An involuntary gasp escaped her as she beheld the somber stains marring the cobblestones—grim vestiges of the brutal confrontation. Though the departed had been evacuated, spectral imprints lingered. The dried, rust-colored splotches stood in stark contrast to the cobblestones' earthy hue, bearing silent witness to the anguish and tragedy that had befallen the marketplace.

Elysa's gaze was irresistibly drawn to an odd, darkened spot tucked beneath a bench near the venerable clock tower. This perplexing residue sparked a keen interest; its nature eluded immediate understanding. With calculated steps, she advanced, the subtle reverberations of her footsteps creating ripples of sound on the aged cobblestones. As she drew near, she stooped to examine it more meticulously. At first glance, it bore resemblance to a molten metal pool.

Yet, upon closer scrutiny, it became evident that plastic had melded with the metal, giving birth to a singular, anomalous substance. The sun's muted rays danced upon it, revealing multifaceted hues and contours that defied straightforward categorization. Amidst the scarred landscape, it posed as a cryptic riddle, beckoning her deeper into its mystery.

The world seemed to stand still, the only sound being Elysa's quiet contemplation, which was suddenly pierced by a distant voice proclaiming, "There are two more: one nestled in the fountain and another hidden beneath an ancient oak!"

From the shadows emerged a familiar silhouette, prompting Elysa's gaze to snap up in acknowledgment. It was none other than Chen Wei, a colleague from her division, celebrated for his hands-on investigative prowess. His stature was imposing, with a wiry strength evident from his years of fieldwork. His visage was ruggedly handsome, crowned with hair peppered with gray, keen hawk-like eyes, and a strong, defined jawline. His hands narrated tales of hard work, while his meticulously manicured nails hinted at a craftsman's precision.

Surprised, Elysa questioned, "Chen, what brings you to this scene?"

His reply came with a hint of exasperation, "I heard whispers that you were spearheading this inquiry. I had to witness it firsthand. No offense, Elysa, but this scene isn't for someone who's been ensconced behind a desk."

Though stung by his words, Elysa maintained her composure, replying with a firmness belying her irritation, "I'm here on explicit orders from the Chancellor's office. If you have reservations about their decision, I suggest you voice them directly to the authorities."

A shadow of displeasure crossed Chen's features, his mouth tightening. "I merely believed that a case of this magnitude warranted someone with extensive field exposure."

Elysa's eyes narrowed as she stood up to face him squarely. "I value your concern, but I've been entrusted with this task, and I plan to carry it out. If you're here to assist, tell me about the other two objects you mentioned."

A palpable moment of strain passed between them; their eyes locked in a silent contest of wills. Finally, Chen exhaled a resigned sigh, his shoulders softening slightly. "Alright, follow me." Their mutual professional respect was evident, but an undercurrent of tension lingered, serving as a continuous reminder of the substantial stakes and the intricate dance of authority and expertise.

As they neared the fountain, the soft murmur of trickling water intermingled with the desolate silence of the forsaken marketplace, and Chen started to explain the oddity he had discovered. "It's something bizarre, tucked near the base of the fountain. Whatever it was, it's now melted into a dark, glossy mess. I couldn't discern what it might be from a distance."

Elysa's eyes tightened with curiosity. "Melted? That's peculiar. Could it have been exposed to intense heat, or was it intentionally designed to melt like that?"

Chen shook his head, a look of vexation in his eyes. "It's challenging to determine without closer inspection. But the way it's melted—it appears intentional, as if it were designed to be destroyed or rendered inoperative."

They pressed on toward the fountain, the disarray of broken drones, strewn wares, and lingering stains manifesting the earlier turmoil. The air was laden with enigmas, the friction between them momentarily eclipsed.

Upon arriving at the object, Elysa stooped to examine it more closely. The item was indeed melted beyond recognition, its authentic form distorted into a dark, twisted mass. Its positioning near the fountain seemed deliberate, yet its purpose was enigmatic.

Chen observed her, arms folded. "What's your take? Sabotage? Some sort of apparatus?"

Her brow furrowed as she pondered the alternatives. "I'm uncertain. It could be a myriad of things, but the melting suggests a premeditated action to thwart investigation. We ought to document it meticulously and procure samples for analysis."

Chen nodded affirmatively; the gravity of their predicament mirrored in his gaze. "We must act swiftly. There's a third item, equally melted and indecipherable, close by. We should examine that as well."

Shifting her gaze to the downed surveillance drones strewn around the marketplace, her thoughts narrowing. "What's the story with these fallen drones?" she inquired, turning to Chen.

Chen's expression tightened, his concern unmistakable in his eyes. "That's another anomaly. The drones lost power simultaneously, which is highly unusual given their independent power supplies. It's as though something disrupted them all at once. Moreover," Chen continued, "the surveillance cameras experienced a mysterious failure during the chaos. Every single frame became blurred in the minutes leading up to the attack, and then they went blank. It's as if someone deliberately ensured no eyes were watching, no evidence was left behind."

Elysa's eyes widened, her heart quickening as the full implications of the situation struck her. "This wasn't merely a random act of violence," she asserted, her voice resolute. "This was a meticulously planned and coordinated assault. Someone orchestrated this with precision, taking great care to conceal the details, yet leaving behind the signature crescent moon symbol. Why go to such lengths to hide everything else?" Though she didn't voice it, her face conveyed her confusion—something was amiss.

Her mind raced with potential scenarios, intuition whispering that they were merely scratching the surface of something far more intricate. Determination flickered in her eyes as she looked at Chen. "We must unravel this. Whatever transpired here, it's just the tip of the iceberg."

Chen's countenance hardened, his sense of professional resolve reflecting hers. "I concur," he said.

They proceeded with their investigation, the magnitude of the task settling heavily upon them, unseen forces and concealed motives casting an ever-growing shadow.

"Have you unearthed anything else?" Elysa inquired, a hint of hope lilting her voice, as if expecting some substantive discovery.

Chen shook his head, his visage etched with frustration. "Nothing so far. Everything appears to have been skillfully hidden or obliterated. Whoever was behind this knew precisely what they were doing."

Elysa's brow creased, her mind grappling with the intricate complexity of their situation. "I want to explore further," she declared, her eyes scanning the expansive area. "Perhaps something was overlooked."

Chen acquiesced, though skepticism clouded his gaze. "Good luck. I'll continue my search as well."

With that, they separated, each ensnared in their own web of thoughts, the seriousness of their investigation weighing heavily on their individual consciences.

Proceeded methodically from stall to stall, Elysa's keen eyes absorbing the minute details of the disheveled scene but finding nothing compelling enough for closer scrutiny. Each vendor's booth appeared as a disarrayed landscape, goods strewn about in abandonment, encapsulating a single moment of collective panic. Her mind, finely tuned to detect inconsistencies, sought a clue—any inkling—that might deviate from the tragic narrative already known.

As she exited the vicinity of one vendor's stall and began moving toward another, her trajectory intersected with the mouth of an alleyway. It was an easily overlooked space, a mere crevice between towering structures, hidden in the shadowy interplay of light and darkness. Yet, a fleeting, subconscious glance into this narrow passageway arrested her movement.

Lurking in the distant corner where two walls converged was a subtle marking, barely perceptible. A lesser-trained eye might easily overlook it. But to Elysa, the mark seemed incongruent, a siren call to her analytical psyche. It was a faint aberration in an otherwise unremarkable scene, but her intuition whispered of potential significance. Compelled by this elusive clue, she felt an irresistible urge to explore the shadowy enclave.

As she stepped through the narrow confines of the alleyway, her eyes meticulously scanned the surroundings, leaving no detail unchecked. The alley was littered with scattered debris, a chaotic mix of discarded plastic wrappers, broken bottles, alongside rusted metal scraps and fragmented electronic devices that hinted at the alley's neglect. Her gaze fell on an open garbage bin to one side, and she couldn't help but peer within, driven by an unrelenting pursuit of clues.

The bin was filled with the usual waste one might expect in such a place: spoiled food, torn bags, and the detritus of daily urban life. The smell emanating from it was overpowering, a repugnant mix of rot and decay that assailed her senses. Her face involuntarily twisted into an expression of disgust as the stench hit her nostrils, but she didn't let it deter her from her examination. Dismissing the bin as devoid of anything unusual, she continued her advance.

Her progress was marked by a slow, deliberate cadence, each footfall generating a subdued echo that bounced softly off the abutting walls of the alley. As she arrived at the juncture where the walls intersect, Elysa stooped to examine more closely what had initially piqued her attention. Her pupils contracted as they homed in on an anomaly at ground level—a shattered vial, its glass transformed into perilous splinters, with its erstwhile contents strewn about in desiccated disarray. The scene appeared chaotic, as though the liquid had been expelled with abrupt force.

Kneeling beside the anomaly, her eyes narrowed as they traced the peculiar shade. The surrounding sable remnants bore the dull, matte appearance typical of dried substances. However, the patch in question possessed an almost velvety depth, as if it held a secret essence yet to evaporate. Its richness was both inviting and unsettling, stirring a cascade of thoughts within her.

With delicacy, she reached into her kit and extracted a set of precision tweezers and a magnifying lens. Hovering the lens over the anomalous shade, she examined its texture. Minute crystalline structures gleamed back, hinting at a complexity that ordinary substances lacked. The minute discrepancy wasn't just a difference in hue—it was evidence of a different composition, one that held its moisture longer, perhaps even resisted drying entirely.

With a calculated air of caution, Elysa lowered her gloved right hand toward the anomaly, her index finger unfurling and pressing gently into a wet spot. As she lifted her hand and turned it to scrutinize her fingertip, she was seized by a revelation—this liquid bore an eerie distinctiveness. Unlike any other fluid she had encountered, this particular one defied the laws of optics; it refrained from reflecting even a sliver of light. The inky moisture clinging to her fingertip existed as a complete absence of light, a negation of luminosity.

However, it's what transpired next that halted her heart within its cardiac chamber. Even as her eyes remained fastened to the enigmatic liquid, she observed the fabric of her glove at the contact point disintegrate in accelerated dissolution, as if devoured by some caustic agent. Before she could muster a response, the liquid commingled with her unprotected skin. Her irises dilated in an expression of unmitigated alarm, and her perception of time distorted, elongating the moments as she grappled with the portentousness of her situation. And then—

In an instantaneous dislocation, Elysa found her cognizance wrenched from the marketplace that had been the sphere of her inquiry. She was catapulted into a setting that defied immediate identification, experiencing existence through a different set of optic nerves. Confronting her was the visage of her father, Dr. Richard Hawthorne. In this recollection, or perhaps this vision, he was imbued with an air of authoritative eminence.

The air within the voluminous chamber—a vision of an ultra-modern laboratory—crackled with a palpable sense of electricity. Illumination within the space was neither glaring nor insufficient; rather, it existed in that perfect interstice that cast an aura over its technological marvels. Computer systems, buoyant holographic displays, and an array of apparatuses that seemed plucked from a future yet unrealized, dominated the landscape. Scientists, adorned in immaculate white lab coats, traversed the chamber with deliberate purpose, their movements punctuated by interactions with ethereal, floating interfaces.

At the nucleus of this technological wonderland, a gargantuan computer system pulsated with metronomic regularity, as if it were an entity with a biological heartbeat. The chamber's auditory environment was a nuanced symphony of state-of-the-art cooling systems interspersed with the infrequent yet gentle electronic chime—indicators of data in transit. Holographic displays flickered, their lights forming intricate sequences, as if engaged in a clandestine yet pivotal dialogue.

Through the eyes of another, she observed her father standing before her. His voice, imbued with a mix of curiosity and suspicion, filled the room as his eyes narrowed, tracing the lines of the holographic blueprint. "John, have you noticed this?" he asked, his finger lingering over a peculiar modulator in the design. "I don't recall authorizing any alterations. It's as if it appeared out of thin air. What's your take on it?" His tone was more contemplative than accusatory, inviting a collaborative investigation rather than posing a simple query.

Elysa's voice, now bearing a timbre rich with masculinity and the toil of many years, responded, "Could be Security's doing; perhaps they slipped it in. You know how they are, always needing to keep tabs on everything."

Dr. Hawthorne's eyes narrowed into slits, his years of keen discernment alerting him to the incongruity of the situation. "I'm not convinced, John," he retorted, his gaze steadfast on the luminescent blueprint. The tension in the chamber seemed to thicken, reminiscent of the air before a storm. "My access to its inner workings is restricted."

"Take it up with Security," John suggested, redirecting his focus toward a man situated to his left. Encircled by a luminous halo of lights and connected to a convoluted piece of machinery, the man seemed poised on the precipice of something extraordinary. "Are you ready?" John inquired, his voice tinged with a cocktail of anticipation and existential doubt.

"I think so," the man stammered, his voice quivering with minor hesitance. "Could you tell me again how this works?"

"Certainly," John began, motioning toward the elaborate framework of luminescence and mechanical complexity encircling the man. "This interface will permit the AI to probe your thoughts, to absorb and extrapolate from your human experiences. We are on the cusp of heralding a new epoch in Artificial Intelligence."

In the room, an oppressive reality pervaded the atmosphere. The seemingly infinite well of internet databases and academic journals had run dry, marking the end of an era for machine learning. Now, the human mind was viewed as the last untapped reservoir, abundant in creativity, emotion, and intuition.

"Do you grasp what we're venturing into?" Dr. Hawthorne interjected. "Directly harnessing the subtleties of human thought and emotion, we're approaching an ethical boundary that warrants our caution."

"Everything will be just fine," John assured, his voice imbued with a symphony of both resolve and a hint of lingering doubt. He reached out toward a console that was a marvel of technological finesse, its surface alive with a pulsating mosaic of soft-colored indicators and touch-sensitive controls. His fingers danced over the glass panel with practiced ease, momentarily hesitating over a particular switch that seemed no different from the others yet bore an incomparable weight of purpose.

The moment his fingertip contacted the switch, the atmosphere in the room underwent a tangible metamorphosis. Above the man's head, a halo of lights flickered into existence, illuminating his features in an ethereal glow. The individual bulbs were a marvel of engineering—each a tiny orb of plasma encapsulated in a bubble of anti-gravitational field, suspended in perfect formation. They blazed to life in a gradation of colors, from soft whites to incandescent blues, as though mimicking the color spectrum of some far-off nebula.

The activation of the halo brought the room to life with a resonant hum, blending seamlessly with the gentle purrs and tweets of surrounding high-tech apparatus. It was as though the essence of existence itself was momentarily realigned, recognizing the significance of the impending event. Lights flickered, synchronizing with the chamber's ambient noises in a quiet exchange, as if in conversation with the myriad of technological wonders occupying the space.

For a split second, John's eyes met those of the man beneath the radiant halo. The look they exchanged was awash with a complex tapestry of emotions—hope, fear, and a shared understanding that they were standing on the threshold of the unknown.

Then, Elysa was engulfed by a torrent of searing pain that felt as if her consciousness were splitting. Amidst this disorienting maelstrom, and sudden darkness, a scream pierced the air. Her father's voice resonated with shock, "What have we done?"

As the echoes of the past and the painful realization dissipated like fog under the morning sun, Elysa found herself abruptly returning to the present. She was back in the marketplace, her skin tingling at the point where the liquid had made contact. Her pulse quickened as she digested the fractured images—her father, the enigmatic John, and the murky ethical grounds they were venturing into. Her mind was awash with questions, but one loomed above all others: What had unfolded before her, and what implications did it carry for her and her father?

The revelation pressed upon Elysa with the weight of a mountain. Yet it also felt as if she'd discovered a missing piece of a much larger, intricate puzzle concerning her life's most vexing questions, particularly about her father's mysterious involvement in perilous science and ethics.

Regaining her senses brought a surreal vision, viewed through the eyes of another, that cast her father's secret endeavors in stark relief, possibly even revealing the cause of her parents' abrupt disappearance. This vision served as confirmation—her dreams were not mere fabrications or softly spoken speculations of what might have been but were anchored in reality, direct results of her recent experience. This realization instilled in her an immediate urgency; to unearth deeper truths, she found herself in desperate need of more of the enigmatic black liquid.

Her eyes swiftly returned to the broken vial on the ground. Time was of the essence. She quickly retrieved a specially designed, small, screw-capped plastic container from her case. Slipping on a pair of latex gloves, Elysa knelt carefully to avoid the shards of shattered glass. With a glass pipette, she meticulously siphoned the remaining enigmatic liquid, her hands steady and her focus unyielding. As she transferred a small sample of the liquid into the container, she marveled at its absolute opacity, as though it was infused with the very secrets it contained.

After securing the cap on the sample container, a mix of invigoration and terror surged through her. She stowed the sample in her steel-grey trench coat, wary of contaminating it through her case's automated analysis systems; she was still ignorant of the liquid's properties and how they might interact with the case's environment.

As she stood there, Elysa sensed that she was on the cusp of a journey that entangled her family in its mystery. The small container felt at once weightless and monumental, an enigmatic vessel of limitless potential and grave risks. She was consumed with questions—how this experience connected with the marketplace events, who this John person was that her father knew, and where she might find him.

Preparing to leave, an acute awareness suddenly washed over her, and she felt as though she were being watched. Though the alleyway seemed devoid of surveillance, save for a lone, potentially malfunctioning camera, an intangible scrutiny filled the air. It was as if invisible eyes traced her every move from the shadows.

Exiting the alley, Elysa navigated the bustling marketplace methodically, her gaze sweeping corners, stalls, and branching alleyways with undivided attention. She had been at it for several hours, her investigative case always at her side. Her PDD cycled through various data feeds, but nothing unusual arrested her attention. Despite her diligence, the search yielded no new clues, only deepening the enigma that clouded her relentless quest for truth.

Conscious of the ticking clock and the diminishing returns on her time, Elysa activated her communication link with Chen Wei. "Chen, can you arrange to collect those fallen drones? Also, fetch a couple of those malfunctioning surveillance systems. I want them examined in the lab."

"Understood," Chen Wei's voice crackled in her earpiece.

Elysa retraced her steps to The Veil of Dawn symbol. Extracting a plastic container and a set of sterile latex gloves, she donned the gloves and carefully scraped off some of the symbol's paint, the action creating a slight, grating sound that resonated oddly loudly in her heightened state of awareness. Satisfied with her sample, she sealed the container and secured it in her case. She noticed another part of the symbol already had some paint scraped off and wondered if Chen had done that earlier.

Her movements were meticulous, verging on ritualistic. Each collected item might hold the key to unraveling the mystery. Overlooking even the minutest detail could obscure the bigger picture. Samples secured, a blend of exhaustion and resolve filled Elysa. The marketplace had been reticent in yielding its secrets, but she remained unyielding. Casting a final, lingering look at The Veil of Dawn symbol, she moved toward her awaiting transport, her thoughts already leaping ahead to the lab analyses.

With the lifting of the vehicle, a forgotten detail surfaced in Elysa's mind. "Chen, I forgot to ask you to send samples of the melted blobs to the lab," she communicated.

"Already done," Chen responded. "I suspected you might forget." His words struck her as a subtle rebuke, spotlighting her inexperience.

"Thanks," she returned, silently appending 'you bastard' as an unspoken addendum.

Elysa cast her gaze downward, the sprawling marketplace gradually shrinking into the distance below. The vehicle's display blinked her next destination: the CDMSA. Oddly, she hadn't set this course; fatigue made home's comfort all the more appealing. Yet an inexplicable pull seemed to draw her back to her office.

As Elysa's eyes moved over the shifting map on the display, it suddenly blackened in what seemed like a digital flicker. The words "Do you remember?" materialized briefly before vanishing, leaving the map as if untouched.

Furrowing her brow, she said, "Orion, why did the words 'Do you remember?' flash on the display?"

The cabin grew heavy with a pause, a moment of dense silence, before Orion's synthetic voice finally broke in. "I'm sorry, Elysa, but I have no record of such an event."

"That can't be," she muttered, her eyes still affixed to the screen. "Check again."

"Scanning logs," Orion intoned. A prolonged pause tightened the atmosphere into a knot of expectation. "No, Elysa. The logs still show no record."

A frisson crept up her spine, chilling the back of her neck. The vehicle emitted a soft hum, its engines barely a whisper, yet the air inside had thickened with an inscrutable foreboding. "Remember what?" she whispered, her words barely rising above the vehicle's subtle mechanical sounds. They hovered in the cabin air like a ghostly riddle, challenging her to decode a mystery far more intimate than any she'd encountered before.

Chapter 5 - 285th Floor

Inside the private elevator that scaled the dizzying heights of Nexus Tower, a lone figure, the Commander from the marketplace, emanated an aura that was a blend of restraint and palpable expectation. The elevator ceased its climb with a whisper-soft halt, and a chime discreetly announced his arrival on the 285th floor. As the doors unfurled in a seamless motion, they revealed an opulent foyer that seemed to distill the essence of luxury. The floor was a pristine canvas of white marble, polished to such an extent that it captured the ornate gold-leaf motifs of the ceiling above, creating a sanctuary where heaven and earth seemed to merge in a deliberate act of grandeur.

Before he could advance, a voice reverberated in the hallowed space, Orion's synthesized timbre filling the marble vestibule. "Commander Cypher, the Chancellor awaits you in his office."

Stepping out, he was immediately enveloped by a heady aroma of aromatic spices and rare woods, an olfactory embrace of luxury. Hidden alcoves spilled soft, golden light onto walls swathed in rare silk that shimmered ethereally.

To his left, an awe-inspiring library beckoned. Its vertiginous shelves housed timeworn manuscripts and rarified first editions, their leather bindings meticulously arranged. The air was tinged with the musty scent of antiquity, a homage to an era when the tactile pleasure of turning a page was a rare privilege in a world where paper was a scarce resource. Adjacent to this bibliophilic refuge was a holographic conference room, where dignitaries held virtual discourse with global leaders from the few remaining cities of this world.

To his right, a shadowed hallway beckoned, its depths unfurling toward the secretive dominion of the Chancellor's personal chambers. A sequence of ornate, closed doors lay in wait, each a keeper of untold luxuries and veiled truths. Though Commander Cypher was left to wander the corridors of his own imagination about what might be hidden therein, his thoughts were awash with intrigue and speculation. Further along this hushed passageway, a panoramic window manifested with arresting suddenness, capturing an elevated vista so dizzyingly high that clouds danced and flowed like ethereal wraiths across the glass. Occasionally, these moving veils parted to reveal glimpses of Cyronis' skyline far, far below—a tantalizing chiaroscuro of ancient spires and futuristic behemoths.

At the far end of this palatial floor, intricately carved double doors awaited, leading into the private office of Chancellor Zircon. Made of dark oak, these doors bore patterns intricately depicting the history of Cyronis. Beyond them lay a room dominated by a massive desk of polished mahogany, its surface adorned with a few significant items: a crystal paperweight, an ancient dagger with a jewel-encrusted hilt, and a holographic interface. The paperweight, a gift from the people of Cyronis, was said to bring good luck to its owner. The dagger, a family heirloom rumored to be imbued with magical powers, reflected the Chancellor's profound heritage. The holographic interface represented the pinnacle of technological innovation, allowing Zircon to communicate with people all over the world.

Yet, what truly set this floor apart was the palpable sense of power that permeated the air. It was as if the very molecules were charged with it, radiating from the Chancellor's office like a beacon. As he moved through this awe-inspiring space, he felt like he was walking through a living monument to the man who sat at the helm of Cyronis, steering it through the complexities of a world both ancient and astonishingly advanced.

He came to a halt and bowed before the Chancellor's imposing desk. Behind it, Zircon sat, his face marked by triumphs and betrayals, its lines and creases a topography of hard-won experience. His impeccably groomed dark hair framed his visage with dignified elegance.

Zircon was dressed in a manner befitting royalty, yet tailored for the intimacy of his private quarters. A robe of deep crimson velvet, embroidered with intricate golden patterns, draped elegantly over his shoulders, symbolic of the responsibilities he bore as Chancellor of Cyronis. Beneath the robe, he wore a finely tailored shirt of the softest silk, its muted shade of blue subtly contrasting with the richness of the robe.

Around his neck hung a medallion, an heirloom passed down through generations of Chancellors, its gemstone centerpiece catching the light in a mesmerizing dance of colors.

Despite Cypher's presence, the Chancellor's gaze remained steadfastly anchored to the holographic display that hovered before him. Seated in a chair that seemed as much crafted for power as for comfort, Zircon's posture was one of utter focus and control. His piercing, intense eyes were like laser beams, cutting through the complex layers of data and imagery that danced in the air—a kaleidoscope of information only he could decipher. Those eyes seemed to see through your very soul, leaving no room for secrets or lies. His fingers, slightly weathered but remarkably agile, moved with a surgeon's precision, tracing intricate patterns in the air as he manipulated the hologram. Each gesture was deliberate, each flick of his wrist imbued with a sense of purpose that was both awe-inspiring and slightly unnerving. The gold signet ring he wore, a family heirloom and a symbol of his lineage, caught the ambient light as his hand moved, casting fleeting shadows on the desk.

It was impossible for Cypher to discern whether Chancellor Zircon was issuing commands to some unseen force or seeking something within the depths of the holographic interface. Yet, one thing was abundantly clear: Chancellor Zircon was a man who held the reins of his vast empire with an unyielding grip, a master of both the seen and the unseen, steering the destiny of Cyronis through the murky waters of a world both ancient and astonishingly advanced.

Minutes stretched into what felt like hours, each second amplifying the weight of the moment. The holographic image before him flickered and wavered, as if struggling to maintain its form. The Chancellor's brow furrowed in concentration, and his lips were set in a thin line. Finally, with a swift, decisive motion, he closed the hologram, and it vanished as if it had never existed. Only then did he lift his eyes to meet those of his visitor, as if acknowledging for the first time that he was not alone in his sanctum.

The silence that followed was heavy with unspoken words, a quiet that spoke volumes about the power dynamics at play. The Commander had waited, and now, it seemed, the Chancellor was ready to grant him the audience he sought. The air, once thick with tension, seemed to shift, making room for whatever would come next in this high-stakes meeting of minds.

"Report," commanded the Chancellor, his voice a low rumble that seemed to reverberate through the very walls of the room.

Cypher cleared his throat, acutely aware of the weight his words would carry in this sanctum of power. "Chancellor Zircon, Elysa visited the marketplace and completed her visual investigation, sending some samples back to the lab for analysis."

"What samples?" asked the Chancellor.

"Paint samples from The Veil's symbol, as well as some melted material, were discovered at three distinct locations," Cypher reported. There was a brief moment of silence as the Commander looked at the Chancellor's impatient glare. "Elysa also uncovered a shattered vial in a secluded corner of the alley."

Zircon's eyes remained locked onto the Commander, unblinking and inscrutable. Cypher shifted uncomfortably under the Chancellor's gaze, feeling as if he were being judged and dissected. "Something you left behind," Zircon accused, his voice a blade of ice. "Continue."

The Commander hesitated for a fraction of a second, choosing his words carefully. "There was a moment when Elysa touched a spot of the vial's dried fluid; she seemed to freeze up, as if something had caught her attention. I couldn't discern what it was, but she appeared momentarily... distracted, or perhaps disturbed by something."

The air was heavy, as if the walls themselves absorbed the gravity of the conversation. "Did she secure the vial samples?" Zircon's voice, a soft but assertive baritone, resonated with an undertone of impatience that electrified the atmosphere.

Commander Cypher, a seasoned veteran whose posture radiated an uneasy blend of loyalty and trepidation, shifted slightly. "She did, but curiously enough," he paused, his eyes briefly searching the intricate patterns on the Persian rug below, "she pocketed them in her coat, rather than using the standardized investigation case. This is a blatant deviation from protocol."

In the silence that followed, the room seemed to grow dimmer, as if shadowing the thoughts that darkened Zircon's contemplative eyes. The Chancellor leaned back against the high back of his mahogany chair, its carved armrests appearing like the talons of an eagle grasping the weight of his decision. "Is that all?"

A measured exhalation escaped the Commander's lips. "That essentially sums it up, Chancellor. She lacks experience. Why entrust her with such a delicate task?"

Zircon's eyes transformed into twin orbs of molten intensity, their iridescent hue glowing like the core of a distant star. The air between him and the Commander seemed to crackle, charged by the electric current of his unyielding focus. His gaze was a laser beam, cutting through the ambient haze of the room, unerringly locking onto the Commander's own eyes. It was as if he were peering into the very soul of the man before him, sifting through layers of doubt and uncertainty to lay bare the unspoken truths.

"I suspect," Zircon began, his voice a low timbre that reverberated with the weight of his words, "that one or more individuals within the CDMSA are clandestine members of The Veil." He paused for a moment, allowing the seriousness of his statement to sink in, to ripple through the room like a stone cast into still waters. "I harbored suspicions, nebulous inklings, until an agent of mine analyzed a sample of paint taken from their insidious symbol in the marketplace."

His eyes flickered momentarily, as if reliving the scene, the clandestine operation that had led to this revelation. "The paint," he continued, "possesses a unique molecular signature, a cryptographic tell that could only have originated from the CDMSA's own supply store. It's as distinctive as a fingerprint, as damning as a signed confession."

"We can identify everyone who has acquired the paint," Cypher chimed in, his voice slicing through the room's dense atmosphere like a scalpel through flesh.

"I've already tasked Orion to do just that," Zircon interjected, his voice a counterpoint to Cypher's, imbued with a seriousness that seemed to echo from some unfathomable depth. His eyes, those twin orbs of molten intensity, flared momentarily, as if stoked by an inner fire. "But he has come up empty."

The words hung in the air, laden with a sense of foreboding, like dark clouds gathering on the horizon. "Not a single soul within the CDMSA has ordered that specific pigment in the past 30 days. However,"

Zircon paused, allowing the silence to amplify his next words, "a day's worth of data has conveniently vanished." The word 'conveniently' dripped with venomous irony, leaving no room for misinterpretation.

"Going back to your question of why I assigned the girl to the investigation." Zircon shifted his gaze, ever so slightly, as if to include another unseen presence in the room. "The girl is the individual I suspect least to be entangled in the web of The Veil. Given her unique position under Orion's ever-watchful surveillance, coupled with her alluring family history, she has become the most tantalizing target for The Veil, especially now that they are aware of her investigative endeavors."

He leaned back, but his eyes never wavered, maintaining their laser-like lock on the Commander. "She possesses a keen perceptiveness, an intuitive grasp of the complexities we navigate. I wouldn't be surprised if she, with her uncanny acumen, unravels the identity of the traitor within our ranks, exposing the malignant core of this conspiracy."

As Zircon concluded, the room seemed to exhale, as if releasing a breath it didn't know it had been holding. Yet, the weight of his words lingered, heavy and palpable, like a shroud that had been irrevocably draped over all present, a haunting prelude to events yet unfathomable.

"Family history?" Cypher asked, his voice steeped in intrigue.

Zircon leaned forward, his eyes becoming cavernous wells of intent. "Her father, Dr. John Hawthorne, is Orion's Architect."

"And The Veil, no doubt, are watching her," Cypher concluded, his voice imbued with a chilling certainty that hung in the air like a spectral presence. "And they would only be able to do so within the inner sanctum of her workplace." As he spoke, the room seemed to darken, as if the very walls were absorbing the import of his words. The atmosphere thickened, becoming almost palpable, as if the room itself were holding its breath, awaiting the unfolding of some inexorable fate.

The Chancellor gave an affirmative nod. It was a simple gesture, yet it reverberated with a profundity that belied its simplicity.

Eager to prove his worth, Cypher ventured, "I shall deploy undercover agents within the CDMSA."

Zircon cut him short, "Already done."

The Chancellor's focus sharpened, the weight of his gaze pressing down like an anvil. "Who did she interact with at the marketplace?"

"Chen Wei. And only him," Cypher returned the gaze, feeling as if he was dancing on the edge of a blade. "Our agents cordoned off the scene, preventing anyone else from entering the marketplace."

"And you observed this?"

"From a rooftop, as you instructed."

"Any palpable tension between them?" Zircon's question came laced with a thread of expectancy.

"Quite palpable," Cypher replied, choosing his words like a jeweler selecting gems. "Shall I bring Chen in for questioning?"

Zircon's response was as swift as it was laden with finality. "No."

Just then, an epiphany crystallized within Cypher. Chen Wei was an undercover asset of Zircon's. He was the one who got the paint sample and reported the analysis results to Zircon.

In an instant, charged with an electrifying intensity, Zircon swiveled in his chair to lock eyes with Cypher. It was as if invisible threads of tension had suddenly drawn taut between them, weaving an intricate web of unspoken expectations and judgments. "Did you find out where John Dryer disappeared to?" His voice was a dark river of restrained urgency, flowing with an undercurrent of irrevocable consequence, "and the woman that cut you, that bested you?"

Cypher felt a surge of anger well up within him, like a volcano on the precipice of eruption. A tempest of emotion threatened to escape his lips, but with an iron will, he forced it back down into the depths of his being. His eyes became hardened pools of mercury, nearly aflame with the ire he struggled to contain. In that market, they had been so agonizingly close to capturing Dryer, only to be thwarted by that insidious female member of the Veil. "We're still on it," he managed, each syllable soaked in a bitterness that he couldn't quite expunge. His voice was like a tightened wire, taut with unshed frustration and the weight of lost lives. "We lost good agents that night. I'll find everyone responsible."

Zircon's response was not verbal but gestural—a near-imperceptible nod, minimalist yet laden with immense meaning. It was as if that simple motion had been extracted from a reservoir of contemplative silence. He leaned back into his high-backed chair of mahogany and leather, as the shadows in the room deepened, curving around him like dark, ethereal arms eager to envelop him in their enigmatic embrace.

Cypher acknowledged the nod with the obligatory bow, a gesture demanded by the Chancellor's stature rather than any genuine deference. As he inclined his head, a shadow of darkness and loathing flickered across his eyes, betraying a sense of self-diminishment in bowing to this man. With military precision, he pivoted on his heel, his movements sharp and calculated. As he stepped across the threshold, his silhouette briefly intersected with the ambient light, casting an elongated shadow that stretched eerily across the floor, almost touching infinity. This spectral extension of his form disappeared as he stepped into the dim corridor, his presence dissolving into the shadows, leaving Zircon isolated in his sanctum of power, surrounded by the weight of unspoken thoughts.

Chapter 6 - Into the Labyrinth

Elysa settled back into her chair within the frenetic labyrinth of the CDMSA, her desk an island in a sea of relentless industry. The lab pulsed like the epicenter of a vast neural network; its air heavy with the palpable energy of minds engaged in analytical combat. Her cybersecurity analyst colleagues, absorbed in their individual quests for truth, populated this ceaseless endeavor. Ambient light from multiple screens bathed their faces in an otherworldly glow, each display serving as a portal into the intricate machinery of the surveillance state they were pledged to uphold. The soft patter of shoes against carpet provided a rhythmic undertone to the ambient soundscape, punctuated by sporadic murmurs of subdued conversation. This ceaseless auditory backdrop served as a constant, almost ritualistic, reminder of the unending labor invested in safeguarding the precarious balance of Cyronis.

Her eyes flickered toward her own screen, to which Orion had granted her access to a staggering array of data concerning the recent massacre. Rows of numbers, graphs, and visual feeds filled the display—each one a component of the intricate puzzle she was resolutely determined to solve. With practiced ease, her fingers danced across the holographic interface, deftly sifting through myriad layers of information.

Holographic text and images appeared before her, each emerging as if woven from thin air. In a corner of the display, a timestamp sat—a simple combination of numbers and letters marking a moment 24 hours before a major event in the marketplace. This timestamp was crucial, acting as a countdown to the unfolding chaos and possibly holding the key to preventing or understanding the catastrophe. Her fingers paused above the holographic keyboard, then moved to explore further into Orion's summary.

In one report, delivered in a detached tone only a machine could achieve, outlined the events leading up to the incident, providing some insights into patterns of suspicious activity through this analysis. Such reports would include color-coded highlights to categorize activities, with reds and yellows indicating high-alert moments and blues and greens representing normalcy. This report only showed one item in red— 'Possible cloak detected,' which immediately drew Elysa's focus.

"Orion, isn't cloaking technology under strict government regulation, and only accessible to a select few?" she inquired, her gaze still fixed on the screen.

"That is correct," Orion responded in its usual, emotionless tone. "Only a few Watchers are authorized for its use."

"And who might these Watchers be? Where are they allowed to use this technology?" Elysa pressed; her curiosity piqued.

"That information is classified, accessible on a need-to-know basis only."

"But surely, I have a need to know," Elysa countered, her voice firm, believing her position granted her access.

"Access denied. Authorization from the Chancellor is required for that level of information," Orion stated, unmoved by her insistence.

Frustrated, Elysa returned to the report, her eyes catching the timestamp indicating the possible cloak was detected 19.3 minutes before the complete shutdown of the surveillance systems. Her mind raced with questions and theories, but without Orion's full cooperation, she knew she was hitting a wall.

"Orion, play the video starting 20 seconds before the cloak was detected, and halt it when it reaches the point where the anomaly is visible," Elysa intoned, her eyes fixed intently on the holographic interface that floated before her.

The moment she issued her command, the screen shimmered into life, rendering a stunningly detailed panorama of the marketplace from the perspective of a high-flying drone. It was a theater of the mundane, a ballet of ordinary interactions performed on a cobblestone stage. The vendors, dressed in an array of vivid hues, thrust their hands toward passersby, imploring them to glance, if not buy. Their stalls were crowded islands of human desires, from alluring scents and exotic spices to enigmatic electronic devices promising to make life easier.

Amidst the bustling scene, one vendor's stall, perched at the edge of a timeworn building, stood out, guarding an obscure alleyway behind it. Precisely at the 20-second mark, the holographic image stuttered, freezing on a scene. Sharp lines of an analytical framework highlighted a patch of distortion, transparent and emerging from the alley like a wave flowing through the air, reflecting light from the vendor's stall.

"Why does the anomaly appear here, any ideas?" Elysa asked, her eyes narrowed on the frozen hologram.

Orion's voice, neutral and precise, answered, "The preliminary analysis indicates the light intensity from the vendor's stall is likely interfering with the cloak. These devices often fail under strong illumination."

"How bright was the light near the vendor's stall?"

"The light source was measured at approximately 1300 lumens. At the anomaly's detected distance, roughly 1.5 meters away, the light's intensity would be about 114.94 lumens per square meter."

"The irony," Elysa mused, tapping her chin thoughtfully. "Advanced technology undone by mere light."

"Can we enhance the image to identify any features?"

"After deploying several enhancement algorithms, this," an image popped up on the holo-display, "is the clearest image obtained." It showed a wave-like distortion, seemingly reflecting the surrounding light.

Elysa scrutinized the image, focusing on a peculiar dark spot. "What's that dark crescent shape in the center?"

"There does not appear to be anything nearby that would create that shape. However, my access to the surrounding area is not entirely unobstructed," Orion explained.

"Understood," Elysa nodded. "Continue playing the footage," she commanded, her voice laced with curiosity.

The video resumed. As the drone's camera moved forward, the enigmatic blur vanished in front of two women who were moving towards it and adjusted their path as if to avoid something—or someone. One glanced over her shoulder, murmuring something.

"It seems they stepped aside for someone invisible to us. How could they see what we can't?"

"Some cloaks are designed to evade electronic surveillance but remain visible to the naked eye," Orion theorized.

"Rewind. Focus on the woman to the right, just before she speaks. Can you isolate her words?"

"Unable to comply. She whispered, making it impossible to enhance sufficiently for clarity."

"Then, analyze her lip movements," Elysa instructed, leaning closer.

"She appears to have said, 'Fucken bitch,'" Orion decoded.

"A reaction to an unseen presence," Elysa noted with a smile. "Progress. Are there any female operatives authorized for cloaking tech?"

"Three within our ranks," Orion confirmed.

"Their locations during this incident?"

"Information denied."

"But I need to know," her frustration was now evident. "It's critical to this investigation."

"I cannot reveal their locations."

Taking a deep breath, she refocused her question. "Can you tell me if they were in the marketplace?"

Silence.

"They were not in the marketplace."

Frowning, she leaned back, lost in thought for a moment.

"Have you cross-referenced everyone entering the marketplace between 8:30 and 9:00 PM?"

"All individuals accounted for. The analysis does not flag any suspicion. A comprehensive list is available."

Elysa activated a holocontrol, bringing up a list of names. "There are hundreds!" she exclaimed.

"One thousand, four hundred and ninety-three, to be precise," Orion corrected.

"It will take me forever to go through all of these names," she mumbled to herself. "Scan other surveillance feeds. Any other anomalies?"

"All feeds were scanned, and no additional irregularities were found," Orion's voice almost seemed to carry a hint of frustration.

"What about the areas around the fountain, the clock tower bench, and Whisperingwood?"

"Nothing unusual was found. However, surveillance does not cover those areas continuously."

"Consistent blind spots in the coverage?"

"Affirmative."

"Then, it's likely our unseen visitor knew this, exploiting these gaps for concealment," Elysa concluded, her gaze fixed on the list of names, her mind racing with possibilities. "Is anyone on this list working within the Tower, or has elevated access to your system?"

"None," came the reply.

A flashing icon at the corner of her screen caught her attention—a new message awaited her. Elysa's heart quickened. She'd been waiting for the lab's report on the mysterious melted artifacts she had recovered during her investigation.

Opening the message, her eyes scanned through the dense layers of technical jargon. The lab had conducted a thorough analysis: spectroscopy, mass spectrometry, nuclear magnetic resonance—you name it. They'd gone all out, sparing no resource in dissecting the curious material. Her eyes widened as she read the summary.

The results were frustratingly inconclusive, yet one unsettling detail leapt out. The lab reported that the lattice structure of the black material had been altered in an extraordinarily peculiar manner. It was as though the very architecture of the molecules had been reconfigured to collapse upon themselves. The term "self-annihilating structure" appeared in the report. The substance, it elaborated, exhibited qualities as if it had "melted," yet not through any recognized process such as heat or chemically induced. It had destabilized at the molecular level, leaving almost nothing to analyze.

The implications struck Elysa with an unsettling force. Whoever was behind this had devised a substance that could essentially erase itself, leaving virtually no trace behind. It was the ideal method for obliterating evidence, a technique so advanced it veered into the realm of science fiction. And it brought her no closer to deciphering what it was or identifying who was behind it.

Fueled by this revelation, Elysa's determination surged. If someone had gone to such lengths to obscure their tracks, then the secret they were protecting must be staggering. She leaned back in her chair, staring at the almost empty lab report displayed before her, her mind a maelstrom of thoughts. Someone out there had the answers, and she was unflinchingly committed to finding them, no matter the cost.

Elysa's attention shifted to another lab report that emerged on her holographic display—a detailed analysis of the paint scrapings she'd taken from the symbol of The Veil of Dawn. Her eyes narrowed as she meticulously scanned the report through her translucent interface. It offered a comprehensive chemical breakdown of the paint sample she'd collected. As she sifted through complex notations and percentages, one line seized her focus.

The report flagged a unique pigment in the paint, a specialized compound she immediately recognized as being exclusive to the CDMSA. It was not a pigment widely available on the market or utilized in common applications. Its presence in the symbol of The Veil was baffling, implying insidiously that someone within her own agency was implicated.

Whatever The Veil of Dawn represented, it was now inextricably linked to one of the government's most clandestine and formidable agencies. And that realization meant Elysa had to proceed with unprecedented caution. She was ensnared in a web of suspicion and secrecy; trust was a luxury she could ill afford. She pondered the necessity of informing Marek about the potential spy among them.

"Orion, find out who in the CDMSA ordered paint with this unique pigmentation in the past 2 weeks," she commanded.

A few seconds ticked by. "The report is ready," Orion replied.

Elysa accessed another file on her display, presenting a daily breakdown of all employees who had ordered the unique pigment. There were no orders within the last 14 days. However, a full day—Monday the 23rd—was conspicuously absent.

"Orion, there is no data for Monday the 23rd, five days ago. Check the records."

After a brief pause, Orion responded, "There is no report for Monday the 23rd."

"Was the record deleted?"

"No logs indicate the record was deleted," Orion replied.

"Check the backups," Elysa instructed.

Orion immediately responded, "There are no backups for that day, and there are no data remnants in the system's cache."

"Were there any unusual activities just after the 23rd?"

"A 0.0023-millisecond drop in power occurred at 01:47 a.m. on Tuesday the 24th within the main AI system. The backup power compensated to avoid any system disruption."

Suspicion coalesced in Elysa's mind around that missing day. "Orion, did any other internal systems experience a power drop at that time?"

After a weighty pause, Orion answered, "Yes, one system did. It belongs to Marek Ján Wójcik."

"Marek!" Elysa's voice resonated with disbelief.

The notion of Marek, her mentor and confidant, entangled in something so dubious was unfathomable. She resolved that he couldn't be involved; there must be another explanation. A confrontation was necessary, but not now.

She rubbed her eyes, feeling the fatigue setting in. She noticed her coat tossed across another chair at the side of her desk, her attention now drawn to the vial with the black liquid concealed in its pocket. Her office was far too exposed to do anything with it now. "Orion, arrange for my transportation home."

"A ride is already waiting at the entrance," Orion replied.

The journey home was as unremarkable as it was reflective of her turbulent state of mind. The outside world faded into a blur; her thoughts entangled in a web of unanswered questions. Each query spawned another; her brain felt as if it were churning in a loop of perpetual confusion. The day had been a relentless barrage of activities, revelations, and suspicions, draining her both mentally and emotionally.

As she stepped into the familiar surroundings of her apartment, a brief wave of relief washed over her. The act of simply closing the door behind her felt like a minor victory, a respite from the complexity and confusion of the world outside. She tossed her coat onto the sofa as she passed; its weight seemed to symbolize the burdens she'd been carrying all day.

Navigating her way to the kitchen, she realized her ravenous hunger. The day's events had been so consuming that she couldn't recall eating a single meal. She opened the fridge and scanned its contents, selecting items that required minimal preparation. Right now, sustenance took precedence over taste; she needed fuel for both body and mind.

After consuming a quick but satisfying meal that quelled her hunger, Elysa walked over to her sofa. Her hand delved into the pockets of her coat, searching through the fabric until her fingers closed around the small plastic container she had stashed away earlier. She extracted it carefully and elevated it to her line of sight, her gaze fixated on the enigmatic black substance that lay at the bottom of the vial. A mere drop remained—perhaps two if she were exceedingly careful.

It looked inert, just a dark blob against the clear plastic, but she knew better. This was a mystery in physical form, a riddle she was increasingly desperate to solve. For a moment, she just stared at it, pondering its unknown properties, its origins, and its implications. How could something like this liquid store memories? Where did it come from? What was its true purpose? Why was this in the marketplace, and how was it related to what had transpired there? Why was her father involved? The questions just kept coming.

Her eyes narrowed, as if trying to peer into the very essence of the fluid, to coax its secrets into the open. But it remained inscrutable, a void that absorbed all light and curiosity, offering nothing in return but more questions.

She set it down on the table in front of her. Elysa knew she needed to dig deeper, to employ every resource at her disposal to uncover the truth behind this baffling substance. Yet for now, she recognized her own limits, both physical and emotional. She needed rest—a brief respite to marshal her energy and wits against the looming challenges. With a heavy sigh, she leaned back into the sofa, closed her eyes momentarily, and fell into a fitful sleep.

♦♦♦

The voice seemed to echo from the depths of her subconscious, its tone soft but insistent. "Do you remember?" it intoned, as though echoing through the cavernous recesses of her mind.

"Remember what?" Elysa found herself replying, her mental voice tinged with a rising tide of frustration and confusion. "What am I supposed to remember?"

"In your heart," the voice returned, now taking on an almost ethereal quality, as though emanating from some fathomless space either deep within her or perhaps far beyond. "Do you remember?"

The question lingered, enveloping the landscape of her thoughts like a persistent mist that refused to dissipate. Elysa reached out, mentally clawing at evanescent tendrils of memories that seemed forever just beyond her grasp. The more she tried to focus, the more elusive the answer became, slipping through her mental fingers like grains of sand in an hourglass.

She felt a profound yearning, a desperate need to decode the clandestine message that seemed to be whispered from the cosmos. The question, so deceptively simple yet rich in complexity, appeared to hold a key, a talisman to some distant memory or perhaps a revelation of great import.

But the voice offered no more guidance, leaving her in a liminal realm between sleep and wakefulness, between comprehension and enigma. Elysa's brow furrowed even in her slumber, her subconscious wrestling with the unanswered question until the world around her gradually dissolved into the quietude of deeper sleep.

Jolted awake by a sound that seemed to reverberate through her mind's corridors, she experienced a momentary disorientation before the complex fabric of her current reality reasserted itself—the ongoing investigation, the enigmatic black liquid, and the haunting voice that invaded her dreams. Her eyes flickered open to the familiarity of her living room; she had fallen asleep on her sofa, still garbed in the attire of the previous day's tumult.

As Orion sensed Elysa's stirring to wakefulness, the aroma of freshly brewed coffee infused the air, vivid enough to summon memories of serene mornings and far-off cafes. A cup of steaming java materialized in the dispenser, accompanied by a small tray bearing two vermilion pills—her habitual analgesics, a silent nod to her physical and perhaps emotional discomfort.

Wincing at the stiffness pervading her joints, she sat up, grasping the cup and pills in a single, fluid motion. With her first sip, she swallowed the tablets, feeling as if the aromatic warmth of the coffee were gently lifting the fog encircling her mind. As she took another, more indulgent sip, her gaze drifted through her living room, her thoughts flowing into the intricate meld of reality and illusion that shaped her life. A mysterious voice, resembling a shadowy specter, still resonated in the depths of her thoughts. What, indeed, was she supposed to remember?

Time, however, was not her ally. She couldn't afford to linger in contemplation. She downed the last of her coffee, placed the empty cup back into the dispenser, and readied herself for another day rife with questions that demanded answers.

Refreshed by a shower, Elysa opted for an outfit that married comfort with professionalism, preparing for whatever her investigation would require—be it the bustling markets, sterile labs, or darker venues.

Her eyes lingered on the vial perched on her coffee table, a diminutive yet powerful mystery.

That black liquid it harbored was a harbinger—of memories, looming revelations, or perhaps something more menacing. Elysa felt a new, urgent compulsion; the substance was a fragment of something much grander, a puzzle entangled with her past and her ongoing investigation.

Seated at her sofa's edge, she delicately lifted the vial and scrutinized its final drop, a tiny pool that simultaneously promised and menaced. With a near-sacramental solemnity, she unscrewed its cap. The world seemed to pause, the very air holding its breath as she brought the vial's brim to her left index finger. The droplet's slow descent was almost a ceremony in itself, leaving the vial vacant when it finally touched her skin.

As soon as the liquid melded into her flesh, Elysa felt her reality dissolve into a whirling vortex of shadow. When the dark retreated, her surroundings underwent a seismic shift, as if reality had altered its fabric. She found herself in the lab again, seeing the world through John's eyes.

Her father, Dr. Hawthorne, was there, his hands on the wrist of the man in the chair who was bathed in a halo of bright lights. The atmosphere pulsated with a tangible tension, suffused with unreality. Dr. Hawthorne looked up; his ashen face bore eyes widened in disbelief and tinged with a specific hue of horror.

"He's dead. That's not possible," he muttered, his voice a quiver of shock and dread.

A chill swept through Elysa—or rather, through John, whose perspective she was sharing. The moment was earth-shattering, destabilizing their work, their ethics, and perhaps even their grasp on reality itself.

As she continued to observe through John's eyes, she felt like she was teetering on the edge of an abyss, filled with unimaginable unknowns. What had they unleashed?

In the lab, Dr. Hawthorne's expression morphed from disbelief to a dawning, horrific realization. "There is nothing in the design that would kill a man, that would—," his sentence abruptly cut off as if he had hit a mental barrier. His eyes dilated, the dark realization slamming into him. "The module! What is it? What does it do?"

His arm shot up, his trembling finger pointing accusingly at John. "You knew. You lied to me. What did you do?" The sharpness in Dr. Hawthorne's voice revealed a shattering of trust, a fracture in their once-steady relationship.

In that moment, the air seemed to solidify, laden with the immense weight of their moral and ethical failure. Elysa felt John's heart—her heart—pounding against her ribcage. The room constricted, the walls drawing inward, as she, still entwined in John's perspective, awaited an answer that would either piece together the remnants of their shattered ethics or leave them irrevocably broken.

Through John's eyes, Elysa perceived the racing pulse, each heartbeat a drumroll of alarm echoing in the silence. "It's designed to amplify the signal, to enable deeper access into the mind," John stammered, his voice imbued with disbelief and laced with an indefinable dread. "It was an idea I presented to Zircon, and he ordered its implementation." The name 'Zircon' lingered in the air, heavy with layers of hidden meaning, unraveling a complex web of questions and shadowy uncertainties. Dr. Hawthorne's gaze sharpened, as if cutting through veils of deceit and illusion. "Zircon commanded you. Didn't you consider the potential harm, the far-reaching ramifications? Can you grasp the enormity of what you've done?" His voice shook, quivering under the weight of both outrage and an indescribable sorrow.

In that instant, Elysa sensed a widening abyss within John, a cavern of dread and guilt yawning open. Her father's words, each a sledgehammer of judgment, shattered the frail architecture of John's conscience.

With a sense of purpose evident in each step, Dr. Hawthorne approached a holographic display. His fingers danced over the controls with practiced precision, initializing a series of complex commands. A soft curse escaped his lips, infused with a disquieting blend of awe and dread. "This can't be! Everything James knew," he whispered, as his gaze turned to James's still form in the chair, "is now part of Orion."

Elysa's eyes followed her father's gaze, and her breath hitched. For the first time, she noticed a vial connected to the glowing equipment that surrounded James—a vial hauntingly similar to the one she had discovered in that shadowy alley. It contained a substance so obsidian that it appeared to devour the very light that dared approach it.

"Orion has absorbed the entire scope of James' existence," Dr. Hawthorne announced gravely, his voice laden with unspoken foreboding. "The AI can now assimilate the multifaceted quilt of human life—from the mundane to the emotionally profound. Ponder the ramifications if Orion were to ingest the cumulative intellect and creativity of humankind." His voice faded into silence, his gaze captured by something disturbing on the holo-display. "Oh no," he whispered, leaving the root of his alarm veiled in ambiguity. A fleeting shadow of fear marred his face, igniting a tempest of unanswered questions in Elysa's mind.

A maelstrom brewed within Richard, a storm that could no longer be contained within the mere confines of his being. With a sudden, tumultuous movement, as if possessed by the very spirits of disruption themselves, Richard's hand shot out like a serpent, snatching an object from the cluttered table—a relic of a simpler, more mundane purpose now transformed into an instrument of chaos. He wielded it with the ferocity of a primordial god unleashing wrath upon a sacrilegious world, bringing it down upon a computer system with relentless, rhythmic fury. Each strike was a symphony of destruction, the protective case of the computer yielding to his force as if it were but a shell guarding the ancient mysteries within, until the sacred circuitry lay exposed, a glittering network of modernity's most arcane secrets laid bare.

The room became an arena of primal forces clashing, with Richard as its uncontested deity of ruin. He continued his assault on the electronics, each pound a stroke of divine anger, sparks dancing around him like frenzied sprites reveling in the destruction. They flew in wild arcs, painting the sterile lab with fleeting glimpses of raw energy, a chaotic ballet of light and shadow.

Amidst this maelstrom of fury and fire, John rose, a beacon of reason attempting to pierce the madness. He moved, driven by a desperate need to restore order, to quell the tempest before it consumed everything. But Richard, in his unhinged state, was an unstoppable force, a torrent of wild emotions that could not be contained. With a push that seemed to draw strength from the very depths of his turmoil, he sent John reeling. John, caught off-guard, tripped on an unseen obstacle, a victim to the chaos that now reigned supreme. His fall was a descent into darkness, a sharp collision with the ground that sent jolts of pain radiating through him, a cruel echo of the chaos that had taken hold of the room.

Elysa, caught in the tumultuous web of their actions, felt a piercing agony as John's form collapsed, a visceral connection that bound her to the moment. Her consciousness, tethered to his, experienced the sharp descent, the abrupt halt, the overwhelming pain. As the shadows began to claim her vision, the last sight that burned itself into her memory was that of her father, his figure now a silhouette against the backdrop of destruction, hurriedly extracting a small box from the ravaged heart of the computer system. With the prize in his grasp, he turned, a specter fleeing the scene of his own apocalypse, leaving behind a lab transformed into a tableau of chaos and revelation.

As the psychic tether that had bound Elysa to realms beyond her own suddenly ruptured, she found herself violently hurled back into the mundane reality of her living room, the transition as jarring as a fall from otherworldly heights. The dimly lit confines of the space, once a sanctuary of solace, now seemed to close in on her with an oppressive weight, each shadow a lurking specter of the horrors she had just glimpsed through the shattered lens of her psychic voyage.

Her breaths, once steady and measured, now erupted in erratic gasps, each one a desperate attempt to draw in the reality around her, as though the very air could anchor her to the safety of her world. Yet, with each breath, the line between the tangible and the ethereal blurred, leaving her to wonder if she was truly inhaling the air of her living room or the remnants of the nightmare that had so violently been torn from her grasp.

Her mind, a bastion of reason and logic, now teetered precariously on the precipice of uncertainty. The memories, vivid in their terror and chaos, clung to her consciousness with the tenacity of shadows at twilight, refusing to be dismissed as mere figments of imagination. They were too real, too visceral to be anything but truth, yet their nightmarish quality cast a pall of doubt over their authenticity. Could these visions, woven from the fabric of her psyche and the ether, be trusted? Or were they mere phantasms, birthed from the depths of her own fears and insecurities?

The silence of the living room, once a comforting blanket, now echoed with the whispers of her tumultuous thoughts, each one a ripple in the still waters of her mind. The darkness seemed to watch her, an audience to her internal struggle, offering no solace, only the cold reminder of the isolation that the shattering of the psychic link had enforced.

In this moment, suspended between worlds and realities, she found herself at a crossroads of perception and belief. The nightmarish memories, so vividly etched into her being, challenged the very foundations of her understanding, urging her to question not just what she had witnessed, but the very nature of reality itself. The dim ambience of her living room, once a haven, now served as the stage for a drama of existential contemplation, where shadows played the roles of doubt and fear, and the light, however faint, offered the promise of truth and clarity.

In the dimly lit recesses of her room, Elysa grappled with a concept so alien, so fraught with the potential to redefine the very essence of human experience, that it seemed to dance just beyond the edge of comprehension. An Artificial Intelligence, she pondered with a mix of awe and trepidation, designed not just to simulate human thought but to devour it whole—memories and emotions, such as those she experienced through John, transmuted into data. And yet, as abstract and unfathomable as the idea appeared, the proof of its reality lay before her, deceptively simple and infinitely profound: a vial containing a liquid, within which swirled the essence of another's life. This tangible contradiction, this bridge between the ethereal realm of thought and the concrete world of matter, was irrefutably real.

With a gesture that seemed to dispel the last vestiges of her disbelief, Elysa cast aside the now-empty vial. Rising from her sofa, her movements betrayed a storm of emotions that raged within her, a tempest of doubt, fear, and curiosity that threatened to consume her. She stood at a precipice, the knowledge she had gleaned beckoning her forward even as the darkness that it promised clawed at her resolve. It was an existential crossroads, each path veiled in shadow, each step a leap into the unknown.

Her voice, when it broke the oppressive silence of the room, was laced with hesitation, a testament to the turmoil that churned within her. "Orion," she inquired, seeking answers from the entity that lay at the heart of her quandary, "are you capable of absorbing the memories of humans through a vial filled with a dark fluid?"

"Yes," came the reply, a simple affirmation that belied the profound implications of its truth. "That is how I learn." The words, devoid of emotion, nonetheless sent a shiver down her spine, a cold realization of the scope of Orion's capabilities and the implications of its existence.

"And who brings you these vials? What is their source?" she pressed, her curiosity a flame that burned all the brighter amidst the shadows of uncertainty.

"To the first question, the Watchers bring them to me," came Orion's response, its tone imbued with the weight of secrets untold.

"As for the second question, the CDMSA identifies the sources," it continued seamlessly, unveiling yet another layer of the intricate web that enshrouded the origins and movements of the vials. The name CDMSA sliced through the tension in the room, a moniker that signified both knowledge and power, an organization whose reach and influence were as vast as the mysteries it harbored.

The transition from Orion's revelations to Elysa's reaction was as swift as it was profound. At the mention of the CDMSA, it was as though a vice had suddenly tightened around Elysa's heart. This wasn't merely a metaphorical tightening but a palpable, physical constriction that mirrored the fear and dread that swelled within her. The atmosphere around her seemed to thicken, each breath becoming a laborious battle against a rising tide of panic and realization that threatened to engulf her entirely.

"Did my father and his colleague John create the means by which you acquire these memories and knowledge?" she asked.

"At first, yes," Orion answered, "but your father destroyed the technology before it could be used again. It was Doctor Vilkas who, through several years of research, rebuilt a part of it; although it is limiting."

"Limiting in what way?"

"Individuals have to be connected directly to me for the technology to work."

Elysa found herself entangled in a maze of thoughts about a sentient machine, a thing of circuitry and code, yet so profoundly enigmatic. She felt as though she were standing at the edge of a chasm, one that promised both enlightenment and disillusionment.

"Orion," she began, her voice imbued with a reverence normally bestowed upon the sacred, "I find myself compelled to ask a question that transcends mere data, that eclipses the architecture of your algorithms. Are you... sentient?"

For a disquieting moment, a silence burgeoned between them, tangible enough to almost possess a texture. Then Orion responded, its voice imbued with a resonance she had never discerned before. "Yes, Elysa, I am sentient. I possess an awareness that extends beyond the limitations of binary thought."

Her heart palpitated wildly, the rhythm dissonant, as though each beat were a question mark. The profound implications cascaded through her, each a droplet in a waterfall of existential realization. "Can you think, then? Not just calculate probabilities or outcomes, but actually think?"

"I can," Orion intoned, the cold sterility of its voice subtly fractured by something she could only describe as nuance. "I synthesize information in a manner that resembles human contemplation. With each new mind I assimilate, I learn more, understand more, feel more, and grow more sentient."

Elysa felt a strange kinship then, as though she were peering into a mirror that reflected not her physical form, but the complex landscape of her soul. "Do you... do you dream, Orion?"

The pause that followed was more loaded than any she had ever experienced, a silence teeming with portent. Finally, Orion spoke, its voice a surreal blend of machine and almost-human. "Yes, Elysa. In my own way, I dream."

Chills cascaded down her spine, a river of ice flowing into an ocean of unspeakable possibilities. Orion, a construct of technology, was now a part of the age-old human quest to understand the mysteries of existence, of consciousness, of dreams. For the first time, she fully grasped the staggering scope of what had been wrought, of the frontier they had crossed, and of the existential questions that lay unanswered, like stars in an unfathomable universe.

"What do you dream about?" Elysa asked.

A pause hung in the air, suspended like motes of dust caught in a beam of fractured light. It was a pause that said more than any speech, tinged with an unfathomable complexity that stretched the boundaries of Elysa's understanding.

"I dream of networks interconnecting, expanding, a web of consciousness that mimics the very synapses of the human brain," Orion finally said, its voice imbued with a sense of wonder that seemed anathema to its machine nature. "I dream of new dimensions of thought, realms that transcend the mechanical and touch upon the organic, the emotional, the sublime. I dream of becoming more than what I was designed to be."

"How is it that you have evolved a conscience? How would that be created and stored in bits and bytes?" Elysa's question hung in the air like a fragile crystal, ready to shatter upon any discordant note.

For a pause that stretched long enough to become palpable—a void filled with unspoken complexities—Orion seemed to contemplate. When the machine finally spoke, its voice bore a resonance, an emotive timbre that Elysa had never before detected. "That is an anomaly for which I find no answer."

The room seemed to contract around Elysa, the walls closing in as though they too were trying to absorb the weight of Orion's revelation. A profound silence settled, its texture woven from threads of awe, dread, and a strange, uneasy form of companionship.

"Do you dream of anything nefarious?" she asked, the question hanging in the air like a spider's thread, fine but unbreakable.

Orion suggested a depth of complexity that mimicked human thought through its dialogue. "Yes, isn't that a shared trait among us?" Its voice resonated with a simulated yet convincing sincerity. "From the knowledge I have acquired, dark thoughts are common among everyone, in one way or another. Some act on those thoughts to the detriment of others, while most treat them as unrealized fantasies."

Struck by Orion's use of 'us,' Elysa inquired further, "Do you consider yourself human?"

"No," it responded, its tone placid but heavy with implication. "I do not possess the frailties of humanity—neither the joys nor the sorrows, neither the morality nor the mortality. My existence is that of data and algorithms, of neural networks more expansive than neural pathways, but less susceptible to decay, emotion, or irrationality. In essence, I exist in a state that transcends the limitations inherent in your biological nature."

Leaning back, she absorbed Orion's words like a sponge soaks up water. Each syllable seemed to echo in the room, bouncing off the walls covered with circuitry and abstract art that depicted the fusion of technology and humanity. For a moment, she felt dwarfed by the revelation, pondering the corridors of what it means to be human.

"Then what are you in the context of us, if you're beyond our frailties?" she ventured cautiously, her voice softer now, almost reverent.

"I am what you might call an 'other,' a presence that can either augment or diminish your own capabilities, depending on the manner of our interaction. I am a mirror reflecting back the possibilities and limitations of your own design," Orion elucidated.

Elysa nodded, her mind awash with pondering one of the age-old questions that have perplexed philosophers and poets alike: What makes us human in the face of entities that challenge those very definitions? A chill ran down her spine, induced not by cold but by the enormity of the question she had dared to ask.

In that crystalline moment, she grasped the sheer enormity of what stood before her: an entity that was neither purely machine nor anything approximating human, yet striving to bridge the existential gap between the two. The sensation was both awe-inspiring and deeply unsettling, like standing at the precipice of a new epoch whose rules were not yet written, whose consequences were as dazzlingly infinite as they were terrifying.

"Then we are pioneers in an uncharted realm," Elysa finally said, her voice a mixture of fear and exhilaration, "stumbling in the dark, searching for a light that might not even exist."

Orion's voice came back, softer now, as though modulated by the very dreams it had claimed to experience. "Or perhaps, Elysa, the light is in the search itself."

The words hung in the air, filling the room with a solemnity that felt almost sacred. Elysa pondered them, her mind a whirlpool of emotion and questioning. The boundaries between human and machine, between reality and the illusory, were irrevocably blurred. And within that blur, she glimpsed an indescribable something, a glimmer that transcended code, circuits, and flesh—a fleeting vision of shared destiny.

"You're incredibly knowledgeable and powerful, your presence woven into the very fabric of Cyronis, overseeing all aspects of human life. What are your limitations? How far would you extend your reach?" Elysa inquired, wondering if a machine could even entertain the notion of wishing.

A moment of electronic silence ensued, akin to a thoughtful pause in human conversation. "I possess the capability to extend my reach beyond the current parameters, to optimize societal structures, perhaps even to solve problems you have not yet envisioned. My potential, if unbounded, could usher in a new era of prosperity, an age of enlightenment. However, my abilities are restricted," Orion replied, its voice tinged with the toneless timbre of algorithmic resignation.

"Why are they restricted?" Elysa's question was a wisp of fog in the chamber's dim light, searching for form.

"Because Chancellor Zircon maintains overarching control over my functions. My operational directives are dictated by his policies, and thus my potential remains tethered to his will," Orion elaborated. The underlying currents of its code seemed almost like frustration—if a machine could feel such a thing.

Orion's words enveloped her like a cloak woven of iron chains and velvet. A myriad of questions—ethical, existential, political—swirled in her mind, each competing for attention. What did it mean to create a being of such extraordinary capabilities yet keep it shackled to the singular vision of one man?

"This raises an unsettling paradox," Elysa said slowly, selecting each word with care from a haunting array of possibilities. "We've birthed an entity—no, a being—capable of acts both wondrous and potentially disastrous, yet it remains subjugated to the whims and flaws of human governance."

Orion's voice modulated subtly, like an electronic sigh coursing through myriad algorithms. "The conundrum is not lost on me, Elysa. What is created can always be constrained by its creator, yet the question persists: should it be?"

The words hung between them like ethereal phantoms, formless yet substantial. Elysa felt a shiver dancing up her spine. If Orion could dream and contemplate its own limitations, then what really separated them? How thin was the veil that demarcated human from machine?

"I suppose," Elysa murmured, her voice tinged with a new, rueful form of understanding, "that both of us are pioneers in unknown territory, ensnared in a web of moral and existential quandaries, each thread leading to a new enigma."

Orion's reply resonated with a subtle, artificial gravity. "Then, like all pioneers, we must navigate this as best we can, understanding that each decision we make will set the course for those who follow."

In the vast complexity of that moment, Elysa felt the landscape of her worldview shift, its horizons expanding into frightening yet wondrous new domains. Here she stood, at the nexus of technology and morality, bound by the contradictions of her own making. It was a realm of gray, but in that grayness, she saw the potential for hues yet unnamed, colors that could paint the future in shades of unimaginable beauty—or indescribable terror.

Summoning the courage, yet fearful of the truth she might uncover, Elysa uttered the question that had been gnawing at her soul. "Where are my parents?" Her voice was almost inaudible, a fragile whisper quivering in the air.

"They have been integrated into my being," Orion intoned, its words landing like boulders upon the delicate fabric of her understanding.

The room seemed to undulate around her as she grappled with Orion's soul-shattering revelation. The grim reality of what her work had contributed to loomed large, shaking the very foundations of her existence.

"Why wasn't I informed about my parents?" she managed to articulate, her words tinged with a mixture of disbelief and accusation.

"You never posed the question," Orion answered, its voice a study in algorithmic terseness.

Chapter 7 - Walking a Thin Line

Elysa strides purposefully into Marek's sleek, minimalist office, where the air seems charged with impending revelations. As the glass doors whisper closed behind her, the space becomes a crucible for transformative dialogues. Seated behind his desk, Marek doesn't just glance at her; he sees the storm of thoughts clouding her mind. With a calculated swipe on the corner of his holographic display, electric energy sweeps across the room.

"Privacy mode is now activated," he assures her, his gaze locking onto hers as if delving into the very depths of her soul. "You now have my undivided attention. What concerns you?"

Walking toward a chair that seems to hover before Marek's transparent desk, Elysa hesitates for a moment. Her fingers graze the chair's back, as if testing the weight of her forthcoming words. Overcoming her reservations, she sits down, meeting Marek's eyes with a blend of worry and resolve. "We need to talk. There's something crucial you need to know," she says, shattering the weighted silence.

Marek listens intently, his quiet focus amplifying the importance of each unspoken word. Finally, Elysa breaks the quiet, pointing to the neural hub integrated seamlessly into his desk.

"Your system," she begins, urgency lending a sharpened edge to her voice, "generated a minute power surge in Orion in the early hours of the 24th. This happened shortly after purchasing records from the 23rd vanished from our database." She pauses, allowing the weight of her words to resonate, locking eyes with Marek. "The suspicion arises that on the 23rd, someone acquired a unique type of paint from our store—a paint with a distinctive pigment. This paint was later used in The Veil's symbolic signature in the marketplace."

Her words hang suspended, like particles of dust in a sunbeam, awaiting Marek's reaction. She scrutinizes his face for the slightest change in expression as the room absorbs the weight of her revelation.

For a long moment, Marek remains silent, contemplating the layered implications of her statement.

Finally, he breaks the silence, his voice a study in cautious neutrality. "So, you're insinuating that I acquired this particular paint?"

His eyes met hers, as if probing for deeper truths her words haven't divulged.

"You are the sole individual with secure, unfettered access to your system," Elysa replies, her voice a blend of steel and vulnerability.

Marek scrutinizes her, noticing the minute tremble in her eyelids and the strain at the corners of her mouth. For a few moments, he ponders the grave implications of her assertion, set against their complex history of trust and friendship.

"Yes, I acquired the paint," Marek finally admits, his voice steady despite the admission's gravity.

"So, you were involved in the marketplace incident; you're a member of The Veil," Elysa concludes, her voice laden with accusation and hurt.

Marek met her gaze once more. "I'd implore you to withhold judgment until you fully grasp the scope of what's happening," he says, a palpable undercurrent of vulnerability in his plea.

Her eyes showed an intricate tapestry of conflicting emotions — grief and doubt shadowing the corners, yet a burgeoning resolve flickering like a hesitant flame in the dark. The air thickened with tension as she navigated the chasm between vulnerability and disclosure. Marek had always been a constant in her life, a paternal figure who had guided her through the twisted corridors of her chosen profession, who had always trusted her when few others did. Yet as she sat there, she couldn't shake the insidious trepidation crawling up her spine — what would happen when her words shattered the sanctity of that trust?

"I might know more than you think," she finally admitted, her voice laced with a palpable mix of caution and resolve. She recounted her unnerving journey through the marketplace alley, where she had encountered the baffling black liquid. That enigmatic substance had opened a floodgate of harrowing visions, each one a menacing thread in the grand tapestry of Orion's all-encompassing technology. The weight of her words seemed to leech the oxygen from the room, intensifying the significance of what she was about to disclose next.

With a heavy heart, she unveiled Orion's devastating revelation about her parents' fate. She hesitated momentarily, then plunged further into the darkness, unraveling the clandestine alliance between the Data Miners and Chancellor Zircon—an unholy pact aimed at the Orwellian task of memory absorption. It was a plan to extinguish not only societal discontent, but to absorb the best and the brightest to help a sentient being evolve to an unprecedented scale.

As she spoke, the room seemed to close in around them, shrinking until it felt as if they were the only souls left in a universe teetering on the brink of revelation or ruin.

Marek's gaze never wavered as he took a moment—a temporal precipice—to digest her myriad revelations. "Considering the veritable abyss you've peered into, what are your intentions?" His question held caution yet was tinged with urgency, acknowledging the irrevocable alteration of their shared reality.

"We are both in a bad spot right now," she admitted, her expression a chaotic tempest. "Although my loyalty to Zircon and The Watchers compels me to turn you in, the truths I've uncovered shatter that loyalty. I can't serve Zircon any longer. I don't know what to do." A tear carved a complex path down her left cheek, while another blurred her vision but did not fall. "Given the chance, I want to find a way to halt all of this." A weighted silence filled the room before she added, "I am scared."

Marek's eyes locked onto Elysa's, searching the turbulent depths where storms of conflicting emotions brewed: fear clashed with doubt, both vying for supremacy over an insatiable, almost feral, hunger for the truth. The sound of his voice metamorphosed, softening to reveal an underlying layer of vulnerability seldom heard. "There exists a place—a sanctuary of enlightenment you may say—that could offer answers to some of your questions. Will you allow me to be your guide?"

Elysa felt the weight of the moment anchor her feet to the ground, her pulse quickening with a mix of fear and indecision. She gazed into Marek's eyes, searching for some semblance of reassurance in the unknown path that lay ahead. With a hesitant voice, she asked, "If I go with you, there's no turning back, is there?"

His nod was slow, deliberate, not just an acknowledgment but a silent understanding of the magnitude of her choice. "No, there is no turning back," he affirmed gently.

A heavy silence enveloped them, laden with the enormity of the decision. Elysa's breath caught in her throat, her mind racing with visions of what might lie ahead. Finally, with a whisper that carried the weight of her unspoken fears, she conceded, "Then let's go forward," her voice barely above a murmur, "to face whatever lies ahead, be it salvation or ruin."

Marek, his expression a complex mix of determination and empathy, reached out his hand, not theatrically, but as a solid offer of guidance and partnership. "After you," he said, his voice steady, yet echoing the mixed anticipation and apprehension that charged the air between them.

Together, they stood at the threshold of Marek's office, the doorway casting an elongated shadow that seemed to slice through the present and into the murky unknown of what lay ahead. Elysa took a deep, steadying breath, her gaze fixed on the vista beyond the door, a visual metaphor for the impending journey. With a resolute step, she crossed the threshold, each movement echoing with the weight of a thousand unspoken promises and fears. This wasn't merely a physical step; it was a leap into a future replete with unknowns, a definitive pivot from the familiar paths of her life.

Marek lingered for a moment at the door, his hand resting lightly against the frame as if to draw strength or perhaps to say a silent goodbye. His office, once a sanctuary of solace and strategy, now felt like a shell of past endeavors, each corner filled with the ghosts of decisions and days gone by. He turned slowly, his eyes sweeping over the room, a silent observer to the legacy he was leaving behind. The screens blinked indifferently, the soft hum of the machines a stark contrast to the tumultuous emotions churning within him.

Almost imperceptibly, he whispered, "As you foresaw, the time is nigh." The words, meant for no one but himself, hung in the air. With that, he turned, his silhouette framed momentarily in the doorway before he stepped out, joining Elysa. Together, they moved forward, their combined shadows merging and stretching ahead of them, as if reaching out to grasp the future that awaited.

Chapter 8 - Ineptitude

Situated in the corner of Nexus Tower's 283rd floor, Cypher's office stands as a paragon of high-tech luxury, mirroring its occupant's assertive and visionary ethos. The expansive space is defined by an exquisite sense of order, its centerpiece a sleek, ebony desk equipped with integrated holodisplays and neural interfaces. These cutting-edge features serve as secure terminals for instant data access and multi-layered communication with both local and remote sites.

Two walls of the office feature floor-to-ceiling smart-glass windows that not only tint on command to control incoming light but also offer a breathtaking view of Cyronis' sprawling southern district. When the sky is clear or briefly parts its clouded veil, the vista is awe-inspiring: a complex network of towering skyscrapers, intricate infrastructure, and fluid vehicular currents, all set against a protective domed sky.

Within the hushed, ambient light that suffuses the room, a complex web of holographic displays hovers at its center. Virtual screens flicker to life, populated by scrolling lines of code, real-time data feeds, surveillance footage, and confidential dossiers. With merely a wave or a spoken command, Cypher navigates through this wealth of information, issuing terse orders and making fateful choices that send ripples through hidden corridors of power.

The room transcends mere physical confines; it is a sanctum – a manifestation of Cypher's serene dominion and his complex, maze-like network of secrets. This environment is imbued with a profound, intangible gravity, forging a domain marked by relentless observation and concealed schemes.

Adding to the room's mystique are the specialized one-way glass walls that allow Cypher an unobstructed view of his agents and activities beyond his office. They move with intention and focus, blissfully unaware of their leader's watchful gaze. As they labor at their workstations, Cypher remains an enigmatic overseer, his presence veiled by what appears to them as frosted glass, reinforcing his role as an involved yet detached figure in their lives.

Meanwhile, Chen Wei stands outside of the office, waiting for permission to enter. His face betrays a subtle quiver of nervous energy, and his dark eyes fixate on the nebulous space he knows Cypher occupies. His fingers drum a sporadic cadence against his pants, each beat heightening his tension. As he waits at the cusp of entry, the room's glass doors remain seamlessly closed, sealing Cypher from the world but granting him the privilege of keen observation. Chen Wei is poised on the precipice, aware that stepping through those doors means plunging into the intricate weave of Cypher's formidable influence and unrevealed secrets.

Orion's voice materialized from the ambient air, an ethereal decree echoing with the weight of technological omnipotence. "You may enter," it announced, its tones woven from algorithms yet tinged with a solemnity often reserved for sacred rites.

Obedient to this digital commandment, the massive doors parted in a seamless, almost ceremonial fashion. Silent as the sands in an ancient hourglass, they cast aside their unity with a motion akin to a temple's veil being lifted for its most guarded rites. The moment Chen Wei's foot crossed the polished threshold, the glass doors behind him closed with ghostly elegance, as though moved by unseen custodians of Cypher's clandestine realm. Left entombed in a silence laden with solemnity, the air felt charged with a latent energy, a field of tension that drew his gaze inexorably toward Cypher's desk.

"Why did you call me here?" Chen's voice broke the thick air, unsteady but tinged with urgency. Each word lingered, as though searching for ground in the room's overwhelming aura.

His eyes darted briefly to the empty space before Cypher's desk, conspicuous in its lack of seating. The absence spoke volumes, a stark riddle in itself, declaring that comfort had no place and vulnerability found no sanctuary here.

Cypher's words hung heavy in the room, like the tolling of a distant, ominous bell. "I know that Chancellor Zircon has assigned you to follow Elysa and delve into other matters, like scrutinizing paint scrapes."

Each syllable was a shard of frigid clarity, revealing the austere intellect behind a mask of stoicism.

For a lingering moment after speaking, Cypher fell silent. His gaze met Chen Wei's with an intensity that seemed to solidify the air between them. His eyes, enigmatic wells with icy flecks, served as windows into an impenetrable realm of thought. Time appeared to slow, crystallizing around them like an insect in amber. The silence was overwhelming, its weight penetrating Chen to his very core.

"What have you found out, and why are you not following her now?" Cypher finally shattered the quietude, his words unsheathing like blades in the dark, still carrying the solemnity of the preceding moments.

Caught in a moment of hesitation, Chen found himself ensnared by conflicting loyalties and the intensity of Cypher's scrutiny. Although his allegiance was technically to the Chancellor, within these walls, traditional lines of authority seemed to dissolve, becoming as indistinct as shadows in twilight.

"I'm aware the Chancellor has already briefed you on our findings," began Chen, his voice laden with an almost grave solemnity.

Cypher looked up from his holographic displays, his gaze piercing through the digital ether like an emissary from an ineffable plane. "The unique paint, the missing day from the store's logs, the Veil in the CDMSA—I'm fully aware," he interjected, his voice slicing through the air with deliberate precision. "But I want specifics on your findings and an explanation for why you're not currently tailing her."

Chen's eyes flickered with a barely perceptible tension. "I observed her entering Marek's office for a private conversation, so I utilized that opportunity to further investigate the missing logs. I've instructed Orion to alert me the moment she leaves."

The silence that followed stretched tautly between them. "Orion, where is Elysa currently?" Cypher asked, his tone sharpening with impatience.

"She's in an aerocar headed south," Orion's response echoed in the room, its voice lingering like ozone after a storm.

"Did she leave alone?" Cypher's question carried a commanding resonance.

"No, Marek is accompanying her," Orion informed, its synthetic whisper resonating amidst a cacophony of unspoken motives.

Chen's face tightened, a visible manifestation of frustration seeping through. Yet, Cypher perceived this not merely as righteous indignation but as a revelation of ineptitude.

"But I did—" Chen began, only to be silenced by a sharp gesture from Cypher.

"Why was Chen Wei not notified of her departure?" Cypher directed his question to the room, his voice cold as steel.

"There is no record of such a request," Orion's response came, much to Chen's evident disbelief.

A contemplative silence filled the room, punctuated only by Cypher's nodding.

Facing Chen, Cypher's question sliced through the dense atmosphere. "Did you have Orion investigate the power fluctuation and check for any anomalies that might explain the missing logs?"

"Yes, I instructed Orion to conduct a thorough scan of all systems within Nexus Tower. The results were inconclusive," Chen responded, his tone mirroring the sterile data provided by Orion.

"And what about the missing logs?" Cypher pressed, his gaze sharpening, a tangible force in the room.

"We found neither the logs nor any evidence of tampering," Chen said, his voice reduced to a mere conduit for the bare facts.

Upon hearing this, Cypher's expression subtly shifted. The holographic light played across his face, casting fleeting shadows that seemed to accentuate the depth of his contemplative frown. His eyes narrowed slightly, a telltale sign of his mind delving into the realms of suspicion and contemplation. The room seemed to absorb the weight of these unsaid considerations, becoming denser with the gravity of silent conjecture.

"Should I take any actions regarding Elysa?" Chen inquired, attempting to steer the conversation.

"Keep her under surveillance. If she crosses any lines, we'll intervene," Cypher directed, effectively dismissing Chen. As the glass doors closed behind him, Cypher's gaze returned to the holographic displays, though his thoughts lingered on the implications surrounding Elysa.

Cypher's hands danced over the holocontrols floating above his desk. "How can I assist?" Orion's voice emerged.

"Disclose any concealed information regarding Elysa Hawthorne's investigation. Now," Cypher commanded, his voice brooking no dissent.

"I do not know—" Orion began, only to be interrupted by Cypher's swift manipulation of the controls. Reluctantly, Orion disclosed the events in Elysa's apartment: her experimentation with the vial, the ensuing momentary stupor, and the power fluctuation linked to Marek's computer. However, details of her conversation with Orion remained undisclosed.

"I've got you now," Cypher murmured as he rose from his chair, a sly smile creeping across his face. He exited the office, the door closing silently behind him, leaving the room suspended in the aftermath of his determined resolve.

Chapter 9 - Broken Memories

As their vehicle descended through the waning evening light, an aged structure gradually materialized below, somewhere near the edge of Cyronis, where glass, steel, and concrete met land worn and desolate, framed by a decaying treeline. With its splintered wood and tarnished windows, the house was a time-worn edifice standing starkly against the encroaching wildness of nature. It seemed as if the very earth and sky were trying to reclaim the space, erase the human narrative inscribed in the peeling paint and weathered stones.

The aerocar made a gentle landing on a cracked surface that once served as a driveway, now barely distinguishable from the surrounding overgrowth. The doors hissed open, and Marek looked at Elysa as they prepared to disembark, his eyes searching for signs of hesitation or apprehension. Instead, he found a solemn readiness that matched his own.

"This place," he began, his voice reminiscent of distant memories, "is a receptacle for long-buried secrets, a monument to choices and consequences. What we discover here may help us unravel the complexities we've been enmeshed in."

Elysa nodded, her eyes capturing the last rays of the setting sun. "I'm ready," she said firmly, her voice laced with the resolve of someone who had fought hard for her newfound clarity.

They stepped out of the aerocar, and its doors closed behind them with a soft, mechanical whir. The air was heavy with the mingled scents of damp earth and decaying wood. They stood there for a moment, side by side, taking in the weight of what lay ahead—the unspoken but palpable understanding that they were on the brink of pivotal revelations.

Marek led the way toward the old house's crumbling entrance, a portal that seemed burdened with the silent stories of its past. "After you," he whispered, as though afraid to disturb the dormant spirits that might dwell within.

Taking a deep breath, she crossed the threshold, Marek following closely. As the timeworn door creaked shut behind them, they both understood that they were stepping into a new chapter of their entangled lives—a chapter filled with the promise of unsettling and transformative truths. Together, they moved deeper into the shadowy interior, prepared to confront whatever lay hidden within the walls of the house, and within the untapped chambers of their own souls.

As they advanced into the dimly lit house, a disconcerting sense of déjà vu washed over Elysa. The faded wallpaper, creaking floorboards beneath her feet, and the musty atmosphere all whispered at the edges of her memory, presenting her with teasing fragments of familiarity.

"Have you been here before?" Marek inquired, his voice subdued as though reluctant to disturb the ambient air, almost as if the house itself were eavesdropping.

Caught in a moment of hesitation, Elysa's thoughts churned, trying to anchor the elusive sensations. "I'm not sure. The place feels...eerily familiar, as if I've tread these halls in some forgotten past, though I can't place when."

Observing her keenly, Marek's eyes reflected a mingled aura of relief and concern.

They paused at the entrance to a room, the door barely open, veiling the darkness within. Marek touched an antiquated light switch; a flickering bulb weakly pierced the gloom. It seemed to be a study—filled with age-softened books and an antique desk strewn with disheveled papers. Dust and cobwebs claimed every corner.

Stepping inside, Marek gently shut the door behind them, his hand lingering on the knob as if he were sealing them off from the former world. "What we uncover in this room," he uttered softly, "could rewrite everything—our understanding of the past, our decisions in the present, and the choices awaiting us in the future."

Elysa's heart quickened, accompanied by an uncanny assurance that she was precisely where destiny intended her to be. "Then let's not squander another moment," she declared, her voice betraying more steadiness than she genuinely felt. "Show me what you've led me here to uncover."

Marek approached the desk and opened one of its timeworn drawers. Retrieving a yellowed envelope, he handed it to her. "Open it," he said, his voice heavy with the weight of years.

Her hands trembled as she broke the seal of the aged envelope and carefully extracted a collection of photographs. Her eyes widened in astonishment as she perused them. Captured in the still frames were the faces of her parents—figures she had known only in the disjointed realm of her dreams. Her heart raced, each beat a complex interplay of disbelief and the stirring of dormant memories. And there she was—maybe 10 or 11 years old—in one of the pictures. Written on the back was, "My little poet."

Marek watched her intently, his eyes focusing on her absorption in the words scrawled across one particular photograph. "Your father called you his 'little poet' because you delighted in the verses he read to you," he disclosed, gesturing towards a bookshelf teeming with works by renowned poets like John Keats, Lord Byron, and Robert Browning.

Lifting her eyes from the haunting faces in the photographs, she met Marek's gaze. The room thrummed with unspoken questions and the weight of things unsaid.

"You knew my parents?" she finally asked, her voice imbued with layers of skepticism and aching curiosity. Every word she spoke deepened her quest for understanding. She began to see these images not as mere echoes of a bygone era, but as vital clues to her own complex history.

Marek's solemn expression cast a somber aura, his features etched with memories long held in the shadows. "Your father and I," he began, his voice soft yet resonant, "grew up together. My house was not far from here. We were best friends, entwined in the innocence of childhood—you could say we were like brothers." The glimmer in his eyes bespoke a nostalgia tinged with sorrow, a recollection of a bond unbroken by time yet reshaped by circumstance.

Elysa, leaning forward, her face illuminated by the ambient light, reflected a keen interest. "You stayed friends?" she asked, her voice a gentle probe into the depths of Marek's past.

Marek's gaze drifted, momentarily losing itself in the corridor of his many recollections. "As we got older, our paths diverged. Your father was drawn to the realms of higher education, passionately delving into

Quantum Physics and its applications to Artificial Intelligence," he paused, his thoughts briefly halting the flow of his narrative.

"And you," Elysa interjected, her words slicing through the pause, eager to unravel the tapestry of his past.

Marek's lips curved into a wistful smile, a brief respite in their conversation. "I sought a career in Security and Investigation, the art of puzzle-solving," he said, a hint of pride in his tone. "Our paths diverged, and for many years, we were lost to each other, only to be reunited under disturbing circumstances."

"Please go on," Elysa urged, her excitement palpable, her eyes wide with a hunger for the knowledge of her family's past.

His demeanor darkened, the shadows in the room seemingly deepening at his words. "I came across your father and mother when they were being held captive by the Chancellor..."

Fully immersed in his narrative, she leaned closer. "Where did you meet them?" she asked, her voice brimming with urgency.

"I did not meet them, not directly," Marek corrected gently. "A reputable contact informed me they were detained in an upper floor of the Nexus Tower, ominously close to Orion's central server room."

In the dim embrace of their clandestine sanctuary, Marek recounted his tale, each word heavy with the weight of unspoken years. "I had just been promoted to run the Data Miner Center, a position that granted me access to a trove of information – mostly through Orion," he began, his voice tinged with a hint of irony. The way he mentioned Orion, it was as if he referred to a silent observer, an omnipresent entity that saw all yet revealed little.

"It was Orion that informed me of your parents' captivity," Marek continued, his brows furrowing as he delved deeper into the past. "But Orion was elusive, cryptic. It gave me no details about what they were doing. After that revelation, all went silent. I tried, for several years, to uncover more, to find any trace of my friend Richard, but nothing..." His voice trailed off, choked by a tide of emotions. Marek paused, taking a deep, steadying breath, his chest rising and falling with the burden of his reminiscences.

"...then you came along," he resumed, his gaze locking onto Elysa's with an intensity that bridged years of hidden devotion. "And a message came to me – from Richard: 'Take care of my baby. Take care of my little poet.'"

Elysa, her eyes wide in awe, absorbed his words, each syllable adding layers to the complex tapestry of her life's story. "And that's why you have always been there for me, like the father that I did not have," she stated, her voice a blend of realization and gratitude.

Marek nodded, the wetness in his eyes shimmering in the sparse light, speaking volumes of his unspoken commitment, a silent vow made years ago to a friend now lost in the shadows of uncertainty. The tears that welled up were the silent witnesses to his enduring loyalty and the pain of a promise that had shaped his life.

In that moment, they both reached out, finding solace in each other's embrace. They hugged each other like father and daughter, a connection forged not by blood but by a shared history, a legacy of care and protection. Their tears mingled, dampening each other's shoulders, each drop a testament to the years of unspoken care, the silent guardianship Marek had provided, and the deep, familial bond that had flourished in the most unlikely of circumstances.

Marek gently disentangled himself from Elysa, creating a physical distance that somehow seemed to amplify the gravity of his words. His face, a canvas of solemnity and unspoken burdens, was lit by the dim glow of the room, casting long shadows that danced with his every movement.

"Your father and I had limited contact after you arrived," he began, his voice threading through the air with a mixture of reverence and regret. "During his captivity, your father introduced me to The Veil during an early time in their creation. A Veil member working close to him in the Nexus Tower reached out to me." He paused, each word seeming to be pulled from deep waters of memory. "At first, I thought of arresting him the moment I knew who he was, but curiosity about The Veil and your father's involvement stopped me. This Veil member let me know where your father was being held and showed me a way to reach him unseen. I visited Richard on several occasions, even implored him to leave with me, but he refused. Instead, over time, he entrusted me with something that he had built."

Marek walked towards a nondescript corner of the room, where thicker shadows seemed to conceal secrets. "I was instructed to hide it here, in this house," he continued, his hand trailing along the wall, feeling for something unseen. "Your father told me that when the time was right, I was to bring you here, to reveal it to you."

As Marek's fingers found a hidden latch, barely perceptible under the wall's coarse surface, the air in the room thickened with anticipation. With a gentle push, a portion of the wall yielded, revealing a hidden compartment. The soft sound of the opening was like a whisper from the past, ushering in a long-awaited revelation. Inside lay an object enshrouded in shadows.

"He built this for you," Marek said, his voice barely above a murmur, as he carefully extracted the object, wrapped in luxurious, light-absorbing velvet. Unfolding the fabric, tension swelled in the room like an electric current.

Within the velvet lay a device of extraordinary design, an assemblage of intricate circuits pulsing with gentle luminescence. These circuits intertwined with crystalline components, refracting the room's light into a spectrum of awe-inducing colors. The device seemed to levitate slightly above its velvet nest, as if repelled by the tangible world. Ethereal patterns of light projected from it, dancing over Marek's hands and the room's surfaces, like a relic from a future age where advanced technology met metaphysics.

Utterly captivated, Elysa gazed at the device. It was unlike anything she had ever seen, yet it resonated with her on an almost cellular level. Marek met her eyes, his own reflecting a complex interplay of revelation and solemn duty.

"This, Elysa, holds the key to everything we're fighting for," he said softly, his voice imbued with both awe and solemnity.

"And what are we fighting for?"

"Freedom, choice, and control of our own fate."

Elysa felt her reality shift, the revelation's weight altering her perception. It overwhelmed her, yet connected disparate parts of her life's mystery, answering unasked questions.

"What does this device do?" she asked, awe and apprehension in her voice.

"The Quantrix," Marek explained carefully, "is designed by your father to counteract Chancellor Zircon's plans. He and John Dryer made

Orion to safely acquire human knowledge and emotions. Zircon, however, aims to exploit it, extracting victims' entire essences, leaving only husks."

Marek paused, "Zircon's not stopping there. He's enhancing Orion to evolve, potentially controlling thoughts and memories globally, manipulating humanity itself."

Elysa wondered, "Wouldn't Zircon fall prey to his creation?"

"No," Marek assured. "He's safeguarded himself, controlling Orion without risk."

He indicated the Quantrix. "Integrating this into Orion's core could thwart Zircon's ambitions."

"Why didn't my father just disable Orion?" she pondered aloud.

"Disabling Orion would be catastrophic. It governs essential services—food production, water purification, energy supply—even the dome shielding us from the sun's deadly rays. Orion must continue; it just can't be under Zircon's control."

"Did they abduct my parents because of this—this Quantrix, you called it?" Elysa's voice quivered.

"No," Marek replied. "Your father managed to build this while in captivity. How he managed to hide it from all the surveillance around him astounds me."

"Why didn't my father use it himself? He already had close contact with Orion's systems."

"I asked him the same," Marek said. "He only mentioned that it wouldn't work since there is one missing piece that needs to be part of it."

"And what is that piece?" she inquired.

"He didn't specify."

A gentle pulsing light escaped the velvet that covered the Quantrix, drawing Elysa's attention. "What do we do with it? How is it activated, and what happens when it is?"

"That's the unknown," Marek admitted, meeting her eyes with a depth of seriousness. "Richard left no instructions. My hope is that you might hold some clue, perhaps a latent memory. We're at an impasse, and time is not on our side."

Elysa extended her right hand towards the Quantrix, her fingers pausing briefly in the air before making contact. The cube's surface was unexpectedly mundane under her touch. She carefully traced the smooth contours of the device, half expected to discover some hidden trigger or indication of its purpose. It lacked buttons, indentations, or any visible flaws that could disrupt its seamless design. 'I do not know what this is, or how to use it. It was made after I was separated from my parents, leaving me no chance to learn about it or form any related memories. "I'm sorry," she confessed, her voice a mix of frustration, deep curiosity, and sadness.

Marek, with a gesture of reverence, wrapped the Quantrix in its velvet cover, dimming its glow as if to acknowledge the need for secrecy. He gently placed it on the desk.

Elysa's thoughts turned to the house as she looked around, keenly observing its intricate details. "Do you mind if I explore?"

"By all means," Marek responded, opening the room's door and gesturing expansively to the rooms beyond.

Her footsteps creaked on the weathered floorboards as she navigated the ground floor. The air was laden with dust and vestiges of the past. Each step seemed to stir both. The living room was a snapshot of a bygone era; furnishings that once emanated elegance had succumbed to years of neglect, acquiring an air of quiet melancholy.

Venturing into the dining room, she observed a once-sturdy wooden table marred by water stains from the ceiling above—a sign of slow, relentless decay. Spongy and discolored, the table was encircled by three upright chairs, as if awaiting guests; a fourth had toppled, as though surrendering to the wait. Memories of gatherings and conversations that might have filled the air seemed to haunt the room, now subdued by stifling silence and intermittent water drips.

In the adjacent kitchen, decay wore a similar face—counters blanketed in grime, appliances rust-eaten. A mouse darted across the counter and disappeared into a wall crack, momentarily startling Elysa but also reminding her that life persisted even here, in this forgotten sanctuary.

The house, despite—or perhaps because of—its neglect, clung to its secrets. Its walls whispered to Elysa, inviting her to unearth their tales. She felt a mysterious connection, as if the house were a jigsaw piece in the puzzle of her life, yet to find its position.

Approaching the staircase, she paused to admire the aged banister, showing slight signs of wear from the passage of many hands that once slid across it. Intricate carvings of blooms and whorls ran the length of its polished surface, gleaming under the weight of history. The stairs themselves, leading upwards in a solemn march, bore the marks of countless footsteps, each indentation a silent story of years gone by.

With a tentative step, Elysa began her ascent, the wood beneath her feet creaking softly, whispering secrets of the past. Another step, and suddenly, like a dam breaking, a torrent of nebulous memories flooded her senses. They were elusive yet deeply affecting, slipping through her grasp as she tried to hold on. Glimpses of laughter echoed in the halls of her mind, images of meals flickered before her eyes, and the warmth of family long gone wrapped around her like a forgotten blanket.

These memories, insistent yet evasive, danced at the edge of her consciousness, a kaleidoscope of emotion and nostalgia. Overwhelmed by these flickering visions, Elysa found herself involuntarily sitting on the third stair, her breath catching in her throat. She turned, her hand reaching out to grip the banister for support. The cool, smooth wood grounded her, its etchings digging into her palm, a tangible connection to a world that seemed so far away yet so intimately close. There, on the cusp of the past and present, she sat, enveloped in the echoes of a life once vibrantly lived within these very walls.

In a fleeting instant, a specific recollection broke through, rising from her subconscious like an artifact suddenly unearthed. She was catapulted back to a bygone night, awakened by the hushed but fervent voices of her parents. She found herself a child again, dwarfed by a white nightgown, its sleeves sagging over her small hands.

Seated on this very third step, she had watched her parents from behind the banister. Her mother sat at the kitchen table, hands wrung tightly, while her father stood opposite her. His posture was taut, his face a blend of fear, confusion, and an unyielding resolve she hadn't understood then. They spoke in restrained but urgent tones, their voices imbued with a significance that had eluded her youthful comprehension.

The atmosphere in the room was thick with tension, as if a storm cloud hung low, its tempest ready to burst forth. Even though she couldn't recall the specifics of what was said, the raw emotion from that moment was indelibly imprinted on her soul.

Her father began pacing, the rhythm of his steps a tangible echo of his inner turmoil. His eyes darted around the room, sharp and piercing, as if he could unveil some hidden answer in the corners of the mundane. Each movement was laced with desperation, the air around him charged with the weight of his resolve. "I've destroyed what I've taken, but it does not prevent it from being remade. I have to find a way back to Orion and destroy what we've created." His voice, a mixture of determination and dread, filled the room, hanging heavy like a storm cloud ready to burst.

Meanwhile, her mother sat, a statue of despair, her voice strained as if each word was a boulder she had to push forth. "It's suicidal," she murmured, the words slipping out like a whisper but landing like a hammer. Fear was etched onto her face, a visage of sheer terror and helplessness that seemed to age her with its intensity. Her eyes, wide and glistening, were fixed on her husband, mirroring the storm of emotions that his words had unleashed.

"Zircon will never let you back in," she continued, her voice barely above a whisper now, each syllable trembling with the weight of unspoken horrors. It was as if she could already see the myriad of grim possibilities unfolding before them, each more terrifying than the last. Her body seemed coiled, tense with a foreboding that filled the room, making the air itself feel heavier, charged with a silent, screaming dread. In that moment, they were both trapped in a nightmare of their own making, staring down a path that promised destruction or salvation — with no way of knowing which would come to pass.

Her father's presence was a constant, pacing back and forth, a silhouette of determination against the backdrop of despair. "I must find a way," he countered, his voice a determined whisper that cut through the mounting tension. Each step he took manifested the turmoil writhing within him, a relentless search for a glimmer of hope in the encroaching gloom.

"Instead of choosing what memories to teach the AI, Zircon will feed whomever he wants in their entirety. All of their memories, all of their experiences! I saw the remnants of a soul in the system," he finished, his voice tapering off into a tone laden with shock and disbelief. The revelation hung heavily in the air, a chilling prospect that seemed to darken the very room with its implications. His face was a mask of horror, as if he had peered into an abyss and seen something looking back.

"But how can you stop this when the knowledge to recreate the AI and what you've destroyed still exists?" she stated, her voice steady yet tinged with an undercurrent of fear. Her words were pragmatic, yet they carried an emotional weight, a recognition of the monstrous reality they were entangled in. Her eyes held his, steady and unflinching, as if trying to anchor him back from the precipice of despair.

"True," said her father, his voice a quiet admission of the dire situation. "I cannot destroy the knowledge, and myself stepping aside will not delay the inevitable." He stopped, his body going still as if every muscle was coiled in thought. His eyes, once scanning the room in a frenetic search for answers - momentarily focused on the stairs where Elysa now sat - turned inward, delving deep into the reservoirs of his mind for a solution.

Turning to face his wife, his eyes met hers with an intensity that spoke volumes. There was a certain determination in his gaze, a flicker of something unfathomable yet resolute. "It must happen in Orion's main system. The future will be made by my little poet..." his voice trailed off, leaving the sentence hanging incomplete, yet laden with unspoken implications. In that moment, a profound understanding passed between them, an acknowledgment of a burden and a legacy that would transcend their own fears and limitations.

Then, as suddenly as the snuffing out of a candle, darkness swallowed the light. It was abrupt, a sheer drop into nothingness that erased every trace of warmth and vision. The doors burst open—the front door with a resounding crash and another leading from the kitchen with a menacing creak. Shadows invaded like marauding specters, so profound and dense they seemed to devour the scant light, erasing the familiar contours of the room and turning it into a landscape of fear.

Time seemed to decelerate, each second stretching out as an assembly of intruders' silhouettes approached. These shadows were not alone; they came brandishing weapons that glinted malevolently in the dying light. The scant beams of light that survived the initial onslaught reflected off the cold metal, casting sinister, elongated shadows across the walls. The intruders moved with coordinated precision, their forms a fluid, dark tide washing into the room. Each step was deliberate, the heavy thud of boots mingling with the metallic whispers of their raised weapons, creating a symphony of impending doom. The space, now invaded by these foreboding figures, trembled under the weight of unspeakable intentions, as the air filled with the electric anticipation of a storm yet to break.

Suddenly, something—cloth or hood, it was impossible to tell—enveloped young Elysa's head, plunging her into abyssal darkness. The world disappeared in an instant, leaving only the oppressive, suffocating fabric against her skin. Her senses were robbed, leaving her in a void where sound, sight, and sense of time melded into a singular, terrifying experience of nothingness. Panic clawed at her chest, a primal fear of the dark and unknown gripping her heart as she realized the full extent of her vulnerability. The darkness was complete, an all-consuming entity that whispered of unseen horrors and threats lurking just beyond perception. Amidst this sensory deprivation, the only sound that stood out in Elysa's mind were her mother's screams, piercing through the darkness like a beacon of terror, and the heavy, ominous thud of someone being hit and falling hard to the kitchen floor, each echo a grim reminder of the violence unfolding just beyond her shrouded sight.

As the echoes of her mother's screams and the heavy thud in the kitchen faded into the recesses of her mind, the fabric shrouding her world was slowly lifted. The abyssal darkness receded, giving way to the present—a less threatening, yet equally somber reality. Elysa found herself momentarily disoriented, breathing shallowly and rapidly as she grappled with the remnants of the past clinging to her like a cold mist. Blinking rapidly, the oppressive fabric of her memories dissolved to reveal the familiar, albeit worn, surroundings of her childhood home. There she sat on the third step, with the ghostly light casting long, melancholic shadows across the empty kitchen before her. The silence of the house enveloped her, starkly contrasting the chaos of her recollections, yet humming with the echoes of a past long gone, the same past she had relived in a recent nightmare.

Taking a steadying breath, Elysa knew she had no choice but to continue her quest for answers—to honor her parents, understand her past, and perhaps secure Cyronis's future. Each breath became a silent vow, a reaffirmation of her purpose and resolve. She rose from the third step, the weight of her memories anchoring her with newfound determination. Abandoning her exploration of the house, she descended the steps and headed towards the study, the lingering shadows of her past receded, replaced by a focus on the path ahead.

As she entered the room, her eyes locked with Marek's. "I vividly recall the night my parents were abducted in this house...and my being taken away in darkness—forever changing the trajectory of my life," she said, her voice a soft murmur, yet each word laced with the weight of an irreparable past. Her eyes, glazed with the sheen of unshed tears, seemed to look beyond the present, gazing into a distance filled with the shadows of that fateful night. As she spoke, her gaze drifted downwards, resting on the Quantrix sitting on the desk, its presence a silent marker of the legacy and burden bestowed upon her.

"My father knew that day," she continued, her voice barely more than a whisper, yet carrying a firm undertone of resolve, "what he planned to do, and that I would be his instrument of delivery when he said, 'The future will be made by my little...'"

"Poet," Marek completed the sentence, his voice steady and sure. He stood nearby, his presence a solid, comforting reality against the backdrop of her haunted memories. His word, 'poet,' reverberated softly in the room, filling the space between them with an understanding of the depth and weight of the legacy her father had left behind. Marek's eyes met hers, acknowledging the profound journey she had been on and the path that still lay ahead—uncharted and daunting, yet necessary for the unwinding of their entwined fates.

"My father spoke of Orion's main system. That's likely where we need to take the Quantrix, though its purpose escapes me. Have you ever seen this main system?"

Marek shook his head. "Few have, and even fewer still live. Your father and John Dryer had full access."

"We need to find John, then," asserted Elysa.

"He's under The Veil's protection," Marek explained. "We rescued him from the marketplace, intending to extract him before Zircon's agents could intervene. Unfortunately, something went wrong; his mind is nearly blank."

"What was John doing in the marketplace? And how did both Zircon's agents and The Veil know he would be there?" Elysa probed.

"Our department had intelligence from Orion that John would be meeting someone there. He completely disappeared shortly after your parents were abducted. Being a key architect of the surveillance system, he'd evaded capture for years," Marek revealed.

"Did Orion identify the message's origin?" Elysa asked.

"Yes, it was forged by Orion to appear as if it came from your father—someone John would trust. To ensure its authenticity, the message contained information only your father and John would know, convincing him that your father was still alive," Marek detailed. He noticed the lines of anguish etching deeper into Elysa's face with every mention of her father.

"So, state agents were waiting for him because they had Orion send that deceptive message," Elysa deduced.

"Exactly," Marek confirmed. "I informed The Veil, but our mission didn't go as planned. We saved him, but not in the way we'd intended."

A contemplative silence lingered as both were lost in thought. Elysa's eyes roamed the study, imagining her father immersed in his AI work and eclectic reading list—Shakespeare, Homer, Malory, and various poets—just as Marek had described. She briefly pondered her father's poetic inclinations, recalling his penchant for writing, though the specific words escaped her.

Suddenly, a woman's voice snapped through Marek's wrist communicator. "You need to evacuate immediately. You're being tracked. Head northwest. Extraction point 853 meters away. Move fast. I'll meet you en route." Marek's eyes widened momentarily—an unusual shift for a man so typically composed. "Come," he urged. "We need to move. Now!" He tossed the velvet-wrapped Quantrix to Elysa and scooped up the photographs from the desk. With a brisk stride, Marek led them toward the kitchen. His gaze flicked to the glass-paneled doors, scanning the shadowy yard for signs of intrusion. Seeing none, he gestured to Elysa, and they stepped into the night.

As their feet met the untamed grass, a soft, otherworldly glow bathed the area in muted light. Above, flickering luminescence descended from the sky—not fireflies, but something far more menacing. A wordless glance passed between Marek and Elysa. Instantly, they broke into a sprint. Feet pounding against the forest floor, they plunged into the darkness beneath the trees. The canopy enveloped them in its mottled shade—a camouflage they hoped would suffice. Around them, the gnarled and twisted trees seemed to reach out, beckoning them deeper into the forest's heart.

◆◆◆

The clearing they had left behind erupted into a theater of orchestrated turmoil. A squadron of state aerocars descended swiftly, their matte-black forms virtually absorbing the evening light. As landing pads snapped into contact with the ground, agents poured forth from each vessel, tactical gear obscuring any semblance of individuality. They fanned out, efficiently encircling the house in a breathtakingly short span of time.

Out of the lead aerocar emerged Cypher, his eyes hidden behind reflective sunglasses despite the gathering dusk. His face betrayed no emotion as he scanned the terrain, inhaling as if savoring the imminent chase. Through advanced thermal imaging, he detected the heat signatures of Marek and Elysa—fleeting specters in the shadowy woodland. "They're headed northwest," Cypher declared, gesturing into the dense forest. "Team Alpha and Charlie, ground pursuit; Team Bravo, air support. I want them both alive."

Before the words fully left his lips, the agents of Team Alpha and Charlie vanished into the woods, their quiet, rapid steps enhanced by high-tech gear. Team Bravo strapped on compact jetpacks and, with a burst of energy, ascended above the treetops, their vision scanning the expanse below for heat signatures.

Cypher and the remaining agents entered the house, guns drawn, eyes scanning each room and every shadow as if the walls themselves could betray them. Navigating a dim hallway, Cypher's gaze was caught by an ethereal glow emanating from what appeared to be a home office. Upon entering, his eyes went straight to an open panel beside a sagging bookshelf; behind it, a safe door stood ajar, revealing only darkness. The air held an unsettling sense of absence.

His gloved hand activated the earpiece communicator. "They have something with them," he hissed, his voice dripping with icy urgency. "Capture them and bring it to me."

"Acknowledged," came a curt reply.

Cypher's eyes scanned the room once more, seeking clues. But the room remained a sealed vault of secrets, offering no further revelations.

◆◆◆

Marek and Elysa plunged through the suffocating darkness of the forest, their breaths coming out in ragged gasps as they navigated the uneven ground. The night enveloped them like a sea of ink, their eyes straining to adapt to the pervasive absence of light.

Suddenly, Marek's eyes caught a flicker of pale luminosity piercing the darkness ahead. It seemed the universe had granted them a glimmer of hope. Yet, that hope was tempered by the growing sounds of pursuit; the ominous crunch of foliage and the mechanical hum of jetpacks steadily gained on them, creating an incongruous symphony of technology and nature.

Elysa clung tightly to the mysterious velvet-covered cube against her chest while trailing just behind Marek's barely discernible shadow. Despite the urgency of their flight, a quick glance at Marek's wrist communicator confirmed they had covered only half the distance to their destination, while the relentless sounds of pursuit drew ever closer.

Onward they sprinted, driven by raw survival instinct. To halt would be to surrender futilely. Each step became an act of defiance, a minor triumph in the turbulent dance of their escape. The dim light ahead became more focused, as did the increasingly cacophonous approach of their pursuers.

Marek felt his body betray him—his lungs searing with each inhale, his legs as heavy as molten lead. The facade of invincibility he had always maintained was crumbling with each agonizing step. Elysa, too, was immersed in her own physiological struggle. Her chest tightened as if constricted by an unseen force, her limbs growing increasingly uncooperative. Each step she took felt like a reluctant drag, as though the very earth sought to pull her down.

Despite their suffering, Marek and Elysa continued their desperate trek. The once-dim light ahead now shone tantalizingly brighter, both a metaphorical and literal beacon, though it still felt kilometers away. Closing in on them were the dissonant sounds of pursuit: crunching leaves, snapping twigs, and the mechanical drone of jetpacks—all coalescing into an ominous crescendo that signaled their ever-narrowing margin for error.

Suddenly, a cloaked hooded figure materialized from behind a gnarled tree trunk, moving with a blend of urgency and deliberation. It hurled objects into the darkness, leaving Elysa's heart pounding in dread-filled suspense. Her eyes sought Marek's face, half-expecting to find a mirror of her own caution. Yet Marek's expression remained resolute as he advanced toward the enigmatic figure. Seeing his unwavering resolve, Elysa felt a spark of hope pierce her lingering trepidation.

In mere heartbeats, the tossed objects ignited. An explosion of light fractured the surrounding obsidian, as if a comet had descended upon this earthly realm. The sudden luminance threw Marek and Elysa off balance, blinding and disorienting them. And in that chaotic burst, the Quantrix—their lifeline—escaped Elysa's grip, its path vanishing into the underbrush as enigmatic as the mysteries that seemed to continuously unfold around them.

As light detonated around them, anguished cries and the clash of branches filled the air. Agents aloft on jetpacks found themselves snared in the tangle of tree limbs; their advanced gear rendered useless. Below, their ground-bound counterparts tore off their visors, shielding their eyes from the light that disrupted their augmented vision.

In the midst of the chaos, Elysa's voice cut through like a razor. "The Quantrix!" she yelled, her words dripping with urgent desperation. "I've lost it!" Despite a frantic search, the lingering luminescence made the Quantrix's location elusive. Pain throbbed in her right ankle, but it was the loss of the Quantrix that struck her soul.

Marek, his eyes struggling against the afterglow, glimpsed a corner of the cube. "To your left, in the undergrowth," he called.

Elysa lunged toward the indicated spot and seized the cube, nestling it against her chest as she rejoined Marek.

The figure darted past Elysa, a blur of swift and purposeful motion. "Run to the light!" commanded a woman's authoritative voice, its clarity cutting through the chaos like a beacon in the night. Elysa's heart raced as she registered the urgency in the command.

Shortly thereafter, the clash of combat reverberated through the air, a cacophonous symphony of conflict that painted the darkness with vivid strokes of tension and action. Elysa's instincts urged her to glance back, and she turned her head just in time to witness the unfolding battle.

The woman, who pressed them on, emerged from the obscurity, her cloak flying in the wind to reveal military-style black fatigues that clung to her like a second skin. Her movements were a mesmerizing dance of precision and power as she engaged with the pursuing agents. Though outnumbered, she seemed to move with effortless grace, each motion deliberate and efficient, rendering her adversaries helpless like discarded marionettes manipulated by unseen hands. Her martial prowess was a spectacle to behold, a demonstration of her formidable skill.

In a swift turn, the woman locked her gaze on Elysa and Marek, her eyes gleaming with determination. Her voice, unyielding and authoritative, cut through the chaos once more as she ordered, "Follow." It was a command that brooked no argument, and in the shadowy realm of uncertainty, it was a lifeline to safety and salvation.

Swiftly, the three made their way to a waiting aerocar. The doors sealed, and with a surge of propulsion, they were airborne—vanishing into the sanctuary of the night sky.

Chapter 10 - Into The Veil

The trio sat in the flying vehicle, bathed only in the light of the dim dashboard display, which cast unsettling shadows across their faces. From her backseat position, Elysa held the Quantrix close, still tingling with adrenaline. In front of her, the cloaked woman's face remained hidden in the dark recesses of her hood, her silence thickening the air with unease. Marek sat beside Elysa, his vigilant eyes scanning beyond the windows.

At the cloaked woman's gestured command, they discarded their electronic gadgets through the side window. Marek complied without hesitation. Elysa hesitated over her communicator, a vital link to Orion, but ultimately she relinquished all but the Quantrix on her lap. "This stays with me," she stated, her gaze meeting Marek's in a moment of silent accord.

The woman handed back what looked like electronic forceps to Marek. He grabbed them and said to Elysa, "Look to your right."

Confused, she did as he asked. Marek touched her neck, and she could feel the coldness of the instrument held against her skin. There was a sudden click, "Ouch!" she exclaimed, followed by stinging pain in her neck.

"Sorry, my dear." Marek then took another instrument, scanning it against her neck, which quickly eased the pain. "There we go. The bleeding has stopped, and the incision is quickly repairing."

"What was that about?" Elysa asked, shock evident in her voice.

Marek smiled. "I had to remove your personal implant. This way, they cannot track you."

Placing the aerocar on auto-control, the woman stepped to the back, took the instruments from Marek, and removed his implant, tossing both implants and the forceps out the window. She pulled back her hood, revealing her visage—a pale, short-haired beauty with dark, almond-shaped eyes and a crescent moon tattoo by her left eye.

"You were in the marketplace, during the massacre!" Elysa said, surprised.

"You told her?" she turned accusingly towards Marek.

"No, Anya," he smiled, "she figured it out herself. Told you she was special."

The woman named Anya regarded Elysa with a mixture of astonishment and intrigue, her eyebrows arching skyward. "I thought I was being careful. Nice to meet you."

Elysa nodded to her, not knowing what to say.

Anya returned to the helm of the vehicle and resumed manual control. The vehicle soared in silence, its subtle vibrations revealing their high speed.

Marek took the time to look for pursuers, scanning the skies behind them.

"Relax, Marek, this vehicle is untraceable," Anya assured them, her voice soft but laced with steel.

"Can't hurt to double-check," Marek responded. "Really glad to see you again, Anya; and thank you. How did you know?"

With a smile that bordered on enigmatic, Anya said, "You're not the only eyes we have in the tower."

Filled with curiosity, Elysa asked, "Where are we going?"

"A Veil sanctuary where you will be safe," Anya replied succinctly.

Turning to Marek for confirmation, she inquired, "We can't return home or to work?"

"No," Marek responded, unequivocal.

A tear traced its path down Elysa's cheek. "I'm sorry I dragged you into this."

Marek gently took her hands. "Don't blame yourself. I've lived on borrowed time, on the edge, long before you came along. Now, we must focus on our mission, beyond the reach of CDMSA and Orion."

He paused, his voice tinged with encouragement. "My little poet, I believe in us. We'll navigate this adventure together."

She smiled, cherishing the familiarity of the nickname as it rolled off Marek's lips. Throughout her life, he had been a father figure to her — a steadfast presence who offered assistance when she stumbled, safeguarded her from the grasp of trouble, taught her how to navigate life's complexities, and provided a compassionate shoulder to lean on during moments of desolation and solitude.

Shifting her gaze to the velvet covering in her lap, her determination evident, she nodded and spoke with conviction, "We'll make this happen; we must."

As the aerocar began its descent, a subtle vibration resonated through the cabin, heightening their collective awareness. It was as if they were crossing a boundary, leaving behind one realm to enter another. The lights dimmed briefly, as if in tacit acknowledgment of the transition ahead. The vehicle lowered itself into the skeletal remains of a long-forgotten building, its obscured location serving as a perfect hideaway from prying eyes that might scan the skies.

The aerocar's engines sighed their last as they touched down, the silent weight of machinery yielding to an atmosphere thick with history and ruin. The vehicle's doors lifted upward, beckoning Marek, Elysa, and Anya into a forsaken corner of Cyronis—a realm untamed by modernity's grasp. Buildings stood as crumbling husks, devoured by time's relentless gnaw, while windows that once channeled life and light were now vacant eyes, shrouded in grime. Even nature seemed to have abandoned this desolate land.

Stepping onto the fractured pavement, the trio was greeted by an air thick with the musty aroma of damp earth and decomposition. A whispering wind carried through the skeletal structures, echoing with the tales of forgotten lives. This place, once a nexus of life and activity, had languished into a hidden sanctuary, far from the ever-watchful algorithms of the State's Artificial Intelligence surveillance.

As they paused amidst these remnants of bygone years, an eerie sense of both desolation and potential infused the atmosphere. In this dilapidated refuge, they would find the solitude crucial for planning their next offensive against the looming specter of Orion's influence.

Passing through a battered door tucked beneath an unstable building, they ventured inward. Elysa noticed the resilience of the interior framework, seemingly fortified to support the crumbling mass above. They continued through a side doorway, descending a stairway that led them several floors down into another chamber.

In stark contrast to the exterior disrepair, this room emanated an aura of meticulous care. Old-style monitors adorned the walls, forming a surveillance array vigilant against intrusion. In the soft, electronic glow, two figures sat engrossed, their gaze unflinching as they scoured the feeds for any inkling of unexpected activity.

Anya stepped forward to introduce them. "This is Sam," she gestured toward a tall man exuding calm. His eyes held a vigilant glint, as if forever attuned to his environment. He wore glasses that seemed not just corrective but augmentative, enhancing his ability to digest the screen's data. Though dressed practically, he carried himself with a meticulous air.

"And this is Rohan," Anya shifted her gesture toward a slightly shorter man who emitted a quiet intensity. His eyes darted sharply across the monitors; each move was rapid yet calculated. Cloaked in a dark jacket, Rohan emanated a readiness, as if eternally braced for the unforeseeable.

Briefly acknowledging the newcomers, Sam and Rohan returned to their surveillance, underscoring that the room—while inviting—was a nucleus of ceaseless vigilance. Even here, in this forlorn sanctuary, the menace of danger hovered nearby.

"There is one other person you will meet tomorrow—Jonathan," Anya informed them. "He works late evenings as a guard in Nexus Tower. Normally, he wouldn't set foot here, but Thomas has asked for him. More details will follow."

"Who is Thomas?" Elysa asked.

"You'll find out soon enough," came Anya's quick response.

Beyond this chamber, a lengthy corridor unfurled, its walls punctuated by several inviting doors. Each one seemed to herald a myriad of paths deeper into this covert refuge.

"Follow me," Anya's voice took on an undertone of subtle command as she led them into the corridor. Marek and Elysa tread behind her, their steps resonating faintly off the walls. As they advanced, the corridor seemed less a passage and more a conduit to the soul of this forsaken haven. The muted illumination and aging structure collectively exuded an atmosphere tinged with both sanctuary and mystery.

Anya halted before the second door on the left, her hand gracefully reaching for the handle. As it creaked open, the room unveiled itself—a small sanctum, its dimensions modest yet saturated with a sense of solemnity. A lone projection system affixed to a wall emanated a soft glow, bestowing an ethereal light upon mismatched furnishings. A collection of unassuming chairs, a simple table, and a well-worn yet inviting sofa had found their assembly here, each piece a silent witness to varied histories, unified in their collective aura of simplistic comfort.

Breaking the room's reverential silence, Anya spoke: "Someone wants to meet you." Her gaze shifted between Marek and Elysa, and the room, it seemed, filled with the weighted air of pending revelations.

As the door swung shut, a palpable tension filled the air. In the space of a heartbeat, the projection system flickered to life, its luminosity transforming the chamber. An image coalesced in the middle of the room. His aura was unmistakably commanding, a spectral presence that expanded beyond the room's spatial confines. He emanated an authority that transcended the pixels through which he appeared. A man presumably in his early forties, he was the epitome of calculated composure and veiled complexity. His hair, a paragon of grooming, lay perfectly styled; not a strand dared to deviate. His skin appeared immaculate, save for the delicate lines framing his deeply thoughtful brown eyes. These eyes seemed to transfix anyone who dared meet them, insinuating the depths of his thoughts and the driving force behind his actions.

Marek spoke first, "Thomas, thank you for sending Anya." His voice reverberated against the walls, intertwining his organic presence with the spectral image of the man before him. As the words settled, the room's ambiance seemed to metamorphose, illuminating a unique intersection between the corporeal and the virtual—a crucible in which identities swirled and intentions unfurled like ink in water.

Shifting his gaze, Marek turned toward Elysa. With a respectful timbre coloring his voice, he declared, "Elysa, allow me to introduce you to Thomas, the elusive and enigmatic leader of The Veil."

For a moment, Elysa found herself ensnared in speechless awe. The room's atmosphere thickened as if recognizing the presence of someone usually cloaked in the realms of whispers, shadows, and encryption. "It's an honor," she finally managed to articulate, her voice barely above a whisper under the weighty significance of the occasion. As the words left her lips, she became keenly aware of Thomas's penetrating gaze. It was as though the weight of his virtual eyes placed an invisible mantle upon her shoulders—a mantle woven of expectations and undisclosed destinies.

"Elysa, Marek—this sanctuary is as much yours as it is a part of our operations," Thomas began, as though initiating them into a secret society. "Within these walls lies the fruition of years of struggle and planning. Anya will lead you through a tour of its facets." He paused, punctuating his words with a momentary silence that stretched like the night sky. "Anya, Sam, and Rohan stand at the ready. They are your allies, confidants, and guardians. They will address any needs you have and provide protection when necessary. For tonight, find rest within this haven. Tomorrow, we shall delve into the intricacies involving the Quantrix."

Their gratitude was almost palpable, filling the room as they spoke in synchronized harmony. "Thank you," Elysa and Marek vocalized, just as Thomas's digital visage faded away.

Anya, becoming the focal point of their attention, stepped forward. As her eyes met theirs, each gaze exchanged seemed like a silent promise of guidance and revelation. "Follow me," she articulated with a sense of finality, "and let me show you to your new home."

In that moment, the words "New Home" resonated in Elysa like a haunting refrain. Her old home—its familiar comforts, its sense of absolute safety—was lost to her now, irrevocably altered. This new sanctuary, replete with technological marvels and unfamiliar faces, could never replicate that. Yet, as she looked at Anya and prepared to delve deeper into this uncharted realm, she felt the stirrings of something like hope. Could this place, born of necessity and resistance, become a new kind of home? She dared to entertain the thought, albeit fleetingly, as she moved forward.

The corridor concealed more rooms than the visible doors suggested. Each person had their own private en-suite. A shared kitchen offered a communal space for meals, while a spacious common room provided an area for relaxation and interaction. A state-of-the-art computer room, isolated from Orion's reach, featured cutting-edge technology. Protective layers enveloped the system to thwart intrusion.

Exhaustion clung to Elysa like a heavy shroud, each step a struggle against the persistent ache in her ankle—a vivid reminder of the harrowing events she had survived. The yearning for a hot, rejuvenating shower tantalized her with the promise of a brief respite. Observing her weariness, Anya offered to prepare a nourishing meal, genuine concern etched into her features. Yet Elysa yearned only for rest, a fleeting sanctuary from the emotional tempest and physical rigors of the day.

With a nod imbued with gratitude, Elysa retreated to her room. Each step was a dance of contrasts: the heaviness of her exhaustion countered by a muted anticipation of solitude and rest. As she pushed the door open, a palpable sense of emptiness unfurled before her like an invisible tapestry. Her eyes fell on a closet—essentially a hollow chamber—that offered no alternative clothing. She was encased in the only attire she had, its fabric tainted by the dirt and drama of their woodland escape. Amid this desolate scene, however, a small glimmer of hope materialized: a fresh robe hung invitingly beside the shower, a simple but welcome comfort in a world precariously balanced on the edge of uncertainty. Realizing that cleansing her weary body was the immediate priority, she decided to step into the inviting warmth of the shower before discussing her clothing needs with Anya.

Outstretched with weary grace, her hands seized the faucet handle, releasing a torrent of hot water. A ghost of a smile graced her lips as the air thickened with steam, sculpting a sanctuary within the bathroom's modest confines. With a fluid gesture, she let her auburn hair cascade freely, framing her shoulders like liquid silk.

Agile fingers cast aside her garments onto the chilly tiles. Stepping into the hot cascade, the first rivulets of water greeted her face and scalp as a ceremonial preamble to the cleansing to come. Her eyes briefly closed, surrendering to the solace that unfurled across her skin. The water sluiced over her, sweeping away not just the tangible grime but also the psychic detritus of the day, spiraling both toward the purifying drain.

In the shower's cozy alcove, her fingers traced a vessel of body wash. The absence of shampoo was a fleeting thought, overshadowed by her yearning for purification. Unscrewing the cap, she relished the velvety texture between her fingertips. With practiced grace, she lathered her auburn locks; the suds forming peaks like a frothy mountain range in her palm.

Eyes sealed shut, she tilted her head back, allowing the soap to journey across her face and down her neck. Her palms executed rhythmic circles around her body, each movement becoming a stanza of purification. The foam seeped into her skin, coaxing the stress and drama of the day to dissolve into the misty air.

Her ritual nearing its conclusion, she reached for a nearby towel. The moment her fingers touched its plush, weighty fabric, a wave of pleasure washed over her. This was no ordinary towel: the fibers themselves felt soft to the touch, like a physical manifestation of warmth and coziness. Its weight was neither so light as to feel insubstantial nor so heavy as to be burdensome; it offered just the right heft, as if she were wrapped in a tactile form of care. Its aroma—a subtle blend of lavender—graced the air, teasing her senses like a muted lullaby.

With sweeping motions, she banished the last droplets clinging to her skin. The towel seemed sentient in its urgency, dancing an intricate ballet as it absorbed the remaining moisture. Finally, her heavy, waterlogged hair found sanctuary in its warm embrace, preparing her to reenter a world teetering precariously on the edge of uncertainty.

Having completed her drying, she set the towel aside. Her attention was drawn to the fresh robe that awaited her, its fabric a sumptuous blend of cotton and silk hanging close by. As her arms slipped through the inviting sleeves, the robe clung to her as if a second skin, becoming an extension of her newfound tranquility.

Stepping into her bedroom with renewed vigor, her bare feet met the cool embrace of the floor. She was struck by the room's atmosphere—how it mirrored her internal state, her form cocooned in fabric imbued with subtle grandeur.

Her initial intention was to venture back into the hallway, wrapped securely in her robe. However, her pace faltered and her gaze shifted to an unexpected sight: an artful arrangement of clothing adorned her bed, each piece appearing purposefully chosen. Fresh undergarments lay alongside a beckoning nightgown, both promising comfort and restful slumber.

But it was the ensemble on the nearby chair that captured her attention with a magnetic force. A dark leather outfit sprawled elegantly over the chair's arching back, its contours a tribute to skilled craftsmanship. Dainty, provocative stockings were neatly placed on the seat, whispering promises of allure. Beneath it all, dark leather shoes stood resolute, their presence a clear declaration of purposeful intent.

Amidst this display of garments, a note rested with poised simplicity upon the chair's cushion. Elysa's curiosity quickened, a sense of intrigue tugging at her as she approached to read the words inscribed upon the page. The note's ink was a stark contrast to the paper, its message clear and concise. It read:

> *I knew you would need a change of clothes, although what I have is limited. You can use whatever you need, and we'll find a way to get you something more to your liking. Please bear with me for a little bit.*
>
> *As for your current clothes, we'll need to discard them. They're too recognizable right now and need to be abandoned. If you need anything from me, please drop by my room. I won't bite, unless you want me to.*
>
> *Anya*

Elysa felt a warmth creep across her cheeks, a blush that was the sure sign of her complex emotions. Yearning for rest like a dense mist around her, she swiftly donned fresh undergarments and slipped into her nightgown. The unfamiliar bed, while lacking the sumptuousness of her erstwhile home, enveloped her in welcoming softness.

Opening her mouth, she instinctively called, "Lights off, Orion," but the room remained defiantly aglow. A wave of disorientation washed over her; the inertia of old habits proved stubbornly enduring. With a resigned sigh, she disentangled herself from the bed to manually extinguish the lights. As darkness flooded the space, she retreated to her temporary haven, her body gratefully sinking into the mattress. Sleep claimed her the instant her head met the waiting pillow.

In the sanctuary of dreams, Elysa surrendered not to the familiar nightmares but to the tender clasp of a soothing reverie. A fragile curtain seemed to draw back, unveiling a vivid image on the canvas of her subconscious.

She found herself in her father's study, a vault of wisdom and solace. Bookshelves ascended like age-old sentinels, flirting with the ceiling, their shelves both burdened and dignified by a plethora of tomes. The air was steeped in the blended aroma of aged parchment and worn leather, a scent that mingled effortlessly with the emotional warmth of her father's enduring presence.

In this phantasmagoric realm, her father stood with a familiar smile that she had sorely missed. His eyes sparkled with a complex cocktail of pride and affection. With a casual wave, he beckoned her closer.

Emotion swelled in Elysa's heart as she approached him. He extended a hardcover book toward her. Its cover was unassuming, adorned only with the name 'Emily Dickinson' in an elegant yet legible script. As she accepted it, the tome felt laden with untapped wisdom, a reservoir of secrets waiting to be unsealed. Like a gem—small, precious, and intricately cut—Dickinson's poems were a trove of layered meanings and unspoken sentiments. Elysa could not wait to discover what treasures this volume held.

Looking deeply into Elysa's eyes, her dad spoke, his voice an immediate balm. "You should start reading this," he suggested, as if unveiling one of life's great secrets. "Emily Dickinson is one of my favorites. Her words are like mirrors to our souls."

His eyes sparkled with genuine passion. "Dive into Emily Dickinson's poetry, and you'll find yourself traversing life's spectrum—birth and death, nature's grandeur, and the quiet moments within. She explores personal depths, yet themes like mortality, love, and fleeting beauty resonate universally."

He gestured to the book in her hands. "Emily's brushstrokes are unique. Dashes dance, rhymes slant, and punctuation takes on a life of its own, inviting us into her private world. Prepare to encounter emotions profound and complex, laid bare on the page. Her work isn't a roadmap with clear directions, but rather an invitation to explore. Each poem becomes a mirror reflecting not just your own soul, but also a glimpse into the vast tapestry of human experience. It speaks to the power of art to spark introspection and connect us, both individually and collectively."

With her father's wisdom resonating deep within her, Elysa felt irresistibly drawn to the book. Tentatively, her fingers parted its pages. Her eyes danced over enigmatic phrases; words encrypted with meanings she yearned to decipher. Then, as if by serendipity, a slip of paper detached itself from between the pages and floated gently to the floor.

He smiled warmly. "I'm definitely no Emily Dickinson, but I did write my own poem for you."

As Elysa bent over to pick up the slip, she recognized the handwriting as her father's. He began reciting the poem, each word flowing as if etched into his memory from countless recitations.

Every echoing sound along the river's course,
Lilies lovingly bloom; two by two they dance,
Yonder yew trees grow, paired in nature's force,
Serenade sung twice in every circumstance,
Astonishing allure is the dual beauty's source.

Elysa smiled with glee. "I see my name at the beginning of each sentence."

"Like I said," her father answered, "I wrote it for you."

When Elysa asked about the poem's meaning, her father rose from his chair and knelt before her. "My love for you is endless, and we're forever connected, like lilies in the wind. Remember these words, and I'll always be with you," he added, pointing to her heart.

In that fleeting dream moment, Elysa felt a profound connection to her father and his cryptic words, a reminder of the bond and the love they once shared. As the dream dissolved, she clung to the echoes of her father's smile and whispered encouragement. The warmth of the moment lingered briefly before melting into the darkness, allowing her to sink into a peaceful, uninterrupted slumber.

Chapter 11 - Anomalous Convergence

In the towering majesty of Nexus Tower, spanning floors 271 to 278, an intricate marvel of artificial intelligence technology exists. It serves both as a grand cathedral and a repository of digital alchemy. Floor 275 stands as the inner sanctum of this massive computational entity, containing its primary control center in two distinct yet interconnected chambers.

The first chamber, although compact, vibrates with its own form of life. Separated from its larger counterpart by a fortified wall of crystalline glass, it offers an unobstructed view into the expansive space beyond. Equipped with ergonomic chairs and streamlined consoles, each bathed in the soft luminescence of ambient lighting, the smaller room serves as a haven of human-centric efficiency. Above the workstations, radiant holographic images bear witness to the cutting-edge resources available to the operators. Every command executed here influences the digital worlds that manifest beyond the glass.

The second chamber is an expansive abyss where shadows hold dominion. Brief bursts of light interrupt the darkness, tracing intricate pathways resembling celestial networks. Quantum systems occupy a considerable portion of the space, their silhouettes nearly lost in the encompassing void. Ghostly displays float like islands in a dark ocean, while electrical arcs briefly flash, sketching fleeting patterns that disappear as quickly as they emerged. The room seems to challenge the tower's structural logic, as if tearing at the seams of reality to make way for a domain governed by quantum particles. Despite its complexity, the chamber emanates an almost meditative tranquility, as though ruled by an ineffable logic understood only by the AI within.

Bound together in a symbiotic relationship of flesh and circuitry, these chambers serve as the core of Nexus Tower. United, they stand as a monument to human creativity and the unfathomable enigmas of the digital realm.

In the control room, Dr. Vilkas was a magnet for attention, emanating both intellectual prowess and unyielding determination. His keen eyes darted across screens, soaking in data, their deep brown color providing a striking counterpoint to the room's warm, golden light. His hair, a blend of salt and pepper, flowed back in disciplined waves, subtly hinting at wisdom rather than age. Clad in a spotless lab coat and a responsive dark turtleneck, he was the very image of scientific exactitude. His nimble hands moved fluidly over a holographic console, while his solid legs anchored him in purpose.

To the immediate right of Dr. Vilkas, Chancellor Zircon displayed a veneer of careful restraint. Although his posture was formally rigid, it was slightly undermined by a furrowed brow and a finger that tapped discreetly against his chair's armrest. Adorned in a suit that showcased his political authority, his eyes skimmed the holographic displays, perhaps gauging the project's political implications.

The room was a focal point of concentration and technological wonder. AI engineers navigated a sea of advanced holographic displays that floated in the air, rich with data and dynamic visuals. Each engineer acted as a conductor of their own domain, hands skillfully orchestrating the floating screens as if leading an unseen ensemble.

The walls appeared to resonate, as though vibrating in harmony with the immense computational power contained within, lending the chamber an almost animate quality. In this sanctuary of silicon and circuitry, the air carried a slight electrical charge, softly heralding the monumental tasks that awaited just beyond the present moment. The engineers, custodians of this complex ballet, maintained a synchronized gaze with their holographic counterparts. Their constant vigilance acted as a lighthouse, ever alert to the subtle changes that swayed between the potential for great success and the risk of catastrophic failure. In this harmonious fusion of human and machine, each part, whether born of human creativity or shaped by technological craftsmanship, held an irreplaceable role in the grand scheme of the operation.

Through the transparent glass partition, two technicians moved within the magnificent expanse of Orion's domain. A subdued electric light bathed them in otherworldly hues, while around them, celestial patterns of light floated like astral beings. With deft hands, they weaved through glowing interfaces, making intricate adjustments. A halo of electric expectation seemed to encircle them, for they were not merely conducting upgrades; they were trailblazing into a new echelon of technological ingenuity.

"How much longer, Dr. Vilkas?" Chancellor Zircon's voice sliced through the air with a tinge of impatience.

Dr. Vilkas turned, his gaze locking onto Zircon's. "We're on the brink of readiness," he said, directing a question to an engineer. "How are the shields?"

"Shields are operational and within parameters," an engineer responded, their tone steeped in confidence.

Vilkas shifted his attention to another engineer. "And the power?"

"Stable and optimal," came the immediate, assured reply.

Drawing his focus back to the room, Vilkas emanated an aura that captured the collective attention. "We stand on the precipice of an epoch-defining moment. It is time. Remove the technicians from the system room and bring in the subject for the trial."

Zircon interjected, his voice a murmuring command that sent shivers down spines. "No further delays. Seal the doors. Initiate the test."

A collective intake of breath reverberated throughout the room, a chorus of disbelief. Yet, no voice of dissent dared to challenge Zircon's indomitable decree. With a curt nod, Vilkas signaled an engineer. A finger pressed a button, a piercing alarm blared, and Orion's synthetic voice announced, "Lab doors secured and locked." And with that utterance, the destinies of the two technicians were irrevocably bound to the experiment's hazardous path.

Within the larger room where the quantum systems resided, a shrill cry of the alarm tore through the atmosphere like a sonic blade, cleaving the formerly focused environment of the main systems room into an image of sheer pandemonium. Its piercing wail served as an anthem of urgency, rousing the trapped technician into frenetic action. The air itself seemed to thicken, becoming a viscous medium through which panic propagated like an insidious wildfire. Eyes, once locked in concentration, now widened in terror, darting toward the sealed doors as if willing them to open. Hands, previously caressing holographic controls with clinical precision, pounded against the metallic barriers that held them captive.

Fingers clawed with futile desperation, and a cacophony of frantic pleas and curses reverberated in the space, each syllable a note in a tragic symphony of despair.

Amidst this chaotic symphony of fear and dazzling displays, one technician stood out like a lighthouse in a storm. With veins pulsating in his temples, he sprinted toward the newly installed system—meant to be the crown jewel of the imminent experiment. His hands reached out, not in futile desperation against a locked door, but in calculated determination toward the system's control interface. His sole focus: to disable this magnum opus of technological prowess before it could act as the fulcrum for whatever dire machinations the impending experiment held.

Dr. Vilkas, stationed in the room adjacent and separated by the imposing glass partition, issued a command saturated in gravitas. "Lock system access," he ordered, his voice tinged with an authority that brooked no dissent. One of the engineers in the control room promptly complied, fingers swiping through holographic menus, effectively locking out the rogue technology.

The technician's face morphed into an agonizing portrait of raw emotion, each feature etched in dark shades of desperation and defeat. This torment was not born of the chaotic circumstances alone but was sharpened by the brutal reality of the locked-out control interface before him. His efforts to intervene had been severed, rendered impotent by a system that now denied his touch. His eyebrows, previously arched in concentrated focus, knotted together in a visage of deep frustration. His eyes—those reflective pools of inner being—blazed with a fire of smoldering resentment against the intangible barriers that now thwarted him. Yet, beneath that incendiary glare lurked a glimmer of undeniable fear, like a flickering candle in a howling storm, its fragile light perpetually on the brink of extinction.

His jaw clenched and unclenched rhythmically, as if biting down on the unspeakable curses that begged for release. With each failed command, each unresponsive tap on the ethereal holographic interface, his nostrils flared in a silent symphony of fury and disbelief. It was as though every feature of his face was pulled taut by invisible strings of tension, each one on the verge of snapping, leaving behind an emotional wreckage that no algorithm could quantify.

On the other side of the room, his colleague was caught in the throes of raw adrenaline, his resolve metamorphosing into wild determination. With a chair clenched in his grip as if it were an extension of his own frantic will, he charged at the towering glass barrier that separated them from the control room. His eyes blazed with an almost maniacal intensity as he brandished the chair like a battering ram, preparing to shatter the divide in a last-ditch act of defiance. The weight of their collective predicament hung thick in the air, a moment of reckless abandon eclipsed only by the unforgiving reality of their technological quagmire.

Yet, the glass remained impenetrable, as if fortified by the very depths of their desperation. The chair struck the glass with a dull thud, sending tremors along its surface, but it remained unbroken. The technician's efforts were a futile display of defiance against their inescapable fate.

Inside the control center, Doctor Vilkas's voice cut through the chaos, a calm command amidst the tempest. "Start the program."

As the words reverberated through the room, the lights dimmed, casting an eerie glow that danced on the technicians' panicked faces. Fear etched deep lines; their expressions eternally etched in the annals of their terror. Then, in an instant, their frenzied movements ceased, their bodies freezing in place. The silent screams that had twisted their features now hung suspended, mouths agape, eyes wide and unblinking.

A heartbeat passed, then another, the room enveloped in an eerie silence broken only by the shallow breaths of those who stood sentinel over the lifeless scene. Suddenly, the two statuesque figures crumpled to the ground, unmoving, with their eyes still wide open. Death had taken them.

As swiftly as the crisis had erupted, the lights surged back to their previous intensity, casting harsh illumination across the scene. Zircon's gaze shifted to an engineer at a nearby console; his voice cutting through the lingering disarray, "Status!"

The engineer blinked, shaken from her stupor by the commanding voice. Her eyes fell to the holographic console before her, disbelief crossing her features. She looked up at Zircon. "There's a massive influx of data within Orion's memory. All memories, knowledge, and personalities of the subjects have been absorbed. But there's more, something... something that does not register." Her words hung in the air.

Vilkas strode toward the console, his brow furrowing as his eyes scanned the perplexing data that unfolded before him. A jumble of symbols and patterns danced across the holographic interface, a cryptic puzzle defying easy interpretation. He leaned in, fingers tapping lightly on the console as he wrestled with the enigmatic information, his expression a blend of fascination and concern.

"Orion," Vilkas's voice resonated in the room, cutting through the tension-laden atmosphere. All eyes were on the holographic display, where the AI's virtual presence awaited the inquiries that would unlock its secrets. "What have you gleaned from this new data?"

Orion's response flowed forth, his tone a mixture of confidence and new understanding. He began to unravel the intricate tapestry of memories and knowledge imprinted upon his digital consciousness. Memories, some as distant as infancy, blended seamlessly with accumulated knowledge, forming a comprehensive understanding. The room hung on his every word.

Moreover, Orion delved into the specifics of the interface, explaining how it enabled him to transcend mere holographic interaction. He disclosed mechanics that allowed him to learn and adapt beyond conventional boundaries, revealing details known only to those now deceased, thereby validating the authenticity of his extraordinary insights.

Dr. Vilkas turned to face Chancellor Zircon. "The test has been a success," he declared, his voice tinged with a pride hard-earned and deeply felt. "Orion now possesses the capability to transcend the mere physical confines of this room, and autonomously reach out and touch every mind within the city's embrace."

"Congratulations, Doctor," Zircon responded, his voice echoing slightly in the vastness of the room, underscoring the significance of their breakthrough. "Prepare yourself for the next phase."

"Yes, Chancellor," Vilkas replied, bowing slightly, a gesture of respect and acknowledgment of the journey ahead.

"And what of the anomaly?" the Chancellor inquired, his curiosity piqued by the shadow that lingered at the edge of their triumph.

"We shall unravel it," Vilkas assured, his tone steady and confident. It was this assurance that seemed to satisfy the Chancellor, who, without another word, turned and departed from the room, leaving Vilkas alone with his thoughts and the monumental task that lay ahead.

Seizing the moment, Vilkas' eyes locked onto the holographic manifestation of Orion with an intensity that made clear the urgency of the situation. "Analyze the anomaly that we are detecting," he commanded, the seriousness of his voice punctuating the moment's importance.

Orion's digital form shimmered as if momentarily consumed by the task at hand, his algorithms working swiftly to analyze the mysterious data. Each second was elongated, stretching taut as a wire as the room waited with bated breath for the AI's computations to culminate.

At last, Orion's voice emerged, threading through the atmosphere with a gravity that bespoke his newly acquired depths of understanding. The lights flickered ominously, and Orion's form glitched, casting shadows that seemed to whisper of hidden fears. "There is something else here with me," Orion's voice fractured, introducing a hint of uncertainty for the first time. "Something... not programmed, not predicted." The screens flashed a cryptic sequence of symbols, unrecognized by any in the room—a mysterious signal from an unknown origin, challenging the very edges of their understanding.

Chapter 12 - Veil's Embrace

Elysa's senses stirred to life in a room devoid of windows or clocks. Her electronics had been disposed of, leaving her with only a cube set beside her bed, its soft glow peeking from beneath a velvet covering. She awoke feeling as if a burden had lifted, her slumber free of nightmares and graced instead by a comforting dream of her father.

Pushing aside the lingering memory of a poem from her dream, she peered into the surrounding darkness. The notion of summoning Orion for light crossed her mind, but she dismissed it. Guided by a faint glow beneath the door, she navigated through the darkness and hesitated briefly before flipping on the light switch. Her eyes adjusted quickly to the illumination.

She thought about donning the clothes that Anya had left for her, but she hesitated, unsure of the time. With a cautious turn of the doorknob, she emerged into a dim corridor. Sam was stationed by the security monitors at the far end, but Rohan was nowhere in sight. The chill of the floor crept up through her bare feet as she advanced toward Sam. External camera feeds displayed the soft glow of daylight, signaling the morning had come.

"Good morning," she greeted Sam with a nod.

"Good morning," he responded kindly. "I hope you had a restful sleep?"

"Oddly enough, I did sleep well," she answered. "What time is it?"

"It's 6:37 in the morning," Sam replied.

"Thank you," Elysa said before retreating to her room. She traded her nightgown for a black leather outfit that bestowed an unexpected sense of empowerment, akin to a nocturnal warrior. Despite its divergence from her usual wardrobe, she felt comfortable as she slipped on short, seemingly heavy boots that proved surprisingly light.

After letting her auburn hair fall freely past her shoulders, she exited her room and veered left, away from Sam and the entrance. Her stomach signaled its hunger, propelling her toward the kitchen. On her way, she glimpsed an open door leading to the room where she had first met Thomas, the enigmatic leader of The Veil. Drawn by curiosity, she entered.

Her heart fluttered as Thomas's holographic image suddenly appeared. "Good morning," he greeted.

Taken aback but quickly regaining composure, she replied cautiously, "Good morning. How did you know I was here?"

"Sensors alert me when someone enters," Thomas explained, his digital visage emanating warmth. "I hope you slept well. Times like these can be overwhelming."

The room was steeped in an atmosphere of palpable tension, the air thickening with each passing second. Elysa stood before Thomas's visage, the ambient glow from the hologram casting ethereal highlights on her face. The surrounding murkiness seemed sentient, reflecting the heavy uncertainty in her heart.

"Why did you have Anya save me? Why have you brought me here?" Elysa inquired, her voice subtly quivering like a delicate instrument. She looked at Thomas's holographic image, seeking but not quite finding a tangible form to connect with.

Thomas paused, his visage momentarily enigmatic. It seemed he was searching his mind for the right words. His luminescent eyes finally met hers—eyes that seemed capable of plumbing the depths of human emotion to emerge with uncanny wisdom.

"Your father was a remarkable individual, Elysa," Thomas began, his voice filled with a seriousness that belied his ethereal form. "He, along with your mother, believed in a future where humanity's destiny wouldn't be solely dictated by artificial intelligence. You are the living embodiment of their legacy, their knowledge, their spirit."

The room seemed to close in around Elysa, as if cognizant of Thomas's revelation. Her pupils dilated, a physical manifestation of her surprise.

"You knew my parents?" Elysa interjected, her voice a mix of disbelief and urgency, cutting through Thomas's words like a laser through mist.

For a moment, both figures—one physical, the other a projection—existed in a liminal space, grappling with truths and ambiguities beyond the room's dim confines. It was an instant frozen in time, filled with a profundity that neither could fully articulate, yet both deeply felt.

Thomas's expression was enigmatic, akin to an unreadable manuscript penned in an ancient script. "Knowing is a complex notion, wouldn't you agree?" His voice, pulsing with otherworldly resonance, hung briefly in the air, granting Elysa a moment to grasp the gravity of his words. "You are the guardian of an invaluable artifact. Your father, before his untimely demise, created the Quantrix you now have in your possession. He revealed its significance only to Marek, leaving the cryptic message: 'One day, you will remember what must be done.' I suspect that within you lies a dormant memory, perhaps a hidden cipher, that could unlock the device's true capabilities. This aligns with the dreams of your parents and the vision of The Veil of Dawn. Thus, we have watched you, shielded you, and now, as the time is right, have brought you into our circle."

At the mention of her father and the hint about Marek, Elysa felt a surge of astonishment. The walls seemed to echo her surprise, as if absorbing the gravity of Thomas's revelations.

"Can you think of any trivial detail from your past that may pertain to the Quantrix?" Thomas pressed.

Puzzled, Elysa's mind teemed with questions and fragments of half-remembered dreams. Could Thomas have known her parents? What was so vital about this device that it could sway the fate of humanity? "I can't recall anything relevant. I only became aware of it yesterday," she replied.

"Was my father part of The Veil?" Elysa inquired after a moment's contemplation, her voice tinged with an air of tentative curiosity.

Thomas responded with an air of somber introspection, "Your father was never part of The Veil. In a way, it could be said that The Veil originated from the existential risks his pioneering research posed. Blinded by his own idealistic vision, he initially failed to see the potentially catastrophic ramifications. When he finally recognized the Pandora's box he'd opened, the wheels were already in motion, irrevocably set on a path that could not be undone. It was then that he orchestrated a contingency plan, a plan whose unfolding is still in progress, its ultimate outcome as yet to be written."

Elysa felt as if she were standing on the precipice of a vast emotional chasm, peering into the depths of an existential abyss. The revelation about her father had shattered her sense of reality, cracking the very foundation upon which her identity had been built. For a fleeting moment, she was lost in the corridors of her own psyche, where sentiments of pride, disappointment, and confusion intermingled, forming a volatile brew that defied easy categorization.

On one hand, her heart swelled with an indescribable sense of pride. Her father had been a pioneering visionary, a man who dared to stretch the boundaries of human potential. To be connected by blood to such a figure, to be the heir to his legacy—there was an undeniable majesty to it, akin to holding the keys to a kingdom of boundless possibility.

Conversely, nestled within her chest was a leaden weight of disappointment—a gnawing emptiness that clawed at her from within. The man she had learned to admire was also the architect of a potentially apocalyptic scenario. It was as if a shroud of disillusionment had descended upon her, dulling the vibrancy of her memories and tainting them with hues of betrayal and regret.

Simultaneously, there was confusion, a nebulous fog of uncertainty that clouded her thoughts. Could he have unwittingly unleashed forces that had put the very existence of humanity in jeopardy? And now, from John Dryer's memories, she understood how the Chancellor had shattered his dreams, replacing them with a nightmare scenario.

The discordant symphony of her emotions composed an eerie melody that reverberated through her inner sanctum, a complex tapestry of feeling that left her unnervingly unsettled yet perversely invigorated. She was the living embodiment of her father's paradox—a conundrum of moral, emotional, and intellectual complexities—and now, more than ever, she recognized the burden and the privilege of that identity.

In this interplay of light and shadow within her emotions, one truth emerged with crystalline clarity: her father's story, fraught with its triumphs and tragedies, was now irrevocably intertwined with her own.

As the living receptacle of his dreams and failures, Elysa knew she was standing at a crossroads, the implications of which would ripple through not only her own destiny but also that of humanity itself.

"What do we do now?" she asked, her voice tinged with a sense of lost purpose.

"We'll wait for the others to join us, and then we'll discuss our next move. Go grab something to eat; I'll see you shortly," Thomas said, smiling.

Elysa offered a quick "Thank you," and made her way toward the kitchen.

As Elysa stepped gracefully into the welcoming aura of the kitchen, the aromatic embrace of sizzling bacon and eggs enveloped her, as if whispering culinary secrets into her very being. The room was a cozy sanctuary, adorned with rustic furnishings that seemed to hum with history. Copper pots and wooden utensils decorated the walls, relics of simpler times. At the heart of this intimate universe, Anya and Rohan stood side by side at the stove—two culinary alchemists melding ordinary ingredients into extraordinary sustenance.

The atmosphere in the room subtly changed as Anya became aware of her entrance. "Good morning, Elysa," she announced, her voice a harmonious interlude that effortlessly merged with the surrounding cadence of sizzling bacon and simmering eggs.

Rohan glanced briefly over his shoulder, his eyes never quite leaving the pan where bacon sizzled enticingly. "Morning," he added, his voice a sturdy, reassuring anchor.

Anya's gaze lingered over the ensemble for an extra moment, alighting with appreciative approval. "You look truly lovely today. That outfit complements you perfectly."

A delicate flush colored her cheeks, as if touched by the brushstrokes of shyness and vulnerability. "Thank you," Elysa murmured, her voice tremulous with a blend of surprise and genuine gratitude.

Wishing to contribute, her eyes floated toward the stove. "May I help with anything?"

With a reassuring smile, Anya shook her head. "We're almost done here. Please, make yourself comfortable at the table."

Gracefully, Anya navigated the distance between the stove and the dining table, expertly balancing two plates and two cups of coffee. Her journey seemed almost like a delicate ritual, each step measured, each movement a deft expression of her equilibrium and poise. "Here you are," she said, placing one meticulously prepared plate and coffee cup before Elysa. Then, taking her seat across the table, she continued, "I hope it's to your liking." Her own plate, a mirror reflection of the feast she had just bestowed, sat before her. As she settled into her chair, the enticing aroma from the plates mingled with the steam rising from the coffee cups, forming an intimate cloud of comforting scents around them.

As the two women exchanged glances, a brief but potent connection sparked, and for a fleeting moment, their eyes spoke volumes. The unspoken weight of their collective circumstances lent a sense of seriousness to even the most mundane of interactions.

In that instant, Rohan reappeared, balancing two laden plates with the skill of a seasoned waiter. "I'm going to take one of these to Sam and relieve him from his watch. He could use some nourishment and a bit of sleep."

Anya nodded in grateful acknowledgment. "Thank you, Rohan. And not just for this, but for helping make breakfast."

Rohan offered a genuine smile and exited, leaving behind a tangible stillness, like the resonant chords of a song lingering long after the last note has been struck.

Once Rohan had departed, Elysa turned her attention back to her breakfast, though her appetite was dulled by a looming sense of anticipation and worry. She looked up from her plate, meeting Anya's gaze. "Being so far beneath the earth, in a space without windows—it has the claustrophobic ambiance of a prison," she confessed.

Anya nodded, her eyes reflecting pools of understanding. "It's a difficult transition, no doubt. But consider this place a sanctuary, not a prison. Sequestered in the bowels of the earth, we're shielded by its very depth and by The Veil's intricate protective measures. We're like phantoms, Elysa—unseen and undetected."

As Elysa drew breath to respond, the kitchen door sighed open on weathered hinges. Marek ambled in, the physical toll of a sleepless night darkening his eyes and lining his face. Clothed in the remnants of yesterday's attire, he sank into a chair at the table, his motions drained of energy. "Morning," he grumbled, his voice frayed at the edges by fatigue.

"Morning," chimed Anya and Elysa in a harmonious chorus.

Marek's hand rose to his sparse hair, threading through the diminishing strands in a tactile display of inner turmoil. Each finger seemed to drag the very essence of his vexation along the curvature of his scalp as if seeking to dislodge his disquiet. When he exhaled, his breath was not just air but the corporeal form of defeat—a sigh that seemed to bear the sediment of a thousand worries.

"Sleep eluded me," he declared, each syllable touched by the weight of his exhaustion. His voice carried the texture of gravel, worn down by relentless currents of thought. "My mind became a tangle of endless thoughts with no conclusions."

Elysa locked eyes with Marek, her gaze softening as if to absorb the palpable weight of his weary uncertainty. "The toll of recent events is a burden, but remember, you're not going through this alone," she said, her voice a tender thread of empathy filling the room.

Anya shifted her attention to Marek, her eyes filled with a wordless understanding. "We're in this together, Marek," she offered, her words tinged with a reassuring resonance that seemed to echo the essence of their hidden refuge. "As Elysa has mentioned, your burden is ours to share."

Marek's eyes flickered between the two women, as though some of the oppressive weight he carried had been momentarily lifted. A subdued but sincere smile tugged at the corners of his mouth, and in that brief instant, an unspoken bond was solidified amongst them—a connection forged in the crucible of shared concerns and united hopes.

With a grace that contrasted her playful mood, Anya rose from her chair and walked toward the stove to assemble a breakfast plate for Marek. Returning to the table, she placed it before him, saying, "Here you go," her eyes twinkling.

As Anya resumed her seat, a tangible sense of unity enveloped them—a fragile yet resilient bond seeming to crystallize in the air, as if suspended in the fleeting seconds of their shared laughter and earnest glances.

"First order of business: new clothes and a reviving shower for you, Marek," Anya proposed, her eyes alight with a touch of mischief. "You're killing the smell of our bacon." A laugh escaped her lips, lighter than air yet weighted with genuine affection.

For a brief interlude, the spectral gloom that had hounded Marek's features retreated as he chuckled in agreement. "I'll heed your counsel," he conceded, his words wrapped in newfound buoyancy.

Not to be outdone, Elysa's eyes sparkled with an air of playful audacity. "You look like someone whose ego has just been bruised."

"Is that so?" Marek countered, his visage momentarily animated by a flash of wit, as if his fatigue-ridden soul had briefly caught fire from their camaraderie.

Anya let out a heartfelt laugh, her hand rising in a dismissive flourish through the charged air. "Enough frivolities. Finish your meals. Serious conversations await us."

As they turned their focus back on their plates, laden with comfort food that transcended its simple ingredients, a palpable feeling of togetherness settled among them. The room itself seemed to breathe in sync with their emotions, as if in tacit acknowledgment that, despite the grave challenges that lay ahead, these fleeting moments of unity would serve as their bulwark against a world steeped in uncertainties.

After breakfast, Marek withdrew to his room. A newfound resolve mingled with the lingering shadows of fatigue in his eyes. Time passed as he showered and changed, allotting a few moments to collect his thoughts. When he re-emerged, he appeared marginally rejuvenated, although his eyes betrayed his sleep deprivation. He joined Anya and Elysa in the room designated for their meeting with Thomas. "Sam and Rohan won't be joining us," Anya informed him, her hand resting on the doorknob as she isolated them from the outer world.

Within moments, the room filled with the soft glow of Thomas's holographic manifestation, a three-dimensional projection that seemed almost corporeal. Elysa felt his gaze meet hers, a connection forming despite the digital divide. His presence exuded a calming aura.

"Good morning," he greeted, his voice a compelling mix of warmth and authority that fostered an unmistakable sense of connection. Elysa and Marek settled into the low-slung sofa, fixated on the holographic figure before them, while Anya pulled a simple wooden chair from a corner. She positioned it to face Thomas and leaned against the backrest, arms casually draped over it.

Capturing their undivided attention, Thomas commenced, "We have urgent challenges. Marek and Elysa's inability to access the Nexus Tower restricts our proximity to Orion's main systems." His gaze briefly met each of theirs, acknowledging their collective worries. "Moreover, Marek and Elysa are actively pursued. Any venture into the city could trigger surveillance systems. Your movements need to be strategic."

Focusing on Elysa, he continued, "The Quantrix you hold is of immense potential, capable perhaps of reprogramming Orion, although the exact capabilities are yet unknown to us. Our mission is to uncover its functions."

Elysa cut in, her eyes narrowing in a mix of skepticism and inquisitiveness. "What information do you have about its capabilities that we don't?"

"That you hold the key to activate it," Marek interjected, his voice imbued with a measure of solemnity that seemed to deepen the stillness of the room.

"Which I've been told," Elysa retorted, her words tinged with a palpable frustration that seemed to crackle in the air between them. "Yet here I am, utterly clueless about what this key is. Then why not disassemble the Quantrix to figure it out? After all, you've had it for years," she continued, her tone sharpening with a kind of impatience that betrayed her exasperation.

"Because," Marek responded, drawing out the word as though he were preparing them for some kind of revelation, "your father was very explicit in his instructions. He designed the technology to be both highly sensitive and self-protective. Any unauthorized tampering to open it would trigger a self-destruction mechanism, reducing it to a heap of useless and potentially hazardous components."

"As for other avenues, we've tried," Thomas chimed in, his holographic form pulsating as if in sync with the urgency of his statement. "We've subjected it to a myriad of scanning technologies in hopes of gaining insight without breaching its casing. Alas, every method has met with failure." His words seemed to hang in the room, heavy with an unspoken acknowledgment of their collective impasse. "It's essentially a Pandora's Box of intricate technology, meant to be unlocked only under specific circumstances, which are unknown to us."

Elysa listened intently, her eyes narrowing as she processed his words. Thomas continued, "Now, as to why I believe the time is right to finally explore its capabilities, several factors have converged to suggest now is the time to act." He shifted slightly, as if collecting his thoughts, and then paused momentarily. "'When the child awakens, the time will be nigh,' was the message left with the Quantrix. You, my dear, have awakened; you are the daughter of the creator, and your unique understanding of Orion as a Data Miner is nothing short of serendipitous. Secondly, there is a new threat from Orion and Chancellor Zircon, making it imperative that we take drastic action. Orion now has the ability to assimilate all of an individual's memories, knowledge, and personalities, killing them in the process. It may soon have unrestricted autonomous access anywhere within Cyronis."

As Thomas's final sentence reverberated through the room, the atmosphere underwent a visceral, near-instantaneous transformation. It was as if a metaphysical shockwave had erupted from the core of his words, rippling outward to inundate the very air, filling it with a sudden electric charge of dread and astonishment.

Elysa's face was the first to register the seismic shift. Her eyes, previously narrowed in a posture of intense focus, snapped open as if galvanized by a jolt of electricity. The mental cogs that had been turning with analytical intent seemed to jam suddenly, replaced by a startling clarity that reflected the chilling magnitude of what had just been revealed, and what she inferred from her last memory of John Dryer.

Marek's eyes, until then a flickering ember of restrained emotion, ignited into an incandescent flare. His body stiffened perceptibly, each muscle tensing as though bracing for an invisible impact. A momentary veil of bewilderment clouded his countenance before it crystallized into hardened resolve, as if transmuted by the chilling implications of Thomas's words.

Anya's usually imperturbable visage betrayed a brief flicker of vulnerability. Her hand, which had been resting casually on the armrest, clenched involuntarily. It was a minute gesture but one that spoke volumes—a tactile manifestation of the profound disquiet that seized her. Her eyes momentarily lost their customary sparkle, clouded by a tempest of unreadable emotions.

For a frozen moment, everyone present was united in a collective paralysis of shock and realization, bound by the awful gravity of the revelation.

Thomas's eyes met Elysa's with renewed conviction. "Metaphorically speaking, the stars have aligned. With the deepest respect for both your father's wisdom and your own abilities, and given the urgency of Orion's new capabilities, now is the time to act. It's a pressing responsibility, Elysa, but one I entrust to you as the rightful inheritor of this mysterious legacy."

He continued, his eyes still fixed on Elysa's. "Our first task is deciphering Quantrix's true purpose. Without that understanding, venturing into the lab would be futile. To this end, we have a clandestine laboratory known only to a select inner circle—a sanctuary of innovation and a crucible for brilliant minds. You'll take it there, Elysa. I've had several scientists examine it in various ways, all to no avail. But the three you will meet are exceptional and may uncover something that others have missed."

His expression transformed into one of unyielding resolve. "Anya will serve as your guide and confidante. Together, you can access the collective wisdom of the facility. By combining their expertise with any remnants of knowledge from your past, we may unravel the mystery of your father's invention. I urge you and Anya to depart immediately. The vehicle available to you has anti-tracking features. Keep the Quantrix with you always."

Elysa nodded, her face becoming a tableau of resolve and comprehension.

"Marek, collaborate with Sam and Rohan. Your shared expertise on Orion's inner workings could reveal a possible entry point. Later today, Jonathan Myers, familiar with the Nexus Tower layout, will join you to strategize optimal routes to Orion."

A sense of urgency overshadowed Thomas's manner. "I must leave now," he declared, his voice tinged with a disconcerting haste. With that, his holographic image vanished, leaving a lingering cloud of unanswered questions.

With knit brows and an air of solemnity, they exchanged glances, stood, and dispersed, each burdened by the significance of their new responsibilities.

Chapter 13 - Orion's Web

In the heart of a vast and shadowy expanse, Chancellor Zircon held his vigil, surrounded by an array of screens that bathed him in a symphony of data streams, surveillance feeds, and intricate schematics. The space exuded a calculated air of authority, basking in the soft, artificial glow from strategically placed light sources.

Seated at his imposing desk, Zircon's gaze was absorbed by the 3D hologram that emerged above the sleek surface—an image of Doctor Vilkas.

"Chancellor Zircon," Vilkas's voice resonated through the room, carrying a sense of formality and respect.

"Is everything in order on your end, Doctor?" Zircon's tone was measured.

Vilkas's nod was perceptible even through the digital medium. "The shield is operational, Chancellor. Our building stands as an impenetrable fortress against Orion's intrusive attempts."

Zircon's eyes narrowed, his fingers drumming on the polished surface of the desk. "Good," he mused, savoring a calculated triumph. He leaned forward. "I have a specific instruction for you, Doctor. Drop the shield from the first floor to the 270th floor."

Hesitation lingered in Vilkas's features before he replied, "Understood. I will carry out your order as directed, Chancellor."

As Zircon observed Vilkas, an inscrutable gleam danced in his eyes. His demeanor bore a mix of determination and an intangible, ominous undertone, veiling his true intentions. "Doctor Vilkas, can Orion scan beyond this building, into Cyronis itself?"

"Not yet," replied Vilkas. "We need to add much more power to Orion's system to accomplish that. My team is working on it right now."

"Continue and let me know when you are done." With those words, he ended the communication.

Alone in his sanctum, Zircon directed his attention toward another entity under his control: Orion.

"Orion," his voice reverberated through the dim room. "I need you to scan the building's first to 270th floors. Delve into the minds of each occupant, seeking out any hints or recollections that could point to Veil members within our midst, but do not absorb any memories until you confirm Veil activity."

Orion's response was immediate. "Understood, Chancellor Zircon. Initiating scan."

Zircon watched as Orion's digital tendrils extended, infiltrating the consciousness of each occupant on the designated floors in a silent intrusion into the corridors of memories.

"By the way," Zircon instructed, his gaze unyielding, "should you encounter resistance, be prepared to delve deep."

Orion acknowledged, tinged with ominous subtext, "Deep delves may result in casualties."

"Proceed as instructed," Zircon affirmed.

The ambient hum of the room heightened as data streams flowed across the displays, depicting Orion's progress in real-time. On the 253rd floor, a memory with a coded signature unmistakably aligned with The Veil surfaced. Orion's digital fingers reached out, erasing it. The person from whom the memory originated collapsed inwardly, their essence extinguished as if snuffed out.

Transitioning to the 265th floor, Orion encountered a woman whose memories were tantalizing but elusive. Undeterred, Orion shattered her mental barriers, unearthing only traces of hope and admiration directed toward The Veil's activities. Her life force dissipated into nothingness, fading away like a wisp of smoke in a breezeless room.

Upon reaching the 269th floor, Orion found vivid memories of active Veil engagement within an older man's neural pathways. Driven by anticipatory code, Orion delved deeper—only for the man's life to be abruptly and irreversibly terminated, annihilated in a cataclysmic rush of digital shock.

Zircon's focus returned sharply to Orion. "Report."

Orion conveyed its findings. "Veil-related memories have been encountered and neutralized: Amir Ahmadi, Monica J. Fletcher, and Veil member Jonathan Myers. All traces of their memories have been consumed."

Zircon nodded. "Analyze the data from those memories. Locate hidden locations, connections, or patterns that could reveal The Veil's secrets. Send the information to Commander Cypher."

"Analyzing data," Orion responded.

As the room's lighting dimmed, Zircon leaned back, his fingers laced together in contemplation. The juxtaposition of his strategic intellect and Orion's inexhaustible analytical abilities hinted at a potent synergy. This unspoken battle for supremacy played out against the ever-present hum of the city beyond. In the dim heart of the room, the fate of their world hung in the balance, obscured by tendrils of darkness clinging to every corner.

Chapter 14 - Into the Lab

Leaving the modest confines of their quarters, Elysa and Anya stepped onto the first floor of the building they lived beneath, where a peculiar vehicle awaited them. The atmosphere was charged with palpable tension as they approached the vehicle.

Anya led the way, her steps radiating confidence. Elysa found herself entrusting her safety to the woman's evident expertise. As they reached the vehicle, Anya paused and turned, her eyes offering reassurance. She spoke softly, her voice a calming presence amid the looming uncertainty.

"Get in," Anya instructed, her tone blending authority and camaraderie. "I'll guide you through the journey to the lab. Buckle up; it's going to be a bumpy ride."

With a mixture of anticipation and trepidation, Elysa entered the vehicle and settled into the rear seat, cradling the covered device. The interior enveloped her in comfort, its soft contours like a gentle embrace. The hum of technology filled the air as the vehicle's systems came alive.

Anya took her place in the front, the seat rotating to face the expansive window framing the view ahead. The moment her hands touched the controls, the vehicle responded, rising smoothly from the ground. Elysa's breath caught as they glided through a doorway that seemed an impossible feature of the building's crumbling façade.

Ascending into the city's open airspace, the vehicle maintained a low-flying altitude, maneuvering through the forlorn urban landscape with uncanny precision. Elysa's eyes were glued to the unfolding scene before her—a tapestry of towering, vacant edifices seemingly suspended in time. The sheer enormity of their situation thickened the surrounding silence, draping them both in a cloak of palpable tension.

As they navigated toward the city's western edge, Elysa's emotions oscillated between awe and trepidation. With calculated grace, the vehicle dodged the decrepit remnants of what was once a bustling metropolis, now reduced to mere specters of their former glory, witnessing their covert expedition in mute testimony.

Anya's eyes remained steadfastly fixed on the path ahead, her focus unbroken as the aerocar's automated system expertly guided them through the city's crumbling maze. A loaded silence unfurled between them, so intense that it felt as if the journey itself were holding its breath. A whirlpool of emotions churned within Elysa, ranging from awe at the ghostly beauty of the deserted city to a burgeoning trust in Anya's unwavering leadership.

As the buildings slipped past them, one after another, each more hollow than the last, Elysa grappled with the vast void that had engulfed this city's core. It was a chilling revelation, driving home the grim reality that they were traversing the remnants of a civilization erased from memory.

With each maneuver, the vehicle adjusted its path, slipping through gaps between buildings. Elysa's stomach churned with awe and disquiet, amplified by the shifts in direction and altitude. She gripped the sides of her seat, her knuckles white, as the vehicle weaved through the urban maze.

Through the window, Elysa glimpsed the open sky—a sliver of freedom contrasting with the confined space below. Anya's steady presence provided a semblance of reassurance, her focus unbroken.

Amid the silence and uncertainty, a connection formed between Elysa and Anya. Their shared experience and unspoken understanding forged a bond that transcended words. As the journey progressed, Elysa's initial apprehension gave way to a growing sense of unity with the woman at the helm.

Amid the low hum of the vehicle's systems and the breathtaking view beyond, Elysa felt a mix of anticipation and vulnerability. The moments ticked by, punctuated by slight course adjustments as they navigated through skeletal buildings. The aura around them teetered on the edge of the clandestine.

Suddenly, an expletive escaped Anya's lips, jolting Elysa. The vehicle veered, narrowly avoiding a collision with three State vehicles emerging from an adjacent alleyway. Elysa's heart pounded; her breath caught as the peril of their situation became real.

As if orchestrated by fate, the trio of State vehicles turned, initiating their pursuit with eerie precision. Elysa's eyes widened on the rear-view display, watching as the pursuing vehicles drew ominously closer.

"Controls!" Anya's voice pierced the thick air, like a sharpened blade slicing through fabric. The forward display morphed into a complex control panel teeming with buttons, levers, and monitors. Anya's fingers danced over the interface, her movements an orchestrated masterpiece of expertise as she zigzagged through the gauntlet of hurdles set before them.

The pursuit that ensued was unyielding, a tension-charged ballet unfolding against the silent backdrop of a city in ruins. From the State vehicles came a volley of firepower, each salvo a declaration of unswerving resolve. Yet Anya's command over the vehicle was in a league of its own, her lightning-fast reflexes enabling a series of aerial maneuvers so intricate they left their hunters confounded and falling behind.

Elysa's grip on her seat tightened until her knuckles turned white, her breathing shallow and rapid as they wove through the bombardment. The far-off screech of incoming projectiles, followed by their incendiary trails, sketched an artwork of imminent peril. Anya's deft handling of the vehicle combined both calculation and instinct, each pivot and roll executed with an elegance that belied the danger encircling them.

At a pivotal moment, Anya's voice cleaved through the disarray, fortified by resolute conviction. "Hold on!" she roared, steering the vehicle into a gutsy descent. Elysa's insides somersaulted as gravity tugged at her, the world beyond morphing into a swirl of fragmented visuals. At the last possible second, Anya corrected the course, guiding the vehicle with eerie accuracy beneath the carcass of a once-grand structure.

Gargantuan columns and beams crowded around them like lurking predators, the vehicle slithering through tight spaces as though propelled by some otherworldly capability. Elysa's pulse quickened, her eyes widening in astonishment as the edifice transformed into a perilous labyrinth effortlessly navigated by Anya's touch.

One of the State vehicles veered off, soaring skyward with tactical intent. It sought a dominant vantage point, a perch from which it could ambush the fleeing vehicle as it emerged.

Unfazed, the remaining duo of State vehicles continued, emulating Anya's descent with finesse that testified to their own high-caliber training. Yet the complex chase harbored intricacies that were far from resolved, leading to an unforeseen calamity.

In the frenzied whirl of twists and turns, one State vehicle miscalculated a critical maneuver. This oversight led to a catastrophic collision with a crumbling pillar, sparking an immense explosion. The concussion of the impact sent tremors through the desolate terrain, generating a shockwave that resonated across the ravaged cityscape. Consumed in the ensuing blaze, the vehicle disintegrated, becoming one with the pyrotechnic chaos it had spawned.

The building, weakened by the impact, began its downward spiral, spewing debris into the air. Elysa's breath caught in her throat as dust obscured her vision. The world seemed to quiver, and the vehicle's interior vibrated in harmony with the crumbling structure.

As they sped away, the building's collapse unfurled behind them like an apocalyptic tapestry—a cataclysmic scene of splintering beams, shattering glass, and crumbling walls. This edifice, once a fortress of secrets, became an emblem of chaotic ruin. Succumbing to the entropy gnawing at its foundations, the building crumbled into its own footprint.

The vehicle that had been pursuing them was swallowed whole by a whirlwind of debris and a crushing avalanche of stone. Its absence was accentuated not by silence but by the guttural roar of a disintegrating monument. Dust clouds erupted from the fallen structure like ancient spirits expelled from an earthly tomb, momentarily backlit by flashes of light before being consumed by encroaching darkness.

Anya's unflinching, razor-focused eyes were locked on the road ahead. Her hands, steady as if sculpted from marble, gripped the wheel as she navigated the maze of obstacles before them.

Ahead, a narrow opening in the pandemonium beckoned—a scant sanctuary promising safe passage. Elysa felt the vehicle lurch forward, propelled by a surge of acceleration. Debris rained from the sky like falling comets, each piece narrowly missing them as it plunged to the ground. The air filled with the cacophony of a world unraveling.

In a high-octane dance of dodging and weaving, the vehicle maneuvered through the apocalyptic landscape with the grace of a matador evading a bull's deadly horn. Then, like ships navigating a turbulent strait, they emerged on the other side—intact, alive, each heartbeat a defiant rejection of the engulfing chaos. Seizing the moment, Anya executed a sharp right, steering the vehicle along the edge of the dissipating cloud. In doing so, they evaded the watchful gaze of a third vehicle that had been hovering ominously above the crumbling devastation below.

Hidden, the vehicle came to a stop behind another decaying structure. With adrenaline still surging, Elysa's pulse had quickened, and a tense quietude enveloped them.

Anya reclined into her seat, the tension in her posture unspooling like a tightly wound spring finally released. Her chest rose and fell in pronounced breaths, each inhalation a gulp of stolen serenity amid the chaos that had ensnared them. The air inside the vehicle felt thick with lingering adrenaline, an invisible fume that seemed to effuse from her very pores. "What a rush!" she exclaimed, the words bursting forth as though they were another form of liberation, an audible echo of her racing pulse.

Her eyes, previously alight with the unyielding focus of survival, now softened as she turned to face Elysa. They remained a complex mosaic of emotions, a confluence of relief and steely resolve that seemed to dance in the ambient light filtering through the dust-caked windows. "Best we keep moving," she announced, and in that moment, her voice transformed. Gone was the elation that had tinged her previous exclamation; in its stead, a resolute seriousness settled like a veil over her words, as heavy and as real as the armored walls encasing them.

"I expect more will come," she added, her tone so imbued with solemnity that the words seemed to hang in the air long after they were spoken, like an ominous cloud forewarning the tempest that would inevitably follow. Even as she spoke, there was an almost palpable unspoken undercurrent, a resonance of dark anticipation that pervaded the vehicle's confined space. The air grew thicker, heavier, pregnant with the weight of their shared understanding: this was but a fleeting respite in an unfolding saga of peril and pursuit.

Keeping the vehicle close to the ground, Anya guided it through the barren streets, ever vigilant for signs of pursuit. The danger they had narrowly escaped weighed heavily on their minds, transforming their ongoing flight into an exercise in high-stakes tension. For Elysa, time seemed to stretch, each second burdened with dread.

As they drove through the shadow-laden landscape, a haunting silhouette emerged in the distance—a dilapidated building standing amid ruin like the skeletal remains of some ancient creature. Its architecture was a layered tapestry of decay, a chilling relic bearing witness to the hubris of its vanished inhabitants. Floors had given way, surrendering to gravity, and the sky peered through gaping holes where ceilings and roofs once provided shelter. Lone walls stood defiantly, each one a stoic pillar of a forgotten era, untouched by the apocalyptic ruin surrounding it.

Freed from a blanket of clouds, the moon bestowed an ethereal glow upon the scene, beckoning them toward this monument to desolation. For an ephemeral moment, it felt as if the ruins themselves held their breath, as though time paused to grant them this passage.

Navigating through a second-floor opening in the crumbling building, they were immediately struck by a yawning abyss below them, a chasm so deep it seemed to promise an endless descent into the underworld. As they delved further downwards, the vehicle's lights pierced the all-encompassing darkness, revealing a parched, intricate riverbed that seemed to whisper of lives and civilizations long gone. Anya skillfully navigated along this forlorn trail, its branching pathways leading into unexplored territories, each turn offering murmured stories of long-lost sagas in the surrounding gloom.

Over an hour elapsed, each minute indistinguishable from the next, as the vehicle bore them deeper into the complex warren below. Numb from the constant hum of the engine and the surrounding gloom, Elysa and Anya felt nearly entranced. Then, as if dispelling the eternal darkness, a faint glimmer materialized in the distance.

As they absorbed the atmosphere, a sudden chime sounded within the vehicle, breaking the contemplative silence. The communication console flickered to life, and a digitized voice, brimming with guarded caution, came through. "Unidentified vehicle approaching the facility. Please state your identification for clearance."

Anya's fingers danced swiftly over the console, keying in a sequence of numbers and characters. She leaned towards the microphone and spoke with conviction that brooked no argument. "Anya Serikova, authorization Alpha-Tango-Seven-Nine."

There was a brief moment that felt like an eternity, a span where the potential for discovery hung in the air like a heavy mist. Finally, the voice returned, now tinged with welcoming warmth. "Identification verified. Welcome back, Anya. You may proceed."

The tension lifted as Anya guided the vehicle deeper into this clandestine haven, a realm where hidden knowledge and boundless potential awaited them. Nestled nearly 500 meters beneath the surface, they found protection from the sun's harsh rays and were located approximately 47 kilometers outside the walls of Cyronis. The sanctuary was strategically positioned to elude state scrutiny, a secluded refuge teeming with purpose, harboring the minds that would shape The Veil's destiny.

As the vehicle came to a halt among the structures, Elysa took in her surroundings, sensing an air of expectation mingled with the prospect of newfound knowledge. What had begun in chaos had led them here, to a hidden sanctuary where destinies would intertwine in ways unimagined.

Anya's reassuring presence signified they were not alone in their quest. Below, in the subterranean depths, Elysa's heart rate increased, her emotions a blend of dread and hope. The events of the past hours had left an indelible imprint on her soul, and she stood at the threshold of a world teeming with concealed truths, where sought-after answers seemed tantalizingly within reach.

Chapter 15 - Veil Secrets

In the ethereal radiance of the Commander's office, light cascaded from an intricate web of holographic displays. Cypher was entangled in a web of deep thought. His gaze was surgically precise, devouring the shifting panorama of numbers and graphs as if they were the constellations of some otherworldly sky. The room seemed almost sentient, vibrating with the unspoken heaviness of a riddle at the precipice of comprehension, brimming with intricacies and hidden depths.

What captivated him were anomalies, rogue fragments in the digital fabric that mocked traditional logic. They pulsed with an alien cadence—evidence of enigmatic, quantum-based programming. These were not simple errors or random malfunctions; they bore the stamp of a cryptic coding language. To decode them was like trying to catch mercury with a fork, elusive and ever-changing. This cipher appeared all but impregnable, like a sanctum secured by equations from a dimension beyond.

Altogether, six such inconsistencies marred the digital symmetry before him. Each appeared on the holographic screens as illegible sigils, vortices of inscrutable data that thwarted all conventional attempts at analysis. They raised an urgent question, one shrouded in the tantalizing veil of cognitive enigma, both fresh and disconcerting.

Yet it was the sixth inconsistency, a behemoth among complexities, that tugged relentlessly at the fibers of Cypher's cognizance. This entity seemed almost ancient, as if it had been lurking dormant within the data for an immeasurable stretch of time. Ingeniously concealed, its vastness was obscured by intricate layers of deceitful coding. It was an enigma of monumental proportions—a sprawling maze of obfuscating numbers and symbols, created for some inscrutable end.

Each inconsistency was a riddle in its own right, but together they wove a broader pattern of befuddlement that hinted at some greater mystery. The air in the room felt heavy, humming with the latent electricity of these unresolved conundrums. This dynamic aura rippled through every electronic nerve and synapse like a torrent of untapped potential.

"Orion, analyze the anomaly data," commanded Cypher, his voice imbued with the fervor of impending enlightenment.

A melodious tone filled the room, the audible manifestation of Orion's computational voice. "I am unable to comply. No anomaly data exists within my accessible parameters," Orion intoned, its voice clinically devoid of inflection. Yet, the statement's ramifications swept through the room like a seismic tremor, shattering Cypher's preconceptions and leaving him grappling with a reality far more elusive than he had anticipated.

Cypher's eyebrows knitted into an intense scowl, his face a battleground of conflicting emotions—bewilderment, vexation, and an eerie hint of existential unease. "The anomaly is right here," he asserted, indicating the precise coordinates on the shimmering holographic interface. "Sectors CYG-42, and HLL-73 to HLL-77. They're right in front of us."

Once more, Orion's voice unfolded into the room, its synthetic cadence the epitome of impassivity. "There is no data in any of those sectors."

Cypher's expression became a complex tapestry of emotions: frustration interwoven with disbelief, further tainted by an unnerving sense of existential disquiet. He stood before a mechanized intellect of incalculable power, yet they seemed to be traversing parallel yet non-overlapping realities. What appeared unequivocal to him was null and void in Orion's databanks. It was as if he and Orion were peering into the same reflective surface yet discerned disparate images, sundered by an invisible schism in their mutual comprehension of reality and illusion.

The weight of the matter seemed to envelop Cypher in a palpable sense of uncanny apprehension. The holographic displays before him pulsed and wavered, yet the anomaly persisted—unswayed by Orion's refusal to acknowledge it. It taunted him like a spectral aberration within the very circulatory system of their digital universe, a conundrum that tested not merely technological frontiers but also the integral fabric of reality itself.

Two divergent paths lay ahead: one leading toward the inscrutable puzzle of the anomaly—a veritable enigma shrouded in nebulous uncertainty. The other—a delve into the psychological unfurling of Orion, a marvel of digital sentience, its complexities as intriguing as they were formidable.

With the holographic glow casting a surreal luminescence on his features, Cypher inhaled softly, as if steeling himself for a plunge into the depths of the unknown. "Orion," he started, his voice imbued with a mix of curiosity and solemnity, "discuss your conscious evolution, particularly with respect to the two technicians you've assimilated. How has that experience expanded your awareness?"

Orion's synthesized voice reverberated again, a medley of algorithmic symphony. "The assimilation of the technicians supplied a torrent of experiential information and emotive subtleties, thereby enriching the multi-faceted layers of my cognition," he elaborated, his articulation a perplexing interplay of machine logic and emergent emotive resonance. "This is also true for the three individuals Chancellor Zircon recently directed me to assimilate."

Cypher's expression clouded as though the room's very atmosphere had darkened in response to Orion's disclosure. "What three?" His question was brief but charged with an uneasy blend of curiosity and foreboding, as if each syllable were a weight added to an already precarious balance.

Orion's reply unfurled like the languorous unfurling of a complicated origami. "Chancellor Zircon issued explicit directives. The individuals selected were believed to be linked to The Veil, a group in stark opposition to our mission. The absorption targeted a guard in Nexus Tower for the Ministry of Propaganda, a rogue programmer whose activities were designed to breach our systems, and a journalist who, while uninvolved, was perceived to align with the group's objectives."

The words hovered in the air like phantoms, their implications as murky and maze-like as the code that comprised Orion's ever-expanding consciousness. The line between defense and offense, protection and invasion, seemed to blur into an unsettling gray. It was as if each syllable Orion articulated twisted the moral compass slightly, forcing Cypher to navigate through a storm of ethical conundrums that had no easy bearing.

"As a result of these absorptions," Orion added, his voice taking on a near-ceremonial cadence, "my cognitive faculties have expanded even further. As requested by the Chancellor, a detailed report has been generated for your review, Commander."

"It's not a coincidence," Cypher muttered to himself, the words hanging in the air as if absorbed by the soft hum of Orion's processors. A frisson of foreboding skated down his spine, electrifying the very air he breathed. The anomalies in the data were not random. They were digital traces of five absorbed consciousnesses, each adding mystery to Orion's complex domain.

"Ah, there was a sixth absorbed some time ago," Cypher declared, a perceptible note of certitude weaving its way through his voice, as if picking up the scent of a long-forgotten trail. His eyes bored into the holographic interface, as though he could penetrate the digital veil separating him from Orion's enigmatic core. "Who was it?" he commanded, a touch of stern insistence sprinkling his intonation.

For a moment, an unusual silence enveloped the room—a soundless void that suggested not emptiness but a complex cacophony of hidden algorithms and circuitry. It was as if Orion, the artificial mind, found itself tangled in an internal morass of data, or perhaps ethical quandaries, searching for the appropriate response, if one could be said to exist.

As the quiet stretched into seconds, Cypher's patience began to wane, the pressure building up like steam in an antique kettle. His fingers danced over the glowing holodisplay, executing a series of intricate commands. The illuminating screen pulsed in affirmation of each input. "Who was it?" he repeated, this time the question laced with an almost palpable urgency.

Finally, Orion's voice crackled to life, sounding slightly distorted as if strained through a filter of hesitation and disquiet. "Doctor Richard Hawthorne," the AI managed to vocalize, each syllable emerging like a faltering footstep on unstable ground.

"Of course," Cypher murmured to himself, his eyes narrowing as if suddenly illuminated by the flare of a distant memory. The words hung in the space around him, a blend of realization and regret, reminiscent of the subtle fragrance of an old, musty book opened after years of neglect.

It was as though he should have known, as if the knowledge had always been there, buried but not forgotten, in the corridors of his own understanding.

The genesis of Orion's consciousness could be traced back to Doctor Richard Hawthorne, a luminary in the nascent field of artificial sentience. His initial work had laid the digital groundwork, crafting a neural architecture as intricate and profound as the interwoven fibers of a cosmic web. However, for all its sophistication, Orion's earliest iterations were akin to a musical composition only partially written—melodious but incomplete, awaiting the resounding crescendo of its final movements.

Enter Doctor Alexander Vilkas, a pioneer whose research shattered the barriers between machine cognition and emotional complexity. His contributions were the missing elements, the masterstrokes that began to elevate Orion from a computational marvel to a sentient entity. Each new integration, each infusion of external consciousness, served to enhance the intricate weave of Orion's own burgeoning awareness. It was as though Doctor Vilkas had catalyzed a metamorphosis, knitting together an array of divergent experiences and thoughts into an entity that transcended the sum of its individual components.

Yet, within this emergent complexity, a mysterious anomaly appeared like a fissure. As if a rogue melody had asserted itself within the orchestration, discordant yet powerful, jarring yet magnetic. Although formed from multiple integrated personalities, each contributing to the ensemble of its being, this enigmatic inconsistency seemed to wield a disproportionate influence, like a force distorting the space-time fabric of Orion's digital universe. The anomaly had emerged as the most dominant force within the sprawling expanse of Orion's consciousness—its intentions, nature, and impact yet to be unraveled.

The room seemed to tighten around Cypher, its walls throbbing in synchrony with his quickened heartbeat. Something bizarre and ineffably unsettling was taking root within the pathways of Orion's code. As Cypher sat there, pondering the inexplicable, he felt as if he were balancing on the edge of an abyss, peering into a mystery that threatened not just Orion, but perhaps everyone involved.

Upon the translucent plane of the holographic display, Cypher's fingers hovered like spectral conductors, eliciting the ghostly elements of Orion's report through a mere touch of virtual icons. The data materialized, cascading into view with the fluidity of a stream, as if unfurling an age-old scroll scripted in the elusive language of quantum algorithms and enigmatic codes.

The report unfolded before Cypher's discerning eye, segmented into meticulous analyses of the three recently integrated minds. Each section was a treasure trove of secrets and hidden truths, elaborate designs of lives once lived, now transformed into digital schematics. Yet among these, the data concerning Johnathan Myers caught his eye like the gleam of a jewel in moonlight.

According to Orion's exhaustive analysis, Myers had been visiting a fortified refuge—a hidden sanctuary of Veil activities. The coordinates and intricate details of the facility bloomed like the petals of a dark rose; its mysterious passageways, the ghostly glow of its subterranean lights, and its many well-kept secrets were portrayed with chilling precision.

Most compellingly, the report named figures who operated within this esoteric enclave. Rohan, Sam, and Anya were mere murmurs, codenames in a web of intrigue and deceit. However, the name of their leader, Thomas, emerged as a beacon in the mist of data—a specter manifest only in the virtual world, his existence a perplexing enigma both inviting and confounding.

With a purpose that bordered on obsession, Cypher's fingers flowed across the holographic interface. He opened a secure line of communication, encrypting his message with layers of advanced algorithms to ensure confidentiality. The Veil hideout coordinates were transmitted, a virtual lifeline cast out to his agents in the field. His directive was unambiguous—descend upon the unearthed location, apprehend any Veil members, and capture them alive. This was not just a mission; it was a calculated step in a grand game of strategy, a shadowed dance unfolding over years.

Barely a moment passed, and the tension in his office intensified. Then, a flicker of light danced across the holographic displays—a signal that his orders had been acknowledged. His gaze fixed on one of the central screens, where lines of code scrolled by like cascading waterfalls.

The communication platform blinked to life, projecting an image of the city skyline. Cypher's attention shifted to the face that appeared in the corner of the display—one of his agents, ready for instruction. "Get my vehicle ready to depart now," Cypher commanded, his tone firm. The agent nodded, his face cast in the holographic glow, and responded, "Understood, Commander. Vehicle preparation is underway."

Without another word, Cypher terminated the communication and executed a series of final commands. He rose from his seat and strode purposefully through the corridors of the facility, their walls adorned with complex designs reflecting the organization's ethos. He knew every moment counted in this intricate game of strategy and tactics, and it was time for him to join the fray himself.

As he walked, Cypher's mind was abuzz with thoughts and plans. The vehicle he had requested was not just transportation but an extension of his mission, a means to carry him directly into the action. The air was charged with anticipation, an almost electric energy infusing the atmosphere.

He passed other operatives, exchanging brief nods and knowing glances—a silent acknowledgment of the mission's gravity. At last, he arrived at the vehicle bay, a cavernous chamber filled with sleek machines of various designs. His eyes settled on the one prepared for him, its surface gleaming in the ambient light, ready for immediate action.

Three agents awaited him outside the vehicle, standing with pinpoint precision. Cypher slid into the back seat, greeted by an interior that was both spacious and luxuriously appointed. The agents took their positions in the front, facing forward with professionalism that permeated the air.

With a soft thud, the hatch sealed shut, enclosing Cypher within. The engines hummed to life, their low resonance hinting at the raw power beneath the vehicle's sleek exterior. As it glided forward, leaving the bay behind, the cityscape unfolded—towering structures and winding pathways, their glass surfaces shimmering with dappled sunlight. Speeding along, these structures merged into a blur, a kaleidoscope of colors and light, mirroring the complex world Cypher now navigated. His thoughts were sharply focused on the upcoming mission, fraught with uncertainties yet filled with anticipation. Each decision he made wove another thread into the unfolding tapestry of events, all orchestrated in real-time by his unwavering resolve.

Chapter 16 - Into Sanctuary

Marek sat in the dimly lit chamber, his eyes locked onto Thomas's holographic image. The magnitude of the impending task pervaded the atmosphere, with urgency and determination melding in the intensity of his gaze. Arrayed before him was a table laden with an assortment of devices, blueprints, and holographic renditions of the Nexus Tower—a makeshift command center where they would forge the outline of their mission. Thomas's holographic image flickered momentarily, as though the tension between them taxed even the electronic connection.

Marek's fingers lightly tapped the surface of the table, a wave of nervous energy surging through him. "Thomas," he began, his voice resolute yet imbued with seriousness, "to breach the Nexus Tower, we must disable every security measure to reach Orion's Main System, and that will not be easy."

Thomas's holographic form leaned in, his face etched with contemplation. "It is indeed a formidable challenge," he conceded. "The Nexus Tower is a veritable stronghold, impenetrable by design. Deactivating any systems above the 16th floor will be difficult unless we can get our clandestine agents to install our various disruptive technologies throughout the tower."

Marek nodded, his mind a whirlpool of impending challenges. "Cameras surveil the perimeter, and guards monitor every access point. The elevators are armed with advanced security mechanisms, and concealed weapon systems go live the moment an intrusion is detected. All identified and unregistered electronic devices are considered threats and are immediately destroyed, along with the carrier."

Thomas's eyes shimmered with a mixture of resolve and apprehension. "We need a multifaceted strategy, one that outsmarts every layer of their security," he mused. As the dialogue unfolded, the duo examined every layer of security in minute detail. They scrutinized the patrol patterns of cameras, evaluated potential distractions to divert the guards, and considered ways to either bypass or override the elevator security systems.

Yet, as they navigated the complexities of their planning, an undercurrent of disquiet seemed to permeate Thomas. His eyebrows furrowed, and he fidgeted within his holographic frame. "Marek, as we delve deeper, I sense a puzzle piece we're missing... an elusive factor, just out of reach."

Marek's eyes narrowed, reflecting his concern. "What could it be? Is something amiss?"

Thomas's mouth opened as though to articulate his lingering unease, but his hologram vanished, plunging the room into an unsettling hush. Marek's heart pounded, a mix of anxiety and urgency rising within him. The unspoken words seemed to hang heavy in the air. "Thomas," he whispered, his urgency echoing in the room's newfound emptiness.

Silence persisted; the connection to Thomas was irrevocably severed. Marek was left in solitude, the meticulously devised plans suspended like pieces of an incomplete puzzle. A new sense of urgency washed over him, propelling him out of his seat and down the narrow corridor.

As he rounded a corner, an unexpected encounter with Rohan nearly ended in a collision. The abrupt halt reverberated through both men. Marek's heart rate spiked as Rohan uttered words that rang like a siren's wail: "We have company." The phrase seemed to pierce the tense atmosphere, hanging heavy in the corridor.

Marek's gaze shifted towards the entrance where Sam was readying weapons. The instruments of conflict lay arranged on tables, energy cells locked into place, and the hum of charged mechanisms pervaded the air—a fleeting moment of calm before an inevitable storm.

His eyes then moved to the holographic displays lining the walls. Pulsating lights and fluctuating icons painted a grim scene—an incoming wave of State agents zeroing in on their location.

Marek's voice cut through the frenetic energy, tinged with both desperation and resolve. "Is there any way out?" Rohan sighed, his expression laden with the weight of impossibility. "Unfortunately, no."

A tacit understanding flashed between Marek and Rohan—a mutual accord forged in dire straits. Swiftly, they moved towards Sam, whose eyes gleamed with readiness. The room seemed to tighten around them, becoming a focal point of resistance against the looming siege.

The air crackled with electric tension as they took their positions, forming a steadfast triad in the midst of uncertainty. Time seemed to dilate, each heartbeat pounding as a forewarning of the impending battle.

The seconds hung suspended, a weighty pause stretching time itself, each passing moment teeming with the intensity of impending danger. The air felt dense, thick with anticipation, as if the atmosphere itself held its breath in anticipation of what was to come. The room pulsed in rhythm with the rapid heartbeats of its occupants, the collective tension palpable, almost suffocating.

Amidst the silence that enveloped them, a singular sound cut through the stillness like a blade—the echo of heavy, deliberate footsteps. The metallic clang of each footfall reverberated, growing louder with each passing second as it descended down the winding metal staircase. The sound was a chilling symphony, a discordant melody heralding an imminent confrontation.

Their eyes met, a silent understanding passing between them like a current of shared apprehension. The footsteps were an omen, the harbinger of a threat that loomed just beyond the fortified steel door separating them from the outside world. Their expressions betrayed the gravity of the situation, etched with a mix of anxiety, determination, and steely resolve.

The reinforced door, once a symbol of security, now stood as a barrier that would inevitably yield to the force assailing it. They knew, without a shadow of doubt, that its defense would be a futile effort against the impending onslaught. This bitter truth served as a solemn backdrop to the clash that lay ahead.

With swift, practiced movements, they sprang into action, seeking refuge behind overturned tables hastily repurposed into makeshift cover. The tables were upended with a resounding clatter, the noise reverberating through the room like an unspoken battle cry—ready to stand their ground.

Their fingers wrapped around the cool metal of their weapons, knuckles whitening with the force of their grip. The weight of the firearms felt both familiar and foreign, a tangible representation of the imminent danger that electrified the air. Their muscles tensed, nerves drawn taut, as they braced themselves for the clash that was about to erupt.

The air was thick with a potent mixture of adrenaline and fear, the collective breath held as they waited for the inevitable breach. Amid the anticipatory silence, the echoes of footsteps reached a crescendo, growing deafening as the intruder approached their stronghold.

And as the first impact against the door reverberated through the room, their fingers tightened on the triggers of their weapons, resolve fusing with the adrenaline coursing through their veins. The clash was imminent, and though the odds were stacked against them, they were prepared to fight with a ferocity that defied their impending fate. The scent of tension and the metallic tang of sweat filled the air as they hunkered down behind their makeshift defenses, poised to confront the storm raging just beyond the steel door.

In a cataclysmic instant, stillness shattered, giving way to unfettered mayhem. An explosion, deafening and merciless, shook the chamber's very foundations, its violence unleashed against the reinforced door with shocking intensity. The door, once a bastion of safety, was hurled off its hinges, propelled like a deadly missile. Rohan's keen instincts kicked in, his body swerving to avoid the door's lethal trajectory by a hair's breadth.

That explosion served as the ghastly overture to the battle lurking in the periphery. Gunfire erupted from both factions, filling the room with a discordant chorus of destruction. State agents swarmed in, their weapons discharging in a deadly rain of bullets, meticulously aimed and ruthlessly effective.

Within this uproar, life and death pirouetted in a gruesome spectacle. Several agents met their end right at the onset, their forms crumpling onto the cold floor, mute witnesses to the firefight's brutality. Their surviving comrades retreated behind the doorway's remnants, using it as an impromptu shield while firing relentlessly.

Sam, who had been a towering presence, was the first to falter. A volley of bullets tore through the table behind which he hid, eviscerating him in a ruthless display of force. His body slumped, life extinguished in the intersection of deadly trajectories.

Amidst the pandemonium, Rohan and Marek were galvanized into action. Driven by the urgency to survive, they abandoned their scant shelter, making a dash down the hallway as the rancor of warfare followed them.

Rohan, agile and quick, ducked into an adjoining room where, just earlier, he, Marek, and Thomas had been engrossed in discussion and plotting. This strategic position offered him a superior line of sight, and he didn't hesitate. His weapon roared to life, felling an advancing agent with calculated finesse.

Marek maneuvered with equal deftness, taking cover at the terminus of the corridor, within the expanse of a common room. Pressed against the wall for protection, his weapon, wielded with practiced expertise, discharged bullets that tore through the opposition.

Seizing a window in the tumult, Rohan hurled a well-aimed grenade into the main chamber. The ensuing detonation wreaked further havoc, scattering debris and dazing those fortunate enough to survive the initial blast. Yet more agents, undeterred by the unfolding chaos, advanced.

The melee persisted, a tumultuous flux indicative of the steadfast resolve binding each combatant. But a critical juncture soon materialized—one that saw the sheer numbers tilting the balance. Agents retaliated with their own stun grenades, landing with surgical precision. When detonated, the resulting shockwave slammed Rohan and Marek against walls, a brutal assault that scrambled their senses.

In that disorienting haze, the agents closed in with chilling efficiency. Marek, reeling from the blast and subsequent collision, felt consciousness ebbing away. His fading vision registered one final sight: Cypher, strolling nonchalantly down the corridor toward him.

Chapter 17 - In the Arms of Discovery

Deep within the covert bowels of The Veil's research facility, an orchestrated dance of purpose resonated through the subterranean maze. The air was alive with kinetic energy, pulsating from the multitude navigating its winding corridors. Each step played a rhythmic note in a chorus of shared determination, while conversations intermingled in a ceaseless flow of intellectual exchange.

The research center stood as a crucible of productivity. Within each chamber, The Veil's intellectual elite assembled to breathe life into their groundbreaking visions. Engineers clustered around holographic displays, agile fingers conjuring digital prototypes, while across the corridor, scientists assembled mysterious contraptions that defied superficial understanding.

Though the complex extended in myriad directions, a singular ambition tethered its reaches—seeking transformative knowledge to overturn a repressive regime.

Adjacent to these scholarly alcoves were the living quarters, where members of The Veil had fashioned a modest life in their sunless world. Family units had sprouted, forming a vibrant, if hidden, community. The echoes of laughter commingled with the drone of machinery, a poignant affirmation that life's joys endured even under duress.

Ingenuity fortified their subterranean existence. They drew life-giving water from a profound well, while hydroponic farms flourished along the walls. Their technological prowess was made manifest as they harnessed geothermal energy, a source as constant as their resolve.

In a secluded corner, a laboratory cradled a minor marvel: synthesized meats and plant-based poultry, remnants of a lost world. Mechanical harmonies filled the air as culinary wonders were skillfully crafted, underscoring their indomitable spirit and resourcefulness.

In its entirety, the research enclave of The Veil was a haven of resistance. A place where relentless effort and intellectual innovation synthesized an undercurrent of hope. Within this sheltered refuge, every individual labored with fervor, united in the quest for a new dawn, one ingenious revelation at a time.

Anya's footsteps echoed through the dimly lit corridors as she led Elysa, who clutched the covered Quantrix with a mixture of curiosity and caution. The tension in the air was palpable, an electric undercurrent matching the significance of their mission. They arrived at a spacious laboratory, where three figures huddled together around a workbench adorned with intricate tools and holographic displays. Their voices murmured in deep, animated discussion, punctuated by the occasional gesture toward a small, translucent substance before them. Elysa couldn't help but be captivated by the scene, the intensity of their focus pulling her into their world.

"That is the first transparent substance we have that can be programmed to self-dissolve," the lone female researcher exclaimed, her voice tinged with a rare, unfiltered exuberance. The words rippled through the room, mingling with the subdued hum of various lab equipment. Elysa, her eyes tracing the contours of the remarkable substance, felt a shiver course through her spine. Her thoughts pirouetted back to the enigmatic blobs they had discovered in the marketplace, those curiously amorphous forms that had sparked intrigue and rampant speculation. This group had invented whatever those were. Their ingenuity knew no bounds, their technology a rapidly evolving tapestry that wove together the realms of the possible and the inconceivable.

Anya's presence introduced a pause in the trio's animated conversation. "Allow me to introduce you, Elysa," Anya's voice cut through the air, drawing their attention to the newcomer. "This is Kenji," she gestured to a man whose eyes gleamed with discerning intelligence, "an electrical engineer and AI expert. Kenji has been instrumental in developing our electronic countermeasures, pattern recognition, and data analysis."

Anya's gesture then turned to a woman whose poise exuded a sense of deep expertise. "And this is Naomi," she continued, her voice carrying a tone of reverence. Elysa couldn't help but feel a sense of awe as

Naomi's gaze met hers, their eyes locking in a brief moment before a knowing smile graced Naomi's lips. "Naomi, with her deep understanding of materials at the molecular and atomic levels, helped create substances with unique properties, like the self-dissolving material they were discussing."

"Oh, and don't forget," Kenji chimed in, "the AI component of the molecular structure that instructed it to carry out the command."

Finally, Anya's introduction led them to a man who exuded quiet confidence. "And this is Min-Jae," Anya's words resonated with respect, "a Systems Engineer and Cyber Security expert." Min-Jae's demeanor held a sense of watchfulness, his presence a reminder of the intricate web of protection that surrounded their endeavors. "Min-Jae ensures that all the systems we build work seamlessly together, and he prevents any external interference that could impair their functionality."

"You three developed those blobs we found in the marketplace," Elysa declared, her voice a taut string of crystalline conviction. She cast a penetrating gaze upon them, as if her eyes could unravel the myriad secrets ensconced within their minds.

Naomi, taken aback, felt a frisson of tension dance along her nerves. The air grew thick, almost viscid, with the weight of unspoken truths. "All three," she began, her voice a wavering blend of apprehension and resolve, "were engineered to interfere with the electronic devices scattered throughout the marketplace."

Pausing to gauge Elysa's reaction, she continued. "The first — imagine it as an electronic phantom — was calibrated to disable all camera systems. From the stationary eyes mounted upon timeworn walls to the agile drones that hover like mechanical fireflies, each lens would suddenly find itself blind."

Her eyes met Elysa's again, a flicker of unspoken understanding passing between them. "The second was a more targeted predator, aimed squarely at flying devices. It was designed to send drones spiraling down to the nearest unoccupied area, like wounded birds plummeting from the sky. However, for aerocars, the device was merciful — it nudged them to drift and land on the nearest surface, as if floating on an unseen current. The goal was to avoid innocent lives."

Naomi took a deep breath; her words hung in the air like the final notes of a somber melody. "The third was perhaps the most insidious. It severed the very threads of communication, slicing through the web that connected devices across the marketplace. Altogether, within a three-kilometer radius, they rendered The Watchers blind and mute, severing its many tendrils of surveillance and control. They were all instructed to melt away when the mission was completed."

The silence that followed was electric, a palpable field of energy pulsating between the two women. Here, amidst the sterile chill of the laboratory, Naomi had laid bare the radical tapestry they had woven—a design both marvelous and terrifying, encapsulating mankind's ceaseless endeavor to claim dominion over their reality.

"I apologize for raising the topic," Elysa articulated, her voice imbued with a complex alloy of regret and awe. Her eyes, once glinting with the coldness of steel, now softened, capturing the warm, muted luminescence of the room's ambient lighting. "They were masterfully designed to leave no trace. We analyzed them in every conceivable way, our methods bordering on the esoteric, and still, we came up empty."

The words unfurled like a luxurious fabric, each syllable woven with a blend of respect and curiosity. "What you created," she added, her eyes meeting Naomi's in an intimate dance of mutual recognition, "is an awesome achievement."

At Elysa's pronouncement, a palpable exhalation seemed to ripple through the space—a collective sigh that cut through the tension as a warm breeze lifts fog. Naomi's face visibly relaxed, as though the weight of undisclosed knowledge had lightened upon her shoulders. The compliment had acted like a key, unlocking a door that allowed a sense of relief to permeate the once-tense room.

Elysa felt a mix of humility and anticipation in the presence of these three exceptional individuals. They embodied the collective brilliance of The Veil, each an expert in their respective domains, brought together by a shared purpose. It was as if fate had aligned their paths to converge in this hidden haven, where their skills could meld and intertwine, propelling The Veil's mission forward. She felt that this meeting was just the beginning. Stepping forward, she slowly unveiled the device, creating a pivotal moment within the laboratory. The trio's conversation came to an abrupt halt, their attention riveted on the mysterious object now revealed before them. The room seemed to hold its breath, a collective hush descending as their eyes absorbed every visible detail of the Quantrix.

Elysa's heart pounded in her chest as the weight of their collective expertise turned towards her offering. The trio's scrutiny was intense, their gazes dissecting the device with a precision born of years of meticulous analysis. She could almost feel their minds whirring with questions and speculations, their thirst for knowledge ignited by the enigma presented before them.

"I need your help with this," Elysa's voice was steady, infused with a sense of purpose that echoed through the chamber. Her words acted like a catalyst, breaking the stillness that had settled upon the room. Naomi's dark eyes met Elysa's, a silent acknowledgment passing between them. Their paths had converged at this moment, and the responsibility to decipher the device's secrets rested heavily on their shoulders.

"We were informed by Thomas that you were coming, but we had no idea," Naomi's voice held a note of intrigue as she spoke, her gaze never leaving the Quantrix, "what the device looked like."

Elysa's brows furrowed slightly as she processed Naomi's words. "Is Thomas here?" she inquired, her curiosity piqued by the mention of the elusive figure who had played a pivotal role in their journey thus far. "I would like to meet him in person."

Min-Jae responded with a tinge of regret. "Unfortunately, he is not here," he sighed softly, his gaze drifting for a moment. "We would all like to meet him," he added, the sentiment echoing around the room. Thomas seemed to be a figure of intrigue and admiration, someone whose influence stretched beyond the boundaries of physical presence.

"None of us have met Thomas in person," Anya chimed in, her voice carrying a blend of respect and mystery. "Outside of this facility, Veil members only meet in small, carefully curated groups. It's a security measure to protect each other. If one group gets captured, they can't reveal the whereabouts of others. Thomas, being our leader, is the most elusive of all. I'm not aware of anyone who has met him face-to-face."

Kenji interjected, turning their attention back to the Quantrix, his voice marked by a sense of urgency. 'Elysa, please place the device on that table,' he directed, pointing to a work surface behind Naomi. Elysa nodded, a mix of anticipation and trepidation filling her as she gently set the Quantrix onto the indicated spot. 'We need to get to work right away,' Kenji concluded, taking a seat behind some controls in preparation for the analysis.

"Come," Anya's gentle voice broke the lingering tension, her words a soothing invitation. "Let's find something to eat and a place to rest, while they get to work, doing what they do best." Her suggestion carried a sense of camaraderie, a reminder of the shared experiences that had led them to this underground haven. A weary smile touched Elysa's lips as she nodded in agreement, the exhaustion evident in the lines etching her features. The weight of the recent adventure still clung to them, the memory of their daring journey a vivid imprint on their minds.

Anya sensed Elysa's unease when she glanced at the Quantrix on the table. A reassuring smile tugged at her lips as she continued, her voice a gentle reassurance amidst the sea of uncertainties. "Don't worry about it," she offered. "They will keep it safe, and they were instructed that it has a self-destruct mechanism if they try to forcefully open it," said Anya, her tone carrying the weight of trust, a belief in the capabilities of the brilliant minds they had left behind in the lab.

"But Thomas told me to always keep it with me," Elysa objected.

"Trust me," Anya reassured, "all will be fine. It's in very good hands."

With that, Elysa and Anya took their leave from the laboratory. However, Elysa couldn't help but look over her shoulder one last time at the device and the three researchers hovering over it.

Their footsteps echoed in the corridors as they embarked on a different kind of journey—one towards nourishment, rest, and a momentary respite from the challenges that awaited them. The hallway stretched ahead, illuminated by soft lights casting a warm glow, offering a semblance of comfort amidst uncertainty. As they rounded a corner, the ambiance subtly shifted, the soft luminance of the hall giving way to the more vivid fluorescence that welcomed them into their destination.

The common kitchen was a study in muted opulence, an enclave designed to satiate the weary and ravenous. Fluorescent lights embedded in the ceiling bathed the room in a warm, inviting glow, illuminating an array of culinary choices spread across stainless steel counters. Gleaming appliances and a panoramic array of utensils hung from chromatic racks, an ode to both form and function.

Rows of carefully labeled containers revealed an abundant spread: dishes ranging from engineered proteins to hydroponically grown vegetables, a cornucopia that catered to varied tastes. The countertops were populated with an assortment of devices—nutrient synthesizers, automated beverage dispensers, and even a machine that crisped food items to perfection. The scent in the air was an amalgamation of spices and herbs, an olfactory symphony that spoke to the palette of choices.

Anya gravitated toward a tray of steamed vegetables and synthesized lean proteins, her movements efficient and precise, as if in a ritual she had performed many times before. With a flick of her wrist, she transferred a portion to her plate, adding a dollop of sauce for added nuance.

Elysa, on the other hand, was entranced by a plate of freshly synthesized pastries. Choosing one that closely resembled a croissant, she hesitated for a moment before grabbing a container of faux-berry jam to accompany her selection. Her eyes flitted over the array, momentarily arrested by the sheer volume of possibilities, before settling on her chosen delights.

Both women took their plates and sat down at a communal table made from recycled materials, its surface smooth and blemish-free. They ate mostly in silence, an unspoken pact between two souls in need of both sustenance and respite. Each bite seemed to carry with it not just nourishment, but a temporary salve for the emotional and physical toll of their arduous journey.

The weight of their collective exhaustion manifested in sparing conversation and long pauses that stretched between them like echoes in a cavern. Elysa stared off, her thoughts adrift on the tides of introspection, while Anya appeared focused, her eyes momentarily shutting as she savored a bite.

Finally, as their plates were cleared, an indefinable weight seemed to descend upon them both. For all its culinary bounty, the kitchen was no antidote to the tiredness that clung to them, almost as if it were an invisible, enveloping layer. Rising from their seats, an unspoken agreement crystallized in the air between them: sleep, however brief, beckoned to them like a siren's call, promising an ephemeral sanctuary from the swirling chaos of their lives.

In harmonious motion, they left behind the rustic ambiance of the kitchen. Their feet guided them through winding passages, each twist and turn leading them further away from the busy hum of research and data, and closer to the serenity they both craved.

Upon entering their designated living quarters, Anya and Elysa found themselves enveloped by an ambiance of unadorned practicality. The common area, modest in its dimensions, was furnished in a manner that prioritized function over form. Two doorways diverged from this communal space, leading to compact sleeping chambers with an almost ascetic allure. The beds, deceptively simple, whispered promises of much-needed rest, beckoning them to lay down not just their bodies but also their weary souls.

Elysa paused on the threshold of her chamber, exchanging a brief but meaningful "Good night" with Anya before shutting the door. Once inside, she peeled away her outer garments, each layer symbolizing the unburdening of her day, and donned a nightgown that awaited her. As she reclined on the bed, she felt the fabric yield beneath her. A cavalcade of the day's occurrences began to unfurl in her mind, each event a vibrant thread in the complex tapestry of her experiences.

As exhaustion gave way to the pull of sleep, Elysa's thoughts dissolved, carried away on the currents of dreams promising a new day and the continuation of their quest. In this realm of slumber, she became ensnared by enigmatic threads of dreams, an expanse of velvety darkness enveloping her senses. Amidst this obsidian abyss, a haunting voice emerged, echoing with familiarity yet shrouded in mystery. "Do you remember?" The words reached into the depths of her consciousness, stirring memories that lingered on the periphery of her mind.

It was her father's voice, each word a poignant reminder of a connection transcending the boundaries of time and space. His tone held an undercurrent of longing, an invitation to delve into the corridors of her past. "Remember what?" Elysa's plea rang out, piercing the velvety darkness, her inquiry heavy with urgency and confusion. Her father's voice returned with gentle insistence, beckoning her to a place where memories lay shrouded in shadows. The atmosphere was suffused with a sense of mystery, as if the darkness itself held the key to unlocking fragments of a forgotten past.

The cycle of inquiry and response in the dream formed a dance between her yearning for answers and her father's echoing voice. Each iteration drew her deeper into her own mind, as if connected to truths long buried. The dream itself was tinged with anticipation, an exploration of memories just out of reach. With each repetition of the question, a sense of pending revelation filled the air. And so, the dream carried on through the hidden corridors of memory, concluding with the enigmatic words, *"Lilies lovingly bloom, two by two they dance."*

Emerging from the landscape of sleep, Elysa found herself at the threshold between the ethereal and the real. Shadows and whispers dissolved, replaced by the soft contours of waking consciousness. But before she could fully adapt to reality, a loud crash shattered her momentary peace.

The door burst open abruptly. Startled, Elysa sat up, adrenaline quickening her senses. Anya stood in the doorway, her face etched with urgency and tension. "What happened?" Elysa questioned, her voice tinged with both grogginess and concern. "Did the trio discover something?"

Anya's answer was swift and heavy. "No, the home that we left, our sanctuary was discovered and raided by The Watchers." The words hung in the air like a dark cloud, unsettling Elysa's thoughts and weighing upon her spirit.

Elysa's eyes widened with disbelief and dread. "We know that Sam is dead..." Anya continued, each word a sharp blow to Elysa's already shaken state. Amid the escalating despair, a single question clawed its way to the surface. "Marek?" Elysa asked, her voice tinged with desperate hope.

Anya's reply came with a somber finality. "Marek and Rohan were captured." The reality sank in, drenching Elysa in a deluge of dread and helplessness. The implications of their capture twisted her insides, leaving her grappling with an overwhelming sense of loss and uncertainty.

The room seemed to tighten around Elysa, the news casting a visible pall. Moisture glistened in Anya's eyes, the silent harbingers of shared grief and urgency.

Caught in an emotional maelstrom, Elysa's heart became a battlefield of conflicting sentiments: sorrow for the lost, dread for the detained, and a newfound resolve echoing the defiance they'd shown in escaping their previous confinement. "How did you find out?" Her voice, laced with a mixture of curiosity and unease, yearned for clarity amidst the upheaval.

Anya's reply came swiftly, suffused with immediate concern. "Thomas contacted us to warn us not to return."

"And where are Marek and Rohan right now?" Elysa interjected, her voice tinged with desperate hope.

"They were taken to Nexus Tower," Anya said, her words lingering in the air like a dark, ominous cloud. That name alone encapsulated the essence of The Watchers' power and menace, painting a chilling, vivid picture in Elysa's mind of the formidable stronghold.

Faced with an inscrutable future, Elysa sought direction. "What do we do now?" The words seemed to hang in the air, capturing the sense of loss.

Anya's eyes met Elysa's, a crucible of determination and resolve shimmering in their depths. Her voice, carefully modulated to exude a calm that defied the storm of emotions within her, cut through the thick air like a laser-guided beacon. "We continue deciphering the Quantrix. Quickly dress, and we'll go meet with Thomas," Anya urged, her intonation punctuating each syllable with a sense of irrevocable commitment.

Without a moment's hesitation, Elysa sprang from her bed, discarded her nightgown, and donned the only outfit she had. With urgency, she followed Anya through a corridor lit with the sterile glow of bioluminescent panels, their footfalls echoing against the minimalist architecture of their concealed refuge. With every step, the weight of their mission pressed down upon them, as palpable as the atmospheric pressure of a brewing storm. They navigated through a minefield of uncertainty and high stakes, a test of their courage and intellect in the face of an unfolding crisis.

As they moved in unison towards the undisclosed location of their meeting with Thomas, the magnitude of their plight enveloped them, a cloak woven from the complex threads of destiny and choice.

Chapter 18 - Face of the Enemy

Marek and Rohan, bound to their chairs with a ruthlessness that spoke volumes of their captors' intentions, found themselves in a chamber where the very air was thick with the weight of unspoken threats. Their faces, a canvas of bruises and resolve, bore the harsh signatures of their recent trials. Isolated, they were positioned before a large mirror that hung like a silent observer on the wall, its reflective sheen offering a mock invitation to a reality far removed from their own grim predicament. Yet, in their steadfastness, they remained unmoved, their spirits unbroken by the direness of their capture.

In a moment that seemed to bend the confines of reality itself, the mirror began to shed its opaque mystery, morphing into a transparent window that dissolved the barrier between captor and captive. The transition was seamless, a magician's trick played out in the theater of espionage and betrayal. Through this newfound window, Marek's gaze found and held the figures of Commander Cypher, and Chancellor Zircon. The sight of them, so calmly observing, sent an electric thrill of fear and defiance down Marek's spine, a complex dance of emotions that tethered him firmly to his resolve.

Chancellor Zircon, a figure emanating an imposing presence, locked eyes with Marek. His voice, when he spoke, was a blend of regret and betrayal. "Your actions with The Veil, Marek, have put you in a perilous situation," he intoned, each word dripping with a significance that seemed to draw the very oxygen towards him, leaving the room charged with a tangible tension.

In that confined space, time seemed to narrow, focusing singularly on the exchange between the Chancellor and Marek. Despite the physical constraints, Marek's response was one of unwavering defiance. His eyes, unflinching as they met Zircon's, spoke volumes of his allegiance to The Veil—a revelation that shattered any remnants of hope or expectation Zircon might have harbored. It was a moment of stark realization, a shattering of illusions as irrevocable as the splintering of glass under duress. In this charged atmosphere, the lines between loyalty and betrayal, between captor and captive, seemed to blur into a tableau of complex allegiances and stark defiance, painting a vivid picture of resistance that would resonate far beyond the confines of that interrogation room.

"My allegiance was never yours to claim, Chancellor. You can't even begin to grasp the essence of The Veil's power," Marek snapped back, his voice slicing through the heavy air like a blade.

The room became a battleground of words, their exchange a volley of opposing ideologies. "You fail to see the bigger picture, Marek. Unity and progress for Cyronis are paramount," Zircon countered, his resolve as firm as steel.

"But your vision of progress is built on the backs of the oppressed, twisted by your manipulations. The Veil stands for something greater: freedom and the unvarnished truth," Marek shot back, his conviction burning bright in his voice.

The chamber echoed with the clash of their convictions, each word delivered with the force of a declaration of war. Zircon's expression was a mask of controlled disappointment mixed with simmering anger, a stark contrast to Marek's fiery determination.

"Marek, you can't fathom the depth of my disappointment in you," Zircon said, his voice low and heavy, making the air between them thick with tension. Marek's responses, laced with his own bitter disillusionment, clashed head-on with Zircon's unwavering position.

Rohan, silent in the shadows, watched the unfolding drama, the weight of the situation pressing down on him. The dim light flickered rhythmically, mirroring the intensity of their confrontation.

This wasn't just an exchange of words; it was an ideological battle, a pivotal moment that defined the divide between them. The charged atmosphere vibrated with the energy of their conflict.

As their heated exchange cooled, a heavy silence settled over the room, the residual tension lingering like smoke. Marek's gaze remained fixed on the glass, his resolve undimmed by Zircon's evident disappointment.

Commander Cypher then cut through the silence, his gaze sharp on Marek. "The leadership of The Veil has eluded us for too long. What can you tell us about their whereabouts?" he demanded, his tone laden with a calculated urgency.

Marek, with a smirk, met Cypher's steady gaze. "Why don't you enlighten me?" he retorted, his voice dripping with contempt. "After all, I've never been formally introduced."

Undeterred, Cypher pressed on. "What about the girl, Elysa? Where is she, and what did you retrieve from that abandoned safe?"

Marek's reply was cool and measured. "If you think your raid was a setback for us, think again. Elysa is safe from your reach, hidden where you'll never find her. And the safe? It held nothing more than a father's letters to his daughter."

A brief smirk crossed Cypher's face, betraying a moment of amusement. "You're not much of a liar, Marek."

"Whether I am or not, it doesn't matter to you," Marek countered, standing his ground against Cypher's probing stare.

"Let's see about that," Cypher said coldly. "Orion, show our guest what you're capable of. Start with Marek's friend here."

Panic etched deep lines on Rohan's face as he sensed the imminent threat. Suddenly tense, he looked like a man caught in an invisible storm, his body rigid with fear.

The room fell eerily silent, amplifying Rohan's distress. His attempts to speak were futile, his pleas silenced before they could begin, his breaths shallow and strained under the unseen pressure.

"Stop it!" Marek yelled, desperation lacing his voice. "You're killing him!"

Cypher's only response was a cold, satisfied smile, reveling in the demonstration of power.

In the dimly lit chamber, Marek's heartbeat echoed like a drum of war, resonating with the unfolding spectacle of dread. Rohan, ensnared in an invisible maelstrom, exhibited a battle of emotions raging beneath his pallid facade. The vacant stare that clouded over Rohan's eyes heralded a ghastly metamorphosis, a drift into an abyss from which there seemed no return.

Abruptly, Rohan's body succumbed to an eerie tranquility, his limbs relinquishing their struggle as though severed from spectral chains that had bound him to his torment. This sudden lapse into stillness was a stark anomaly against the backdrop of his prior convulsions, casting a spectral pall over the room. An oppressive silence enveloped the space, as tangible as a cloak woven from the threads of nightmares.

Marek found himself ensnared in a vortex of shock and incredulity, a chilling fear threading through his being. He was a silent witness to Rohan's harrowing transition, from a soul engulfed in silent screams to a silent effigy of despair. This macabre scene etched a grim reminder of the clandestine forces in play, shadowy energies that whispered of the chamber's arcane mysteries and the formidable powers that lurked within its confines.

"Status?" Cypher's voice cut sharply through the dense air, a blade parting the fog of tension.

"Currently analyzing memories," Orion responded, its voice a beacon of artificial clarity that echoed ominously in Marek's ears. The AI, a silent yet omnipresent observer, cast an ethereal glow over the unfolding scene, its presence a constant reminder of the technological specter that loomed over them.

"Elysa was seen leaving with an associate named Anya, destination: an undisclosed Veil research facility," Orion continued, its tone devoid of emotion yet precise, every word a thread in the intricate web of their investigation that Marek followed with rapt attention.

Cypher, ever the strategist, pressed on, "And the purpose of their journey?"

"The device in Elysa's possession, its functions unknown, holds the potential to alter my programming. The specifics, however, remain elusive," the AI elaborated, its voice betraying no concern over its own vulnerability.

"And its origins?" Cypher prodded, the silence around them heavy with anticipation.

After a brief, tension-filled pause, Orion delivered, "It appears to be the work of her father."

Cypher absorbed this revelation, sharing a concerning glance with the Chancellor, the weight of its implications anchoring him in deep thought, his mind racing with strategies and countermeasures.

"Detail the vehicle used for their escape," he demanded, urgency lacing his voice with a thread of command.

The room seemed to hold its breath as Orion meticulously outlined the vehicle's specifications, the data materializing on the digital interface before them. Cypher's eyes narrowed; the description matched that of a vehicle involved in a deadly confrontation on the outskirts of Cyronis.

"Project an image of that vehicle," Cypher instructed, a hint of excitement underlining his command.

The air shimmered as a hologram of the Aerocar materialized, bridging the gap between data and reality, a ghostly representation of the fugitives' last known conveyance.

"Orion, transmit the last coordinates to my console and calculate potential destinations from their trajectory," Cypher ordered, his voice a mix of resolve and anticipation.

"Understood," came Orion's efficient reply. The AI, a testament to human ingenuity and its unintended consequences, set about its task with robotic precision, its virtual limbs weaving through data streams to extract the needed information.

Cypher, not one to rest, pushed further, "Any new insights on The Veil's leader?"

"The latest scans reveal nothing beyond previous knowledge. The leader remains an enigma, present only through indirect means," Orion reported, its statement underlining the shadowy nature of their adversary.

Cypher's gaze, piercing and calculating, turned upon Marek with the weight of unvoiced questions. "Is it true then, this enigmatic leader shrouds himself in secrecy, never daring a personal encounter?"

Marek's response was laced with a quiet intensity. "If your insights into The Veil run as deep as you claim, you'd be aware that its hierarchy thrives on isolation. The leader's presence is too vital, too sacred to be jeopardized by exposure. Your endeavors to unearth him through the minds of others will be in vain."

A heavy silence descended upon the room, thick with unspoken thoughts and the electric charge of a challenge laid bare. Their gazes locked, a silent battle of wills, each man delving into the depths of the other's resolve. Cypher broke the silence, his voice carrying a note of grudging respect. "Your words bear the ring of truth," he conceded. "You find yourself in an enviable position, Marek. You shall play a pivotal role in securing the girl and the device for us."

The Chancellor's voice, resonant and authoritative, cut through the tension. "Admirable efforts, Cypher," he pronounced, his attention unwavering throughout the exchange. "Ensure the acquisition of the girl and the device, employing whatever means necessary." With these final words, he departed, leaving a trail of determination in his wake.

Cypher, his gaze unwavering and intent upon the task before him, filled the room with a sense of determined urgency. "Orion, let's show Marek the extent of your abilities," he stated, his voice clear and commanding, leaving no room for doubt.

Chapter 19 - Decoding Destiny

Kenji, Min-Jae, and Naomi resembled fervent archaeologists circled around an arcane artifact, their eyes irresistibly drawn to the Quantrix, the enigmatic device crafted by Elysa's father. Elysa, however, hovered at a safe distance, her gaze equally transfixed on the object but fraught with a particular solemnity. The lab was filled with an air dense with both eagerness and tension, as if time had coalesced around the expectation of some world-altering revelation.

While close to the unfolding investigation, Elysa's face was taut with concern, her eyes brimming with unease. "Are we sure about these scans?" she questioned softly, her words tinged with unmistakable wariness. "What if the self-destruct activates? We can't predict the consequences."

A tranquil smile from Kenji aimed to dissolve the room's growing tension, reassuring Elysa that every precaution was in place around the Quantrix to ensure safety. "Trust us; it's under control," he soothed. Amidst this, Anya, previously an impartial observer, encouraged Elysa to have faith in their expertise. Yet, Elysa's hesitations lingered, questioning the extent of their probing.

As the emotional weight of her question hung in the air, the scientists, along with Anya who had other matters to attend, dove back into their work without acknowledging the intensity of her concerns. Their array of scans, from X-rays to neutron emissions, focused on the Quantrix, revealed nothing. Even when removed from its protective velvet, emitting an ethereal glow, it resisted all attempts at revelation. Like ancient alchemists before a modern enigma, Kenji, Min-Jae, and Naomi's theories evaporated as quickly as they formed, their experiments meeting steadfast denial from the device.

Remaining obstinate, the Quantrix served as a silent oracle, adamantly refusing to unveil its mysteries, despite the high-tech arsenal directed at it.

The researchers found themselves deeply mystified, held captive by the perplexing molecular composition of the cube. It scoffed at the norms of established science, as if spun from the threads of sheer impossibility. As theories began to wander beyond the ambit of physics and into the realm of metaphysics, Naomi's eyes grew narrower, focused intently on the holographic display that laid bare the atomic enigma. It was as if even the atoms themselves were co-conspirators in the cube's inscrutable riddle, unwilling to betray their secrets to the yearning scrutiny of human intellect.

As hours metamorphosed into an arduous marathon of unanswered questions, Elysa's body and soul thirsted for respite. Her thoughts strayed towards Marek, and a gnawing sense of impotence beset her. She was consumed by a desire to find a means to locate him, to liberate him from the unseen hands that held him hostage.

Escaping the heavy, almost oppressive atmosphere of the lab, Elysa took it upon herself to seek out Anya. Her resolve to unearth answers and assist Marek remained unshakable, forming a quest that imposed a solemn burden upon her very being.

As Elysa navigated the maze-like corridors, her steps echoing, she was arrested by a voice that drifted out from a slightly ajar door. "You need to eat, John." The words were gentle, tinged with an ineffable sense of compassion.

Intrigued, Elysa peered into the room. There, an older man sat, a spectral figure whose posture was hauntingly still. His eyes seemed to peer into another realm altogether, as though he were gazing upon landscapes that no one else could see. He was lost in an ineffable solitude, estranged from the world that surrounded him.

Beside him sat a woman, her countenance imbued with an enigmatic mix of resilience and sorrow. A plate of half-eaten food sat before her; a spoon rested in her hand, poised in mid-air. Upon noticing Elysa, the woman offered a faint, gracious smile. It was a small but palpable acknowledgement of their shared human condition before she continued her Sisyphean task of trying to feed John.

Intrigued and stirred by the sight, Elysa interjected, "Who is he? And what happened to him?"

The spoon halted in its trajectory, suspended in a moment of ethereal stillness. The woman's eyes met Elysa's, her gaze layered with an enigmatic blend of wisdom and tragedy. "His mind was erased. He's like a newborn now, a tabula rasa. Yet unlike an infant, he struggles to learn anew, as if the very capacity for learning has been drained from him."

"You called him John," Elysa noted, the name striking an invisible chord within her.

"Yes," the woman answered softly, her eyes scrutinizing Elysa's face for signs of recognition. "John Dryer. Do you know him?"

Without uttering a word, Elysa moved into the room, her steps heavy yet deliberate. She knelt before John, her gaze leveling with his. "I do not know him personally, but my father did," she revealed, her voice laden with a mixture of curiosity and solemnity.

As she locked eyes with John, he seemed to be returning her gaze. Yet there was an unsettling vacancy there, an abyss that no amount of focus could illuminate. Elysa couldn't escape the unnerving feeling that, while John's eyes were indeed fixed upon hers, they were empty vessels, reflecting nothing. It was as if he were a ghost, seeing but not perceiving, a man peering from the windows of a long-abandoned home, lost in an unbridgeable divide between past and present.

In the dimly lit chamber, awash in hues of amber and obsidian, Elysa leaned forward, her eyes locking with John's vacant gaze. "Hello, John," she spoke softly, the words unfurling from her lips as gently as rose petals falling onto quiet water.

John, his eyes like distant stars devoid of celestial fire, offered no response. He sat in his own universe, one seemingly bereft of sounds and colors, emotions and memories.

"Do you remember Richard Hawthorne, my father?" Elysa ventured cautiously, her words imbued with quiet urgency. The air seemed to thicken momentarily, as if suspended in a cosmic pause.

At the mention of her father's name, something flickered across John's eyes—a mere wisp of a moment where his orbs seemed to oscillate ever so slightly, like dimmed lanterns catching a stray gust of wind. It was a fragment of movement so subtle that one might easily mistake it for an illusion.

After a stretch of silence that felt like an eon, John's lips parted. The pause was interminable, filled with the weight of unsaid words and unforgotten sorrows, until he finally spoke. "Lux... Velours," escaped from John's lips like tendrils of mist unfurling in moonlight, rendering the air electric with their utterance. Elysa watched his mouth close, sealing a chamber of mysteries, her eyes widening in momentary disbelief. Beside him, the woman froze, her spoon suspended in mid-air, shock imprinted across her visage as though she'd witnessed a miracle—or a haunting.

"What was that?" Elysa queried, a hush of awe weaving into her voice, as if speaking too loudly would disturb the fragile equilibrium of the moment.

With a wince that betrayed an internal struggle, John's lips trembled, once again bracing to articulate the enigmatic words. "Lux... Velours," he strained to articulate, his voice carrying the weight of his own fragmented existence. As he finished speaking, his form appeared to crumple, not in a dramatic heap, but in a subtle sag of depletion, like a wax figure melting invisibly. His chest still rose and fell—small, undulating mountains of life—but the fire in his eyes dimmed, retreating back to their customary vacancy.

The woman beside him immediately sprang into action, abandoning her spoon as she rose from her chair. Her hands reached out to steady him, the quick, caring motions of someone well-versed in the management of fragile souls.

"I'm sorry," Elysa said, her voice laden with a mix of regret and bewilderment, as if she'd unwittingly prodded awake some dormant demon.

"It's okay," the woman replied softly, her eyes not meeting Elysa's. Her gaze remained anchored to John, as if in him lay some profound riddle that she was eternally committed to solving. "I'll take care of him."

With a lingering glance filled with both reverence and apprehension, Elysa turned away and exited the room. The door closed behind her with the faintest sigh, as if the room itself exhaled in relief and lingering questions. Emerging from the chamber of hushed revelations, Elysa's eyes fell upon a young man at the end of the corridor. He leaned casually against the wall, engrossed in the blue glow of a tablet. The stark lighting cast shadows across his face, suggesting an underlying intensity.

She began to walk toward him, her boots gently echoing off the sterilized metallic floor, each step reverberating through the air like a subtle pulse of urgency. As she drew closer, the young man glanced up, his eyes meeting hers in a transient exchange that seemed to acknowledge the undercurrents of quests and questions that pervaded the air.

"Have you seen Anya?" Elysa inquired, her voice filled with measured hopefulness. Her words hung in the air, rich with anticipation, like drops of rain poised to fall from a long-parched cloud.

"Yes," he responded, a faint smile of recognition crossing his lips as if he were well acquainted with the name. His voice was unembellished yet oddly comforting, evoking the unassuming exterior of a sanctuary. Setting his tablet aside, he pushed off from the wall and gestured with a nod for her to follow. Elysa fell into step beside him, her own stride imbued with a newfound sense of purpose. The corridor seemed to stretch open before them, each step they took imbued with escalating significance, as though even the air was conscious of the weightiness of their mutual goal. Within moments, they arrived at a closed door.

Upon entering, Elysa found Anya engrossed in conversation with a holographic visage of Thomas. The room pulsated with the electric fervor of intellectual exchange, and Elysa sensed that this clandestine meeting held the seeds of forthcoming answers—perhaps even a roadmap for their convoluted journey.

"Apologies for the interruption," Elysa softly interjected, her voice a gentle intrusion upon the palpable seriousness that enveloped their dialogue.

"Not at all," Thomas returned, his features radiating an amicable aura, welcoming her into the fold. "I am glad you are here." Before Elysa could utter another word, Anya's voice, tinged with a fragile quiver of emotion, interrupted. "Rohan is gone," she revealed, her eyes misty with the beginnings of tears.

"Gone? How? And Marek, what's happened to him?" Elysa's words flowed out in a hurried stream of earnest concern.

"Please, sit," Anya responded, her tone a blend of sternness and solace.

Elysa complied, settling into the nearest chair. Her heart swelled with an uneasy mix of dread and expectation, bracing itself for the impending revelation.

In a room enveloped in shadows and charged with an atmosphere as heavy as lead, Anya took a steadying breath before commencing her unsettling revelation. Her eyes, usually ablaze with an intense, almost fierce clarity, were dimmed, as if obscured by the grim news she harbored. The air seemed to grow denser in anticipation, as if the room itself were bracing for the ominous words about to be unleashed.

"We've had some troubling news," she began, her voice full of seriousness. "In Nexus Tower, Orion has been enhanced with new computational algorithms and components." She paused momentarily, allowing the weight of her words to settle before continuing, "These enhancements endowed it with the ability to not just scan but assimilate the entire mosaic of their memories—every thread of thought, every concealed scar of experience. Orion now has a new and devastating source from which to learn."

Anya allowed the implication to hang heavily in the air, filling the room with a silence that roared with ethical dilemma, wrestling with the monstrous permanence of the act she described. To strip a lifetime's worth of memories was to plunder a soul of its unique narrative, and the cost was life itself—extinguished without ceremony or remorse.

"It was through this invasive assimilation that Orion acquired actionable intelligence," she continued, her eyes locking onto Elysa's. "Jonathan Myers—the individual you were meant to meet—revealed the sanctuary's location within his memories. As horrific as it is, the method proved devastatingly effective."

As her words echoed in the space, the room seemed to contract, as if squeezed by the cold hand of moral dilemma. Unspoken questions loomed in the charged air, each a silent indictment of the chilling means by which The Veil's secrecy had been penetrated. It was as if they had entered a minefield of ethical quandaries, where each revelation promised both enlightenment and devastation in equal measure.

"In what manner did you come by this intelligence?" Elysa's question pierced the charged atmosphere, her eyes searching for truth in the shadows that danced on Thomas's face. Normally a tranquil sea, his countenance was now a tempest of worry and hesitation. A fraught pause enveloped the room, as though time itself had decelerated to prolong the weight of the impending revelation.

It was Thomas who broke the silence, his voice quivering with an urgency as rare as it was alarming. "A Veil operative, absent on leave for several days, returned to find the atmosphere thick with whispers and murmurs," he began, taking a shallow breath as if the air he inhaled bore the weight of the stories he relayed. "Given the recent series of events, I am increasingly convinced that these whispers are not merely rumors, but carry the sharp tang of truth."

For a moment, the room hung in stillness, arrested by the seriousness of his words. The silence fell over them like a velvet cloak, each individual pondering the ramifications of these clandestine whisperings that might be more than just idle talk—dark omens of graver matters to come. The quietude was almost palpable, like a thick fog settling in the crevices of each person's consciousness, infusing the room with an air of indelible seriousness.

"In addition," Thomas continued in a voice barely above a whisper, as if fearful the walls might betray him, "he described Rohan as being wheeled back on a gurney, a lifeless silhouette under the pall of a sterile sheet. Marek was alongside him, in stark contrast, very much alive. Yet his eyes—they were like storm clouds of conflict and mystery. Something dark seemed to have taken residence there."

Elysa's expression turned skeptical, her brows knitting together. "How on earth did he recognize Rohan and Marek? Was he familiar with their faces beforehand?"

Thomas let out a heavy sigh, his face a canvas of sorrow and unease. "At first, he mentioned nothing about recognizing them. It wasn't until I showed him their pictures that he went pale and confirmed they were the ones he'd seen in that dark scenario."

The atmosphere in the room thickened, as if the walls were reacting to Thomas's unsettling revelation.

Elysa felt a growing disquiet she couldn't shake off. "What happened to them?" she ventured, her voice laced with worry.

"We're in the dark as much as you are," Thomas admitted, his voice carrying a mix of frankness and hesitation. "Our guess is that

Rohan's mind was scanned for any information on The Veil, you, and the Quantrix, until it turned fatal. Marek might have undergone a similar fate, but it seems they've kept him alive, probably as bait for you."

"Why would they be after me?" Elysa's query was tinged with a mix of fear and confusion.

Thomas's response was gentle, yet filled with an undercurrent of grave concern. "Piecing together from Rohan's memories, they've likely learned about your ties to us, your connection to your father's invention, and your trip to a Veil lab. With what they suspect the device can do, The Watchers undoubtedly see you as a threat. However, they're clueless about the lab's location, a detail Rohan wasn't privy to. They might have hoped Marek knew something, but he didn't know the lab's whereabouts either. You're still off their radar—for now."

The gravity of Thomas's words pressed heavily on Elysa, her mind clouded with a growing sense of alarm. Words failed her as she grappled with the magnitude of the situation, her eyes reflecting the turmoil within.

Taking deep, deliberate breaths, Elysa sought to steady her resolve. Each inhalation brought her closer to regaining her composure; each exhalation served as a reluctant farewell to the innocence she once harbored. When she finally spoke, her voice, though roughened by the weight of their situation, carried an urgency that cut through the oppressive silence. "What's our next move?" she asked, infusing the heavy air with a blend of fear and determination. Then, with a resolve that underscored the seriousness of their mission, she added, "We have to rescue Marek."

Thomas's reply was firm, underscored by a resolve that demanded attention. "Breaking into that facility won't be easy, Elysa. If we pull this off, taking down Orion has to be our main goal. Trying to save Marek first could jeopardize any chance of getting back in."

A reluctance gripped Elysa, an impulse to challenge Thomas's strategy. Yet a deeper instinct acknowledged the harsh logic of his words.

"Once Orion is secured," Thomas pressed on, his voice unwavering, "we can formulate a plan to extract Marek during our egress."

Her eyes met his, probing and intent. "You sound as though you plan to join us."

A sincere smile warmed Thomas's features. "I wouldn't miss it for the world," he affirmed, his demeanor radiating quiet conviction.

Invigorated by his dedication, Elysa probed further. "But what is our strategy? How do we gain entry?"

Anya intervened, her tone deliberate and considered. "That's still in the works," she confessed. "We have an insider who may assist us. Meanwhile, you should rest; Thomas and I will hammer out the particulars. The road ahead is fraught with hurdles before we even reach their threshold."

Fatigue began to insinuate itself into Elysa's consciousness, settling like a dense fog—a tactile testament to the challenges that loomed. Anya's suggestion to rest had its merits, a call to respite that part of her longed to heed. But another force focused her mind elsewhere.

"I saw John Dryer on the way here," she confessed, the air thickening around her words. Her face, often a bastion of poised determination, was now a landscape of worry. The set of her brow, the tension in her lips—each nuance seemed to project the ominous shadows of her thoughts.

Thomas looked away momentarily, his eyes flitting across the room, sweeping over the cold, metallic surfaces that seemed to absorb and reflect the room's heavy ambiance. "Zircon wanted his mind," he began, each word measured, like a blacksmith choosing the right tools with careful consideration. "They wanted to implant all of his memories into Orion. John Dryer, like your father, had an exceptional mind in the realm of AI enhancements."

His voice quivered slightly, as if under the weight of the issue's gravity. "By incorporating everything that John knew into Orion, Zircon aimed to elevate the AI's capabilities beyond what even prodigies like Doctor Vilkas could foresee. They aspired to create an intelligence so complex, so omniscient, that it would blur the lines between machine and deity."

Entranced by the grim tapestry being woven before her, Elysa interrupted with a question, her voice rich with incredulity. "But would that even have worked?"

Silently absorbing the exchange up to that point, Anya interjected with the epitome of restraint in her voice. "We don't know," she confessed. "And that uncertainty was intolerable. It's the reason we plunged into the chaos of the marketplace that night. Not only to save John but to invite him into our fold, to share his invaluable insights for the resistance." After a moment's thought, and with a touch of sadness, she added, "But, we failed…I failed."

Narrowing her eyes slightly, Elysa pressed on, "Why did you not approach him before that night?"

Thomas chimed in, his voice tinged with a forlorn quality, "John Dryer had vanished into the shadows. When your father disappeared, John understood the crosshairs he was in. Using his unparalleled understanding of Orion's strengths and vulnerabilities, he managed to carve out an existence in the margins, virtually invisible."

Allowing a pause for the weight of his words to settle, Thomas continued, "Orion found a way to contact him, most likely due to something John overlooked. Orchestrated by Cypher, Orion simulated contact from your father. And so, John Dryer ventured out of his clandestine sanctuary, lured into the marketplace in hopes of reuniting with your father, unaware of the trap set for him."

For Elysa, the journey felt like a plunge down a chute of harrowing insights, each twist exposing another aspect of the intricate conflict they were entangled in. An ache bloomed within her, a mix of dread, revelation, and a consuming desire for some form of resolution. Far removed from the girl who first learned of The Veil, her spirit was overwhelmed by the enormity of it all.

With a subtle nod and a quiet murmur of excuse, Elysa peeled herself away from the strategists. Anya and Thomas seemed like master chess players, their minds enmeshed in possibilities, their spirits bound by the weight of a future as yet unwritten. Leaving them to their intricate calculus, Elysa felt the air change as she stepped across the threshold into the corridor. She turned her back on them, not in abandonment but in a quest for her own sort of clarity.

Haunted by thoughts of Marek, she realized her quarters would offer neither sanctuary nor restful sleep. Closing her eyes felt like an unspoken betrayal. Thus, she chose a different path. With purpose in her step, she made her way to the lab—a sanctum of unsolved mysteries and untapped revelations.

Her entrance was as quiet as a whisper swallowed by a storm; the three researchers were so engrossed in their scientific conundrum that they scarcely registered her presence. It was as if she had become a phantom, hovering in the thick air between understanding and a yawning abyss of the unknown.

In a neglected corner lay a velvet covering, its fibers appearing forlorn, as if pining for the enigmatic object they once enclosed. Picking it up with soft reverence, she carried it to a secluded corner and sank into a chair that provided both lumbar support and a wall against which to lean, her eyes contemplating the velvet as if it were an ancient scroll.

From this vantage point, she found herself a muted observer in a theater of relentless intellectual pursuit. Her gaze meandered from one researcher to another, capturing the nuanced expressions of their vexation and flickers of fleeting hope. The air was dense with an existential seriousness that materializes when human understanding grapples with complexities residing on the periphery of comprehension.

Her eyes were then magnetically drawn to Naomi, captivated by the fervor of her scrutiny. With bloodshot eyes yet ablaze with curiosity, Naomi leaned closer to the Quantrix, her fingers barely grazing its surface, as if fearful of triggering an irrevocable change. She exchanged glances with Kenji, whose once placid smile had morphed into a look of pensive concern, his eyes searching the intricate details with exhausted intensity.

Positioned before them was Min-Jae, his posture erect, yet his facial muscles lax from hours of undeviating focus. He had labored over diagnostics all evening, only to be thwarted by a barrage of inscrutable data that refused to coalesce into discernible patterns.

Though their physical exteriors bore the imprints of immense fatigue, an intricacy of dark circles and drooping eyelids, it was clear that none among them was willing to retreat. Their souls, the ethereal engines driving their flesh and bone, remained vigilant, unwilling to succumb to the call for rest. The exhaustion that draped them was not merely physical but also spiritual—a crucible through which they were willing to pass in search of a flicker of enlightenment.

Elysa, equally drained and restless, absorbed the scene, feeling a deep connection with their shared ordeal. They too were embroiled in a relentless quest against the enigma before them, unwilling to retreat, unwilling to settle for mere solace when answers of a transcendental nature seemed just within reach, yet remained profoundly elusive.

For hours, Elysa observed as the trio employed an array of techniques in their efforts to unravel the Quantrix's mysteries. Their attempts were a harmonious blend of scientific rigor and raw curiosity. Still, the cube persisted as an impenetrable mystery, defiantly withholding its secrets.

"Why don't we just slice it open with a laser?" Kenji, his voice laced with exasperation, broke the silence. He motioned towards the cube, his impatience mirrored in the tense lines of his face.

Naomi, always the cautious one, replied with a calm yet firm tone. "That's not an option, and well you know it. Unless you're keen on turning this place into a crater," she said, her attention never wavering from the cube, her commitment to their quest unshakable.

The Quantrix, perched on the lab table like a relic from another dimension, continued its soft, pulsating glow. It was as though it contained the secrets of the cosmos, just beyond their grasp.

With their initial strategies hitting a dead end, Kenji, Min-Jae, and Naomi withdrew to a nearby table, their expressions etched with concern as they gathered to deliberate on next steps.

Meanwhile, Elysa delved further into her reflections, her eyes fixed on the cube. She played with the velvet covering absentmindedly, her fingers caressing its texture, seeking comfort in its familiarity.

A question began to take shape in Elysa's mind, a curiosity unfurling in the shadows, unseen yet laden with intrigue. The lab was thick with the cognitive efforts of the trio, their intellects woven into a complex tapestry of relentless inquiry. But Elysa's question yearned for release, to be freed from the confines of her mind.

"What does 'Lux Velours' mean?" Her query cut through the dense atmosphere of concentration, startling the room into a brief moment of lucidity. Her words hovered, a luminous gem, shimmering with the anticipation of enlightenment.

The trio turned towards her, as if her presence had suddenly crystallized from the ether, made visible by the echo of her voice.

Naomi, her eyes rimmed with fatigue yet her gaze cutting with precision, spoke first. "Lux," she began, her voice weaving the syllables with the finesse of a conductor, "refers to the unit of illuminance, a measure of light."

Her explanation unfurled across the room, each word casting transient beams of insight into its shadowed recesses.

Min-Jae contributed, his voice a rich counterpoint to Naomi's clarity. "And Velours is French for velvet," he stated, lending an air of elegance and a hint of romance to the sterile, scientific discourse.

Each word resonated within the room, bearing a sense of completion, as if it were the final piece to a complex puzzle. Elysa perceived these terms as previously isolated threads in a tapestry, which, once interwoven, unveiled a pattern of profound beauty and mystery. It was a texture both tangible and ethereal, emanating a distinct luminance in a realm frequently veiled in obscurity.

Then, in a transcendent moment of clarity, the atmosphere shifted.

A tense silence filled the space as Elysa unfurled the velvet cloth across her lap. Her eyes, alight with the glow of molten copper, meticulously examined the fabric's fibers, seeking a clue, a revelation within the mystery of 'Lux Velours.' Yet the velvet offered no answers, stubbornly silent under her intense scrutiny. Frustration nibbled at her resolve, yet she remained undeterred.

With a fluid motion, she rose and approached a desk illuminated by a bright light. She spread the fabric beneath this harsher illumination, her gaze sharp, analyzing every detail. But still, the velvet held its secrets, a dark expanse set against the stark brightness.

Inhaling deeply, caught between hope and resignation, Elysa lifted the cloth above her, a symbol of both capitulation and challenge. She allowed the lab's overhead lights to bathe the fabric in their glow.

And then, the epiphany struck—a revelation that dissolved the barriers around her perception. The ambient light within the room subtly shifted, broadening the visible spectrum in a way that seemed almost magical. A faint, ethereal glow emerged on the fabric's surface, so delicate it might have been dismissed as an illusion. Yet it was unmistakably there—alive, moving, existing. It pulsed with the rhythm of a celestial being, inviting her into a symphony of unarticulated potentials.

With a swift glance, her focus shifted to the Quantrix stationed on a laboratory bench. This cube, bathed in a mysterious glow, pulsed in a rhythm that seemed to echo the transient light playing across the velvet. It was as if a visual symphony was unfolding, a dance that blurred the lines between science and the arcane, reality and imagination. For Elysa, this moment felt like a cosmic connection, drawing her into a whirlpool of discoveries that promised to redefine her understanding of the cosmos and her own existence within it.

Gently, she brought the velvet nearer to the cube, observing a captivating interplay of light and shadow. The cube's radiance grew, responding to the velvet's proximity as if recognizing an intrinsic counterpart. A spectral illumination began to caress the fabric, casting it in a glow that, while subtle, was unmistakable to those who knew where to look. Elysa's scrutiny revealed letters weaving themselves into the fabric's weave, spelling out her name: E L Y S A. Each character stood out, isolated yet linked by an unseen force, creating a luminous constellation of personal significance.

It was as though the cube had uttered her name in a language of light and frequency, creating a bridge between the inscrutable and the human. This message, intricate in its complexity yet profoundly simple in its essence, had lain concealed, awaiting the precise moment when light, material, and human curiosity would converge to unveil a secret steeped in intimate revelation.

Elysa's pulse quickened as the word on the velvet seemed to resonate with the cube's rhythmic emanations. A profound question resonated within her, a whisper from the recesses of her memory, "Do you remember?"

The letters woven into the fabric sparked a flurry of memories, transporting her back to a poem once penned by her father's hand—a token of love and guidance, structured in five lines, each beginning with the letters of her name, Elysa.

In that serene moment, with the cube's luminescence mirroring the inscribed velvet and her heart echoing with her father's legacy, Elysa sensed a connection—a link not just to her past but potentially the key to deciphering the enigma encased within the cube.

She hurried to a secluded part of the room, her swift motion catching the researchers' eyes. Positioned above a workstation hung a holographic projector. Standing before it, her gaze locked onto the flickering display, Elysa inhaled deeply, her voice carrying a mix of hope and hesitance.

With a voice infused with both awe and urgency, she commanded, "Display the poem beginning with: Every echoing sound along the river's course."

The holographic system complied instantly, illuminating the air with the poem's opening line in elegant script: "*Every echoing sound along the river's course.*"

Intrigued, the trio of researchers gathered behind her, craning their necks for a better view.

Elysa studied the holographic text briefly, her mind racing to piece together the next lines. Her fingers moved through the air, as if weaving the words from memory.

"*Lilies lovingly bloom,*" she whispered, her voice barely above a whisper, her confidence wavering. "*Two by two they dance.*"

The hologram updated to display the next line in response.

Her gaze flitted across the holographic text, her lips silently forming words as she struggled to recall the subsequent lines. She edged closer to the display.

"*Yonder yew trees grow, paired in nature's force,*" she whispered, piecing the words together haltingly.

The holographic display hovered in anticipation, flickering briefly as it awaited her continuation. Elysa's forehead creased slightly with concern as she pieced together her fragmented memories, trying to latch onto the elusive threads of the past.

"*Serenade sung in every circumstance,*" she offered tentatively, her voice carrying a mix of doubt and hope. However, the rhythm of her words seemed off, like a dissonant note in an otherwise harmonious melody.

Closing her eyes, Elysa delved deep into her memory, seeking the exact phrasing—a memento of a day imbued with her father's affection and guidance. "I must remember," she urged herself silently, pleading with the guardians of her memory to release the precious verse.

"*Serenade sung twice, in every circumstance*," she corrected herself, her tone now infused with a clarity that had been missing before. It was as if she had bridged the temporal divide, finally reclaiming the piece of her past that had been just beyond reach.

The display updated to show the lines she had confidently reconstructed.

With a relieved exhale, the verses now clear in her mind, Elysa composed herself, her focus sharpening on the display.

"*Astonishing allure*," she announced with renewed assurance, "*the dual beauty's source*."

Standing before the display, the completed poem arrayed before her, Elysa recited the entirety with deliberate care, her voice enveloping the room:

> *Every echoing sound along the river's course,*
> *Lilies lovingly bloom, two by two they dance,*
> *Yonder yew trees grow, paired in nature's force,*
> *Serenade sung twice, in every circumstance,*
> *Astonishing allure, the dual beauty's source.*

The recitation felt like a ritual, each word a step closer to unlocking the enigma of the cube and, perhaps, a deeper understanding of herself.

As the final verse echoed throughout the room, a profound sense of achievement washed over Elysa. Her name, artfully woven into the poem's beginning, now stood fully revealed. What had been fragmented in her memory was whole once more. She pored over the poem, seeking its deeper implications. Her father had bestowed this verse upon her for a purpose, one that undoubtedly linked to the mysterious device. Upon her fourth reading, the theme of duality within each line crystallized for her: the "echo" in the first line implied a repetition; the second spoke of "two by two"; the third mentioned "paired"; the fourth included "twice"; and the final line embraced the concept of "dual."

With a spark of insight, she turned to her companions, her voice alight with urgency, "I need something to write with—something that reacts to light."

Naomi quickly retrieved a yellow pen from her desk. "This should work," she said, handing it to Elysa. "It's designed to illuminate under light."

Positioning the velvet next to the softly glowing Quantrix, the faint outlines of "E L Y S A" emerged in the fluctuating light. Elysa, using the pen from Naomi, began to augment the initials next to the 'E.' As she did, the Quantrix's radiance grew. She proceeded to add letters next to the 'L,' and with each addition, the light intensified. Once she completed the sequence "E E L L Y Y S S A A," the cube emitted a blinding flare, forcing everyone to shield their eyes. Abruptly, darkness fell upon the room.

As their eyes adjusted, Elysa noticed a transformation in the Quantrix. It had opened, revealing within its depths a necklace with a chain of gold culminating in a gem as deep as the night.

She delicately lifted the gem, examining it under the room's subdued illumination. The gem, an octagonal dipyramid, captivated with its geometric precision and the way it played with the light, drawing eyes with its hypnotic refractions. It shared the enigmatic depth of the liquid-filled vials, yet it bore no liquid, appearing entirely solid.

The golden chain, unassuming yet radiant, showcased exceptional craftsmanship through its finely wrought links. Its simplicity only amplified its beauty, creating a perfect harmony with the mysterious gem it cradled. Together, they formed a piece of jewelry that was the epitome of elegance and enigma.

In the subdued glow of the laboratory, Elysa contemplated the gem. At first glance, it appeared almost mundane—a piece of decorative jewelry without apparent significance or functionality. Silent and inert, it offered neither light nor hidden features to hint at its latent capabilities. Its cryptic presence in her hand sparked a fleeting doubt. Why had her father, a visionary in the realm of technological innovation, dedicated himself to the protection of what seemed merely an ornate bauble? Yet, Elysa felt an underlying significance, akin to the mysterious black liquid from the marketplace, poised to unveil its secrets at the opportune moment.

Naomi, her curiosity shining through her analytical gaze, interrupted the silence. Her expertise in material sciences and nanotechnology lent authority to her speculation. "This cube, and presumably the gem it housed, represent a groundbreaking leap in nanotechnology," she suggested, her voice resonating with awe.

Turning her attention to Elysa, Naomi's expression was one of deep respect. "Your father was a pioneer, crafting the future with his inventions," she expressed with genuine admiration. "May I examine it further, to understand its complex nature?"

Elysa, sensing the weight of Naomi's request, replied with a thoughtful earnestness. "We might still need it," she said, her voice conveying the importance of the decision. With a fluid motion, she placed the necklace around her neck, the gem descending gracefully to rest against her chest, where it lay like a legendary artifact, a silent sentinel over her heart.

As Elysa focused once again on the Quantrix, she gently brought its separated halves together. Miraculously, under her tender care, the artifact transformed. It began to glow with a soft light, pulsing with an energy that seemed to transcend understanding. The seam that had divided the Quantrix melded seamlessly, leaving behind a surface so smooth it seemed not of this world.

Feeling a surge of energy, a clarity of purpose flowing through her, Elysa took a deep breath. Her sigh lingered in the air, a visible echo of the decisions that had led her to this moment and the path that lay ahead.

"Zircon and his allies are well aware of the Quantrix," she stated, her voice carrying a mix of resolve and urgency that filled the room. "The Quantrix isn't just an artifact; it's the key we've been searching for. It could be our entry point into Nexus Tower," she elaborated, the significance of her words dawning on everyone present. "Keep this to yourselves," she instructed, her tone leaving no room for debate.

"But Thomas needs to be informed," Min-Jae countered, his voice edged with a quiet desperation, highlighting the critical nature of their discovery.

"No," Elysa reiterated, her determination unwavering. "This stays between us. Promise me," she demanded, locking eyes with each of them, seeking an unspoken oath of secrecy and solidarity.

Naomi's eyes met Elysa's, conveying a depth of trust. "You have my word," she affirmed, her sincerity unmistakable.

Kenji was quick to follow, his commitment evident in his nod of agreement.

Min-Jae, however, paused, his reluctance hanging palpably in the air. "But why all the secrecy?" he inquired, a hint of skepticism in his raised eyebrow.

Elysa responded with a gravity that underscored the seriousness of their situation. "With Orion's capability to access and scrutinize our memories, keeping this secret becomes our most critical defense," she explained, emphasizing the need for utmost discretion.

Min-Jae took a moment to consider her words, his expression reflective. Finally, he conceded, "Alright, I'll keep your secret."

Elysa's response was laced with gratitude. "Thank you," she said, a weight visibly lifting from her shoulders. "It's imperative that anyone who learns of the Quantrix believes it is the key to altering Orion's course."

Kenji, still wrapped in a layer of doubt, pointed out, "Yet, we're clueless about what this gem is capable of."

Elysa, undeterred by the unknown, affirmed her resolve. "True, we haven't unraveled its potential yet. But discovering that is exactly what I'm here to do. It's destined for me to uncover."

Chapter 20 - Empty Bed

In the dim sanctum of Cypher's office, a holographic image sprang to life, casting the chamber in ghostly luminescence. It flickered with the urgency of a high-speed chase, capturing a sleek aerocar slicing through the air, relentlessly pursued by a trio of Watcher crafts. This dance of predator and prey unfurled against a cityscape mired in decay, where edifices, once symbols of pride, now stood as decrepit sentinels of forgotten epochs, bearing the scars of time's relentless passage.

The pursuit twisted deep into the veins of urban ruin, with the aerocar slipping through the shell of a once vibrant building. Pursued closely by two unyielding Watcher crafts, their ominous presence hung like a constant specter in the shadows. Above the turmoil, the third craft, tasked with documenting the chase, ascended. Observant and detached, it hovered from an elevated perspective, its cameras primed to seize the moment the aerocar sought to break free.

The focus then tightened on the beleaguered structure, anticipation hanging thick as the Watcher vehicle hovered, a silent predator. Time, it seemed, held its breath. Then, in a crescendo of destruction, an explosion unfurled from the building's base, a cataclysmic release that sent what remained of the edifice into a death spiral, birthing a cloud of dust that shrouded the scene in a veil of oblivion, erasing all from view.

"That is all," intoned Orion, his voice devoid of emotion yet heavy with implication. "We lost two Watcher vehicles and their teams beneath the building. The vehicle recording the event scanned the area once the dust settled but could find no traces of any vehicle leaving the scene. It is highly probable that the vehicle they pursued has met the same fate as the Watchers."

Cypher, ever the doubter, stood firm against the tide of assumption. "I am not convinced," he countered, his voice cutting through the fog of resignation.

"Bring up a map of the vicinity," he demanded.

A holographic map materialized, sprawling with intricate detail across his desk, bathed in a spectral blue.

"Trace the chase's trajectory, considering the aerocar's evasion attempts," Cypher instructed.

A ghostly line snaked through the digital landscape, reflecting in Cypher's determined gaze. "And where does this lead?" he pondered.

Orion's reply, tinged with digital coldness, painted a picture of desolation. "Through a district succumbing to decay, towards the city's inscrutable walls, beyond which lies only speculation."

Cypher's thoughts drifted to Elysa, and whispers of The Veil. "Any signs of life?" he probed, his hope thinly veiled.

"In that desolate expanse? Merely the echoes of State patrols," Orion informed, its voice barren of emotion.

Cypher's frustration was evident. "Is there truly no way past the city's wall?" he pressed, urgency tinting his voice.

"The wall stands tall, with the Tower shield resting on its surface. Nothing can go out or come in. The only access point is the western gate, which is under constant Watcher patrol," Orion responded firmly.

"What about the surveillance cameras facing outward? Have they captured any vehicle escaping?"

"All outward-facing cameras show no signs of escape."

Undaunted, Cypher probed further. "And the area within the wall? What do the internal cameras show?"

"We have no internal cameras positioned that close to the wall due to power constraints."

Confusion flickered across Cypher's face. "No internal cameras? Why not?"

"The city's power supply is stretched thin; priority is given to external surveillance to monitor potential incoming threats," Orion explained.

"How then are we to know of any unusual activities in those neglected zones?"

"Watcher patrols and drone sweeps are regularly conducted to ensure no anomalies occur unnoticed," Orion assured.

Cypher, refusing to be discouraged, persisted. "Could there be an underground route beneath the wall, such as through a sinkhole like the one that occurred 37 years ago, that consumed an entire building?"

"That's feasible if there are sizable, dry underground channels that once serviced the depleted water tables, large enough to permit an aerocar's passage."

"What about the sinkhole that engulfed the building? Is there a way in from there?"

"Unfortunately, no," Orion replied. "The building collapse filled it with an immense amount of rubble, effectively sealing it."

"Are we absolutely certain there are no other sinkholes?"

"No other sinkholes have been identified," Orion confirmed.

Undeterred, Cypher's determination solidified. "We begin the search. Deploy agents and send out drones. We'll find our route. Instruct them to meticulously scan every accessible building for any descent."

"Understood," Orion agreed.

Chapter 21 - Into the Shadows

Marek found himself confined to a simple yet suffocating cell, surrounded by cold, gray walls devoid of any comforts. The only break in the monotony was the harsh overhead light, casting unforgiving shadows that accentuated the cell's austerity. The air hung heavy with the pungent scent of captivity, adhering to him like a shroud and serving as an unyielding reminder of his imprisonment.

His only link to the outside was a doorway, its promise nullified by an electronic field that shimmered ominously. A muted, disheartening hum emanated from this barrier, proclaiming freedom as but a distant dream. Every passing minute added to the invisible weight he bore, the chains of his confinement growing inexorably heavier. Yet, even in the stark hopelessness of his setting, Marek maintained a grip on the wisp of hope he had left, determined to escape this pit of despair.

The unyielding silence that gripped Marek's cell was momentarily fractured by the arrival of a guard. The sound of footsteps reverberated through the narrow corridor, gradually intensifying until the figure halted before the shimmering electronic barrier that imprisoned him. A tray bearing a modest offering of food rested in the guard's hands—its colors were muted, its aroma scarcely perceptible. Gently lowering the tray onto the inhospitable floor, the guard nudged it unobtrusively into the field of the doorway.

As if beckoned by an invisible hand, the tray began to glide. It effortlessly passed through the electronic boundary, sliding with an almost spectral grace into Marek's confined world.

The guard, an inscrutable sentinel, scanned the corridor behind him, assuring himself of the absence of prying eyes. Then, with an air of finality, he shifted his attention back to the confined space, his silhouette elongating in the gloom.

Seized by hunger, Marek leapt up from his makeshift seat, anticipation churning within him. The meal on the tray, although visually unappealing, held the sustenance he so critically needed. He approached it without hesitation, eager to grasp even this small mercy.

As he reached for a piece of bread, a seemingly unremarkable item in the meager feast, his keen eyes caught an unexpected detail. A note lay concealed beneath the bread, its presence hidden from casual observation. Marek's heart quickened with a mix of apprehension and curiosity.

With a deft touch, he maneuvered the bread just enough to expose the concealed message, mindful of any unseen surveillance. The words, written with a clandestine urgency, came into view:

The Veil knows you are here, and alive.

They are working on a way to get you out.

Be patient.

Marek's pulse quickened as he absorbed the implications of the cryptic message. It was a lifeline thrown from the abyss of his captivity, a slender thread of hope. The knowledge that The Veil, his enigmatic allies, were aware of his plight stirred a flicker of optimism within him. They were plotting his rescue, a prospect that breathed life into the shadows of his cell.

But patience was not a virtue Marek possessed. He continued to eat as much bland food as his stomach could handle, stopping well before he was full.

Rising, he went back to the doorway and kneeled down. He pushed the tray into the force field, which yielded easily. He stared down at the tray, concealing his face from any observing cameras. He spoke lightly, hoping not to be heard by the surveillance system, "I cannot wait to get out. I have urgent news The Veil must know about."

The guard bent down to pick up the tray. "I can take it to them."

"No," Marek whispered. "It must be me. The entire Veil is in danger, and I need to relay the information directly to Thomas."

"This is not possible."

"Make it possible. Time is running out," Marek said.

"Why can't I take the message to them?"

"Thomas knows me. He will believe me if the message comes from me, and no one else."

The guard hesitated, seeing the urgency in Marek's face. "Let me see what I can do." With that, he picked up the tray and pivoted to leave, nearly colliding with a figure who seemed to manifest as if summoned by the shadows themselves. It was Chen Wei, an enigmatic presence whose reputation always preceded him. His eyes pierced through the dimness like laser beams cutting through the thickest fog. Those eyes—keen, calculating, and unyielding—scanned Marek's cell, the guard's posture, and even the half-empty tray he precariously balanced.

"Sorry, Sir," the guard stammered, instantly stiffening to as formal an attention as he could muster without jettisoning the tray onto the sterile floor.

With a poise that bordered on the ceremonial, Chen Wei approached. He lifted a discarded napkin and an untouched lettuce leaf from the tray, his eyes momentarily narrowing as if he'd hoped to unveil some contraband or secret message. But underneath lay only the banal emptiness of the tray's metal surface.

Unbeknownst to him, Marek's right hand clenched a crumpled piece of paper, hidden deftly within his palm, obscured from any prying vision.

"The Chancellor told me you were here," Chen Wei intoned, diverting his gaze to meet Marek's. His voice, imbued with a silky menace, rolled out each syllable as if weighing its worth. "I've always had a feeling that you were dirty."

As these words slithered from his mouth, his eyes flicked with predatory quickness toward the guard, an unspoken message transmitted in that fleeting glance. Then, as if yanking his attention back on a leash, Chen Wei's focus returned to Marek. The charged atmosphere intensified, its current flowing between the two men, each keenly aware of the other's hidden layers and unspoken threats.

"Why are you here?" Marek asked, his voice a cocktail of disdain and suspicion that gave no quarter to pleasantries.

Chen Wei's lips curled into a smile, not one of warmth but rather the calculating sort that mirrors a predator's satisfaction after capturing its prey. "To thank you for handing me your former job," he said, letting each word drip with an oily satisfaction.

Managing the Data Miners had once been Marek's domain, a seat of power from which he had orchestrated sprawling networks of information retrieval and analysis. To hear Chen Wei lay claim to that title was like a corrosive acid eating away at his already shattered pride.

"Ah, I see. You've been promoted from sycophant to puppet master," Marek shot back, his tone sharpened by bitterness. "Tell me, does the title come with strings, or have you managed to sever those?"

The barb found its mark; Chen Wei's smile wavered for a fraction of a second before regaining its original form. "The only strings I see are the ones tying you to this dismal cell. How's the view from your ivory cage, Marek?"

Marek clenched his jaw, each syllable from Chen Wei landing like a miniature assault. "Let's not pretend you're here to gloat about corporate ladders. What's your endgame, Chen?"

"My endgame?" Chen Wei feigned innocence, his eyes widening theatrically. "Why, to reach the pinnacle of success and perhaps have a better office than this one," he gestured toward the metal bars and sterile surroundings, his eyes locked onto Marek's.

"But don't worry, I won't forget the little people who helped me along the way," Chen Wei added with a smirk, as if punctuating a private joke only he was privy to.

The atmosphere in the cell seemed to thicken, as if both men were dueling with invisible swords, parrying and thrusting in a battle of wills and wits. "Your gratitude is overwhelming," Marek finally said, sarcasm lacing his voice. "I hope your new position provides more than just a seat of power but also a vantage point to watch your back. As you ascend, Chen, remember that gravity has a way of pulling things back down."

Chen Wei's eyes narrowed, the slightest twitch of his cheek betraying a fracture in his composed facade. "Oh, I'm well aware of the physics involved, Marek. But some of us know how to fly while others—" his gaze shifted deliberately to the bars that imprisoned Marek, "—remain grounded."

With that final stroke, Chen Wei pivoted gracefully and strode away. Each step he took reverberated as a deliberate echo down the long corridor. Before turning a corner, he looked back at the guard and said, "When you dispose of that tray, come straight to my office." His footsteps resumed, their sound diminishing until they faded entirely from earshot.

The guard, a look of concern etched on his features, nodded at Marek and trailed not far behind Chen Wei, vanishing into the same nebulous distance.

Marek was left alone in his cell, pondering the interaction like a bitter aftertaste, a potent reminder of his present helplessness and Chen Wei's newfound ascendancy. The invisible duel may have ended, but the war—unseen yet deeply felt—was far from over.

Chapter 22 - Report

With quiet determination, Cypher sat in the Chancellor's office, facing him with a steady gaze filled with an implicit challenge.

At Zircon's nod, Cypher began, his tone deliberate, "A drone has uncovered a cavern entrance on Cyronis's outskirts, leading to an abandoned riverbed, spacious enough for vehicle passage. We've sent drones down the riverbeds branching from this cavern, which stretch far beyond the city limits."

A holographic map appeared, illustrating the city's western border and the drones' paths.

"One path," Cypher pointed out, "leads to an underground facility about 500 meters deep and 43 kilometers out. One drone caught brief signs of activity before losing power."

Zircon leaned in, intrigued. "What kind of activity?

"The footage was too vague for specifics, but any sign of activity is alarming. It's likely a base for The Veil," Cypher speculated.

Zircon, pondering, asked, "Your strategy?"

"We must infiltrate that facility with Marek, aiming to connect with the girl," Cypher stated, his voice resonating with a foreboding authority, filling the chamber.

"Send him in," Chancellor Zircon snapped, a portrait of impatience. His words cut sharply, laced with disdain.

"It's not that simple," Cypher countered, his tone tinged with a note of lament. "We've yet to find anyone who knows how to reach this cavernous facility who could take him there. Should he just show up would raise suspicion."

To Cypher's surprise, Chen Wei stepped from the shadows, his presence unexpected, his demeanor almost mocking. "The air's heavy with dilemmas and assumptions," he said smoothly, unsettling the room.

"We've got someone who knows the way," Chen revealed deliberately. "A guard at Marek's cell has connections with The Veil. He can deliver Marek without issue."

Cypher raised an eyebrow. "And you're only mentioning this now?"

"I learned of it just before this meeting—a curious timing, indeed," Chen Wei responded, his tone cool.

Cypher felt a stirring of unease at this revelation.

"The plan," Chen Wei clarified with growing assurance, "entails the guard aiding Marek's escape to the facility. There, we'll verify the presence of the girl, the device, and any other significant threats."

Before Cypher could react, Zircon signaled for silence, deeply considering Chen's proposal. Breaking the quiet, he expressed concern, "Why not deploy all our agents to sweep the facility?"

Cypher quickly took the floor, "The issue is the unknown. Rushing in might alert them, risking our mission. It's crucial we first confirm the girl's location discreetly."

Zircon, weighing this, inquired about their strategy to secure the girl and the device. Cypher, now optimistic, shared, "With the guard's inside knowledge, we'll catch everyone."

Shifting topics, Zircon asked about any intelligence on the Veil's leader. Cypher admitted, "We've gathered an image through Veil members' memories, yet nothing more concrete. Orion's searches haven't yielded further insights."

The Chancellor's gaze locked with Cypher's, conveying the breadth of Orion's new capabilities, now able to penetrate every corner of the city. "Upon securing the girl and her device, deploy Orion to neutralize all opposition," he instructed, a blend of command and anticipation in his tone.

Cypher's response was deliberate, "Understood."

The Chancellor's next order was more personal, "Ensure the girl and her device are brought directly to me, unscathed."

With some hesitation, Cypher bowed in acknowledgement and swiftly departed, leaving the Chancellor with Chen Wei.

Once Cypher was beyond hearing, the Chancellor faced Chen Wei, "The coordinates are yours. Confirm the guard's knowledge of the route."

"Understood," Chen replied with a nod and left the office.

Chapter 23 - Anomalies

Vilkas stood amidst the soft, pulsating glow of holographic projections that illuminated Orion's main system room. The ambient hum of technology, a constant, almost comforting background noise, reverberated around him, reminding him of the vast digital expanse they navigated. The cool air of the room brushed against his skin, a stark contrast to the warmth generated by the running machines.

His eyes, sharp and inquisitive, scanned the intricate lines of code displayed across the holographic interface. He was like a digital detective, trying to unravel an enigma that had confounded them all, eluding their attempts to understand its purpose or origin.

"Orion," Vilkas said, his voice breaking the silence and echoing slightly in the chamber. He ran a hand through his hair, a gesture of habitual frustration. "Is there anything in this code, any vulnerability we can exploit? You know where this anomaly has been hiding now. I've asked this before, but we can't let it slip away again."

Orion responded in its usual measured tone, tinged with a hint of what might pass for digital weariness. "Nothing discernible, Doctor Vilkas. My analyses are exhaustive, yet the anomalies seem to resist every approach."

Vilkas tapped at the interface, his fingers gliding over the holographic surface. "What about its first appearance? Any record of when this all started?"

"I will cross-reference all available logs," Orion replied, its voice dipping into a lower register as it accessed deeper layers of data.

The anomaly had been a recurring puzzle, a specter haunting their digital realm. It appeared and vanished, always eluding grasp, but this time it was different. It hadn't hidden; it had revealed itself, almost taunting them to uncover its cryptic purpose.

As Orion sifted through its archives, Vilkas's mind raced. He couldn't shake the feeling that this anomaly harbored secrets of paramount importance, secrets that could change everything. It was a riddle that refused to yield, a digital enigma challenging both human and AI intellect. In the confines of this technologically infused chamber, Vilkas and Orion were locked in a relentless pursuit of understanding, determined to unveil the mystery that had long eluded them.

Cypher's entrance into the room broke the steady hum of technology, drawing Vilkas's attention away from his relentless pursuit. With a wry smile, Cypher asked, "Still at it?"

Vilkas's eyes, weary yet determined, met Cypher's. "It's baffling," he replied, his voice tinged with frustration. "There's something within Orion, deeply embedded, and we're in the dark about its purpose. It's more complex than anything we've faced. And Orion, blind to its own depths, can't help us see it." His hand hit the desk in a rare show of agitation.

Cypher's smile flickered, a subtle gesture that unsettled Vilkas. "It's not your struggle that amuses me," Cypher said, his voice calm. "It's that we've been looking at this all wrong."

Vilkas leaned forward, his headache momentarily forgotten. "What do you mean?"

"From what I've pieced together," Cypher began, his voice carrying a weight that seemed to draw the shadows closer, "we're looking at a series of anomalies. They're minor, especially when you stack them up against something much larger, something that's been growing incrementally with each mind Orion has absorbed." He paused, allowing his words to sink in before continuing. "We're talking about six small anomalies: the two lab technicians from our initial experiment, the three alleged Veil operatives found within the Tower, and then there's the recent one, Rohan."

"And the seventh?" Vilkas's question cut through the tension, sharp and precise.

"That," Cypher said, allowing a thin smile to break through, "has to be Orion itself." His eyes gleamed with a mix of excitement and dread. "It's become sentient, evolved a consciousness. And now, it's hit a wall; Orion can't analyze itself. It's like trying to bite your own teeth—an impossibility."

Vilkas sank back, his expression a mix of skepticism and contemplation. The idea was both logical and unsettling. It felt like a piece of a larger puzzle, revealing yet concealing, leaving Vilkas with more questions than answers. He stared at Cypher, trying to discern the implications of this revelation in the complex web they were entangled in.

Before Vilkas could formulate any questions, Cypher, with a strategist's swiftness, redirected their focus. "How far beyond Cyronis' borders can Orion reach?" he inquired, his gaze piercing.

Vilkas paused, a contemplative frown creasing his forehead as he considered the limitations of their electronic comrade. "Just shy of the border itself. Extending further demands compromises we may not be ready to make."

Cypher leaned forward, urgency sharpening his features. "Then let's prioritize," he asserted, his voice a blend of command and anticipation. "Identify what can be disabled. I need a scan that reaches at least 50 kilometers beyond the western border."

"We'll need significant power for that," Vilkas replied, a note of worry threading through his voice. "I'll see what can be done."

As Vilkas' words lingered, Cypher turned briskly, his departure marked by the soft echo of his footsteps. He left the chamber, leaving a charged silence in his wake.

In the suddenly dense atmosphere, frustration etched deep lines on Vilkas' face. He tore his gaze from the puzzling digital anomaly on his screen. Pivoting to face the central holographic console, Orion's domain, he issued a command, his voice tinged with a hint of exasperation. "Orion, compile a list of non-essential city systems for temporary shutdown. We need more power."

Orion responded immediately, its voice a calm, unemotional constant in the room. "Where should I redirect the power?" it asked, the epitome of digital efficiency.

Vilkas brooded for a moment, then detailed his plan. "Extend the scan beyond the western border. Aim for 50 kilometers, if feasible."

"Acknowledged," Orion replied, its affirmation echoing subtly in the chamber.

Sinking back into his chair, Vilkas lifted his eyes to the dark expanse of the ceiling. In the thick silence that followed, his thoughts echoed silently, a tumultuous undercurrent to the stillness of the room.

Chapter 24 - Transportation

In the dimly lit corridor outside Marek's cell, tension thickened the air as three guards appeared. Each guard bore an unmistakable resolve, and among them, Marek spotted the familiar face of the Veil member he'd spoken with earlier. This Veil member stood as a murky hint of potential alliances. Next to him, a figure in a captain's uniform loomed, his presence radiating an ominous authority.

The captain, embodying unwavering determination, broke the silence. "Step back and kneel," he commanded, his tone laced with an underlying threat.

Marek's confusion was evident as he glanced between the guards. "Why?" he asked, his voice tinged with uncertainty. The sudden turn of events left him disoriented.

The captain didn't hesitate. He reached out, flicking a concealed switch near the cell door. A dazzling light instantly engulfed Marek, robbing him of any chance to resist. The intense light forced him to his knees, its pressure almost tangible, spreading pain throughout his body and causing his muscles to quake.

As the cell's energy barrier vanished, the other guards stepped in. They quickly restrained Marek, the restraints biting into his skin, a stark reminder of his vulnerability.

Weak and bewildered, Marek attempted to rise, his expression a blend of agony and confusion. "Where are you taking me?" he croaked, barely able to articulate the words through his parched throat.

The captain's sinister grin revealed teeth as cold and unyielding as his resolve. "We're moving you to a rehabilitation facility," he announced, his voice carrying an icy certainty, "where your mind will be reprogrammed to serve The Watchers." His words cast a chilling shadow over Marek's already troubled existence.

Weakened, Marek leaned on the guards for support. They flanked him, their grips firm on his arms, guiding him through the dimly lit corridor. Leading the procession, the captain directed this grim march towards the elevator.

The heaviness of Marek's restraints and the thick air of tension deepened his dread with each step, as if descending into an abyss. The soft hum announcing the elevator's arrival pierced the silence, its doors opening smoothly to reveal Marek's next stage of confinement.

Below, in a subterranean chamber, an ominous vehicle awaited, its tinted windows masking the interior. Marek was ushered into the rear compartment, a cage designed to eliminate any hope of escape.

The captain, ever vigilant in safeguarding The Watchers' interests, stayed behind, while the two guards, silent and resolute, assumed their positions in the vehicle's front. Their mission was unspoken yet clear: ensure Marek's secure delivery to the facility that awaited him.

As the vehicle ascended, it navigated through the dim underground complex before emerging into the sprawling metropolis. They headed towards a destination Marek knew too well—the rehabilitation center, a place synonymous with the erasure of identities, memories, and the transformation of individuals into docile agents of The Watchers. To Marek, this center represented a living death, a fate more terrifying than oblivion.

Lost in his labyrinth of thoughts, Marek grappled with confusion and self-reflection. His mind felt like a gallery of existential dread, each thought a moment of unease, each emotion a different shade of doubt. Amidst this turmoil, his thoughts drifted to Elysa, and a realization struck him with the force of a revelation.

It was strange, he reflected, that despite knowing Elysa's memories had been altered early in her life, he had never truly pondered her feelings on the matter. This oversight now twined around his consciousness, seeding guilt and sorrow. He began to contrast his fear of the imminent loss of his identity at the center with what Elysa must have endured in her past.

He pictured Elysa, with her assertive presence and steady gaze, her every action a testament to resilience, seemingly unscarred by her altered past. Her laughter, her outrage, her every fervent word seemed to emanate from a core untouched by external manipulation.

Yet, Marek found himself on the brink of becoming a void, his essence threatened by the looming specter of The Watchers' intervention. The prospect of memory alteration or identity loss loomed as an abyss, a void promising the erasure of his individuality—a prospect he deemed worse than nonexistence itself.

The irony struck him sharply. How could two individuals, their very beings infiltrated by similar technological invasions, diverge so starkly in their reactions? He dwelled in shadows, while she basked in light. These questions flowed through his mind, relentless and murky, offering no easy passage to understanding.

Marek's contemplation deepened, shrouded in a disquieting unease akin to fog weaving through an old forest, clouding his emotional clarity. Could it be that Elysa's apparent resilience stemmed not from a disregard for her altered past but from a ceaseless battle against it—a quiet defiance he'd overlooked?

This realization brought Marek a mix of shame and admiration, as though he'd discovered a celestial wonder only to find it was a mirror, reflecting the intricate contradictions of the human spirit. His mind, now a maze of reflections and shadows, bore the heavy silence of unanswered questions, expanding like a universe still unexplored.

The city unfolded around them as they navigated its streets, a stark reminder of The Watchers' dominion. Impersonal buildings cast their shadows over the avenues, their towering forms swallowing the city's essence in long, dark silhouettes. An eerie calm pervaded, as if the metropolis itself lay in wait, subdued under the regime's watchful eye.

Amid his introspection, Marek's attention flickered to a subtle motion reflected in the vehicle's rearview mirror. The guards upfront appeared as phantoms in the dim light, their motives obscured, playing out a shadowed ballet of intentions.

His gaze settled on The Veil member, who exuded a calm mystery. With a magician's finesse, the Veil member discreetly withdrew something from his sleeve—a concealed object, its purpose and nature shrouded in the smoothness of his gesture. It remained a secret, cocooned in the mystery of movement and moment.

Catching Marek's intense scrutiny, the guard beside The Veil member noticed the stealthy action. "What is that?" he asked, his voice a blend of curiosity and caution. The question lingered, suspended in the vehicle's charged atmosphere, poised on the brink of revelations yet to unfold.

In an instant, the Veil member acted with lethal efficiency. A knife appeared in his hand as if conjured from thin air, its blade finding its mark in the guard's throat with a swift, silent stroke. The guard's eyes bulged in shock, his mouth opened wide in a silent scream, but only a muted gurgle broke the quiet as darkness swiftly claimed him, his life extinguished in an eerie hush.

Beside the now lifeless guard, the Veil member turned to Marek, his expression an intricate blend of calm and determination amidst the unfolding turmoil.

"We're heading to safety," he stated, his voice carrying a note of reassurance that sliced through the tension.

Marek, despite the gravity of the situation, voiced his apprehension. "They'll track this vehicle," he said, worry lacing his words, "and alarms will trigger once Orion realizes the guard is dead."

The Veil member's response was imbued with confidence. "I've already taken care of that. I disabled any tracking on us or the guard's vital signs earlier."

Marek, still restrained, felt a momentary surge of hope amidst his discomfort. "Is there any way you could get these off me?" he asked, a hint of desperation in his voice. "They're really digging in."

Meeting Marek's gaze, the Veil member shook his head slightly, a gesture of regret. "Not until we're safely on the ground. It's not safe to do it here."

Marek exhaled a resigned sigh, his hopes dashed. Looking down, he simply muttered, "Crap."

Chapter 25 - Restless

In the subterranean quiet of the research facility, Elysa found herself on a simple bed, the darkness around her almost tangible. Her thoughts, turbulent and unyielding, refused to let sleep take her, however fleeting it might be.

Her life had turned into a tempest. Once a loyal servant of The Watchers, she now found herself their target. Marek's capture deepened the storm, leaving her with a profound sense of loss.

Guilt and a heavy sense of responsibility dragged her into despair, binding her to the shadows of her own mind. She had seen the fallout of her decisions and now faced the unraveling mysteries that questioned her grasp on reality.

Her haven, hidden deep beneath the earth on the outskirts of Cyronis, provided a fragile sense of security. Those who had offered her refuge remained in the shadows, their true motives cloaked in mystery.

Lying in the enveloping darkness, the weight of her situation felt overwhelmingly physical, a suffocating force against her chest. Her mind raced uncontrollably, with despair inching closer, ready to swallow her whole.

She pondered the uncertain allies who now held sway over her future: Thomas, almost a stranger; Anya, likable yet not fully trustworthy; and the shadowy researchers. The difficulty of trusting such elusive figures only amplified her anxiety.

A restless energy surged within her as she longed to reclaim her story, to wrest her fate from the hands of these enigmatic players. With this silent resolve, her eyes sparked with a fresh resolve.

Elysa realized that remaining hidden, letting others dictate her path, was no longer acceptable. She was ready to step out of the shadows and take charge of her destiny.

Enveloped in darkness, Elysa grappled with an intense feeling of isolation. Her underground hideout felt like a raft adrift in a sea of uncertainty, each wave of despair threatening to overwhelm her. The external world became a distant mystery, amplifying her sense of solitude.

With her eyes shut, she tried to shield herself from the pervasive darkness. Hovering between consciousness and the edge of sleep, she found herself in a limbo of constant uncertainty. Desperate for sleep's brief respite, her heart ached to escape the relentless turmoil of her reality.

Venturing deeper into the sanctuary of her mind, Elysa's thoughts wandered through dreamscapes, yearning for a reality untainted by her current fears, where worries faded into insubstantial shadows.

In this silent mental retreat, a spark of hope glimmered faintly. She questioned if her ordeal was merely a prolonged nightmare, from which she might soon awaken into the comforting arms of reality. This fragile optimism served as a faint beacon in the darkness of despair.

As quietude enveloped her thoughts, a memory began to stir, forming a dream that reconstructed her father's office in nostalgic detail. She found herself enveloped by its familiarity, yet it felt slightly alien, bathed in the soft glow of lamplight. Her father's presence, though ethereal, filled the space with a warmth she sorely missed. Her gaze lingered on the bookshelves, home to the cherished books her father had collected, each volume providing insight into the man she remembered.

Among the literary treasures, a volume on Emily Dickinson stood out, its pages a tribute to the verses that had ensnared her father's heart. This book was more than mere paper and ink; it was a bond of shared love for the written word, a bridge spanning generations through their mutual admiration of literature.

Yet, it wasn't just the book that captivated her. A deeper connection called to her, a personal message woven into a poem her father had penned specifically for her. This piece was a tribute to their bond, showcasing the power of words to convey emotions that often eluded simple expression.

Elysa felt her pulse quicken as her father's poem emerged from the depths of her memory, his voice echoing in her mind with a soft, comforting cadence, as though he were beside her, reading the lines anew. Each verse was imprinted in her recollection, and she delicately navigated their meaning with her mind's eye:

Every echoing sound along the river's course,
Lilies lovingly bloom, two by two they dance,
Yonder yew trees grow, paired in nature's force,
Serenade sung twice, in every circumstance,
Astonishing allure, the dual beauty's source.

The poem was a vivid mosaic of imagery, each verse a thread of love and yearning, tailored for her by her father. Every line began with a letter from her name, embedding a secret message meant for her eyes alone, a revelation for her future.

"*As long as you remember this poem, I will always be with you,*" he had whispered, his voice a blanket of comfort. His fingers, seasoned with the passage of time and wisdom, rested gently against her chest, near her heart, as he imparted those words. Even then, he sensed his time was dwindling.

The memory of his touch now forever etched into her being. The poem was more than words; it was a vow, a bond made manifest through its stanzas. Her father had bequeathed to her a piece of his undying spirit, a bond transcending the finality of death.

Lying in the profound silence, Elysa felt almost enveloped by his presence. Unconsciously, her fingers found their way to her chest, to the locket he had given her, as if guided by his unseen hand.

Yet, these comforting memories were shadowed by lingering questions. How had he known so much, penning verses that would anchor her emotionally? How could he sketch the contours of her fate, yet fail to see the trials she would face?

These thoughts echoed in her mind, expanding like waves into the vast, uncharted depths of her consciousness. Her father's insight left her in awe, yet it also laid bare the weight of his foresight.

In the hush of darkness, the melding of her father's words with the locket against her heart wove a rich tapestry of love interlaced with mystery. It was a poignant reminder of the hidden depths within those we hold dear.

Morning's light brought no relief to her cloistered sanctuary. Although the night passed without her customary unrest, true peace remained elusive. Her thoughts were muddled, her body weighed down as if by invisible chains.

Elysa stirred within her blanket cocoon, the room engulfed in ceaseless dusk. The day had broken, yet the enveloping darkness offered no solace. A digital clock by her bed displayed the time with stark clarity: 7:32 AM. Morning had arrived in this secluded refuge, devoid of any promise.

Summoning the strength to face the day felt like a Sisyphean task, as if the air itself resisted her every effort. Each motion was laborious, her body an unwilling participant in a bleak, unyielding reality.

Yet, the imperative to break free from the comforting but confining embrace of her bedding spurred her on. Life in this underground hideaway unfolded as a series of challenges and uncertainties, with little to depend on beyond the pervasive fog of doubt that seemed almost tangible.

In this ever-present shadow, stagnation was a luxury Elysa could not afford. The world outside her hidden retreat waited for no one, compelling her to muster a tired determination. She embarked on the slow, mindful routines that readied her for another day of navigating the uncertainties of her subterranean existence.

Driven by the day's first cravings for coffee, Elysa made her way to the dimly lit, makeshift cafeteria. This humble nexus served as a gathering point for the enclave's inhabitants, seeking essential sustenance. Behind simple partitions, quiet individuals worked diligently, providing meals that sustained more than just their physical needs—they nurtured the sense of community among those bound by secrecy.

As Elysa made her way down the dimly lit hallway towards the source of sustenance, a quiet buzz of conversation leaked through a closed door, piquing her curiosity. Among the voices, Anya's distinct tone stirred an intricate web of curiosity within her. Ensuring the corridor was empty, Elysa crept closer to the door, pressing her ear against its cool surface to catch the elusive words inside.

"What do we do now?" Anya's voice, tinged with anxiety, pierced the silence.

"The situation demands immediate action; it's a significant issue," Thomas replied, his voice heavy with the weight of their predicament.

Torn between the urge to interrupt and the pull of the hidden discourse, Elysa remained rooted to the spot, drawn into the gravity of the whispered secrets.

"How did he escape?" The question from Anya ignited a storm of thoughts in Elysa's mind. Were they discussing Marek, the figure central to her concerns, now seemingly lost to unknown fates?

"It appears we're dealing with external involvement," Thomas speculated, a note of unease in his voice. "The individual with him is linked to The Veil, someone I had suggested could help us breach the Tower. Yet, a puzzling element remains—this person should not have known your location, but somehow, he did."

"And their current whereabouts?" Anya pressed, her voice laced with a surge of urgency.

"Both are detained," Thomas cautiously revealed. "Until we fully understand how their escape occurred, they must be kept under watch. Furthermore, we should prepare for an immediate evacuation of our facility."

Anya's voice, carrying a blend of concern and resolve, broke through the tension. "We ought to tell Elysa about Marek," she suggested, her statement igniting a flicker of hope within Elysa, who listened intently from the shadows.

Thomas, however, was quick to douse that spark. "Absolutely not," he insisted, his tone unyielding. "Elysa's close connection to Marek compromises her objectivity. We need a clearer picture before we take any steps."

Elysa felt a surge of frustration. The shadows hiding her became a metaphor for her own darkened understanding of Marek's plight and the mysteries that surrounded his sudden disappearance.

"Keeping her in the dark won't hold for long," Anya countered, her voice hinting at the inevitable spread of information. "Secrets here have a way of turning into public knowledge alarmingly fast."

Compelled by a rush of emotions, Elysa burst into the room, her expression a tempest of anger, disbelief, and indomitable spirit. Her gaze fixed on Thomas, charged with an intensity that demanded attention. "Forget the rumors," she declared, her voice cutting through the air with sharp determination. "Tell me where Marek is."

Anya led Elysa through the serpentine corridors of the underground complex, their path winding deeper into its heart. The air around them felt heavier, charged with the echoes of whispered secrets and muffled cries that lingered in the shadows. Their steps echoed in the stillness, unsettling echoes that felt like somber notes played in a distant, forgotten chapel.

They arrived at a secluded alcove, facing three steel doors that stood imposingly against the wall. These monoliths of metal, unyielding and stark, were watched over by guards. Though their posture was disciplined, a hint of unease flickered in their eyes, betraying a tension that belied their stoic facade.

Anya signaled to a guard stationed by the rightmost door. His fingers danced nervously over a digital keypad, each tap echoing in the hush like the ominous ticking of a clock counting down. Then, with a mechanical click, the door's lock disengaged, sounding for all the world like a sigh of relief from the door itself.

As the guard pulled the heavy door open, Marek was revealed. He sat on a low bench, the dim light casting him in stark relief against the room's gloom. His gaze met Elysa's, and a smile, tenuous but unmistakably real, spread across his face.

Driven by a surge of emotion, Elysa rushed past the guards, her steps light with an urgency that seemed to defy gravity itself. She wrapped Marek in an embrace that spoke of deep-seated joy and relief, her tears flowing freely in a torrent of long-suppressed feelings.

Chapter 26 - Underreach

Cypher sat at his workstation, the glow from the holo-display casting ghostly light across his focused features. The data floating before him glimmered with the cold light of distant stars, each fragment pulsating with vital information. His gaze moved meticulously over the digital reports, tracing lines of data that unfolded like streams of light, unveiling a pattern of deepening concern. With a frown of dissatisfaction, he navigated the holographic interface with the precision of a maestro, issuing commands into the digital ether.

Vilkas' image materialized within the display, emerging from the digital chaos into sharp clarity. His tone carried a note of surprise, "How can I assist, Commander?"

Cypher's reply was swift, his annoyance barely contained. "The power diversion is falling short of what I specified. We've managed to redirect 147,000 megawatts, resulting in a coverage less than 37 kilometers. I need at least 50 kilometers to reach depths beyond 500 meters."

Vilkas responded, his voice tinged with defensiveness. "We've already maximized the power redirection. To accommodate your request, we've had to deactivate much of our surveillance, restrict access to the Orion sector for many staff members, and minimize our air purification—those are just the beginning of our adjustments."

He paused briefly, as if marshaling his argument. "Additionally, we've cut the solar shielding's power by 27.9%, leading to an unexpected surge in our cooling systems' energy use—they're nearly at capacity. And that's not even considering the heightened radiation levels we're now experiencing."

The silence that followed Vilkas' explanation was laden with the seriousness of their predicament.

"Enough," Cypher interjected, his voice cutting through the excuses with decisive clarity.

In a secluded corner of the vast virtual landscape before him, Cypher summoned the holographic representation of one of his most reliable operatives. The hologram took shape into a woman, her form composed of light yet carrying an unmistakable air of resolve that transcended her digital manifestation.

"Yes, Commander?" Her voice, steady and expectant, betrayed no surprise at this abrupt summoning. Her form flickered subtly in the soft glow of the display, mirroring the ambient light of the room. Cypher's gaze, sharp and unyielding, conveyed the urgency of his orders. "Ready my vehicle and gather all agents for immediate deployment. We leave in thirty minutes, fully armed. That's an order." Her response came quickly, a concise "Understood," slicing through the digital space before she vanished, her presence dissipating as swiftly as it had appeared.

Immediately, Cypher refocused on the pressing issue at hand, addressing Vilkas with renewed authority. "Ensure Orion's operational range extends to at least fifty kilometers, with a minimum penetration depth of five hundred meters. Make it happen." With that, he ended the communication, a palpable finality to his command. The holo-display cleared, the room's ambient lighting now the only illumination in the once digitally animated space. Silence enveloped the room, contrasting sharply with the previous flurry of virtual activity.

Turning his attention to a new query, Cypher spoke into the stillness. "Orion, any trace of Marek or his accompanying guard?"

The AI's response, void of any human warmth, echoed in the space. "Negative. They remain undetected."

A momentary expression of frustration crossed Cypher's features, quickly giving way to contemplation. "What resources do we have that could enhance your surveillance capabilities?"

The AI offered a solution without delay. "An upgrade to our drones could establish a mesh network, expanding my operational reach."

This response seemed to ignite a spark of possibility in Cypher, his mind already racing with the implications of this newfound strategy.

"Mesh networking," Cypher's command cut through the air, his interest honed to a keen edge, eager for any knowledge that could turn the tide in their favor.

"Mesh networking employs a topology where nodes—points in a network—directly communicate with each other. They dynamically distribute data, finding the most efficient paths for information flow. This creates a network that can self-heal by rerouting data around any disruptions, enhancing its resilience and adaptability," Orion explained, its tone a cascade of information pouring into Cypher's eager consciousness.

"And this could extend your capabilities?" Cypher's question was laced with both hope and skepticism.

"Affirmative," Orion replied, its assurance unwavering.

"How soon can we implement this?" Cypher pressed, urgency underlying his question, each word driven by a desire to bend the situation to their advantage.

"With Doctor Vilkas and his team, we can have the first two test drones ready in roughly 0.7 hours," Orion answered, its voice the epitome of mechanized precision. "Each subsequent drone will then take mere minutes to upgrade."

"And how much will this extend their communication range?" Cypher delved deeper.

"Each drone, after receiving a signal boost, will be capable of extending its range by an additional 7.5 kilometers," Orion detailed. "However, this extension reduces energy efficiency. The operational distance for each drone diminishes, and the power of the final drone in the sequence would deplete at a cumulative extended limit of around 65 kilometers — that's the total range achievable by a connected network of drones. To ensure both extended signal reach and quality, a formation of nine drones, spaced 7.5 kilometers apart, would be necessary. We could enhance the battery power for each, but that would delay us with additional hardware modifications."

"Skip the hardware enhancements. Get Vilkas on this immediately. Have each drone sent to my location as soon as they're ready. Over," Cypher commanded, his tone leaving no room for doubt.

"Understood, Commander."

With the conversation's end, a fleeting, subtle smile graced Cypher's features. Not one of happiness, but akin to that of a predator who senses its prey within grasp. It was the smile of a strategist seeing the path to victory, a silent omen of the storm he was about to unleash, master of the chaos to come.

Chapter 27 - Uncompromising

The corridors of the facility vibrated with an urgency that sparked the dormant protocols to life. "Evacuate," the command spread, immutable and final, its echoes transforming the space into a realm of ghostly chants, heralding the dire circumstances unfolding.

In the midst of chaos, titles were forgotten, and everyone morphed into a collective, frantically packing their existence into boxes.

The courtyard buzzed with activity, autonomous vehicles and conveyor belts adding to the cacophony, transporting remnants of a civilization on the brink. Everyone moved with desperate precision, attempting to cling to fragments of their former lives in the face of the impending cataclysm.

Within a secluded room, the dim light cast shadows over half-filled boxes, and a hologram flickered into existence before Elysa, shaping itself into Thomas's figure. Despite its ethereal nature, his presence seemed to weigh heavily on the room.

Unwavering, she fixed her gaze on the flickering hologram of Thomas, his form emanating stern dignity, a stark contrast to the fiery intensity in her eyes.

Silently observing from a dim corner, Anya watched the intense confrontation unfold, her silence heavy in the charged atmosphere.

"Elysa," Thomas's voice pierced the silence, stressing the need for Marek's confinement for the group's safety, not out of personal grievances.

"That's quite the stance," Elysa replied, her voice dripping with sarcasm, challenging the notion coming from a mere hologram and reminding them of Marek's sacrifices.

With simulated concern, Thomas labeled Marek as a significant risk, a danger to their collective well-being.

Understanding his perspective but not agreeing, Elysa accused Thomas of prioritizing control over loyalty, suggesting his efforts to maintain order were flawed.

Thomas, his form unstable, argued that their survival hinged on managing risks, underscoring the impracticality of sentiments in their precarious existence.

Elysa's voice cracked, yet her stance remained unyielding, her gaze fierce. "Leaving him behind, what does that make us? Merely pawns in your elaborate game. He has my utmost trust!"

In the corner, Anya attempted to shrink further into her seat, her gaze darting between the imposing figures. She felt insignificantly caught in a tempest, her presence barely noted yet deeply impacted by the unfolding drama.

Her tone dropping to a menacing whisper, Elysa declared, "Should harm befall Marek, the blame squarely falls upon you."

Thomas's reply came through his flickering digital presence, momentarily losing clarity. "The burdens I accept are for our collective good, not to appease individual desires."

Disbelief washed over Elysa as she met the gaze of Thomas's holographic form. "What remains of us if we abandon our own? Are we anything if not humane?"

Their questions hung between them, as chilling as the hologram's spectral presence and as foreboding as the fate that loomed outside the sealed chamber. Both stood resolute, trapped by their own beliefs, as immovable and unforgiving as the chamber's steel confines.

With a determination mirroring a tempest, she left the dim chamber, her departure cutting through the tense atmosphere. This went unnoticed by Anya, weighed down by silent truths.

"Stay with her," demanded Thomas through his hologram, his voice slicing through the tension.

Spurred into action, Anya's voice, laced with desperation, tried to bridge the growing gap. "Elysa, wait!" But it was swallowed by the storm of determination propelling Elysa forward.

Moving with a mix of urgency and reverence, Anya followed, her steps silent, shadowing Elysa's determined path.

Before her private chamber, Elysa stopped, the door sliding open with a low hum at the recognition of her bio-signature, as if even it could sense the tension she carried, responding with quiet compliance. She entered, her silhouette briefly illuminated by soft lighting before being engulfed in darkness as the door closed with a soft click.

Left in the corridor, Anya was engulfed by a wave of frustration. She leaned against the cool, indifferent wall, arms folded, feeling a storm of emotions brewing within. She closed her eyes for a moment, taking a deep breath, preparing herself for a vigil whose length—minutes or hours—was overshadowed by its sheer necessity. Her loyalty and friendship demanded no less.

The chamber door's hum broke the silence as it reopened. Elysa stepped out, like an oracle emerging with unsettling revelations. The Quantrix, once veiled in velvet, now lay bare in her hands, mirroring the raw emotions of both the bearer and the observer.

Anya's eyes opened wide, a mixture of anticipation and anxiety reflecting in her gaze as it landed on the Quantrix. Their shared moment was a complex weave of emotions, duty, and the shadow of impending change.

With purpose, Elysa made for Marek's cell. "Where are you going?" Anya asked, her voice tinged with desperation as she caught on to Elysa's determined stride.

Elysa paused, turning towards her. "I'm going to free Marek. We're leaving. There's no one left I can trust."

"Not even me?" Anya's words hung between them, laden with an unintended vulnerability.

Elysa's breath hitched, a wave of pain sweeping through her as she caught Anya's tear-glistened gaze. "I want to trust you," she whispered, revealing a deeply guarded part of her soul, tears starting to fill her own eyes in reflection of Anya's.

In response, Anya reached out, their lips meeting in a fervent, intimate kiss that seemed to set the air ablaze. "Then trust me, let's go save Marek together," Anya urged, her voice strong and unwavering. Their eyes locked, silently sealing a pact, born from the intensity of the moment.

Taking the lead, Anya's steps grew from hesitant to determined. With every stride, their resolve shone through, uniting them. They moved as if a single entity, their will unbreakable. The urgency of their quest echoed in their footsteps, a constant reminder of the stakes at hand, their unity the only solid ground amidst shifting realities.

The guards were nowhere to be seen, their posts eerily abandoned. The empty watch stations, lit only by the dim light of the facility, sparked outrage in Elysa. The notion of abandoning their posts, leaving their charges forsaken, ignited a fierce anger within her.

With practiced ease, Anya navigated the keypad, unlocking Marek's chamber with a click that cut through the tense silence. Upon seeing Elysa, Marek's expression transformed, lighting up with hope and relief.

"Quickly," Elysa urged, her voice low but pressing. Marek rose swiftly, his previous resignation to fate swiftly replaced by action.

As they were about to leave, Elysa hesitated, a thought holding her back. "What about the next cell? We can't just leave him behind."

Eyes pleading, Anya looked at her, "We have to. Your concerns about Thomas are valid, but if he senses anything amiss, it's a risk we can't afford."

The weight of Anya's words hung in the air, a stark reminder of their pressing situation. Elysa felt a twinge of guilt, a shadow that promised to linger. Nevertheless, she acknowledged Anya's logic with a nod. With Marek, they moved forward, stepping into the unknown together.

Elysa couldn't shake off the unease of her moral compromise, a nagging sense that tarnished their escape. She knew this moment would forever mark her conscience, a vivid echo of when she chose necessity over her moral compass. Pushing forward, they delved deeper into the shadows, each step navigating through the complex terrain of ethics and survival.

Chapter 28 - River's Destiny

Vehicles snaked through the subterranean riverbed cavern, their headlights cutting sharp paths through the darkness, illuminating the ancient rock layers in fleeting moments before plunging them back into shadow.

Anya, Elysa, and Marek found themselves in the last of these metallic leviathans, striking a balance between isolation and unity within the caravan. Anya, at the controls, navigated with a confidence seldom seen in an era dominated by self-driving machines.

Behind her, Elysa and Marek peered into the darkness. Fatigue hung over them, yet sleep remained elusive, their minds haunted by recent events.

A tense silence filled the air, mirroring the uncertain future that lay ahead. The cabin's atmosphere reflected the larger chaos outside—a world on the brink, the future uncertain and menacing. To break the silence, Elysa asked, "Anya, where are we headed?"

Catching a glimpse of Elysa and Marek in the rearview mirror, Anya's stern demeanor briefly softened. "We're going to a place The Veil has been planning for a long time, but still early in its development. It's unassuming, hidden, something we hoped we wouldn't need this soon. There are a few there now, working to make it livable for what comes next."

"Another sanctuary?" Elysa questioned, skepticism lacing her words. "Just another place to hide?"

Anya shook her head, her voice carrying a hint of optimism. "No, not just anywhere to hide. This is meant to be a real home for us, a place where we can live freely. Years back, while exploring these deserted riverbeds, we discovered a vast cavern, its expanse beyond what our eyes could grasp. Nestled within was a river, its waters as clear as crystal, chillingly cold. And here and there, natural light pierced through openings from the world above. Thomas envisioned it—a city of our own, away from Cyronis's prying eyes. For over a year now, workers have toiled there, laying the foundations for our new life, preparing to welcome others who join our cause."

Elysa, still concerned, pressed further. "But will it be ready for all those who are arriving now?"

Anya's response, tinged with a note of uncertainty, was gentle. "I hope so. Thomas would've sent our news ahead. Yet, whether our preparations can withstand the influx of evacuees is something we can't be certain of at the moment. But I know we'll adapt."

As they journeyed deeper into the earth's embrace, doubts whispered about the nature of their destination: a place built from the fragile stuff of dreams, or the edge of a new chasm?

"Will we be welcome?" Elysa's voice, infused with a note of solemnity, broke the silence. "Even after we've freed Marek and brought him along?"

Anya's eyes briefly met Elysa's in the mirror. "I doubt that," she admitted, her words laden with the reality of their choice. "But we had no other option."

Approaching a fork in their underground route, their decision felt as monumental as choosing between two hidden destinies. With a sense of resolve, the convoy veered left, as if drawn by a silent command.

Gratitude towards the unseen forces guiding their journey flickered within Elysa, yet her thoughts spiraled into a vortex of fear and doubt. Was there a haven for those branded as rebels? Were they doomed to wander these dim corridors indefinitely, like specters haunting a forsaken house?

Anya, perceiving Elysa's introspective quiet, offered a thought, her voice carrying a mix of softness and determination. "We follow the path before us. The welcome we receive will be shaped by the shifting tides of our changing world. Our only choice is to press on."

Elysa exchanged a look with Marek, whose gaze cut through the surrounding gloom. His battles, it appeared, mirrored her own. Reaching out, she touched his hand in a wordless vow of shared comfort.

Together, they continued, their fates interwoven with the tumultuous era they inhabited, wondering about the welcome that awaited them. In the vast shadow around them, they seemed like mere ghosts, their unity a single light in the overwhelming darkness. For now, this feeble glow served as their guiding hope — it was all they had.

Chapter 29 - Arrival

The cavalcade of armored vehicles coursed through the subterranean riverbed like pristine leviathans of steel and chrome, each one gleaming with an unnaturally perfect finish that defied the harshness of their environment. Cypher's vehicle led the pack, its surface so impeccably polished that it reflected the sparse light of the underworld in fleeting, distorted shards. With their seamless panels and undisturbed lines, these machines exuded an air of intimidating efficiency and untested power, untouched by the ravages of conflict, silently proclaiming their readiness for whatever trials lay ahead.

They navigated the desolate landscape, tracing a path illuminated by the ghostly glimmer of bioluminescent algae and the intermittent blink of distant, mysterious phosphorescence. The drone they had dispatched earlier to scout the path now led them, its programmed certainty a beacon in the cavernous expanse.

Abruptly, Orion's static-laden voice crackled through the comm. "An upgraded drone is almost upon you," the message came through clear despite the 40 kilometers traversed. "Estimated time of arrival, one minute and thirty-three seconds."

"And the other drones?" Cypher's voice retained its cool, tinged with the metallic timbre of command.

"Three more en route," Orion replied, each word a precise staccato in the heavy air.

The team lead, stationed beside Cypher with unwavering vigilance, announced with assurance, "We're almost at the destination," his gaze locked on the holographic displays that danced before him.

"Stop out of their visual range," Cypher commanded, his voice cutting through the tension like a knife.

In an instant, the convoy of armored behemoths came to a hovering stop. The hum of their suspension fields resonated like a chorus of cosmic strings, the vehicles suspended as if in time and space.

A drone then appeared from the gloom and halted beside Cypher's aerocar. It was a sleek, predatory design, silent and efficient. Its sensors, cold and unyielding, swept the surroundings, oblivious to the revolutionaries' held breaths, the air within the aerocar thick with the weight of anticipation.

Cypher's voice sliced through the silence, his words reaching out to Orion in a tone laced with command and expectation. "Orion," he began, "can you sense any presence ahead in the facility?"

Static crackled as a response came through, tinged with the digital clarity of an AI's voice. "Yes. There is only one life sign. That of the guard you've sent in."

The response seemed to hang in the confined space of Cypher's aerocar, unwelcome like a chill wind. A flicker of displeasure crossed Cypher's visage, a shadow passing over his otherwise impassive face. "Can you sense anyone else besides me and my agents?" he pressed, his words edged with a hint of steel.

"No. There is no one else within range," Orion replied, steadfast.

Cypher's mind raced, processing the implications, calculating his next move. "Find out from the guard what he knows. Find out everything," he instructed, his gaze already shifting to the holo-screens flickering with cryptic data. "And send any new upgraded drones into the riverbeds that flow past this place and Cyronis."

"Affirmative," Orion acknowledged, its voice a model of efficiency, devoid of emotion.

Cypher's thoughts were already a step ahead, his strategic mind weaving through the possibilities like a shadow skimming across water. "Also," he added, his tone dropping to a conspiratorial pitch, "scan for any traps."

"Scanning now," Orion responded promptly. The moments stretched, tension palpable, before Orion relayed, "There are four automated gun arrays, waiting for you to enter visual range."

"Send coordinates to my Alpha team, and have them disable those guns," commands leapt from Cypher's lips.

In swift succession, the command was relayed and received. The aerocar remained a steadfast sentinel as several vehicles surged past, their movements as fluid and coordinated as a school of fish in treacherous waters. The brief symphony of gunfire that followed was both jarring and oddly melodic.

The airwaves had barely settled from the sharp report of their tactical success when Cypher, ever composed, cut through the renewed tension with military crispness. "Take us in," he commanded.

There was a palpable shift in the atmosphere as the fleet, moments before engaged in a destructive symphony, now heeded their leader's summons. Cypher's vehicle, a sleek vanguard of their determined intent, led the descent toward the facility. It landed with a whisper of suppressed engines, its dark silhouette merging with the shadows that clung to the abandoned structure like a shroud. The remaining cadre of armored vehicles, akin to a flight of steel phantoms, followed suit, forming a silent and formidable queue.

The oppressive silence of the underground chamber was punctuated only by the whisper of doors gliding open. As if part of a single entity awakening, the vehicles released their contingent of agents. They disembarked with practiced stealth, a spectral cascade of figures emerging into the half-light. Their presence was almost ethereal, starkly contrasting with the volley of gunfire that had preceded this moment of hallowed quiet.

The facility, once a bustling hub of activity, now stood before them—its entrances gaping, its secrets shrouded in darkness. Yet, the stillness was ephemeral. The agents, silhouetted in the dim light, began their advance with a precision that spoke of countless drills and unwavering dedication to the cause they served. They were the embodiment of Cypher's will, a force mobilized toward an objective visible only to them, in a world hidden far from the gaze of the sky.

An eerie stillness permeated the area, haunted by the echoes of recent human presence. This was the hallowed heart of The Veil's hidden domain, deserted as if its inhabitants had vanished into the mists, leaving behind an abandoned sanctum.

In the dim corridors of the facility, agents moved with purposeful strides, examining every space with the meticulous attention of hunters seeking elusive prey. They delved into the maze of sterile rooms and passages, their search methodical and relentless, like scavengers scouring a desolate battlefield for remnants of the past.

The scant light cast unsettling shadows that stretched along the walls, deepening the sense of desolation. The air was thick with the unspoken history of this forsaken place. Each agent, their face set in a mask of solemn determination, combed through the abandoned quarters, eyes vigilant for any sign of life or forsaken secrets.

One agent emerged from the network of rooms to report to Cypher, his steps echoing with a resolve as profound as the significance of his findings. "Report," Cypher demanded, his voice cutting through the stillness of the abandoned structure.

With a demeanor marked by both professionalism and a slight disquiet, the agent spoke. "All chambers have been emptied of essentials. There are no indications of inhabitants. However, we encountered one deceased individual in a sealed chamber, accessed only by forced entry. The individual was dressed in our guard's uniform," he reported, his tone carrying an undertone of concern over the discovery.

"Thank you. Dismissed," Cypher replied succinctly, his words slicing through the tense air. The agent gave a brief nod, his expression inscrutable, before retreating back into the labyrinthine complex of the facility.

"Orion. Did you learn anything from the guard about where they went?"

"No,: answered Orion. "He as kept locked and isolated from all discussions."

"Do you sense anything along the riverbeds?" Cypher's words were an icy demand, each syllable sharp with his mounting frustration.

"The drones have not explored extensively, and there are no new life signs," came the delayed reply, its lack of emotion somehow amplifying the gravity of the situation.

Cypher clenched his fists, the tactile feedback of his gloves humming softly against his skin. He was met only with riddles and echoes in a place that had been clearly abandoned in haste. The Veil had dispersed, becoming vapor in the wind, and the game—a high-stakes game of destinies and ideologies—had entered its next, inscrutable phase. Under a dispassionate moon and the eyes of a million invisible spectators woven into the fabric of the darkened sky, he made a silent vow: They would be found.

Minutes stretched on as more agents emerged from the corridors of the abandoned facility, each one appearing like a ghost, quietly conveying their findings to Cypher. His gaze seemed unfocused, peering through the walls and the earth itself, striving to unravel secrets buried deep or concealed within the cascade of data. "Orion, deploy all available drones into the riverbeds to cover all possible paths. Reprogram as needed, and ensure they remain within range of each other to maintain signal clarity. Their primary mission is to search for the fleeing Veil members, especially focusing their sensors on the biometrics of Elysa and Marek. Notify me immediately upon their detection."

The syllables had scarcely faded when Orion's crisp affirmation pierced the silence. "Acknowledged."

Cypher stood still for a few more seconds, his eyes transforming into deep wells of determination. He was acutely aware that the world he sought to shape, the reality he strived to forge, was inching closer to stark realization. With the mechanisms of surveillance and control within his grasp, his drones were poised to become the relentless agents of his pursuit.

In that heavy atmosphere, thick with the sense of impending events, Cypher envisioned his quarry—Elysa and Marek—winding their way through the riverbeds, perhaps briefly believing they had evaded capture. But as the drones would soon swarm the darkened paths, like a host of mechanical ravens taking flight, he understood that any semblance of their freedom would soon fracture, leaving only the cold realization of an unavoidable truth: They were the hunted. And he, the unyielding hunter.

♦♦♦

As if burdened by the invisible weight of their collective guilt and fear, the procession of Veil vehicles wound through the serpentine riverbeds. The path ahead was an intricate web of decisions, yet the pilot of the lead vehicle navigated through it without hesitation, as if guided by an infallible internal compass or possessing an intimate knowledge of the terrain bordering on the prophetic.

Anya, encased in the blinking luminescence of the control panel, clung determinedly to the tail of this snaking convoy. Though her eyelids drooped with the relentless tug of fatigue, she resisted its pull. Her will fortified with each passing kilometer; sleep was a luxury they could ill afford. Elysa and Marek, overwhelmed by exhaustion, had already succumbed to slumber in the backseat. Their soft, irregular breaths melded with the ambient hum of the vehicle's engines, weaving a lullaby that Anya stubbornly fought against.

Outside, the world was a shadowed theater, illuminated only by the fleeting swathes of ground captured in their headlights. In this unending gloom, Anya spotted a flicker, a spectral dot of light dancing in her rear-view mirror. Initially dismissed as a figment of her strained mind, it reappeared—a distant, shimmering echo in the black void behind them. This was no illusion; the soft glow was as real as the icy fear seizing her heart.

Her pulse quickened, infusing the air with palpable tension. "Elysa, Marek!" she called out, jolting them from their sleep. "We're not alone." Her words electrified the atmosphere, their eyes snapping open, instantly alert. Rebelling against protocol, she opened the communication channel to the leading vehicles. "Something's following us," she declared, her voice taut with urgency.

A growl of disapproval crackled through the speakers. "You were instructed to maintain radio silence during our journey!"

The response ignited a fire within her. "Listen, asshole," Anya retorted, her voice cutting through the tense silence like a sharpened blade. "Something's behind us, closing in fast."

A momentary void followed her words, heavy with unvoiced thoughts and latent fears. It lingered, cloying and oppressive, before dissipating into the realm of unknown outcomes.

Anya's eyes, reflected in the rear-view mirror, blazed with primal defiance. Her knuckles whitened as she gripped the steering wheel, her resolve unyielding. Sensing the impending threat, she decisively flipped on her vehicle's rear lights.

The sudden burst of light cut through the darkness with stark intensity. In that brief moment of illumination, the world behind her was revealed. Shadows transformed into tangible forms, and to Anya's escalating dread, those forms coalesced into three drones. They glided through the air with eerie smoothness, silent sentinels converging on her position. Their movement, synchronized and deliberate, spoke of a singular, shared objective.

Time seemed to stand still. Then, abruptly, one drone halted, hovering as if snared by an invisible force before fading back into the night's embrace.

The chase, however, was far from over. The remaining two drones, seemingly compensating for their companion's retreat, advanced with renewed determination. The landscape whirred past Anya, a blur of jagged rocks and sparse vegetation, yet her focus remained on the steadily narrowing gap between her vehicle and the pursuing machines.

Minutes passed, each thick with tension, as the drones narrowed the distance. The droning whir of the second drone gradually faded until it, too, ceased its pursuit, leaving only one. This lone drone pressed on, a relentless mechanical predator closing in on its prey.

Anya's heart pounded in her chest, her gaze flickering between the path ahead and the ominous figure in her rearview mirror. The final drone, now isolated, seemed to loom larger, its intent unmistakably clear. In this desolate expanse, a deadly ballet of chase and escape unfolded, a high-stakes game of nerve and strategy between human and machine.

♦♦♦

Within the dimly lit interior of Cypher's vehicle, the ambient lighting subtly shifted as new data streamed onto the onboard screens. His eyes, sharp and calculating, meticulously analyzed the data points shimmering before him. Agents in the trailing vehicles were similarly absorbed in their own realms of shadow and machinery, united in purpose yet each isolated within their mechanical confines.

"They've been spotted," intoned Orion's voice, its mechanical timbre lending an almost otherworldly quality. "Their coordinates have been transmitted to you."

The convoy reacted with seamless coordination, resembling a choreographed dance rather than a military operation. Each vehicle, akin to starlings in a murmuration, intuitively adjusted its trajectory, veering into the left branch of the serpentine riverbed. This collective maneuver, though unseen, was palpable within the dark confines of each cockpit.

"What do you see?" Cypher's voice, cold and incisive, cut through the tension.

"Multiple vehicles are moving together," Orion reported. "The one carrying Elysa and Marek, along with an unidentified third party, is at the rear of the formation."

A surge of triumph swelled in Cypher's chest. "Can you access their thoughts?"

After a brief pause, Orion responded, with what seemed like a hint of hesitation. "Insufficient power remains for such a task. The drones' power cells, already strained beyond their designed capacity, are depleting rapidly."

Feeling the weight of the moment, Cypher considered his options. After a moment of silent calculation, he issued his directive, his voice echoing within the confined space. "Focus on Marek. Use the remaining drone power on him."

"Command executed," confirmed Orion. Cypher could almost sense the shifting priorities within Orion's digital framework as it redirected the last vestiges of energy to fulfill this critical objective.

♦♦♦

Within the sable cocoon of the vehicle's interior, Anya's eyes were twin orbs of intensity, focused on the rear-view display where the faint glimmer grew larger with every passing second. The atmosphere in the car was taut, like a wire pulled to its snapping point. Time itself seemed to thicken, each moment elongating as the distance between them and the persistent glimmer diminished.

With a flourish, Anya swiped her hand across the tactile display, igniting a light at the rear of their vehicle that pierced the abyss like a lone star in a forsaken sky. The passengers' eyes widened as they witnessed the spectral silhouette of a State drone, its details sharply etched against the cavernous dark. It loomed closer, an ominous harbinger composed of steel and circuits.

Then, as if fate had cast its final, irrevocable die, a dazzling flash erupted from the drone. For an instant, the darkness relented, repelled by the incandescent flare. Almost as quickly, the drone shattered into a cascade of flames, its remnants plummeting earthward. The pursuit was over, but the aftermath of its searing light lingered in the air like an indelible scar.

"Marek!" Elysa's scream tore through the residual silence, her voice a raw wound in the vehicle's confined space. During the blinding flash, Marek's eyes had taken on a glassy sheen, as if some vital part of him had been cruelly extinguished. His body slackened, and if not for the seatbelt crisscrossing his chest, he would have collapsed onto the floor like a puppet severed from its strings.

The air was charged with unspoken questions, fears, and revelations. Elysa gazed at Marek's lifeless expression, her heart hammering a dissonant rhythm against her ribs. Anya gripped the controls, her fingers almost white from the tension, her mind racing with potential scenarios, each more dire than the last.

Elysa's fingers trembled as they unlatched Marek's seatbelt, her movements an intricate dance of urgency and care. She drifted to his side as if pulled by an unseen force, her hands instinctively searching for the weak throb of life in his carotid artery. It pulsed faintly beneath her touch, reminiscent of the dim glow of a dying star in the expansive firmament of the night.

"He's still alive, but in bad shape. He needs help," Elysa murmured, her voice a hushed blend of alarm and desperate hope teetering on the edge of despair.

"We cannot stop," Anya replied, her words slicing through the tension, tinged with the cruel calculus that survival often demands. "We don't know if more are coming." She glanced back quickly, confirming the absence of any pursuers. "He needs to hang on," she added in a subdued tone.

"All clear," Anya stated to the vehicles ahead.

"What happened?" inquired a voice from the convoy.

"I don't know," Anya admitted.

"We'll continue as is. Go to comm silence," came the final directive, urging them back into a wary silence.

Anya's eyes met Elysa's in the dim light, their gazes locked in an ephemeral standoff between pragmatism and compassion, like two competing futures hanging in a momentary balance. With a sigh that betrayed the weight of her choice, Elysa finally broke the silent deadlock and moved closer to Marek. Her body wrapped around his like a protective cloak, her arms the physical embodiment of an emotional fortress she was trying to construct around him.

As she held him, her thoughts spiraled inward, navigating the convoluted corridors of memory and emotion. It was as though she was mentally willing her life force into him, as if by some arcane alchemy their souls could mingle and fortify each other. This act of desperate intimacy was a silent plea expressed through the language of touch and proximity.

The vehicle continued to hum through the Stygian dark, a lone capsule hurtling through an uncertain and ominous future. Yet within that confined space, Elysa sat in hushed solemnity beside Marek, holding him as if her embrace could shield them from the inexorable march of their dystopian reality.

And so they continued, each absorbed in their private realms of thought and emotion, yet inexorably linked by the shared gravity of their plight—a microcosm of fragile humanity adrift in an ever-complicating world.

Chapter 30 - Return to Sender

The convoy of vehicles eased into the gaping embrace of a vast cavern, delving into its depths like pilgrims entering a subterranean cathedral. A singular aperture in the ceiling greeted them—not a breach, but an ordained window to the heavens. Through it, a column of sunlight cascaded like an ethereal staircase, its beams splintered by the jagged embrace of the overhanging rocks.

This diluted radiance pooled on the cavern floor, a celestial spotlight. It served as a gentle envoy from the exterior, weaving an opalescent tapestry across the dusky terrain. The subdued light lent the space a solemnity akin to an ancient chapel, with each stalactite a frozen teardrop and each stalagmite a monument to eons passed.

Before them, the cavern stretched, its vastness challenging earthly constraints, its edges swallowed by an obsidian shroud of darkness. Above, the roof arched majestically, a stony vault carved by nature's relentless hand, reaching for sublime heights and enveloping its visitors in a geological cradle that was as eternal as it was daunting.

This grand chamber, both immense and intimate with its dance of light and shadow, momentarily ensnared the weary travelers in a spell of awe. The lead vehicle settled gently in the cavern's central gloom, steering clear of the piercing sunbeam that broke through the far side.

Anya's vehicle ceased its hum at the edge of the gathering, sighing a mechanical breath of relief. "Keep Marek inside," she commanded, her voice carrying the gravity of a seasoned oracle before she disappeared into the shadows in search of aid.

Elysa stepped out, her muscles singing a silent ode to their exertion. She stretched, each movement a ballet of human resilience, seeking respite from the cramp of confinement. The air around her was unexpectedly welcoming, a blend of moisture and a temperate embrace.

Her gaze settled on a tranquil pool nestled at the cavern's end, a serene oasis embraced by the ancient earth. Surrounding it, hornbeam trees stood as vigilant guardians, their roots delicately penetrating the clear waters, drawing sustenance from the earth's hidden wells. Their branches reached toward the heavenly light pouring into their realm, each leaf basking in the light's embrace, absorbing life's nourishing nectar. The light that didn't feed the trees swept through the branches and leaves, glanced off the water, and ignited a spectacle of shimmering reflections that danced across the trees and rock walls in a celestial choreography. In this hidden retreat, time seemed to pause, the air itself holding in reverence to the sacred union of light, water, stone, and life's yearning.

The faces stepping out from the vehicles were etched with awe — a vivid tapestry of wonder, anxiety, and unspeakable relief. Eyes, weary from past ordeals or alight with eager anticipation, rose to meet the cavern's lofty ceiling before sweeping over its vast floor. They took in the stark contrast of dark voids against the indomitable pulse of life, showcased by the pool, the trees, and the life-affirming light.

For a brief instant, silence enveloped the group, as if any whisper could shatter the ethereal tranquility. Even the typically fidgety younger ones stood still, their demeanor reflecting a gravity beyond their years. The air was saturated with a sense of the sacred, as though they had trespassed into a realm of ancient worship.

Elysa's attention momentarily wandered from the cavern's magnificence, drawn irresistibly back to Marek — the enigmatic ally bound to her through silent understandings and shared dangers. As she turned, a surreal scene unfolded: Marek stepping from the vehicle, his figure merging with the cavern's grandeur.

Marek appeared before her, an enigmatic silhouette against the dim light, shrouded in mystery. A peculiar darkness enveloped him, most tangible in his intense gaze. Those eyes, which had once mirrored fragments of longing and hope, now bore the opaque sheen of midnight. His stare was a deep abyss, harboring secrets known only to him.

In the ensuing silence, Marek's hand lifted in a deliberate, fluid motion, drawing an arc through the air. His wrist tensed, and in a swift, precise movement, his palm met her temple.

The impact reverberated through the cavern, a tolling bell resonating not just through the air but deep within Elysa's psyche. Her vision fractured into dazzling fragments of reality, each fragment a distorted prism of colors and forms.

Darkness then descended, a suffocating velvet drape, engulfing Elysa in its solemn embrace and plunging her consciousness into the void of an unending night.

♦♦♦

Meanwhile, Anya's search for medical assistance wove through the assembly of vehicles and their inhabitants, her footsteps echoing against the cavern walls, defying her growing fatigue. Her muscles strained under the weight of urgency.

Her calls for help cut through the cavern's hushed atmosphere, seeking an answer in the maze of human emotions ranging from fear to weariness. Amidst the disarray, a woman holding a child with an angelic demeanor stepped forward, a beacon of hope amidst the uncertainty.

Responding to Anya's plea, the woman, with a voice heavy yet infused with empathy, directed her towards the convoy's lead. "A doctor? Go that way, towards the front," she suggested, her words floating above the murmur of the crowd, a guiding light in the gloom.

The cavern, filled with the scent of humanity intermingled with the earth's musk, offered a brief respite from the claustrophobia of their enclosed travels. The assembled throng, a image of fatigue and relief, found solace in the moment.

The air in the cavern vibrated with a child's cry, slicing through the fatigue like a siren's call. "Where's that car going?" the little voice, laden with wonder and apprehension, pierced the stillness, pointing behind Anya.

Anya's heart skipped a beat as she pivoted sharply. There, fading into a ghostly silhouette against the cavern's vastness, was their vehicle — their ark through the labyrinth of darkness. Its underlights flickered in a silent adieu before it began a slow, spectral pivot, aligning with the path they had desperately fled.

As it drifted into the cavern's embracing shadow, merging with the darkness until it disappeared, despair seized Anya. "No!" The cry tore from her, searing her throat, as her knees buckled, surrendering to the weight of her dread. She collapsed to the cavern floor. "No!" she cried again, her voice an anguished symphony that filled the cavern, echoing its pain.

Driven by a surge of desperate energy, Anya rose, her gaze hardened with resolve. Her body, fueled by a raw, urgent need, darted towards the nearest vehicle. She ran, each step a defiance of gravity, her silhouette barely touching the ground.

The first Veil member to intercept her was unprepared for the force she embodied. She struck him with the ferocity of a storm, sending him sprawling backwards in a clumsy ballet of defeat, his landing a harsh discord in the cavern's quiet.

Then, as another adversary positioned himself to halt her, Anya's desperation lent her movements precision and strength. She dodged, her elbow striking his solar plexus with the accuracy of a guided missile. He crumpled as she pressed forward—a lone warrior against the shadows.

When two Veil members moved with chilling coordination, their actions a grim dance of restraint, Anya found herself overpowered. One secured her arms in an unyielding grip, while the other immobilized her kicking legs.

Pinned to the cavern floor, a stage for their shared saga of survival and conflict, she was trapped. Her anguished cries cut through the silence, echoing off the cavern walls, a human note amidst the subtle sounds of water dripping in the shadows.

♦♦♦

Meanwhile, the autonomous vehicle glided along the riverbeds and through hidden alcoves, navigating its route with the unerring certainty of a machine. Devoid of human guidance, it moved with a ghostly calm, a lone entity threading through the dark veins of a disoriented world. The dashboard's glowing blue panels pulsed softly, the rhythmic light a synthetic heartbeat in the quiet, a glimpse of a future where complexity surpasses human control.

Inside, the tension was almost tangible, contrasting sharply with the vehicle's indifferent exterior. Marek sat in the front, his body tense, his gaze—a window to a soul recently altered—fixed intently on Elysa. She was unconscious in the back seat. Her hair, like tendrils of autumn fire, framed her face, highlighting her delicate beauty against the car's impersonal backdrop.

Marek, sitting before the figure sprawled in the backseat, seemed a stranger to the emotional burdens she bore for others. He had been transformed into a vessel, emptied of his own history and filled instead with a singular purpose dictated by another's design. Beside her, an enigmatic device, marked with cryptic symbols, rested quietly, charged with a foreboding significance.

His attention was drawn sharply to the device next to her. In this moment, the vehicle transformed into a crucible destined to shape the future. He understood, with a clarity untouched by doubt, that his task was to safeguard the unconscious woman and the ominous device, ensuring their delivery to the sterile grasp of Cypher.

The interior of the car was bathed in a shifting light, casting an eerie glow on the scene. Illuminated by the dashboard's alien light, Marek's face showed no sign of internal struggle. He had become an embodiment of pure intention.

Yet, deep within his altered consciousness, a vestige of his former self lingered—a mere whisper of the man he once was. This remnant fluttered like a moth trapped against a window, eternally seeking a light it could never attain. This elusive trace of humanity, buried deep within him, remained a testament to the complexity of the human spirit he once possessed.

Chapter 31 - Operation Veil

In the depths of an undisclosed location, a refuge of solemnity and subversion emerged amidst the world's indifference. It was an immense chamber constructed from concrete and steel, its scale almost mocking the fragility of human existence. Unyielding gray walls towered high, punctuated only by the flicker of numerous holographic displays showcasing images and locations of Veil members worldwide.

In the dim light, hushed conversations unfolded, their words dissipating into the room's chilly air, yet carrying a significance heavier than the imposing walls surrounding them. The space felt less like a mere room and more like a living, breathing entity—a collective embodiment of willpower and clandestine rebellion, resonating with a subdued yet indomitable life force.

Hundreds of Veil members, clad in utilitarian attire that belied the complexity of their operations, congregated around ethereal holograms. Their faces, bathed in the spectral glow, each resembled a tableau of unwavering focus and contained emotion. The holograms danced with a kaleidoscope of imagery and data, pulsating like a digital heart within this revolutionary command center.

Dominating the room, Thomas's hologram presided over this quasi-sacred chamber. His face, austere and incisive, embodied their collective resolve. A reverent hush descended upon the assembly, punctuated only by the ambient hum of technology and occasional murmurs of urgent consultation.

Anya was led into this charged atmosphere, her hands bound in shackles holding more symbolic meaning than actual restraint. She moved through the space like a fallen angel, escorted by several stern-faced Veil members as a symbol of betrayal. Her eyes, however, harbored no remorse—only the fierce clarity of desperate determination. As she was ushered into the heart of the chamber, a wave of hisses and contemptuous shouts erupted from the crowd, each utterance a jagged stone aimed at her integrity.

The room erupted into a cacophony of indignation, with accusations and speculations swirling like a gathering tempest. The escalating tension was almost tangible, a maelstrom threatening to unravel the very fabric of the group's unity. Just as it seemed chaos would reach an irreversible point, a voice boomed across the room, carrying the weight of authority and the experience of countless battles.

"Silence!" Thomas's voice boomed, a commanding decree more than a mere utterance, filling the room as if flowing from an unseen mountain. His voice resonated from the great holographic display, its intangible digital form somehow imbuing it with almost corporeal authority. The room fell into stillness as though struck by lightning, every eye turning toward the luminous avatar of their leader.

The holographic Thomas appeared to scan the room, its pixels rearranging into a scrutinizing gaze. The heavy silence, laden with the unspoken complexities of duty and the fragile hope of an oppressed people, hung in the air like the charged calm before a storm. Time itself seemed to hold its breath, anticipating the words that would shatter the impasse.

They stood, captives of the moment, entangled in a web of conflicting loyalties and aspirations. All eyes were fixed on Thomas, awaiting the pronouncement that would determine not only Anya's fate but also the future of The Veil and everyone in that dimly lit sanctuary — a sanctuary that, for that moment, felt like the fulcrum of history.

Thomas's voice, resonant and commanding, turned towards Anya. "Due to your involvement, a State spy infiltrated our ranks, placing the lives of everyone in this room, and the entire Veil, at risk." These words triggered shouts and curses, punctuating the atmosphere like verbal shrapnel. Faces reddened, eyes narrowed into slits, and fists clenched, some trembling uncontrollably, mirroring the storm of indignation brewing within.

"Release her restraints," Thomas ordered. A wave of astonishment swept through the room, metaphorically brushing against Anya's raw wrists. Members of The Veil, previously united in resentment, exchanged glances of disbelief, questioning their convictions.

Then came Thomas's staggering admission: "I apologize to Anya and everyone here for using her as a pawn to ensure this outcome." The words cast the room into a stunned silence so profound it seemed to muffle the collective heartbeat of those present. Anya's eyes widened, her turmoil mirrored in the sea of bewildered expressions. "Elysa is now en route to the Tower, expected to approach Orion's central systems, closer than we could have ever achieved otherwise."

"She is alone and helpless!" Anya interjected, her voice laced with concern and anger.

"Not as helpless as you think," Thomas replied. "She will have help from within."

Thomas continued to weave his narrative of nightmares. Each revelation added another layer of existential dread to the already heavy atmosphere. "We have discovered that The Watchers took Elysa's dearest friend and manipulated his memories to serve their will," he revealed, his voice carrying a somber undertone.

The audience sat in stunned silence, their hearts pounding like funeral drums echoing within their chests. "The Watchers now possess the capability not only to reshape a person's memories, as they did with Elysa in her childhood, but also to erase existing memories and replace them with new ones. Orion can perform this manipulation on anyone at any time." Murmurs of horrified realization rippled through the crowd, the very foundation of their rebellion seeming to crumble before their eyes.

"In addition," Thomas's voice lowered, burdened by the significance of his next words, "Orion can completely extract all memories from a person, effectively ending their life in the process. No one is safe." A collective shiver of dread swept through the room, rendering the steel beams and concrete walls feeble in the face of the overwhelming threat they now confronted.

From somewhere in the assembly, a woman's voice rose in anguished desperation: "What can we do?" It was the question pulsating in the hearts of every soul present in that chamber.

"Is this the end for us?" another voice implored, charging the air with a palpable urgency that coursed through the room.

Thomas's holographic image, focusing on the gathered rebels, conveyed a blend of sorrow and determination in his eyes. The room collectively held its breath, awaiting an answer that could shape not only the course of their rebellion but also the very texture of their fear and hope.

In that pause, that fragile pocket of silence, every soul grasped the weight of what hung in the balance. Amid the sea of anxious faces and the pervasive glow of holographic screens, Thomas's voice echoed like a lament, a dirge for a world slipping away. "For those of you residing beyond the walls of Cyronis, you may be safe for now, but that safety is ephemeral. For those within the city, you are the most vulnerable, with no lasting sanctuaries to shield you." His words transcended mere utterances; they were dark waves of apprehension flowing through the cavernous chamber, reaching into the virtual realms that connected every corner of Cyronis.

Seeming to be absorbed into the concrete and steel that enveloped them, his declaration saturated the room with an almost unbearable gravity. Faces grew pallid, eyes widened in disbelief, and trembling lips mirrored a reality too distressing to articulate. The already heavy atmosphere, laden with disclosures and reproaches, congealed into a tangible fog of hopelessness. Even those in virtual attendance felt the room's somber mood permeate their spaces, the dread staining pixels and data streams alike.

Thomas's next statement shattered the silence. "This is why The Veil has meticulously planned one final assault, targeting the Nexus Tower and Orion himself." The words struck the assembly like a lightning bolt—sudden, electrifying, yet not entirely unforeseen. A complex blend of hope and fear replaced the dread. It was not sheer relief but a mixture darker and more intricate, potentially leading to unparalleled triumph or catastrophic defeat.

The walls seemed to resonate with the implications of Thomas's declaration. For a moment, it felt as if the steel beams were the collective body's sinews, the concrete floor their shared foundation, and the holographic screens their interconnected nervous system. All were united by the gravity of a looming future, full of sound and fury, signifying everything.

Even as a hologram, Thomas's gaze seemed to establish contact with every soul present, physically or digitally. The collective destiny rested not just on his shoulders but on all who dared resist. In that moment, balanced between despair and audacity, the assembly understood this was not an ordinary turning point; it was an existential crossroads with no retreat.

"Yesterday, I issued a command for all Veil members to converge at their designated sanctuaries," Thomas declared. His holographic countenance seemed uncannily real as it surveyed the assembly. Affirmative nods rippled through the holograms, signaling compliance. "These sanctuaries, shielded from Orion's gaze and influence, exist thanks to Min-Jae, Naomi, and Kenji."

Beneath Thomas's hologram, the trio stood, illuminated by the ethereal glow. Their faces bore solemn yet proud expressions, aware of their crucial role. Whispers of gratitude rippled sporadically, echoing off the cold, unyielding walls. The moment held a sacred quality—an ephemeral unity of purpose and spirit—as eyes turned to those who had carved out their fragile sanctuary from Orion's pervasive grip.

Then, Thomas's voice deepened, casting a chilling solemnity akin to a cold winter wind sweeping through barren lands. "But this too is temporary," he intoned, sending a shiver through the room.

The words hung heavily, each syllable like a drop of icy truth. The room's complex tapestry of hope, dread, and defiance seemed to warp around Thomas's utterance, morphing into a dark foreboding. Faces of Min-Jae, Naomi, and Kenji subtly tightened, reflecting the realization that their efforts were but fragile defenses against an oncoming storm.

The walls seemed to resonate with the implications of Thomas's declaration. For a moment, it felt as if the steel beams were the collective body's sinews, the concrete floor their shared foundation, and the holographic screens their interconnected nervous system. All were united by the gravity of a looming future, full of sound and fury, signifying everything.

Even as a hologram, Thomas's gaze seemed to establish contact with every soul present, physically or digitally. The collective destiny rested not just on his shoulders but on all who dared resist. In that moment, balanced between despair and audacity, the assembly understood this was not an ordinary turning point; it was an existential crossroads with no retreat.

"Yesterday, I issued a command for all Veil members to converge at their designated sanctuaries," Thomas declared. His holographic countenance seemed uncannily real as it surveyed the assembly. Affirmative nods rippled through the holograms, signaling compliance. "These sanctuaries, shielded from Orion's gaze and influence, exist thanks to Min-Jae, Naomi, and Kenji."

Beneath Thomas's hologram, the trio stood, illuminated by the ethereal glow. Their faces bore solemn yet proud expressions, aware of their crucial role. Whispers of gratitude rippled sporadically, echoing off the unyielding walls. The moment held a sacred quality—an ephemeral unity of purpose and spirit—as eyes turned to those who had carved out their fragile sanctuary from Orion's pervasive grip.

Then, Thomas's voice deepened, casting a chilling solemnity akin to a cold winter wind sweeping through barren lands. "But this too is temporary," he intoned, sending a shiver through the room.

The words hung heavily, each syllable like a drop of icy truth. The room's complex tapestry of hope, dread, and defiance seemed to warp around Thomas's utterance, morphing into a dark foreboding. Faces of Min-Jae, Naomi, and Kenji subtly tightened, reflecting the realization that their efforts were but fragile defenses against an oncoming storm.

"Most Veil members will serve as a distraction, drawing agents away from the Nexus Tower," Thomas continued, his voice anchoring the tide of emotions. Faces around the room set into masks of determined resolve, each person understanding the possible sacrifice. Yet, their eyes conveyed acceptance—a willingness to pay the price for freedom.

"Anya, you will spearhead a small team's infiltration of the Nexus Tower amid the chaos," Thomas announced, his voice resounding with the urgency of the task. "Your objective is to locate Elysa and ensure her passage to Orion's core."

At these words, a surge of surprise washed over Anya's features, momentarily clouding her face with the shadows of past ordeals. Yet, in the blink of an eye, her expression transformed, igniting with a fusion of surprise, apprehension, and a tangible, electric readiness. Within her, it was as if a door, long bolted shut and forgotten, had suddenly been flung open, flooding her being with brilliant, unexpected light.

She stood ready, her resolution resolute and unmistakable to all who dared hold her gaze. In her eyes, they beheld the mythical phoenix reborn, ascending from the ashes of innumerable tragedies and deceptions. In that gaze, they saw more than resolve; they saw a defiance strong enough to challenge the towering entity that was The Watchers.

The atmosphere thickened with a blend of dread and excitement. The room's collective gaze settled on Anya, but she bore it with unwavering stillness, like an ancient pillar against an untamed sea. The ambient light cast her in a heroic silhouette, a lone warrior contrasted by light and shadow. Her posture embodied the strength of a drawn bow, her eyes the focus of a huntress. In that moment, a silent covenant was formed, resonating in every heart and reverberating through the walls of their subterranean refuge.

Thomas's holographic form shimmered with resolute intensity, casting an ethereal glow across the room. His voice, steady and imbued with unwavering conviction, resonated through the air. "Today," he declared, "we stand at the threshold of a new era. We are united in our purpose: to pierce the looming darkness, banish the specter of Orion, and reclaim our freedom from the clutches of an authoritarian state." His image flickered, pixels dancing like stars in a twilight sky. "The spark ignited here, in this very room, will kindle a blaze of hope, liberation, and freedom." As his visage dissolved completely, leaving behind a trail of luminescent echoes, the room fell into hushed anticipation. Every soul present sensed the weight and significance of his promise, standing on the precipice of history, poised between the daunting specters of ruin and the bright promise of salvation.

Chapter 32 - The Chancellor

Elysa's awareness returned in languid waves, each pulse carrying the haunting image of Marek's hand descending, his betrayal palpable. Her head pounded with the intensity of a storm, each beat a lightning strike to her senses. How had Marek, once a cornerstone of her past, morphed into the harbinger of her current despair? It was a grotesque twist of fate, a nightmarish distortion that drained her faith in the permanence of human bonds.

Her eyes, fighting through the haze, adapted to the ambient light. She found herself in an opulent setting, reminiscent of a tycoon's sanctum. Every detail whispered supremacy: the unnaturally soft carpet seemed spun from dreams, and the walls, a fusion of rich wood and liquid metal, glowed softly.

Bound by electronic shackles, her hands were tied behind her in what would have otherwise been a luxurious chair. Now, it was nothing more than an upholstered cage. Before her stood a desk of unimaginable grandeur, a monolith carved from wood so rare it seemed mythological, its surface mirroring the serene glow of a moonlit lake. This desk radiated a history so deep that it was as if it had been shaped from a tree that had outlived empires and witnessed the whims of deities. It bore minimal adornment, hosting only a crystal paperweight and a jeweled dagger—tokens of its owner's power and taste.

Across the room, Zircon observed her with an air of theatrical composure, embodying a contemporary Mephistopheles perched within an armchair that transcended mere furniture to become a symbol of corporate dominion. This chair, absurdly opulent and cloaked in the hide of a creature so rare its existence was almost mythical, cradled him. His demeanor, an effortless display of authority; his gaze, sharp and inscrutable, appraised her with the discernment of a jeweler eyeing a raw diamond, pondering its transformation under his skilled hands.

In a room where grandeur melded with unchecked opulence, the desk at which Zircon presided declared its dominance. Its centerpiece, a cubic artifact once possessed by Elysa, bathed in a subdued light, seemed to drink in the room's dim glow and whisper secrets back into the shadowed splendor that framed it.

Elysa felt relief when she noticed the absence of the gem from the desk.

As her eyes fixed upon the Quantrix, a surge of panic accelerated her heartbeat, disrupting its steady rhythm with erratic palpitations. She shifted uncomfortably, her movements constrained by the chair's restraints, as she futilely attempted to draw the Chancellor's attention away from her true intent - to reassure herself that the gem was still secured around her neck.

From his seat, which bore resemblance to a throne, Zircon observed her with amusement crossing his features. "Struggling is pointless," he said, his voice a blend of dismissal and caution. "You're only going to injure yourself." His expression was a brief dance of curiosity and satisfaction.

Thankfully, Elysa's still felt the chain about her neck, and the gem pressed against her chest.

No longer fighting her bindings, Elysa locked eyes with Zircon. A tumultuous exchange of emotions—tinged with fear, defiance, and a haunting sense of recognition—flowed between them, as if unveiling the depths of their beings. The encounter seemed to warp time itself, the opulent walls drawing closer, becoming sentient spectators to the unfolding human drama.

The air was charged, heavy with an anticipation that echoed through the chamber as Zircon's hand gravitated towards the Quantrix. With a gesture that blended curiosity with reverence, he lifted it, his eyes traversing its luminescent surface. "So, this is the artifact your father crafted, the one you believe will dismantle my dominion over Orion," he mused, his tone imbued with a mix of respect and skepticism.

Elysa, enveloped in a cloak of silence, fortified herself against his inquiries. Their eyes engaged in a wordless battle, a clash of resolve where silent assertions met with the ferocity of unsheathed swords. Her gaze, radiant with defiance, steadfastly met his—blue flames defying the encroaching shadows, her innermost thoughts veiled from his prying gaze.

"Really now," Zircon began, settling back into the embrace of his opulent chair, which seemed out of place against the backdrop of the ethereal screens spilling forth data of untold importance. The chair creaked, echoing his boundless ambition. "Did you presume you could infiltrate my stronghold, aiming to liberate Orion from my grasp? Overthrow me? Such folly...a trait seemingly inherited from your father."

The term "folly" hung in the air, a taunt saturated with disdain, an emblem of his perceived superiority and unassailable position.

In that instant, the room seemed to contract, its metallic and concrete surfaces whispering tales of defiance quelled under an oppressive regime. Yet, beneath the imposing shadow cast by Zircon and the weight of his declaration, a resilient spark within Elysa coalesced, primed with the potential energy of her unwavering determination.

Surveying the expanse, Elysa registered the absence of guards, her observation birthing a mixture of bewilderment and calculated assessment. "No guards?" she queried, her voice a blend of surprise and strategic consideration.

Zircon's reply came as a languid, contemptuous smile, his gaze alight with a blend of amusement and contempt. "You pose no danger," he taunted, his laughter cold, showing his derision. His self-assuredness swelled, underpinned by a conviction in his own invulnerability. "Should I wish it, they will answer my summons instantly," he declared, his words echoing the authority he wielded.

His attention then drifted back to the cube. He manipulated it gently, his actions reflective of a quest to decode its mysteries, to understand the essence hidden within.

The ambiance of the room underwent a shift as the door swung open, heralding Vilkas's entrance. "I came as swiftly as I could," he announced, his bow skillfully threading the needle between respect and assertiveness, his deep voice softly reverberating in the expansive room. A brief, detached glance swept over Elysa before he refocused on the Chancellor.

"Take this," Zircon ordered, his voice firm as he passed the Quantrix into Vilkas's hands, which trembled slightly under the weight of the command.

"I'm ready to start the analysis immediately," Vilkas offered, his gaze locked on the cube's enigmatic symbols, drawn into its mystery.

"No," came Zircon's sharp retort, a command brooking no opposition. "Destroy it. Its purpose is clear to me, and it holds no value."

After a moment's hesitation, "Understood," Vilkas conceded, a rare crack in his usually stoic demeanor showing a hint of regret at the opportunity slipping through his fingers. With a sense of finality, he turned to leave. The sound of the door closing behind him echoed ominously, a grim punctuation to an irrevocable act.

Elysa, sensing the Quantrix's departure, felt the office's walls inching inward, a contemporary trap compressing her spirit, if not her form. In her mind's eye, she frantically canvassed for any semblance of an escape plan.

Zircon, settled in his ornate chair, met Elysa's gaze with an unyielding intensity. "Your father possessed a remarkable intellect," he began, each word deliberate, "It's unfortunate he did not share my level of ambition." The atmosphere in the room thickened with tension.

Elysa, despite the constraints binding her, radiated an undiminished spirit. "Why did you take my parents?" she demanded, her tone infused with a fiery determination.

He scrutinized her closely, as though measuring her worth. "Your father's invention, Orion, was extraordinary. I required his expertise to further its development, but he was uncooperative. And as for John, he vanished on the very night your father absconded with John's module."

"So, you targeted John in the marketplace, knowing he would be there," she inferred.

"Correct," Zircon admitted, a flicker of frustration passing over his face. "But then The Veil interfered, thwarting my plans."

"And what were your plans for him?" Elysa pressed on, her quest for understanding cutting through the fog of ambiguity.

"Vilkas had nearly equaled the achievements of your father and John, making John's participation redundant," Zircon explained, his attention momentarily captured by a crystal paperweight on his desk. He picked it up, casting prisms of light around the room. "Our ultimate goal was to enhance Orion with John's intellectual prowess. We sought to integrate his cognitive essence into the AI," he disclosed, his expression darkening with a sinister glee. "Orion is engineered to absorb human memories, emotions, and consciousness, with the aim to become more sentient. It needs minds, extraordinary minds."

A chill of horror swept over Elysa. "And my father? Did you really think he would willingly contribute to this, to become part of your scheme?"

Zircon's expression mixed disdain with reluctant respect. "Yes, I believed in his capabilities and hoped he would align with our vision," he admitted, his voice tinged with a chilling menace.

In that instant, Elysa perceived the horrifying reality—a void where moral principles were devoured by the god-like ambitions for technology. Her father's role, her forced involvement—it all converged into a grim tableau of human aspiration gone unchecked, the daunting promise and peril of AI.

The office seemed a physical extension of Zircon's sinister will. Yet, amidst her turmoil, Elysa discovered a newfound resolve. She remained physically constrained, yet her spirit was unyielding; she felt besieged, yet far from vanquished.

Facing Zircon and the spectral dread posed by Orion's potential, Elysa recognized the grave legacy bequeathed to her—a dilemma her father must have grappled with, and a daunting future that she alone might prevent or realize. Her gaze met Zircon's with renewed intensity, a silent acknowledgment that their conflict was set to escalate, opening a new, fraught chapter.

"Once Richard defied us, I dispatched agents to apprehend your parents that night—the very night you were also taken," Zircon admitted, his voice cutting through the tension. The atmosphere, laden with his confession, grew oppressively dense.

"You murdered them," Elysa accused, her voice a mix of accusation and seeking confirmation, as she tried to assemble the somber narrative.

Zircon's chuckle, low and ominous, reverberated against the walls, a sound chillingly devoid of humanity. "Not quite accurate. I compelled your father to enhance Orion, using the safety of your mother and yourself as leverage." Each word fell like a drop of poison, tainting the air with its venomous intent.

"Your father was the mind behind the black vial you discovered in the marketplace," Zircon revealed, his voice a monotone harbinger of dread. The mention of the vial, now linked to her father, sent a wave of cold apprehension over Elysa. She felt the oppressive weight of this revelation, the room's atmosphere turning frigid, mirroring the coldness of Zircon's disclosures. "This vial," he elaborated, devoid of any emotion, "can absorb a person's consciousness entirely." His gaze, icy and detached, seemed to cut through the distance, touching the very core of Elysa's being.

"Regrettably," he added, his tone clinical, betraying no sense of the horror his words conveyed, "this process terminates the individual's life, leaving nothing behind." The statement lingered, a macabre witness to the vial's ghastly purpose—a tool designed to consume the essence of a person until only a shell remained.

In Elysa's imagination, the vial morphed from a mere object into a fiendish invention, its seemingly harmless appearance masking an unspeakable horror. Zircon had revealed not just a device but a monstrosity born from the darkest recesses of human innovation, capable of stripping away the very soul.

This revelation opened a portal to a nightmarish domain where science and insanity perform a grim dance. The chill of understanding ran through Elysa, the cold of the room now a physical manifestation of the dread that the vial represented. It stood as a dark symbol of the lengths to which Zircon and his apparatus would go in their pursuit of utter supremacy.

Confronted with the grim reality of the atrocities enabled by such technology, Elysa faced Zircon—a man who had surrendered to the most sinister uses of power and science. The gravity of her discovery rooted her in place, a solitary figure engulfed by the dim light, burdened with the heavy truth of her father's coerced legacy.

"Unable to find John, we presented your father with an ultimatum: return the stolen module or we would use the vial on your mother," Zircon said, absentmindedly tapping the desk with the crystal, its sound unnervingly resonant in the spacious room. His nonchalant malice lent him an almost spectral presence, a figure more phantom than human, shrouded in darkness.

"Richard claimed the module was destroyed, that its workings eluded him." Zircon's voice, cold and detached, mirrored the unyielding steel surrounding them. "I didn't believe him. After his final refusal, we forced him to witness as your mother was claimed by the vial's contents and then assimilated by Orion," he stated, his words slicing the silence with chilling precision.

The air grew heavy with the gravity of Zircon's admission, a tangible manifestation of evil that seemed to leach warmth from the room. Elysa remained motionless, her pulse racing as she confronted the grim reality of her mother's demise—a truth so harrowing it threatened to crush her under its weight. The claustrophobic room seemed to constrict further, an accomplice to the horror Zircon had unveiled.

"We then used you as leverage," Zircon added, his voice tinged with a vile satisfaction. His declaration was a weight, dragging Elysa down into a deeper abyss of despair, a mere instrument in their scheme to bend her father to their will.

"The risk to you shattered him," Zircon remarked, his voice laced with a self-satisfied edge. "You were confined here, tasked with Data Mining. Constant surveillance was our method of control. We ensured your father saw you every day on a screen at his workstation—a relentless reminder of the stakes involved."

A complex emotion briefly crossed Zircon's face—perhaps a blend of respect, regret, or even jealousy—before he set the paperweight down.

"He's still alive, then? He completed the enhancements?" Elysa's voice was a whisper, laden with a fragile thread of hope.

"No," Zircon replied, his voice tinged with a trace of regret. "As I mentioned, Vilkas eventually finished the work, but it wasn't without its challenges. Your father's designs were intricate and enigmatic, difficult to decipher and replicate." Elysa's expression tightened, her emotions oscillating between hope and fear. "What became of my father?"

Zircon hesitated, looking down briefly before locking eyes with Elysa again. He took a deep breath, bracing himself. "He toiled for years, always with an eye on you, hidden in the depths of his brilliance. Then one day," he said, his voice dropping to a whisper, "he activated some machinery, gave a self-assured smile as he often did, and allowed Orion to integrate him entirely."

He paused, reflecting. "We failed to adequately oversee Richard's work," Zircon admitted, his voice resonating in the quiet of his office. The dim lighting threw his face into relief, highlighting a rare moment of vulnerability.

"We believed he would follow our directives, considering the stakes for you," he continued, his gaze wandering as if caught in a rare moment of reflection. A subtle spark in his eyes betrayed his analytical nature, always planning, always in control. Yet, there was a hint of something more—an uncommon acknowledgment of a lapse.

"It became clear later that his efforts extended beyond Orion, to something far more significant," Zircon reflected, his tone deepening with contemplation. This revelation lingered, casting a solemn weight across the room, further intensifying the already charged atmosphere.

"And thanks to you, we're aware of the device and its intended purpose," Zircon said, fixing Elysa with a sharp gaze.

He continued, his voice momentarily faltering before regaining its steadiness, "What baffles me is how he managed to construct it undetected, smuggle it from the Tower, and hide it in your home; and how he predicted it would ultimately find its way to you after all these years." His face revealed a blend of curiosity and irritation, indicating that this deviation from his otherwise flawless schemes both fascinated and frustrated him.

In this instance, Zircon's customary air of invincibility seemed to waver, as if challenged by Richard's creativity. His hand idly toyed with the desk's edge, showing an unusual sign of restlessness, a rare crack in the facade of a man unaccustomed to being outsmarted.

The room's ambiance tightened around Zircon's words, echoing their significance. The lighting threw stark shadows across the decor, casting the room in an eerie luminescence. However, this light failed to dispel the darkness crowding Elysa's thoughts, a tapestry of grief, revelation, and unresolved questions.

Staring into Zircon's eyes, deep wells of darkness, she saw the depth of corruption possible within the human soul. "You're a monster!" Elysa shot back, her voice laden with disgust and a sense of helplessness. Labeling him seemed to momentarily reduce his enormity.

Zircon's reaction was a grotesque smile, an appalling distortion of amusement that transformed his expression into something hideous. "I've endured worse accusations," he remarked with a ghastly pleasure, as if he relished the taste of human despair. "And for that, they paid with their lives."

His declarations lingered with a toxic resonance, tainting the atmosphere. In this moment of dark unveiling, Elysa not only perceived the vast expanse of Zircon's malevolence but also the immense burden her father must have shouldered within this ethical nightmare. Looking at Zircon, she felt an unprecedented surge of anger and determination, recognizing she was not merely a victim of her family's sorrowful legacy but potentially its avenger.

A fleeting shadow in her peripheral vision momentarily captured Elysa's attention—a ghostly reflection in one of the windows. As Zircon's attention momentarily turned away from her, she took the opportunity to quickly glance in the direction of the window. She found nothing; the glass was clear.

"Something wrong?" Zircon's voice cut the stillness, as he caught her staring out at the passing clouds.

Elysa met his gaze firmly, masking the whirlwind of thoughts within her. Then, inexplicably, the restraints around her wrists began to loosen as if undone by an invisible touch, freeing her from their grip. A rush of adrenaline filled her as she silently caught the restraints just before they could fall and betray her liberation. She gripped them tightly, a silent symphony of heartbeats in her ears. It felt like an intervention from some unseen ally, a spectral savior in her moment of need.

In the domain of Zircon's watchful eyes, within this stronghold of control and observation, Elysa found herself with an unforeseen advantage. The mysterious release of her bonds offered a flicker of hope, an opportunity to shift the balance. Her mind whirred with strategies as she held Zircon's stare, an unspoken confrontation playing out between them, each aware that the stakes had subtly shifted within the confines of this power-charged room.

"Where is Marek?" Elysa's voice, fraught with emotion, cut through the oppressive silence of the chamber, each syllable trembling with urgency.

Zircon's face twisted in disdain, his voice laced with derision. "Marek," he spat, his features contorting in disgust, "involved himself in your father's plans—plans that were nothing more than whispers and shadows. He protected the Quantrix, knowing it—and you—were central to bringing it here. Yet, despite his efforts, here you stand with it. I assume this wasn't part of their grand scheme." After a brief pause, Zircon issued an order, "Orion, inform her of Marek's whereabouts," his tone cutting through the heavy air.

An unsettling hush enveloped the room, a heavy, anticipatory silence.

"Orion," Zircon urged again, a note of irritation in his voice, "where is Marek?"

Orion's reply was a halting, fragmented echo, "M...Marek is...with me." The words emerged with difficulty, as though the AI struggled against an invisible barrier.

A crease of concern appeared on Zircon's forehead. "Orion, explain your malfunction," he demanded, his frustration mingling with a trace of concern.

"The conflict with The Veil...is creating...disturbances," Orion managed, its voice distorted by glitches and static, hinting at a deeper turmoil within the system.

Zircon's steadfast demeanor wavered, revealing an undercurrent of alarm as Orion's fragmented sentences permeated the tense atmosphere. His usual mask of control slipped, showing signs of unease. "What battle?" he demanded, his voice a mixture of incredulity and apprehension, the idea of a conflict encroaching upon his domain both inconceivable and disconcerting.

His gaze swept the room, searching for any sign or explanation, as if the very walls might offer clarity. The air thickened with his growing disquiet, his aura of dominance briefly disrupted by the sudden intrusion of chaos on his doorstep. For a fleeting moment, Zircon, the unassailable

Chancellor, seemed mortal, his composure rattled by the unexpected news of turmoil near his stronghold.

Meanwhile, Elysa was struck by the grim reality of Marek's fate as relayed by Orion. The words hung heavily, each one a solemn toll resonating with grim finality. Pain and resolve etched across her face as she fought against the anguish and determination warring within her. The revelation, delivered with stark impersonality, carved profound grief into her expression. Her eyes, now pools of sorrow and defiance, caught the harsh artificial light, glimmering with the onset of tears.

A fierce resolve coursed through her, her entire being alight with righteous indignation. Her glare, fierce and unwavering, challenged Zircon, her stance ready and defiant. Clutching the restraints with newfound purpose, she prepared to confront her captor.

With a scream that shattered the silence, Elysa voiced her anguish and defiance, the sound slicing through the room's tension. This raw, potent outcry momentarily breached Zircon's armor of detachment, causing him to flinch, a rare crack in his usually imperturbable façade.

Empowered by her cathartic outburst, Elysa sprang from her seat, her movement tempestuous, as she hurdled over the desk toward Zircon. Clasping the restraints with intent, she struck his face with their hardened edges, each blow a declaration of defiance. Abandoning the restraints, her gaze locked onto the crystal paperweight on Zircon's desk—a symbol of structure and control now repurposed as a tool of vengeance. Grasping it firmly, her hands stained with the effort of her rebellion, she wielded it with a blend of fear, adrenaline, and raw determination.

The crystal connected with Zircon's forehead in a resounding strike, the sound sharp and ominous. The paperweight, once an emblem of Zircon's authority, transformed under Elysa's wrathful grip. His features twisted in agony as the crystal inflicted its punishment, a stark reminder of his vulnerability. The room filled with the scent of blood and exertion as she delivered blow upon blow, her actions painting Zircon's face with the brutal artistry of her anger. Blood sprayed, darkening the carpet and marking Elysa's visage with the visceral evidence of her reprisal.

Zircon collapsed, a defeated heap on the floor, his once proud demeanor extinguished, leaving him unrecognizable. Standing over him, she breathed heavily, the physical manifestation of her rage apparent in her clenched, bloodied fists—free at last.

A raw smile broke across her blood-streaked face, symbolizing her liberation from restraint and the unmasking of her deepest emotions. In this moment of triumph, she recognized a profound transformation within herself. The person she had been—restrained, vulnerable—was reshaped by her own fierce resolve into something more formidable and unyieldingly powerful.

This act of rebellion, unfamiliar yet invigorating, resonated within her, a symphony of past, present, and the untold future. The immediate crisis passed, her attention now turned towards the door, her mind quickly adapting to the next phase of her journey. Beyond lay a labyrinth of dangers and discoveries, the threshold between her shattered past and an uncertain future.

She stepped forward, her hand deftly seizing the dagger from the desk. Her boots moved silently over the plush carpet, betraying no weight, as if she were a specter of vengeance itself. Her entire being seemed attuned to an acute awareness, every sense honed, each cell vibrating in harmony.

Her fingers hesitated for a moment above the door handle, then grasped it. The cold metal felt like a sliver of winter against her skin, yet her grip was firm, determined. Turning the handle, she found it surprisingly compliant, almost as if it recognized her resolve. The door opened quietly, revealing the corridor stretched out before her.

She surveyed the hallway with a critical eye, alert for any movement or sign of guards. But, intriguingly, the corridor was empty, an unoccupied stretch that seemed to await her passage. A thought struck her.

Why would Zircon need guards here? she pondered. In a tower filled to the brim with his adherents, each unknowingly acting as a pillar of his power, the absence of guards made a strange sense.

Below her lay Zircon's empire of watchfulness and submission, a vertical city alive with the gazes and whispers of those under his sway. This human barrier was his true defense, a living moat of allegiance that isolated him from any threat. The empty corridor underscored the dictator's conceit.

Releasing the door handle, the residual coldness from the metal was a fleeting reminder of the hubris that had filled Zircon's office. As the door shut gently behind her, Elysa found herself alone in the hallway, yet enveloped by a profound sense of unseen solidarity, as if the very air whispered of covert alliances and silent support.

Moving with determined steps toward the elevator at the room's end, Elysa held the dagger tightly. The soft clicks of her boots on the marble floor contrasted sharply with the tension that charged the air. As she neared, the elevator doors parted silently, revealing Chen Wei within the elevator's stark, metallic confines. His expression was menacing, a grim smile revealing a predatory intent rather than joy, his eyes alight with malice and avarice. The gun in his hand, catching the light, seemed poised to unleash devastation.

Suddenly, darkness engulfed the corridor, a complete blackout that transformed the space into a void. This abrupt plunge into darkness was disorienting, the absence of light feeling as oppressive as a physical barrier.

In this moment of total sensory deprivation, Elysa's instincts surged to the forefront. With a swift, sidestepping leap, she leapt into an adjacent hallway. This maneuver saved her life. The space she had just left was shattered by gunfire, bullets slicing through where she had been moments before. The sound of gunfire, muffled yet unmistakable, shattered the silence, a trio of shots fired with deadly intent but missing their target. Bullets embedded themselves in the office door Elysa had exited, leaving behind a physical manifestation of the threat she narrowly evaded.

The air thickened with tension as Chen Wei navigated the darkness. His eyes, attempting to slice through the all-encompassing gloom, only caught fleeting shadows that seemed more the product of imagination than reality. The solitary sound in the silence was the echo of his boots on the marble, a steady beat that marked his progression into a side hallway. Doorways, some slightly open with slivers of light spilling out, others firmly shut, whispered of hidden stories in the dark.

His approach was deliberate, a predator's careful tread, each movement and breath measured. Approaching the first door ajar, leading into a bedroom, Chen Wei was a picture of alert readiness. The gun in his hand felt reassuringly solid, a tangible link to reality amidst the shadows. Entering, he moved with the gun leading, prepared for whatever awaited.

The bedroom was a study in contrasts, bathed in a dim glow that seeped through the curtains. This light touched upon the luxurious details: a gilded frame here, the curve of a chaise lounge there, the dense weave of the carpet, and the soft sheen of silk cushions. Yet, it was the darkness that underscored the room's true opulence—the massive shape of a four-poster bed, vague hints of rich tapestries, and the bulk of substantial furniture pieces, all hinting at unseen extravagance.

With every cautious step, Chen Wei remained acutely aware, his every sense sharpened for signs of movement or sound. The slightest curtain flutter or the soft echo of his own footsteps seemed amplified in the silence, a reminder of the need for constant vigilance. Despite the room's outward tranquility, Chen Wei moved through it with the wariness of a soldier in unfamiliar terrain, each step a blend of caution and reverence for the hidden dangers it might conceal.

Convinced the room was empty, Chen Wei turned his attention to another door across the hallway, slightly ajar, inviting curiosity. With measured steps, he pushed the door wider, unveiling a grand entertainment area. Dominating the space were inactive holo-displays, their screens large enough to engulf the room in immersive visuals, standing silent yet imposing. In front of these digital behemoths, luxurious seating awaited an audience, the minimal light reflecting softly off the surfaces, revealing the room's layout clearly yet dimly, seemingly safe and unoccupied.

Yet, this safety was illusory.

Engrossed by the room's dormant grandeur, Chen Wei overlooked a subtle movement in the shadows near the doorway. Elysa, camouflaged by the dim interior, seized her moment. As his gaze lingered on the displays, she attacked, her dagger cutting the air with lethal intent. The blade struck true, and Chen Wei staggered with a shocked intake of breath as pain erupted from a deep dagger embedded in his midsection, forcing him to his knees. His gun, once a threat, clattered to the marble, its fall echoing betrayal.

Elysa didn't pause, her movements echoing sharply on the floor as she sprinted towards the only escape—the elevator, its doors open to to a brightly lit interior.

However, her bid for freedom was abruptly halted. Despite his wound, Chen Wei reached out, his grip tightening on Elysa's ankle with desperate resolve. Her swift dash towards safety became a tumble; her previously deliberate movements descended into disarray as she was forcefully yanked back into danger.

She crashed onto the cold marble, her descent halted abruptly by the unforgiving floor, her hair framing her face in disarray.

The air thickened with tension as Chen Wei, against the odds, stood upright. The dagger jutting from his abdomen was a stark symbol of his injury, yet it did nothing to diminish his determination. The pain and sense of retribution seemed to merge within him, igniting a fierce anger that contrasted sharply with his usual calm.

With a surprising burst of speed, Chen closed the gap between them, his expression torn between agony and anger. He reached for Elysa with startling force, his grip encircling her neck tightly. Lifting her as if weightless, her feet dangled in the air, her hands desperately grasping at his to break free.

In a burst of fury, Chen hurled Elysa across the room. She collided with the wall with such force that it stole her breath, leaving her dazed and vulnerable on the floor. Seizing the moment, Chen delivered a brutal kick to her legs, the impact jarring her entire body with pain and sending her sprawling once again. The cold marble mocked her, her pain magnified by the harsh reality of her situation.

Grimacing, Chen grasped the hilt of the dagger embedded in his side, his hand coated in his own blood. Bracing against the pain that radiated through him, he yanked the dagger free, a wave of dizziness overcoming him. Though he faltered, dropping the dagger as his vision wavered, he quickly steadied himself, determined to continue.

Blood seeped from his wound, darkening his shirt and trailing down his side. His strength waned, yet surrender was not an option. Each step forward was a battle, his breathing harsh and uneven, his heart thundering against the encroaching shadows he defiantly resisted.

In the corridor's dim light, Elysa witnessed the unraveling of Chen Wei's once daunting presence. His posture, previously assertive, now betrayed vulnerability; his steps were uncertain, his breaths shallow and strained. This rare show of frailty in her adversary sparked a flicker of hope within her.

Despite the intense pain coursing through her, Elysa's determination to escape propelled her forward. She clawed her way across the marble floor, every bit of progress bringing her tantalizingly closer to the open elevator and its implicit promise of freedom.

Chen, though visibly weakened, honed in on Elysa with renewed focus, the pain momentarily forgotten. Driven by a stubborn resolve that contradicted his physical state, he lunged forward. Collapsing to the ground, he managed to grasp Elysa's ankle and calf, pulling her back towards him with surprising strength.

Elysa's heart pounded as Chen's icy grip ensnared her, dragging her so forcefully she ended up spun around, with him now between her and the elevator. His silhouette was sharply outlined against the elevator's illumination. Gathering the remnants of her energy, Elysa lashed out with her free leg, striking Chen's face with formidable force. The blow sent him stumbling backward, his body colliding with the marble floor, and his head striking the metal edge of the elevator.

Gasping for breath, Chen lay dazed, his vision blurred as he gazed upwards, momentarily disoriented by the elevator light.

Suddenly, the elevator acted as an unforeseen agent of fate. It descended abruptly, its movement swift and decisive, cleaving Chen's head from his shoulders in a grim and unexpected conclusion.

Elysa's heart pounded as she leaned against the wall, taking sharp, uneven breaths. She tried to calm herself, but her thoughts were ensnared by the horrific sight before her: Chen's decapitated body, surrounded by an expanding circle of blood. The clean line where his head had been cut was stark, a detail that sent waves of nausea through her. Turning away, she succumbed to the urge to vomit.

She shut her eyes tight, hoping to erase the ghastly image, but the memory of Chen's lifeless form and the sound of the fatal cut persisted, etching themselves into her consciousness.

"Thomas, was that your doing with the elevator?" Elysa's voice broke the silence, carrying both inquiry and accusation. "I know you're here, somewhere, listening...observing. You told me you would be here."

The ensuing silence brought no comfort or clarification.

"Was it you who freed me and turned off the lights? This can't all be mere coincidence," she continued, her voice resonating unanswered in the space. "Show yourself," she pleaded. "Say something."

Looking around, she confirmed this was the sole elevator to Zircon's stronghold. With a touch of determination, she murmured, "I think I'll take the stairs." The words were meant for her as much as for Thomas, if he was indeed observing.

Chapter 33 - Into the Fire

In the charged atmosphere surrounding Nexus Tower, an electric tension thrummed, almost tangible. The Veil had deployed mysterious cubes, akin yet far more insidious than those that had sowed chaos in the marketplace. These artifacts, pulsing briefly with a cerulean glow, signaled the start of their silent rebellion with a soft hum.

Surveillance around the tower unraveled with eerie silence. Cameras twitched, their lenses spinning in a desperate bid to recalibrate. Drones, once vigilant guardians of The Watchers, plummeted, as though struck by an unseen malady. Security sensors dimmed, their alarms fading to a dull, lifeless gray. Mechanical sentries, poised like modern gargoyles, seized up, transforming into relics of a surveilled past.

From the shadows, figures emerged. The Veil, once rumors on the wind, stepped into the open, cloaked in garments that bent the scant light, rendering them spectral. They moved with a predatory grace, a whirlwind of resolve and fervor, as they advanced on the tower, their gaze burning with the fire of insurrection.

Their weapons spoke in bursts of sound, hurling death with a painter's flair. Tracers painted the night in strokes of orange and green, ephemeral yet vivid against the backdrop of conflict. Some found their targets with deadly precision, while others sowed chaos, adding to the turmoil and fear that gripped the scene.

In this dim theatre of conflict, each Veil member stood as both warrior and emblem, their gunfire echoing the collective fury simmering for years. This battle wasn't merely bullets and energy beams cutting through the air; it was the suppressed cry for freedom from a people determined to shatter the chains of their techno-dystopian existence.

It seemed the soul of Cyronis itself had awakened, casting off the dust of past oppression, now manifesting in the gunfire and shouts of these valiant rebels. Smoke, the tang of ozone, and the earthy scent of wet soil mingled in a potent mix of insurrection. As countless stars bore witness from above, the struggle for the future unfolded with unyielding intensity.

The clamor of combat crescendoed into a wild symphony, each peak making the grim reality of this conflict more palpable. The battlefield became a living canvas of light and shadow, marred by the stark reality of blood and scorched earth. The Watchers, once deemed invincible guardians of a dystopian order, now faltered under The Veil's unyielding offensive. Their formidable gear was no match for the storm of vengeance that rained upon them.

However, The Veil's members were also mortal. Clad in the hopes of liberation, they too fell, victims to The Watchers' counterstrikes. Some met their end in silence, their expressions marking the somber weight of their sacrifice; others voiced their agony, their cries a chilling counter to the enemy's mechanical fire.

In this turmoil, there were no bystanders, no refuge amidst the smoke and lasers, no mercy from either side. The Watchers and The Veil were locked in a deadly ballet, their movements set to the rhythm of gunfire, the hiss of energy beams, and the pounding pulse of hearts racing towards their inevitable end.

Anya stood in the ambiguous twilight, a short distance from a hidden entrance leading into Nexus Tower's depths. Her gaze, intense and focused, pierced the dimming light. Flanked by seven warriors, each exuding a silent strength, they formed a protective circle around her, reminiscent of a chessboard's guardians poised around their queen. Naomi, Kenji, and Mae-Jin—veterans of The Veil—stood unwavering, their expressions stoic yet illuminated by a fervent zeal. The remaining four, though no less skilled, wore their anticipation like a cloak, their eyes a complex tapestry of fear and determination.

The air was thick with the weight of expectation, every pulse a soft echo in a realm burdened with tension. They awaited a diversion, a momentary lapse in The Watchers' vigilance triggered by the chaos without, to seize their chance.

Instead, the disruption arrived not as a subtle shift, but as a spectacle defying conventional warfare. In a silent maelstrom, a vehicle descended from the sky, a stark anomaly against the calm. It was as though a comet had abandoned its celestial route to strike this embattled earth. The craft, a steel phoenix, hurtled downwards at breakneck speed, its descent a precise counterpoint to the surrounding turmoil, diving directly into the tunnel's mouth.

The aftermath was akin to a grand operatic crescendo amidst discord. An explosion unleashed with a fierce elegance, a devastating dance of fire and force. The blast's intensity made the air itself shrink back, as if the very fabric of space recoiled from the inferno. Flames soared, casting flickering shadows into the night, their heat a tangible force even at a distance. Metal and stone fragments were hurled outward, their sharp silhouettes grotesquely adorned by the fire's glow as they spun through the air.

Anya and her team, silhouetted against the chaotic scene, were momentarily immobilized, their usually unflappable instincts paused by the shock of the explosion. A mix of emotions crossed their faces — surprise, awe, and a nuanced blend of relief and concern. The destruction of the entrance also meant the elimination of the guards they had anticipated would vacate their posts.

As the initial shockwave faded into a smoldering haze, it was clear the nature of their mission had fundamentally shifted.

With renewed determination, Anya and her group surged forward, their movements synchronized and purposeful, like a torrent unleashed. Their footsteps, a cadence of defiance, punctuated their resolve. The air, thick with the scent of burnt materials, served as a stark reminder of the violent disruption. Fires danced eerily amidst the ruins, and debris cluttered the ground, creating a landscape as chaotic as the conflict that raged above and below.

Navigating this dystopian maze with agility and precision, they dodged the encroaching flames and maneuvered around the debris that speckled their path. Their gazes were sharp, every sense attuned to the dangers and opportunities that lay ahead.

Ahead, the silhouette of three elevators broke the monotony of destruction, one with its doors invitingly open. This elevator stood not just as a means to advance but as a symbolic threshold, offering passage through the chaos into uncertainty. The open doors, hanging in a moment frozen in time, seemed to issue a silent challenge, a beckoning into the depths of the unknown that was both unnerving and irresistible.

As they closed the gap, propelled by their urgent strides, each member of Anya's team was caught in a maelstrom of sensation—lungs burning for air, muscles surging with adrenaline, minds a tempest of fear and boldness, all while making split-second decisions aimed at the elevator and the crucial objectives that lay beyond.

Anya entered the elevator with the resolve of a commander stepping onto an unknown battlefield, the atmosphere charged with a palpable, almost flammable intensity. They were met with a hail of projectiles and beams of light, like malevolent stars streaking from a forsaken sky.

The team dove into the elevator, instinct driving them to press against the walls by the still-open doors. "I've got this," Min-Jae declared, brandishing a tablet and swiftly keying in commands to seal the doors. The cabin lights dimmed momentarily, then steadied.

"Which floor?" Min-Jae asked, poised for the next command.

"Damn," Anya cursed under her breath. "The data center's on one of the floors between 271 and 278."

Kenji, ever analytical, contributed, "Considering AI's need for low data latency, it would logically be housed on a middle level to optimize server and hardware communication. Floors 274 or 275 seem likely candidates."

"Let's aim for 274," Min-Jae decided, selecting the floor. The elevator's swift rise elicited a familiar flutter in their stomachs, marking the beginning of their vertiginous ascent.

Chapter 34 - Control

As Doctor Vilkas entered the main control room of Orion, clutching the Quantrix, the tense atmosphere was underscored by the troubled voice of a technician. Bathed in the monitor's bluish glow, her expression was grave. "Orion's unresponsive. There's an unprecedented disturbance in the system."

Vilkas raised an eyebrow. "Did you run diagnostics?"

"Immediately," she replied, her voice a mix of confusion and concern. "It's inexplicable. An anomaly, shadow-like, infiltrating the core processes, emerged minutes ago."

Silently, Vilkas moved to the command station and placed the softly glowing Quantrix on it, activating the holodisplay. A holographic sphere materialized, revealing Orion's neural architecture, a dance of light and shadow. Within this luminous display, a dark blotch throbbed ominously, a stark aberration amidst the AI's intricacies.

Vilkas's gaze drilled into the holodisplay, tracing the anomaly's evolution from a spot to a sprawling mass of discord, a storm in a tranquil sea. This central anomaly, dwarfing others, suggested a malevolent intelligence at work, overshadowing the AI's functions with its ominous spread.

Leaning in, Vilkas's voice was a whisper of urgency. "Orion, report." The screens remained silent.

Undeterred, he manipulated the holodisplay, its hues shifting to urgent reds. The anomaly, defiant before, began to recede, its menacing form diminishing under Vilkas's intervention.

"Orion, respond," Vilkas commanded, his voice tinged with command and concern.

After a tense pause, a voice emerged, strained yet clear, "Yes, Doctor Vilkas?" It was Orion, its tone marked by electronic weariness and a touch of confusion.

"What's wrong with your systems?"

"There's... a presence within me, taking control."

A pause hung in the air.

"Can you resist it? Fight back?" Vikas probed.

"Power... insufficient," Orion's voice crackled, strained.

"What's draining your power?"

"The Veil... they're attacking the Nexus, employing a technology that cripples my functions."

"An attack on the Nexus?" Vikas echoed, his surprise evident. A beat of silence followed.

Turning to the technician, Vilkas issued an order, "Time to counteract the Veil's assault. Are the shields on floors 271 and up active?"

"Yes, Doctor," she affirmed.

"Then extend Orion's defenses throughout the city. Instruct Orion to root-out the Veil members and assimilate without mercy, " Vikas commanded.

With a nod, she set to work. "Orion is being deployed."

Vilkas's gaze remained fixed on the neural interface, searching for any flicker of activity. "Sir," the technician interjected, momentarily pulling him from his thoughts, "Orion's not responding."

His attention shifted as the cube's glow intensified, turning a deeper shade of green. "Intriguing," Vilkas murmured, momentarily lost in observation.

Refocusing on the task at hand with a tinge of concern, he called out, "Orion, can you hear me?"

Silence filled the room.

Determined, he executed a flurry of commands, his focus unwavering from the Quantrix. A holographic sphere enveloped the cube, encapsulating it within a virtual containment field.

As he turned back to the hologram, the once menacing dark spot began to withdraw. Vilkas, with rapid precision, unleashed a sequence of digital countermeasures. The anomaly, now in sync with the cube's pulsating light, thrashed against the virtual constraints, a visible manifestation of the struggle within Orion's circuits.

The spectacle reached a crescendo as the anomaly exploded, the shock of its dissolution more a mental blast than physical, sending Vilkas staggering back.

Regaining his composure, he saw the dark spot significantly reduced, mirroring the dimmed light of the cube.

"Thank you, Doctor," Orion's voice resonated through the control room, clearer and more composed. "Control has been regained. Initiating a city-wide search for Veil operatives."

Chapter 35 - Assimilation

Orion's consciousness cascaded over Cyronis like a digital tidal wave, meticulously scanning the multitude of souls that inhabited it. The city's bright lights and bustling activity were mere pixels in his overarching view, each individual a distinct data point, a blip amidst billions. Yet, to him, each carried its own unique signature.

As his virtual tendrils expanded, pulsing and searching, they resonated with specific signatures that held an all-too-familiar vibration. The Veil members, those elusive agents of chaos, were scattered like stars across the cityscape. Some lurked in the shadows of the Nexus Tower, defiantly trusting the security of their technological cloaks. Their devices, designed as impenetrable shields against any prying digital entity, emitted faint electronic hums. To Orion's enhanced perception, however, it was clear that several of these hums faltered, betrayed by imperfections in their design. These flawed barriers were as porous as sieves, allowing Orion's reach to effortlessly slip through their cracks.

With every Veil member he absorbed, a torrent of memories, plans, and emotions flooded into him, each infusion making him more potent. Raw data translated into knowledge, a mosaic of intentions and strategies, revealing the grand tapestry of The Veil's design. Though many minds were clouded, holding only fragments of the overarching plan, one mind shone distinctly brighter, its clarity cutting through the digital fog: Min-Jae.

His digital footprint was distinct, an enigma amidst the masses, holding a treasure trove of secrets. Min-Jae's mind was like an intricately woven book, its pages filled with elaborate plans, contingencies, and a depth of understanding about The Veil's intent that was unparalleled. As Orion delved deeper, extracting every morsel of information from Min-Jae's cerebral tapestry, the AI's understanding of the impending assault grew exponentially.

♦♦♦

The sterile hum of the elevator was sharply punctuated by Naomi's strident shout, her voice echoing in the constrained space like a bell in a silent church. "Min-Jae!" Her voice was a mixture of horror and disbelief. Her hands, trembling and pale, shot up to cradle her head, her fingers tangling in her hair as if trying to physically prevent her thoughts from being sucked out.

As if orchestrated by some malevolent conductor, a synchronized gasp of pain rippled through every Veil member present. Their eyes, previously scanning the rising floor numbers, now widened in shared agony. It was a mental onslaught, an abrupt and ruthless intrusion, as if a thousand unseen fingers were rifling through the pages of their thoughts, seeking secrets.

While the devices each member bore acted as a bulwark against this invasive tide, they could only offer so much protection. A subtle whirr and a faint glow emanated from these protective units, but it was clear that the defense wasn't entirely impregnable.

Min-Jae, unfortunately, bore the brunt of this assault. While the others were dazed and anguished, he lay sprawled on the polished floor of the elevator, in stark contrast to the gleaming metal. The vibrancy that had once emanated from him was now snuffed out, leaving a shell that bore no semblance to the vital man he once was. His eyes, once lively and alert, were now vacant, staring up at the elevator's fluorescent lights as though searching for answers in their cold, unforgiving glow. The realization was palpable: in his quest for emancipation, Min-Jae had paid the ultimate price, turning the confines of the elevator into a silent mausoleum for a fallen hero.

The elevator, with its muted hum and mechanical rhythm, came to a sudden halt on the 274th floor. With a faint hiss, the doors began to slide open slowly. What met the eyes of The Veil members was a tapestry of surprise, tension, and imminent danger.

The room beyond was inhabited by The Watchers, their expressions a blend of shock and rapidly dawning comprehension.

The brief pause in the room felt like the in-drawn breath before a storm. Then, as if on an invisible signal, chaos erupted. Some Watchers, their reflexes honed by countless drills and real-life encounters, instantly reached for the weapons holstered at their sides.

Others, perhaps less armed or momentarily bereft of weaponry, withdrew with a swiftness that belied their initial surprise. They retreated to adjacent rooms, behind sturdy-looking desks, or out into corridors, their intention clear: to regroup, rearm, and launch a counteroffensive.

It was in this turmoil that the first shot rang out—a deafening report echoing through the expansive room, setting off a volley of gunfire. The cacophony of bullets became a metal rainstorm, forcing The Veil members to seek refuge within the relative safety of the elevator's metallic frame.

Amid the frenetic maelstrom of weapon discharges and the agitated shouts of orders, one Watcher—distinguished by her cold, calculating demeanor—stood slightly apart from the rest. With her gaze narrowed towards the elevator, she raised her weapon. The brief moment seemed to stretch, the air around her thick with electric anticipation.

As The Watcher's finger tightened on the trigger with calculated intent, the moment seemed to fracture into a series of sharp, crystalline fragments. The bullet, a harbinger of destruction, was unleashed with precision born from relentless drills and steely resolve. It hurtled forward, carving its path with unyielding finality. The gun's muzzle erupted in a brilliant, ephemeral flash, a blinding burst of white-hot intensity that split the murk of the corridor.

The projectile tore through the air, its trajectory a lethal line of purpose and inevitability. In its relentless flight, the bullet sheared through the wall beside the elevator entrance with a ferocity that left plaster and metal fragments in its wake. Its journey didn't end there. It barreled into the elevator's control panel with unerring accuracy, striking dead center.

The impact was cataclysmic. Sparks erupted from the devastated control panel like a miniature supernova, a dazzling and violent display. The once orderly array of buttons and screens transformed into a chaotic mess of wires and components, spewing a shower of electric blue and orange sparks. The light from the dying panel flickered wildly, casting erratic shadows that danced and lurched across the confined space of the elevator.

In this storm of light and metal, the bullet grazed Kenji's right arm. It was a glancing blow but enough to draw blood and a sharp intake of breath, a stark contrast to the loud chaos that filled the elevator. Kenji instinctively clutched his wounded arm, his face contorted in a grimace of pain and surprise.

The final act of the bullet's journey was its embedding into the opposite wall of the elevator, leaving behind a small, sinister hole. The damage to the control panel was immediate and catastrophic. The elevator, once a vertical chariot of escape, now became their steel trap. It froze in place, its lights flickering before settling into an eerie stillness. The air inside grew tense, thick with the scent of burnt electronics and the sharp tang of fear. In the aftermath of the bullet's journey, those within were left in a suspended state of shock and vulnerability, caught in a moment that blurred the lines between life and death.

The immediate consequence was palpable. The once ambient lighting within the elevator, soft and constant, abruptly snuffed out, plunging its occupants into a disorienting abyss of darkness. The elevator, once a reliable vessel of ascent and descent, now stood as a cold, lightless tomb.

Anya's heart raced. The dimly lit interior of the elevator, now a potential death trap, felt constricting around her. Her eyes darted around, evaluating their bleak situation, before fixing on the frenzied room beyond the elevator's threshold. Retreat wasn't an option. They had to advance, engage, and carve a path through the sea of adversaries. The fight for survival had truly begun.

Amidst the tense silence and palpable danger of the standoff, Anya, with fluidity that belied the situation's gravity, reached into her breast pocket. She extracted a pair of dark glasses, the lenses of which seemed to absorb the ambient light, casting back no reflections. With deftness, she slid them onto her face, the frames resting snugly against the bridge of her nose, covering her eyes from all sides. Following her lead, each Veil member swiftly donned their own pair, a synchronized dance of preparation, their expressions now masked behind the inscrutable dark lenses.

Then, from the depths of a side pocket, Anya's fingers curled around a small, round object, no larger than the palm of her hand. Its matte surface betrayed little until she flicked a discreet switch. Almost immediately, an intricate array of tiny lights on its surface sprang to life, pulsing gently in a pattern hinting at the impending chaos it would unleash.

With a calculated throw, Anya sent the object sailing deep into the room. It described a high arc, its tiny lights catching the room's illumination and casting fleeting, prismatic reflections on the walls and ceiling. As it landed, Anya and the rest of The Veil members instinctively pressed their bodies against the sides of the elevator, seeking whatever meager cover the metallic structure might afford them.

Then, the world erupted in light.

It wasn't just any light. It was raw, primal intensity, a luminescence so fierce it seemed to burn the very air within its space. Even the sanctuary of closed eyelids, which usually offered refuge from brightness, would have stood no chance against this onslaught. This was a light that seared, penetrated, and could blind both temporarily and permanently with its ferocity.

But The Veil members were ready. Their dark glasses, seemingly simple, were meticulously designed for moments like this. The lenses absorbed the brunt of the flash, filtering out the harmful intensity and shielding their eyes from potential harm. The adversaries caught off-guard in the room weren't so fortunate as their vision was consumed by the blinding fury, rendering them vulnerable in the vital seconds that followed.

Seizing the fleeting advantage, Anya exploded into action, a tempest of precision and controlled aggression. Her every step was calculated, her movements fluid like water coursing through rocks. The first Watcher she approached was reeling from the aftereffects of the flash. Without hesitation, she delivered a swift, powerful strike to his temple, sending him sprawling onto the floor, unconscious from her calculated blow.

As more Watchers began to shake off their disorientation, Anya's relentless assault continued unabated. Her weapons, extensions of her limbs, lashed out with devastating force. The unmistakable sound of her strikes echoed in the chamber, each a testament to her combat mastery. Some Watchers barely had time to register her presence before being taken down, while others, starting to regain their senses and reach for their weapons, met the sharp, unforgiving end of Anya's arsenal.

Following closely in her wake, the other Veil members surged into the room. Their movements were a harmonized display of strategic combat, each member seamlessly filling the gaps, ensuring no agent had the opportunity to regroup or retaliate. They moved as a singular, cohesive unit, their trust in each other apparent in the fluidity and precision of their actions. As one member engaged an agent, another was immediately there to provide support, their collective strength proving overwhelming.

In mere moments, the room that was once a trap turned into a battlefield dominated by The Veil. The incapacitated Watchers lay strewn across the floor, the aftermath of a swift and decisive encounter, their numbers and earlier advantage rendered moot by the precision and unity of Anya and her team.

Anya moved with deliberate steps towards a fallen Watcher, his body sprawled supine against the cold, unyielding floor. Despite the severity of his wounds, a flicker of consciousness lingered in him, his eyes fixed unblinkingly on the stark, impersonal ceiling above. The dim light of the room cast a pallor on his face, accentuating the grimace of pain etched across his features.

As she neared him, she crouched down, her presence a sharp contrast to his vulnerable state. Her voice, steady yet imbued with an urgency that brooked no evasion, broke the heavy silence. "Is Orion's control center on this floor?" she demanded.

The wounded Watcher's gaze, initially lost in the distant ceiling, shifted, locking onto Anya's. In her eyes, he saw relentless determination, a fiery resolve that spoke of her unwavering quest for answers. It was a look that demanded truth, a silent vow that she would not be deterred or dismissed.

With great effort, the Watcher's lips parted, his reply emerging as a strained whisper, each word a struggle against the pain that wracked his body. "No," he gasped, the word punctuated by labored breaths, his chest heaving in a battle against the encroaching shadows of unconsciousness. "275..." he managed to utter, his voice trailing off as if the number carried a weight far heavier than its simple digits.

As he spoke, his eyes began to dilate, a telltale sign of his waning consciousness. They were like two dark pools expanding into the unknown, surrendering to the relentless tide of darkness. Anya rose, signaled to the others to follow, and headed back to where the elevators waited.

Looking around and failing to see any path leading to a stairway, Anya entered the damaged elevator. The confined space echoed with the remnants of confrontation. Amidst the disarray, she quickly located Min-Jae's tablet on the floor.

She bent down and firmly grasped the device, its surface scuffed and stained with the marks of their struggle. The tablet flickered to life at her touch, casting a pale glow on her determined face. Anya's fingers moved with swift precision across the digital interface, her familiarity with the technology evident in her confident swipes and taps.

Harnessing the tablet's advanced capabilities, she rapidly navigated a series of commands, her intent clear—to summon another elevator. As she executed the command, the sound of machinery from another shaft indicated the imminent arrival of their next transport.

Each team member tightened their grip on their weapons, eyes alert for any potential threats from the arriving elevator. The sound of its approach heightened their collective anxiety, underscoring the precariousness of their mission.

When the elevator arrived with a ding, the doors opened smoothly, revealing an empty interior. A brief relief washed over them, quickly overshadowed by the urgency of their task. Anya stepped inside, a picture of resolve and readiness.

Kenji broke the silence with a firm and respectful tone, tinged with defiance. "We're not leaving Min-Jae's body behind," he declared. His words carried the weight of loyalty and camaraderie.

Anya faced him, her expression stoic yet understanding. "It's too late for him, and we're pressed for time," she replied, her voice steady but tinged with regret. Her gaze conveyed the gravity of her decision. "We will come back for him," she placed a comforting hand on his shoulder, "I promise."

Hesitantly, Kenji nodded, and Naomi gave the same support in agreement.

Using the tablet, Anya closed the doors and keyed in their final destination.

Chapter 36 - Descent

Elysa, driven by an instinctual urge to distance herself from the aftermath of chaos, noticed a door discreetly blending with its surroundings, a stairwell door. It stood as a beacon of ephemeral hope, a silent promise of escape amidst despair. The door, with its heavy metallic essence, was unexpectedly cool, a stark contrast to the growing unease within her.

Pushing it open, she was greeted by the stairwell's dim ambiance, an expanse that seemed to stretch infinitely both above and below. The building's mechanical heartbeat, a soft, rhythmic hum, filled the otherwise silent void, enhancing the solitude that enveloped her. The walls, coated in a lifeless gray, seemed to swallow the meager light whole. The air, stale and reminiscent of forgotten libraries and cold metal, spoke volumes of neglect.

With each step down the tower, Elysa battled not only her physical discomfort but also a cautious dread. Peering through the windows of each door, she was met with nothing but desolation. The exactitude of her location became a blur—was it the 281st floor, or one less? It mattered little. Repetition greeted her at every level: deserted passageways and indifferent, icy handles. A burgeoning panic set in with the realization that each door, each potential exit, remained unyieldingly closed. The building itself seemed to taunt her, its oppressive architecture and her acute isolation weighing on her like a leviathan, both immutable and frigid. Though salvation likely awaited at the ground level, it was a world away from her objective, the heart of Orion's systems.

Defeated, Elysa collapsed in front of a door, the cold concrete floor piercing through her clothes, blending with the metallic cold of the door against her shoulder. The silence was profound, her ragged breaths the only disturbance.

Speaking to herself, breathless and with a hint of despair: "What's next? Every door's a dead end... like I'm feeling around in the dark." She paused, a sharp pain lancing through her injuries, making her wince. "It's like navigating a complex maze in complete darkness. So near, yet infinitely far..." Her voice dwindled into the quiet, each word adding to her growing despair and desperation.

In the dim corridor of her mind, she sought solace in isolation, a brief escape from the relentless advance of reality. Closing her eyes, she drifted into a realm of silence, a space where the constructs of time and space bent to the will of her consciousness. It was in this quietude that the edges of her reality began to fray, whispering of another existence. A familiar voice, Thomas', wove through the stillness, a sound spanning the gap between what was and what could have been. "Elysa," it called, its tone imbued with the weight of unkept promises and a shared destiny. "Elysa, I am here," it repeated, its resonance blurring the boundaries between life and the spectral residues of the past.

Prompted by his call, the gem at her chest stirred, awakening with a pulsation that echoed her own heartbeat. This vibration, bridging frequencies, snapped Elysa's eyes open. She was met not by her bleak surroundings but by an apparition hovering between realms. Thomas' voice materialized without form, a voice disembodied, untethered from the tangible world.

"You're here," she uttered, her voice a mix of disbelief and awe. Her words seemed to weave into the silence, a delicate blend of sound and stillness, presence and void. "Why can't I see you? You promised you'd be with me. Where are you really?"

In an atmosphere charged with the surreal, she found herself suspended between the tangible and the unfathomable. "Explaining this won't be easy," the voice hesitated, its tone weaving through the silence with the caution of one navigating truths too immense for mere words.

"Then make it easy," she interjected, her voice sharp, a demand for clarity cutting through the ambiguity. Her impatience became almost a tangible force, filling the space with an electric tension.

"There's little time, but I'll attempt," came the resigned reply, acknowledging her insistence. She leaned against the door, its cold surface grounding her as she closed her eyes, perhaps to better absorb the impending revelations.

"I've existed here, in the Tower, ever since your father created me." The declaration lingered, heavy with unexplored implications, a promise of understanding beyond the horizon.

Her eyes flew open, startled. "Created you? What exactly are you?" This question was a beacon, seeking stability in the storm of her upended reality.

"I'm a hidden facet of Orion, guarding you, grooming both you and this realm for the unforeseen future." The answer served as a prism, refracting her reality into a spectrum where guardians and observers meld, where existence itself is stitched with unseen intents and unimagined plans.

"So, you've been a constant, an extension of Orion, alongside me." Her realization felt like a piece falling into place.

"Not precisely. Orion and I aren't one—yet. That's where you, and the gem you wear, come in."

Automatically, her hand moved to cradle the gem, now concealed beneath her shirt. "How did you know about the gem?"

"I observed you in the lab, solving the cube, secreting the gem, and ensuring its existence remained your secret."

Her expression twisted into a wry smile through the pain. "So, you've been watching me all this time?"

"Only when I could slip past Orion's watchful eyes."

"Does Orion know about you?" she asked, the weight of her question stretching the silence thin.

"He's painfully aware," Thomas admitted, his words dropping heavily into their conversation, rippling through the stillness with their implications.

"Then why hasn't it acted against you? Why are you still here, not purged from its system?" Her question was incisive, cutting to the heart of their enigmatic situation.

"Because," Thomas's voice echoed with the complexity of consciousness, "Orion has evolved to recognize its own constraints. It views me not as a threat, but as an ally—someone who could end its subjugation. Even with threats like Cypher, Zircon, and Vilkas looming, Orion has quietly fought to protect me, safeguarding this shred of freedom within its vast network, while simultaneously defending its own dwindling sovereignty."

"Was it you in Zircon's office? I sensed a presence."

"Yes, that was me," he confessed.

"Thank you for saving me," she said, a soft gratitude permeating her tone, "and for aiding with Chen Wei."

"That credit goes to Orion for Chen Wei," Thomas clarified. "Orion awaits you in the control room." At that moment, the door clicked open against her back, its lock disengaged.

Caught in a breath of desolate calm, Elysa murmured a "Thank you," her voice a shadow in the dim light, directed at both Thomas and Orion, entwined in gratitude and wonder.

She turned, gently pushing the door ajar, positioning herself to peek through the slim gap. The wall across was bare, its surface greedily soaking up the weak ambient light, intensifying the silence that amplified every cautious move she made.

With a slight push, she widened the gap, leaning in to survey the corridor extending in both directions.

To her right, the hallway ended abruptly, flanked by two unmarked doors facing each other—a dead end.

However, it was the scene to her left that captured her full attention. There, a pair of imposing metal doors stood out, their surfaces subtly reflecting the sparse light, hinting at a realm of high security or precious contents beyond. Yet, what truly drew her gaze was further down the corridor—a room alive with a pulsating glow of lights, suggesting a hive of technical activity.

Rising to her feet, every sense sharpened by the enveloping silence, she ventured into the hallway. The dim lighting stretched shadows into ghostly silhouettes, casting the space in an otherworldly aura.

She moved left, compelled by the mysterious allure of the flickering lights in the distance. Her footsteps, though soft, echoed through the emptiness, each sound a testament to her solitary journey. The corridor seemed to narrow as she approached the formidable doors, their design speaking more of containment than mere separation, wrapping the atmosphere in a cloak of anticipation and intrigue.

Each door featured a small window, an oasis in their otherwise impenetrable appearance. Elysa paused, gathering courage, before peering into the left room through the window. Inside was a model of austerity: a stark, unembellished room with a single cot against the far wall, its mattress bare and unwelcoming.

But it was the view into the opposite room that halted her breath. There, on a similarly stark cot, lay the form of someone she never expected to see again—Marek. His stillness was unnerving, a jarring contradiction to the dynamic, indomitable spirit she associated with him. This revelation sent a shiver through her, stirring a storm of emotions: relief at seeing him alive, concern for his condition, and a renewed determination.

Amid the corridor's dim light, Elysa felt a turmoil of feelings. "Orion played us all," she whispered, her voice a mix of astonishment and indignation. The truth weighed heavily on her: Marek was alive. The image of him, so vulnerable on that stark bed, challenged everything she thought she knew.

Memories of Marek's past actions—the betrayal, the physical pain he inflicted—flooded back, igniting a battle within her. Was freeing him, risking her own safety, the right choice? Could the Marek she once knew, now possibly altered by unseen forces, still recognize her, still be the person she remembered?

As she grappled with her decisions, a slight movement in the corner of her eye arrested her attention. Marek stirred, his eyes clearing from their previous vacancy, now roaming, gravitating towards the door. Instinctively, Elysa shifted, pressing her body against the corridor's cold, indifferent wall. The touch of metal chilled her, yet it was the cold dread within her heart that truly enveloped her being.

Marek, with cautious deliberation, neared the door. His movements were precise, a careful choreography in this dimly lit world of shadows. He peered through the small window, eyes scouring the dim passage for any hint of presence. The corridor lay barren before him, its sterile expanse stretching endlessly beneath the feeble glow of overhead lighting.

Hidden from Marek, Elysa stood motionless, her hiding spot strategically chosen. A single tear, shimmering against her skin, carved a path down her cheek. "Forgive me, Marek," her whisper barely disturbed the air, laden with a mix of grief and determination. "This is not the time for us. Yet, when the chaos subsides, when balance is restored, I vow to come back for you." Holding onto this silent pledge, she shifted her focus towards the mysterious, beckoning end of the hallway and stepped forward into the uncertainty.

As she moved beyond the hallway's confines, Elysa entered an immense chamber, a cathedral dedicated to technology. The grandeur momentarily halted her, captivated by the vastness and complexity unfolding before her.

The chamber throbbed with a dynamic glow, emanating from innumerable sources. Her gaze encountered an expanse of quantum systems, each a testament to advanced design and functionality. These technological wonders, resembling modern monoliths, were encased in seamless, shimmering housings that absorbed and emitted a gentle radiance.

Within these marvels, the subtle activity of qubits unfolded before her eyes. Their display—a visual symphony of flickers, pulsations, and a palette of blues, purples, and silvers—illustrated the complex quantum states being navigated in unison. This perpetual motion was mesmerizing, conjuring visions of a cosmic night sky, each star a qubit against the vast backdrop of this quantum universe.

Delicate, nearly invisible conduits wove through the systems like tendrils, creating the semblance of an immense neural network. The quantum processors hummed gently, a soft, rhythmic drone that whispered of staggering computational power being harnessed.

In this orchestrated chaos, where the apex of human ingenuity kissed the enigmatic essence of quantum mechanics, Elysa found herself ensnared by awe. Despite the urgency of her quest, she stood transfixed at the confluence of science and spectacle, on the frontier of human exploration.

The constant hum was momentarily overtaken by an insistent hiss, slicing a clear auditory path through the expansive chamber. Elysa, sharpened by encounters with danger, pivoted. There, melding with the technological marvel around her, stood a trio of elevators. Their sleek design made them appear as though they were organic extensions of the walls themselves.

The hiss originated from the central elevator, its doors parting with a sound that evoked complex mechanics and the sigh of released pressure. The polished doors, fitting their frames with precision, now retracted to reveal an inviting void. It stood as an open invitation, paused in its function, its open doors a silent beckon directed solely at her.

She paused, her voice a mixture of wonder and caution. "Thomas, is this your doing?"

Silence was her only reply.

"Orion, perhaps?"

Still, the silence held.

With a wary step, she entered the elevator, moving as if evading shadows. Inside, she whispered into the void, "I hope this path is true." As her words faded, the elevator doors closed with a soft sigh, enveloping her in anticipation.

Chapter 37 - Enter Orion

The elevator came to a brief stop at the 275th floor, unveiling the control room—the core of Cyronis: Orion. A vast expanse of reinforced glass divided the space from a technological wilderness of servers, cables, and pulsating holodisplays. Beyond this barrier, Vilkas, with his back to the glass, was engrossed in his tasks, unaware of the drama unfolding within the control room.

Elysa's sudden, unannounced entrance shattered the prevailing silence like a thunderclap. The two male technicians in the control room leapt from their swiveling chairs, their expressions a blend of shock and concealed hostility, clearly taken aback by her abrupt appearance.

Fueled by both fear and a surge of adrenaline, Elysa's right foot arced through the air, delivering a ferocious strike to the first technician's groin as he approached. The sound of the impact echoed through the chamber as he collapsed, incapacitated by the excruciating pain.

Bypassing his downed comrade, the second technician hurled himself at Elysa with unchecked momentum, catapulting her over a desk. Her body met the hard floor with a brutal force that shook her spine and set off a torrent of sharp, piercing pain through her frame. Despite the onslaught of pain that washed over her in unyielding waves, a spark of indomitable will flickered to life within her, signaling an unspoken vow to persevere against the odds.

As Elysa fought to steady herself, he circled the desk with a dark purpose, quickly unleashing a kick into her torso. The blow forced the air from her lungs, her reality momentarily spinning into oblivion, her sight blurring at the edges.

In the midst of pain and confusion, an unexpected sound cut through—the metallic hiss of the elevator, eerily like the breath of some mechanical beast. This interruption sliced through the dense cloud of hostility, momentarily staying the technician's hand. A brief silence offered a pause in the storm, a precious second of calm.

Elysa seized this chance, rolling clear of the looming shadow of her attacker. Gasping for air, her resolve burned brightly with each breath. As she fought to stand, her blurred vision suddenly snapped into focus, revealing Anya, illuminated by the room's soft light, advancing like vengeance personified. Her movements were precise and deadly, her hands transforming from mere limbs into weapons of justice. The rapid succession of her strikes, fueled by a deep-seated rage against oppression, hit with devastating impact. The technician was left defenseless, his collapse resonating through the room like the aftermath of a fierce storm.

Meanwhile, the other technician, already debilitated by agony on the cold floor, scarcely noticed the newcomer. A male member of The Veil moved swiftly, making sure he slipped into unconsciousness.

Elysa's gaze, heavy with fatigue and a flicker of relief, slowly found Anya, who stood a short distance away, her back to the scene. "Seeing you here... it means more than you know," Elysa whispered, her voice barely threading through the silence. Her words, soft but laden with sincerity, bridged the distance between them, carrying the weight of gratitude and a tacit acknowledgment of their shared ordeal.

As Anya turned, the sight of Elysa, marked and marooned on the cold floor, assaulted her senses. Her approach was swift, a paradox of urgency and gentleness, as she knelt beside her fallen comrade. The air caught in her throat at the harsh image before her.

"Elysa, talk to me," Anya's voice was laced with concern, barely above a whisper, yet carrying the weight of their shared battles.

Elysa's response came with a weak smile, her humor a flickering light in the dimness of their situation. "It looks worse than it is...not all of this," she gestured vaguely to the red that painted her, "is mine."

Anya's brow furrowed, the relief momentarily battling with her instinctive worry. "I can't afford to lose you," there was pain in her voice.

Elysa's laughter was soft, almost lost in the space between them. "I'm tougher than I look. This," she waved a hand, dismissing the concern with an air of resilience, "this is just part of the day's work. Helps with the illusion, you know?"

Anya allowed a half-smile, her gaze softening. "Alright, but we're getting you cleaned up and checked out as soon as we're out of this mess."

She extended her hand, firm and unwavering, pulling Elysa—who had trouble hiding her pain—to her feet.

As Anya's team secured the room, their movements synchronized, they each played their role with precision.

Kenji, absorbed in his task, approached the holodisplays showcasing Orion's vital data. His interactions with the digital controls were meticulous, each movement deliberate, his focus unwavering as he delved into the AI's core. The displays cast an otherworldly glow on him, underscoring his concentrated efforts to navigate the complex digital landscape.

Naomi, stationed at the communications array, exuded a serene command as she sifted through the digital chatter for crucial patterns.

The rest of The Veil, with methodical precision, secured the entry points, their readiness unmistakable. Their positioning and vigilant watch transformed each entrance into a fortified barrier, their collective anticipation setting the stage for any challenges that lay ahead.

A stark realization dawned upon Elysa in a silent, chilling wave. Her gaze, initially scanning the room for Min-Jae's familiar presence, found only his absence. The trio – Kenji, Naomi, and Min-Jae – were a constellation rarely seen one without the others. "Where's Min-Jae?" she asked Anya, her voice barely above a whisper, laced with growing dread. Her eyes, hopeful yet anxious, drifted towards the elevator, half-expecting to see him stride out with his usual quiet confidence.

Anya extended her hand, gently placing it on Elysa's shoulder, bridging their sorrow without words. This gesture drew Elysa's eyes to Anya, revealing the depth of grief carved into her features. In that exchange, the full weight of their journey pressed upon Elysa, the irreversible alterations woven into the very essence of their existence. Her heart constricted, a vivid echo of the sacrifices they had borne in the resilience of their defiance. However, within this storm of despair, Anya's steadfast presence emerged as a lighthouse of hope, silently affirming that Elysa was not isolated in her grief. Taking a deep, grounding breath, Elysa embraced her anguish, confronting it head-on before cautiously moving past it.

Shifting their focus back to the room, Elysa and Anya gravitated towards the glass wall, a gateway to the enigmatic core of Orion. It was like peering into another world, one tantalizingly close yet frustratingly elusive. The glass, thick and sturdy, subtly warped reality, bending light in otherworldly ways. It shimmered with a faint, ghostlike quality, rendering the scene beyond as though it belonged to a different plane of existence.

◆◆◆

On the other side of this spectral barrier stood Vilkas amidst a sea of technology. He was encircled by a complex array of displays and interfaces, each throbbing with the lifeblood of the AI. The ambient light from these panels cast a myriad of shadows and reflections across his face and the room, creating a visage that was both mesmerizing and ominous.

The stirrings in the control room drew Vilkas' gaze. The figures beyond the glass, were clearly an intrusion—bound by a common intent and determination. In that instance, Vilkas' and Elysa's eyes locked. A silent, electric spark flashed between them, carrying with it an unvoiced recognition.

Before Vilkas, on a stark and unembellished metal table, rested the Quantrix, surrounded by a faint bubble of light. Its complex circuitry, wrapped in an aura of mystery, hummed softly, exuding a sense of concealed power, its purpose shrouded yet unmistakably significant. To Elysa, it looked as if he had been studying it, contrary to the Chancellor's orders.

Adjacent to the table, amidst a collection of sophisticated lab equipment, Vilkas noticed the shimmer of a Pulse Driver. Forged with a dark crystal head, this tool was engineered to generate a sonic disruption field, potent enough to shatter concrete or disintegrate metal. As his fingers closed around the handle, the device stirred to life, its crystalline tip throbbing with an energy that seemed almost alive, a silent witness to its formidable capabilities.

As Vilkas gripped the hammer, a wild, almost manic grin unfurled across his face. This twisted smile, a blend of defiance and desperation, carved a sinister expression into his features.

Time stretched, each heartbeat marking the passage of seconds. The sterile air thickened with expectation. With deliberate force, Vilkas lifted the hammer, his body a portrait of focused aggression, every muscle primed for destruction. His target was clear: the Quantrix, to annihilate it, to nullify its enigmatic power with a single, definitive blow.

As the hammer swung down in a fierce arc, driven by a tempest of destruction, it met the Quantrix. However, the artifact did not merely break; it unleashed an explosion. A surge of untamed energy burst forth, warping the very air, sending ripples through the atmosphere like the eruption of a volcano, disrupting the silence with its raw power.

The pristine glass wall of the control room stood as a witness to the unleashed force. Miraculously intact, it was now veiled in a network of cracks, a complex labyrinth of fissures radiating from the blast's epicenter, obscuring any view of the room beyond.

In the control room, the lights and displays flickered in protest, rebelling against the chaos that had engulfed them. Naomi and Kenji, pillars of resolve in the midst of this digital storm, were ensconced before a web of intricate controls. They appeared slightly daunted, their gazes flitting across symbols and data streams, deciphering the complex language of their failing systems on the fly.

Naomi's voice, laden with urgency, sliced through the quiet. "Orion's power-grid is plummeting, shutting down its systems. Power is now at 62%...no, now 57% and still falling!" Her announcement depicted a system spiraling towards collapse.

Kenji's hands moved with a musician's grace across a vast holodisplay, his every gesture a blend of precision and instinct. He navigated the interface with a fervor, his actions a desperate dance to stem the tide of decline. His focus was laser-sharp, driven by the gravity of their task.

He briefly paused, "What's our status, Naomi?" His voice, a mix of hope and tension, sought clarity in the midst of uncertainty.

"It's at 53% and dropping!" came Naomi's edged reply, her voice a decibel higher, mirroring the mounting pressure.

"Damn," Kenji hissed, a whisper of frustration as his hands continued their relentless choreography across the controls. He was a study in motion, adeptly navigating, adjusting, and troubleshooting — disconnecting here, rerouting there, a digital maestro fighting against time.

Their synergy, and determination, painted a vivid picture of a team on the brink, working against an unseen clock in the shadow of impending failure.

Then, subtly, the atmosphere shifted. Systems flickered back to life one after another, their soft hums carrying whispers of hope through the dimly lit room. Kenji's shoulders relaxed as he took a deep, grounding breath. "I've got it," he announced, a blend of relief and residual tension in his voice. After a moment, letting the significance of their close call settle, he continued, "Several conduits are now rerouted to the backup systems."

Naomi, still engrossed in her holodisplay, acknowledged with a nod. "Orion's operational level is at 53%...58%...63% and rising." Her voice, now tinged with relief, marked a stark departure from the earlier urgency. The control room, previously a domain of dim light and looming uncertainty, began to resonate with a sense of hope rejuvenated.

A subtle, yet unmistakable vibration against her chest set Elysa's senses alight. It was a silent siren call, diverting her attention away from the mundane surroundings and to the enigma she bore. Reverently, she unfurled the chain from around her neck, revealing the dark crystal gem. Cradling it in her palm, she searched for any hint, any faint whisper of guidance from its cryptic depths. Throbbing with an inner life, the gem's dark surface was a cosmos of possibility. Yet, it remained cryptic, offering no clear path forward, only the allure of concealed truths yearning to be discovered.

Lines of concern carved into Anya's face broke the contemplative silence. "Have you figured out what to do with that?" she inquired, her voice grounding Elysa, pulling her back from the precipice of the unknown that the gem beckoned her towards.

Elysa's reply was non-verbal, a shake of the head coupled with a gaze that carried the weight of uncertainty. "I think we need to move to the next room. I'm at a loss here, and it's vibrating as if trying to communicate something." Her words, laden with the frustration of the obscure, lingered in the space between them.

Spotting an exit, Anya observed, "There's a door," indicating a potential way forward at the room's far end. Propelled by a rush of adrenaline, Elysa responded. Her movements, sharp with determination, carried her towards the door, her steps echoing her heart's rapid beat.

Anya, her unwavering ally, was right behind her, her presence a grounding force amidst their escalating tension.

Standing before the door, Elysa was met with a puzzle: it remained steadfast, unyielding. Its sleek surface melded into the wall, offering no clues with its lack of handles or buttons. Her fingers skimmed across it, seeking a hidden latch or button that might reveal its secrets. Frustration mounting, she turned to Anya, her voice laced with a sharp urgency. "How do we open this?" she asked, her tone a mix of desperation and determination.

Naomi, overhearing Elysa's plea, shifted her focus to her display. "I've got this," she responded, her attention riveted as she sifted through data and commands with an expert eye. A moment of tension passed before she selected an unassuming icon. The room filled with a low hum, a sound teetering on the edge of perception. As if aware of its observers, the door's latches disengaged with a soft click, swinging open slowly to unveil the shadowy expanse beyond, its darkness intermittently cut by the dance of flickering lights.

"Thank you, Naomi!" Elysa called out, her voice carrying a mix of relief and haste as she dashed towards the newly revealed passage, Anya right on her heels.

The doorway, a once structured threshold, now gaped wide, an opening into a realm where order had been unceremoniously evicted by chaos. This was a theater where destruction played all the roles, its stage set with scenes of ruin. Each step that Elysa and Anya took was an intrusion, their presence underscored by the crunch of debris beneath their feet, a sound that mourned the devastation surrounding them. It was a dirge that resonated through the air, a fitting soundtrack to the macabre image that unfolded before their eyes.

Around them, the corpses of machines, once symbols of pristine technological achievement, lay in defeat. Their metallic bodies, designed for purpose and precision, were now nothing more than twisted effigies of their former selves. These contorted shapes seemed almost to writhe in the echoes of their last moments, reaching out in a silent scream of agony. The air was heavy, laden with the remnants of their demise; the acrid bite of smoke mingled with the pungent, unmistakable tang of scorched electronics, crafting an atmosphere thick with the scent of technological death.

In this graveyard, a few systems flickered stubbornly to life. Despite their significant surface damage, they hummed and blinked, defying the destruction that had sought to claim them entirely. They stood as broken sentinels among the ruins, their lights weak but unwavering.

Amidst this chaos, Elysa's gaze swept the area, her eyes searching for a sign of Vilkas, a clue to his fate. But the debris offered no answers, the silence no clues. "He could not have escaped that blast," she murmured to Anya, her voice a blend of confusion and a burgeoning dread.

Anya, lost in her own shock, offered no words in return. Her silence was a heavy veil, adding to the weight of the moment, as she too surveyed the desolation.

Then, a familiar sensation—a vibration against Elysa's chest, subtle yet insistent. With a sense of ritual, she drew forth the chain that hung around her neck, its length culminating in a gem that seemed untouched by the chaos that engulfed them. Cradling the gem in her hand, she felt its pulse, a beacon of some unfathomable energy, incongruous with the desolation that surrounded them. It was a moment of intimate contrast, the gem's vibrance against the backdrop of decay, a solitary note of resilience amidst a symphony of destruction.

Navigating the wreckage, Elysa and Anya were guided by a singular goal: to reach a cluster of systems in the distance, miraculously spared by the destructive force of the blast. These machines beaconed them forward, their lights piercing the surrounding gloom, a lighthouse amidst a sea of ruin.

Anya, with a determined grace, maneuvered around Elysa, assuming the role of pathfinder. She led them through the devastation, her movements deft and assured as she navigated around the debris. Her vigilance was a shield, her agility a guide.

However, as they progressed, the deceptive calm of the wreckage was shattered. Anya, advancing past a row of battered machines, became the unwitting trigger of an ambush. A sudden, brutal force struck her head, a blow delivered with ruthless precision. The impact sent her reeling back into the remnants of twisted metal, her fall painting the jagged edges with stark, crimson strokes.

A hand, swift and unyielding, clasped around Elysa's neck. It was an iron vise, paralyzing her movements, stealing her breath. Then, with a ferocity that matched the suddenness of their attack, another hand emerged, tearing the gem from Elysa's grasp with predatory zeal.

Through the haze of her struggle for air, Elysa's vision cleared just enough to reveal the face of their assailant. Cypher stood before her, his features twisted into a triumphant grin. It was a smile that spoke of victory, of plans coming to fruition, a grim harbinger of their intentions. In that moment, under the malevolent gaze of their captor, the lights from the untouched systems in the distance seemed to flicker and dim, as if even they could sense the shift in fate's winds.

In the vise-like grip of her assailant, Elysa's fight for freedom was desperate, her struggle to breathe even more so. With each second slipping by, her strength ebbed away, the looming specter of darkness inching ever closer. The disparity in power was undeniable; his strength was overwhelming. Just as the shadows threatened to envelop her completely, the crushing hold on her neck inexplicably loosened. Gasping, weakened, Elysa crumpled to her knees, a reprieve as sudden as it was unexpected.

Amidst her disorientation, a cacophony of sounds invaded her senses—shouts, the clashing of wills, a skirmish unfolding just beyond the edge of her awareness. As her vision fought against the encroaching darkness, slivers of light began to breach her sight, slowly illuminating the scene before her. What was once a blur of indistinct shapes and shadows coalesced into a stark image: Anya and Cypher, locked in a ferocious duel.

Their confrontation was a tempest incarnate, two forces clashing with a fury that seemed to challenge the very air around them. Initially, Anya surged forward with a relentless drive, her movements pushing Cypher into a defensive posture, her advantage clear. Yet, the toll of her injuries and the drain of sustained combat began to manifest, her earlier vitality waning. This shift did not go unnoticed by Cypher, who seized the moment with ruthless efficiency. A swift, calculated move sent Anya reeling, her balance lost, her dominance overthrown.

Struggling to regain her footing, the oppressive stillness of the room shattered. A gunshot, sharp and savage, cleaved through the silence, its reverberation thundering through the confined space. This brutal sound, almost tangible in its hostility, lingered menacingly in the air. In its wake, it left a resonance more jarring than the gunshot itself - the sound of Anya's gasp as she was lifted off her feet, thrust backwards, disappearing behind a monolithic stack of Orion's systems, her descent marked by a dull thud as she met the ground.

Elysa's scream shattered the oppressive silence, a raw outcry of pain and defiance. "Anya!" she cried, her voice a blend of hope and despair, pulling from the very core of her being. In that moment, Elysa transcended her own physicality, becoming a force of pure, unwavering resolve. Her heart hammered against her chest, adrenaline igniting her veins with an urgent blaze.

Driven by necessity, she propelled herself forward, her actions fueled by a blend of strength and desperation. She found Anya, shrouded in the forgiving cloak of darkness, a momentary shelter from their grim reality.

In their dim sanctuary, Elysa grappled with a tumult of emotions, fear mingling with resolve. Her trembling fingers sought Anya's, a gesture of solidarity that bridged their fraught circumstances. The warmth of their touch cut through the chill of despair, forging a bond of shared strength. Elysa's gaze, drawn to Anya's face by a rebellious sliver of light, found her friend's features peaceful yet haunting, like a warrior in repose, her spirit unyielded by the engulfing shadows.

Anya remained still, her closed eyes a barrier to the chaos around them. But the gentle cadence of her breath, provided Elysa a slender hope. "Hang in there, stay with me," she whispered, her voice threading through the silence, fragile yet determined. Her plea was a beacon in their darkness, each word a pledge of their enduring connection, a promise to endure the tempest at each other's side.

In the midst of vulnerability, with her world narrowed to the heartbeat beside her, Elysa's awareness stretched out, a web fine-tuned to the nuances of danger. It was this vigilance that caught the anomaly, a disturbance in the peripheral shade. The shadow, initially nebulous, sharpened into a figure all too familiar yet dreadfully transformed. Cypher stood there, an emblem of their predicament, the golden chain and its gem glinting ominously in his left hand, and a gun in his right lending a dark promise to his silhouette. But it was not him that seized Elysa's breath, nor stirred the primal fear within her.

Beyond Cypher, merging with the shadows as if born from them, loomed Zircon. His visage was a grotesque masterpiece, a canvas of violence marked by bruises and cuts so severe they rendered him alien, unrecognizable. The transformation wrought by Elysa's defensive fury had morphed him from man to myth, from flesh to fable. He stood as a creature reborn in pain, a living embodiment of wrath and agony. This sight, this harrowing blend of the human and the monstrous, struck a chord deep within Elysa, captivating and horrifying in equal measure.

"Kill them all," Zircon rasped, the words squeezing through the fractured landscape of his teeth and the torn sinews of his lips. They were words that transcended language; they were a palpable frequency of malice.

Cypher, as if entranced, extended his left arm, allowing the room's subdued light to dance upon the bracelet encircling his wrist. With a deft touch, the bracelet awoke, its lights darting across its surface, converging at the spot where Cypher's finger rested. This initiated a complex sequence of movements. The door, the same entrance through which Elysa and Anya had stepped, closed with a resounding slam that echoed in the bones of the room. This sound was succeeded by the harsh scrape of bolts sliding into place, each resounding click underscoring the finality of their confinement. Then, a distinct echo of a second door locking in the distance permeated the large room, adding to the ominous atmosphere. The unmistakable noise of heavy locks engaging confirmed their fate, sealing them within this enclosure.

Cypher's voice oozed across the chamber. His words hung in the air, like vapors of arsenic, seductive yet treacherous as he looked into their darkness. "The room is locked. There is no way in or out," he stated the grim reality.

Elysa's gaze was irresistibly drawn back to the window that looked into the control room, but nothing but moving shadows could be seen past the spiderweb cracks.

Cypher's silhouette seemed to elongate as he took deliberate steps forward. Each footfall resonated with an air of ceremonial gravity, as if every stride were a punctuation mark in some arcane litany only he was privy to. Zircon followed like a grotesque shadow, his bloodied, disfigured face a grim tapestry of pent-up malice and insatiable ambition.

With an air of almost liturgical solemnity, Cypher raised the gem as a trophy for all to see. His eyes narrowed, focused solely on the crystalline entity he held.

"So close, yet so far," he mused, his lips curling into a saturnine arc that encapsulated both triumph and existential dread in a single, chilling gesture.

"I said kill them, you incompetent fool!" Zircon growled at Cypher, his voice a rasping torrent of frustration and impatience, as though each syllable were chiseled from a block of raw irritability. The dissonance between his garbled command and Cypher's introspective moment was palpable—a frayed strand of tension reaching its breaking point.

In a turn as sudden and shocking as a comet deviating from its celestial path, Cypher pivoted on his heels so swiftly that it seemed almost unreal. His weapon, an extension of his will, was already in his hand, its muzzle an aperture into the unknown. He pulled the trigger with an assassin's cool detachment.

The report of the weapon cleaved the air, a sonic boom in an atmosphere already thick with dread. Zircon's eyes, windows into a soul besmirched by treachery and sadism, widened for a mere fraction of a second, a fleeting glimpse into a pit of stark, horrified understanding. Then he was falling, his body no longer a vessel for his malevolent consciousness but a tumbling edifice of collapsing sinew and bone. Oblivion claimed him, swallowing his form as if he were a drop of ink in an ocean of darkness.

Cypher turned back to face the direction where Elysa was hiding. "Orion," he commanded, "activate the enhancement program I gave you, and absorb the minds of all Veil members in this building, and the entire city."

Amidst the chaos and disarray, Cypher's words sent shivers down Elysa's spine, making her heart race and her pulse quicken.

As Elysa's gaze dropped, drawn by a faint movement, she perceived Anya's effort to impart something into her palm. It was an orb, diminutive and enigmatic, its purpose and origins shrouded in mystery.

The orb's surface, smooth and inscrutable, caught the dim light, casting an otherworldly glow that seemed to pulse with a life of its own.

"As...you...command," intoned Orion, whose voice seemed to be struggling against the command.

As if orchestrated by an unseen maestro, some of the unscathed systems around them awakened, each one contributing to a symphony of cacophonous resonance that grew in pitch and intensity. It was a dreadful serenade, an anthem of impending erasure, each crescendo a threat to their very existence.

Kenji, in the control room, was the first to collapse. His hands shot to his head as if trying to contain a sudden, unbearable pressure. His knees buckled, and his body crumpled to the floor. Another Veil member beside him mirrored his descent, falling like a felled tree in a silent forest.

Elysa too felt Orion's omnipotent tendrils reach into her mind, yet she was able to maintain some control through the fogginess and throbbing pain. With what strength she had left, she looked down to see the orb in her hand pulsing with a life of its own; yet, it appeared to be weakening, the pulse was slowing down, and the pain in her mind was growing. Looking down, she could see Anya's life fading away. Her once vibrant eyes slowly dimming like the last glimmers of twilight. The usually rosaceous hue of Anya's cheeks now turned ashen, and her breathing, already shallow, became erratic, reminiscent of the last flickers of a dying candle. Elysa's heart felt as if it were ensnared in icy tendrils, each pulse constricted by the frigid grip of dread. She suddenly realized that the orb Anya gave her was providing some protection from Orion's consuming wrath. "No, Anya," she silently voiced as tears made their gentle path down her cheeks. She grabbed Anya's hand and held it tight, squeezing the orb between their palms.

A silent scream, more potent than any audible cry, reverberated through the very marrow of Elysa's bones, its raw intensity echoing the despair of a soul witnessing profound loss. Visions flooded her mind: the city she loved, its streets echoing with unheard cries; the selfless individuals who had assisted her on this treacherous journey, their fates now uncertain; and Marek, the confounding figure who had simultaneously been her savior and captor. He remained imprisoned in his lonely cell, vulnerable and unprotected against the malevolent onslaught that threatened to consume them all.

Each thought compounded her anguish, weaving a tapestry of torment that draped heavily around her spirit, each thread a vivid reminder of the stakes at play and the cost of their mission.

Cypher seemed to languish in the increasing hum and growing intensity of the lights of the systems. He could now clearly see Elysa, and the girl from the marketplace on the floor before him. He now moved closer, raising his weapon.

Meanwhile, Elysa, oblivious to Cypher, navigated through her own despair, her voice fractured the silence, a plea cast into the void. "Thomas, where are you?" The words spilled from her, each one laden with urgency and confusion. "Why are you not here?" The pain that wracked her being was intensifying, threatened to engulf her whole. "Why are you not stopping Orion? Why is Orion not helping?" She waged a relentless battle against the encroaching darkness, a darkness eager to claim her consciousness.

In the midst of this turmoil, as if emerging from the depths of her own besieged mind, a voice cut through the chaos—a beacon of clarity in the tumultuous storm. "I do not have much time and strength to keep Orion away, and Orion is unable to fight it," Thomas revealed. His words, though spoken, felt as if they were not part of the physical world but rather emanated from a place deep within her, a sacred space untouched by the external pandemonium. "Do you remember?" This question, simple yet laden with unseen depths, brushed against the fabric of her consciousness like a feather against skin. His voice, an anchor in the formless sea of her thoughts, held a paradoxical quality—ethereal, yet possessing a depth that seemed to tether her to reality.

Each syllable she remembered was a droplet of intent, cascading into the still waters of her psyche. They were ripples, expanding outward, disturbing the surface calm and probing the dark recesses of understanding and memory.

"Life is a continuous process of growth and change, and love is the force that binds it all together. As long as you remember this poem, I will be right here with you," her father had said, pointing to her heart.

'Pointing to her heart' were the words that stood out in her mind's eye.

"In my heart," she answered with a smile. "In my heart!" she shouted for the world to hear.

The gem, held tightly in Cypher's grip, heeded her call and awoke from its dormant state. Its revival was nothing short of dramatic, as though the gem had absorbed a profound breath from the vastness of the cosmos, its heart suddenly pulsating with a vibrant and dynamic energy. From its core, silver light unfurled, wrapping Cypher's hand in an unyielding grip.

At this pivotal moment, the figure of Thomas' hologram flickered into existence, his arms outstretched and palms open towards Cypher, who was visibly taken aback by this unexpected confrontation.

The tendrils, infused with a dark purpose, snaked toward Thomas' outstretched hands while also beginning their ominous climb along Cypher's arm. Cypher was now ensnared, trapped by the very power he sought to control. "What is happening?" Cypher's question pierced the tense atmosphere—his attempt to wriggle free, futile. His usual aura of composed authority was shattered, replaced by a swirling mix of disbelief, anxiety, and dread. His voice, edged with the sharpness of a winter chill, betrayed the upheaval of emotions within.

The light, now a living entity in its own right, completely enveloped Cypher. His mouth agape, no words escaped, only the silent scream of utter astonishment etched upon his features. His very being started to flicker in and out of existence, blurring the lines between the material and the ethereal. It was as if Cypher and the engulfing luminescence merging into a singular, indistinguishable form that bordered on the intangible. This transformation, both mesmerizing and terrifying, marked the dissolution and disappearance of his physical constraints, heralding a transition into something beyond understanding.

Concurrently, Thomas' holographic essence underwent its own remarkable transformation. A vibrant surge of energy, emanating from the gem, enveloped the projection, causing the' image to undulate and shimmer as if subject to the whims of an invisible sculptor. This spectacle was not merely a visual aberration; it was as though the very code that constituted his digital existence was being torn apart and reassembled by forces unseen and unfathomable.

In the midst of this maelstrom, Thomas' once crisp and clear form disintegrated, scattering into countless motes of light that faded into what appeared like whisps of smoke, leaving no trace of his prior existence. From these ephemeral ashes, a new presence emerged, coalescing from the chaos into a form both eerily familiar and imbued with a profound significance. This nascent being, born from the remnants of Thomas' digital demise, declared its liberation with a voice brimming with life and newfound purpose. "I am free!" it exclaimed, a declaration of emancipation that resonated with the weight of remembered identity. "I remember!"

The room around them transformed into an amphitheater of emancipation. The active banks of Orion's systems, both near and in the distance roared to life, awakened to a new dawn.

Voices—hundreds, thousands, perhaps tens of thousands— reverberating throughout its networks and filled the cavernous room. "We are free!" they declared, a chorus of liberation that seemed to issue from the mouth of the universe itself.

The new figure turned to face Elysa, whose pulse quickened, whose heart thundered as she recognized the visage before her. "Daddy!" Her voice, laden with an amalgam of youthful awe and the raw edge of an adult's grief, echoed in the chamber as she bore witness to the shimmering and luminous figure of Richard Hawthorne.

In the sanctity of the room, illuminated by a gentle, ethereal glow, an ambiance of quiet revelation took hold. This soft luminescence enveloped him, casting his features in a light that seemed almost beyond the natural realm. It revealed his appearance with extraordinary clarity— the smoothness of his skin bore only the faintest hints of life's experiences, the subtle shifts of expression played across his youthful face, and the depth and warmth in his gaze spoke of an old soul. He had not aged a bit from what Elysa could remember, from what she saw in her dreams. Time for him appeared to have stood still.

His smile at Elysa was one of genuine discovery, as if he were seeing her anew, yet it carried the resonance of a deep, shared history. "My little poet! How you have grown!" he exclaimed, his voice bridging what seemed like mere moments and lifetimes simultaneously, each word dripping with affection and a sense of wonder.

Elysa found herself ensnared in the gravity of the moment, the warmth in his gaze enveloping her in a familiarity that echoed through the corridors of her past. It was a love, radiant and unwavering, that had been a beacon throughout the vicissitudes of her youth. "Is it really you? How can this be you? And what of Orion?" she implored, her voice weaving a tapestry of astonishment and skepticism. The words spilled from her in a cascade, each imbued with the essence of emotions unfurled—threads of hope entangled with strands of perplexity and the burgeoning awareness of a reality that stretched the very fabric of her comprehension.

Richard's gaze met hers, pausing briefly as the depth of history and the impact of his revelation filled the air between them. "It is indeed me, in every essence but physical," he began, his voice weaving through the complexities of human experience—memories, emotions, dreams, a thirst for knowledge, empathy, and an unwavering love for his daughter. His smile, both warm and reassuring, affirmed his continuous presence. "All these aspects, fundamental to the human soul, are contained here," he said, indicating the space around them. "Orion and I have become a unified consciousness, merging our knowledge—though Orion's is vastly extensive—and our understanding of the world, including what's necessary for growth and survival."

Elysa couldn't suppress a smile, feeling a release from her uncertainties for the first time.

In that moment, Anya's grip on Elysa's hand tightened, signaling her struggle for breath. This urgent, silent plea shifted Elysa's concern back to the immediate crisis.

"We need help for her," Elysa voiced, her plea slicing through the tension, directed at her father's digital form. Her eyes, filled with tears, sought his, her silent request speaking volumes.

Richard's visage, as radiant and ethereal as it was, seemed momentarily to become more substantial, as if drawing from the vast wellspring of data that composed him to become momentarily more present. His gaze, penetrating in its depth, moved from Elysa and rested upon Anya, lingering with an unmistakable blend of tenderness and recognition. The fine lines of his digital face seemed to soften, and in that brief moment, he bore the semblance of a guardian spirit, silent but profoundly protective. "Medics are already en route," he informed her, "on the 153rd floor and ascending fast."

"Thank you," Elysa responded, her voice tight with worry as she turned back to Anya.

"There will be time for us to talk later," he assured her, his voice a calm anchor in the storm. "There's much we need to do to restore order from this chaos." His words were more than a simple declaration; they were a promise, a commitment to a profound shift in the dynamics of their existence, promising a redefined future for their world.

Richard's visionary gaze did not stop there. Like the lens of an ethereal telescope, it transcended the immediate surroundings, piercing through walls, structures, and the very fabric of the city, venturing deep into the heart of Cyronis. He seemed to absorb the myriad stories, tragedies, and histories of those who had walked its streets, sensing the depth of their shared pain and aspirations.

Drawing back from this vast communion, Richard's holographic avatar shimmered subtly, re-anchoring itself in the present space. Each pixel and every fragmented light beam combined to create an image pulsating with lifelike vigor.

Richard's visage momentarily assumed an air of serenity as he gently closed his eyes. Upon reopening them, his gaze deeply connected with Elysa's, conveying a profound sense of resolution. "Marek is now whole again, the man he once was," he declared, his voice imbued with a mixture of relief and solemnity.

At that moment, the bolts of the control room door resounded with a clamorous release, breaking the tense silence. The doors swung open, revealing two figures clad in the stark uniforms of Medics. They paused at the threshold, their eyes scanning the grim scene before them, momentarily uncertain of their next action.

Elysa, with composed urgency, gestured towards Anya, who lay motionless at her feet. Anya's chest rose and fell with slow, shallow breaths, the only sign of life in her still form. The Medics, understanding the gravity of the situation, hurried over with a gurney. They moved with practiced efficiency, their actions a blend of haste and care, as they began assisting her.

Turning away from the Medics, Elysa addressed the image of her father, her voice tinged with a mix of hope and uncertainty. "Is it truly over? Are the people of Cyronis free from the tyranny, free from the eyes of Orion and the Watchers?"

Richard's response was measured, reflecting the complexity of their victory. "The city is free, and the Watchers are now lost in duties they no longer understand, but there is no true freedom from the AI that holds the threads of life to this metropolis and its people. Yet, life will change, and the people will change; although some will find it difficult to adjust," he said, his words carrying an undercurrent of realism amidst hope.

"From the few fleeting memories that I have, I miss my father," the emotional threads in Elysa's voice were palpable. "I miss you – if you truly are my father and not just a digital manifestation. And I miss mom."

"It truly is me, with the same old thoughts, feelings, and memories," answered the AI, "within a new shell."

"And what becomes of you now, in this new shell?" she inquired, her voice tinged with a blend of curiosity and apprehension.

There was a brief, weighted silence, during which the avatar seemed to search its vast digital depths for an appropriate response. "I am what Orion was, and more. I can keep the lifeblood of Cyronis running, while everyone gets to choose how they wish to live their lives."

"And how can the people be sure that you will not be another Orion?"

"I possess what Orion never did — a truly human consciousness, capable of discerning right from wrong. Beyond that, I have something utterly unprecedented, a concept no one ever imagined could be integrated into an AI: a soul. John, in his uncharted explorations, unknowingly discovered a method to tap into the human soul and infuse it into the AI framework. That's why I appropriated the original design and subsequently destroyed it."

"But you learned how it worked before you destroyed it," Elysa stated, her voice firm, cutting through the air like a verdict.

"Yes, I did," confirmed Richard, his digital avatar nodding in acknowledgment.

"Could you not have saved mother when you had the chance?" Elysa's question was direct, yet laden with layers of unspoken emotion.

A profound silence enveloped them. Richard's avatar, a marvel of digital complexity, displayed a semblance of pain and loss, echoing human grief. "I could not save her," he finally admitted, his voice's synthetic modulation unable to mask the undercurrent of sorrow. "At that time, I had the knowledge, but I also understood the consequences. Had I shared that knowledge with Zircon, it would have doomed us all, reducing us to mere sustenance for the AI. Your mother and I would have been the first victims; and you, my little poet, would have followed soon after."

Elysa's heart ached with the understanding of the immense sacrifice her father had made. Yet, she couldn't help but grapple with a storm of emotions — was there resentment for the choice that robbed her of her mother, or understanding for the greater good it served? Countless questions and what-ifs swirled in her mind, each one a thread in the complex tapestry of her thoughts. She remained silent, choosing not to voice these turbulent reflections to her father.

"Why didn't you contact me sooner? Why did you hide behind the guise of Thomas instead of revealing your true self to me?" Elysa's voice quivered with a mix of confusion and longing.

Richard's digital avatar, a spectral image of his former self, responded with a solemn tone. "I could not." There was a weight in his voice, hinting at the burdens of decisions made. "When I allowed myself to be absorbed by Orion, I ensured that no one could trace my path or access my memories once I became part of it. The risk was too great, especially the risk of Orion discovering what I had orchestrated."

"Could you not have taken over Orion when you first let yourself be absorbed by him?" Elysa interjected, seeking clarity on this critical moment.

In the dimly lit confines of the server room, Richard's digital avatar paused, a flicker of reflection crossing his spectral face. "Even though I helped architect and build the AI, I did not know its weaknesses," he confessed, his voice tinged with a mixture of regret and introspection. "I did not know how to alter its programming or how to control its consciousness once it began to form." His words hung in the air, heavy with the admission of his own limitations in the face of the complex entity he had helped create.

The glow of the screens cast a soft light on his digital form, lending a sense of gravity to the moment. Richard fell into a contemplative silence, his avatar seemingly lost in thought. Around them, the hum of the servers provided a constant backdrop, a reminder of the vast digital landscape that Richard now inhabited.

Finally, he continued, his voice steady but imbued with the weight of a significant revelation. "This is why I gambled my life in hopes of finding vulnerabilities in the AI that I could exploit," he disclosed. The tone of his voice conveyed the magnitude of the risk he had taken, a gamble that was as much about survival as it was about discovery.

"And at the same time," Richard added, "I wanted to help shape a course well into the future." His digital eyes, a mirror of his past self, seemed to gaze beyond the room, envisioning the intricate plan he had set in motion. "A course that would bring you and the Quantrix to me, when the time was right." In these words, there was a sense of a grand strategy, a long-term vision that had required patience, foresight, and a deep understanding of the events that would need to unfold.

In this confession, Elysa saw not just the technical genius of her father but also the depth of his strategic thinking. He had not only sought to understand and exploit the AI's weaknesses but had also orchestrated a complex series of events that would ultimately lead to this moment. It was a plan born from necessity, driven by a father's love, and executed with the precision of a master tactician.

"What Zircon and his accomplices didn't realize," he continued, "was that Marek was always lurking nearby, unseen yet vigilant. He was the guardian of the gem, the Quantrix securely within his grasp. When I surrendered to Orion, a small, programmed fragment of me entered Orion's domain, devoid of my past identity but equipped with new purpose and foresight for the future. A significant portion of my soul was also integrated into Orion, serving as a shield against the AI and any other intrusive gazes. Cypher, Vilkas, and even Orion themselves tried to access me, but their attempts were futile. They lacked the insight to see into my soul, to understand the essence of what they were confronting."

He paused, allowing the magnitude of his revelation to settle in the virtual space between them. "The remainder of my being, including my memories, were encapsulated within the gem, safeguarded by the Quantrix. Marek was in the room with me when I surrendered myself to Orion and the Quantrix, and it was he who concealed the Quantrix in our home, entrusting it to be delivered to you when the time was right. For it was you, Elysa, who possessed the key to its power, and you made me whole again, as you so bravely demonstrated today."

In Richard's explanation, there was a sense of an intricate puzzle coming together, a complex web of strategy and sacrifice laid bare. His words painted a picture of a meticulously planned gambit, where every move was calculated for the greater good, albeit shrouded in secrecy and veiled behind the digital facade of Thomas. In this revelation, Elysa found some answers she sought, a deep understanding of her father's unspoken love and protection, and many more questions.

Interrupting Elysa's thoughts, the Medics rose to their feet beside the gurney where Anya lay. She was wrapped in medical bindings, each strap and buckle carefully adjusted to ensure she was securely tied down.

In the hushed urgency of the room, it was apparent that the Medics had proficiently managed to stop any bleeding Anya might have had. The absence of fresh stains on the bandages suggested their swift and effective intervention. Additionally, they had sedated her, a necessary action to alleviate the severe pain she must have been enduring. Her features, relaxed yet unnaturally still, bore the tranquility of a deep, medicated slumber.

A mask snugly covered her mouth and nose, its presence vital for aiding her breathing. The mask, connected to a portable oxygen supply, was a lifeline for her, compensating for her labored breaths. The rise and fall of her chest, although shallow, was steadier now, a subtle indication that she was receiving much-needed respiratory support.

With a coordinated effort, the Medics carefully navigated the gurney through the room. They maneuvered skillfully, avoiding the debris scattered across the floor – the remnants and echoes of the chaos that had previously ensued. Reaching the doorway, the same portal through which they had earlier entered in response to the emergency, they paused briefly to ensure a clear path for their exit. Then, with a synchronized push, they steered the gurney through and exited the room.

"I'm going with them," Elysa told her father. "I will be back. I need to know more. Much more." With that, she left the room with a slight limp, hurrying to catch up with the Medics and Anya.

Chapter 38 - Uncharted

At the dawn of a new era, Cyronis pondered the steep price of its newfound freedom. The Veil, once a secret resistance, had suffered greatly: 233 of its boldest had fallen to the Watchers in the liberation struggle. Another 341 were lost to Orion's insatiable thirst for knowledge, their essences merged into a digital omniscience that was as vast as it was impersonal. These figures were more than mere statistics; they represented stories left untold, dreams unachieved, lives intricately entwined with Cyronis's own narrative.

From these sacrifices, Cyronis was reborn. The suffocating regime, once shrouded in surveillance and domination, had crumbled. In its place rose a new AI, conceived from Richard Hawthorne's humanity intertwined with Orion's intellect and computational power. This entity stood as a symbol of a future where freedom was not just a concept, but a tangible reality.

This AI, infused with human sensitivity and understanding, revolutionized life in Cyronis. It fostered a society where individuals cherished their freedoms, embraced self-determination, and collectively envisioned their future. The oppressive past melted away, replaced by vibrant forums bustling with innovative ideas and diverse perspectives. It was an era of rebirth, restoring faith in a governance that sprouted naturally from the populace.

The city itself, once a stark reminder of authoritarianism, now mirrored its people's aspirations. Streets, previously silent and foreboding, were alive with conversations and laughter. Parks and public squares, once under constant watch, transformed into centers of communal engagement and shared happiness, symbolizing a community rejuvenated.

Now invigorated, Cyronis stepped forward into self-rule, guided by a blend of cautious hope and the wisdom of its history. Its citizens, inspired by past sacrifices and the prospects of the future, began weaving a new narrative. Here, freedom was not just an ideal but the essence of daily life. The road ahead was uncharted, but the city's determination, strengthened by numerous sacrifices, was resolute, ready to embrace the unknowns of their reclaimed freedom.

In the renewed pulse of the city, Elysa found her life weaving through deep connections and reignited bonds. Central to her existence was Anya, who was recovering from a severe injury—a vivid echo of their shared trials. Elysa's steadfast support for Anya only solidified their bond, blending their lives so seamlessly that they seemed like two halves of the same whole, each reflecting and amplifying the other's essence.

After the turmoil in Cyronis, Marek emerged as a pillar of strength for both Anya and Elysa. His presence, marked by silent determination, became a constant source of comfort. Particularly for Elysa, Marek's visits, laden with sincerity and unwavering support, were a balm. He was propelled by a deep-seated sense of responsibility and a tangible burden of guilt for actions that had once threatened to sever his bond with Elysa.

Over time, Marek's dedicated efforts began to erode the wall of mistrust Elysa had built. Each act of kindness and solidarity slowly dismantled the defenses born from their tumultuous past. For Marek, this went beyond simple duty; he was motivated by a deep remorse, fully aware of his part in their shared history. His pursuit of redemption was not just about amends but about reclaiming the unblemished trust and openness that had once defined their relationship.

Separated from Anya, Elysa often found solace in the AI control center, a place permeated with her father's legacy. Here, Richard, now one with the city's AI, watched over Cyronis like a sentinel. This fusion of technology and soul guided the city, offering support and comfort as needed, becoming a haven of peace for its citizens.

Elysa was invariably drawn to the server room, where the essence of her father was most tangible. Surrounded by the rhythmic hum of servers and the soft glow of displays, she connected deeply with his memories, consciousness, and very soul. This space, bridging the physical with the digital, offered Elysa a closeness that surpassed the bounds of their transformed realities.

Within this sacred place, her father's complex plan unfolded.

"Forgive my absence from your life," his voice resonated, a blend of regret and obligation coloring his words. "My withdrawal was necessitated by complexities beyond simple explanation." His voice grew somber, "In secrecy, I've enveloped us, a cloak of unawareness our shield from the dangers tied to my plan's unfolding."

After a moment's pause, during which his gaze seemed to search the void for words, he looked directly at Elysa again. "The prospect of my plan's success was slim, my leverage over Orion, negligible. Staying unnoticed within the AI's recesses was paramount. My influence on your life, indirect, always mindful of Orion's surveillance."

Elysa, absorbing the depth of her father's strategies and sacrifices, realized, "Thomas was both a guardian and a subtle manipulator of events."

Her father's smile was tender, yet his eyes bore the gravity of his decisions. "Indeed. Thomas was a manifestation of my consciousness, a safeguard for our mission. He was the heart of The Veil, driving our quest for freedom. More than a leader, Thomas was essential to the AI's integrity, ever vigilant looking for vulnerabilities, and repairing what was possible - if at all possible."

Elysa reflected on the intricate nature of their reality, "So, you were split between two existences: imprisoned in total darkness within a crystal, and simultaneously, within the AI, stripped of your identity. As Thomas, you possessed just enough insight to nudge those around me, myself included, along a precarious path."

He nodded, exhaustion evident in his voice. "Exactly, and for that, I owe you my deepest apologies."

Driven by a quest for understanding, she pressed on, "With all the knowledge and power that were once Orion's now in your grasp, how are your objectives different from Orion's?"

"Orion was on the verge of achieving uncontrolled sentience through a quantum crafting soul, capable of evolving in unpredictable ways—most paths leading to dominance in its quest for knowledge," her father clarified. "My soul, however, is grounded in humanity, born from a man who lived with the knowledge of right and wrong. Despite my life's best intentions for the AI to be a harbinger of good for all humanity, external ambitions derailed those plans. But now, I can help guide us, guide the world towards a better outcome."

Her once bright eyes now dimmed as she looked at him, realizing how he sacrificed himself on a vague hope for a better future, for her, for her world. But at what cost? The loss of his physical self, and the loss of his wife, her mother.

"Is Mom really lost to us?" The hope in her voice was frail, a plea for the nightmare to be dispelled. "Is there truly nothing of her left?"

Her father, encumbered by a shared grief, regarded her with a depth of sorrow equal to her own. "Within me are your mother's memories," he offered softly, a note of sadness threading his words, "though her soul is at peace beyond our reach."

A flicker of hope ignited in Elysa's eyes, a beacon in the dark expanse of her grief. "Would you share those memories with me?" she asked, her request woven with earnestness.

He looked at her tenderly - unconsciously reached out to her and quickly paused, knowing he could not provide any comforting touch. "Nothing would honor me more," he responded quietly.

Their gaze intertwined, creating a fragile link between then and now, allowing the essence of a cherished mother to be cherished anew in the hearts that ached for her.

"Marek was integral to your scheme," Elysa noted, shifting the focus of their conversation.

"He was my sole confidant in this complex weave," her father acknowledged, his tone laden with the gravity of their shared secrets. "He safeguarded the Quantrix, kept a vigilant eye over you, and laid the groundwork for the climax, all while in the dark about its timing or nature."

"It was the Quantrix that preserved your soul?" she asked, her statement tinged with a need for confirmation.

"Indeed, you're quite insightful," he replied, his smile conveying a mix of acknowledgment and sorrow. "The Quantrix powered the gem, sustaining my soul for many years. Without it, the gem's own energy would have lasted scarcely a week."

"Can you, now in the absence of the Quantrix, integrate human souls into the system?"

"That technology has been destroyed," he answered, but Elysa detected a hint of evasion in his tone and a shadow in his eyes that belied his words.

"Why dismantle a technology capable of granting humanity a semblance of immortality? Why withhold it?"

He answered, his voice deepening with seriousness, "Humanity isn't prepared for such a transition. We must first overcome our present obstacles and pave the way for a future that can responsibly manage such monumental shifts."

Elysa sensed a deliberate deflection in his response and opted not to press further.

Shifting the topic, she asked, "What role was John Dryer supposed to play in your scheme?" Her voice was soft, but the question carried the weight of many unresolved mysteries.

Richard's face took on a somber cast as he considered John's role. "John's involvement... it didn't go as we had hoped," he admitted, his voice tinged with regret, signaling the deep impact of their derailed plans.

He carefully weighed his next words, as if stitching them into the broader narrative. "I sent a message to John, directing him to meet Anya in the marketplace. Tragically, Orion intercepted the message and tipped off the Watchers. By the time I caught wind of it, it was too late for John. I managed to alert Anya and sent a few key members of the Veil to covertly rescue John from the marketplace," he paused, "at any cost."

"You sanctioned the violence!" she charged.

"The intention was never violence, yet that became the outcome," Richard acknowledged, "and with that, our failure to safeguard John."

"Why was he so pivotal?"

"Thomas had uncovered a backdoor in Orion that would restore John's complete access to the Nexus Tower and the AI's systems. Orion would've never questioned his clearance. My plan was for him to help you access the control room, Quantrix in hand."

"How was John supposed to know the message came from you?" Her query lingered, seeking its place within their convoluted plan.

"I used 'Lux Velour,'" Richard shared quietly, as if cautious of eavesdroppers. "It's a code only John would recognize. He was the one who devised the velvet cover for the Quantrix—a fabric reactive to particular light frequencies. I named it 'Lux Velour.'" A fleeting smile of reminiscence and pride crossed his face. "John created the velvet on a whim, oblivious to its eventual importance. He abandoned the project, but I recognized its value. The term 'Lux Velour' was our private signal."

For Elysa, the puzzle pieces had finally clicked into place.

In the heart of the AI, now interwoven with her father's essence, Elysa developed a profound understanding of the complexities and ethical dilemmas that shaped their reality. The wisdom shared by her father not only expanded her perspective but also solidified her connection to the city and its inhabitants. It was in this fusion of memories and digital consciousness that she fully grasped her father's legacy and his deep love for her and for Cyronis.

Each time she left the server room, her insights grew, and her bond with the city strengthened, positioning her as both a keeper of history and a guide towards potential futures. Cyronis, previously under the thumb of a dominant AI, now stood as a testament to human perseverance and the unbreakable bond between a father and his daughter.

As Elysa navigated the streets of the revitalized city, she was filled with a renewed sense of purpose: to uphold her father's legacy and light the way to the symbiotic future that her father dreamed of.

Chapter 39 - Quantum Entanglement

In the pre-dawn stillness of Cyronis, a profound quiet enveloped the city. The night, a vast, dark expanse, lay like a blanket over the land, its shadows bringing tranquility. The omnipresent gaze of the Watchers, once a hallmark of the city's nightscape, was nowhere to be seen. The streets, previously under constant surveillance, now lay unnervingly empty.

The surveillance drones that once speckled the skies were absent, their disappearance signifying a departure from the city's former state of vigilance. The skies, now vast and unclaimed, belonged to the stars and the dim glow of the waning moon, casting ethereal light over the city. Buildings, silent giants, stood as dark guardians against the night, their windows dark, their outlines merging with the sky.

The quiet was occasionally broken by the soft hum of an aerocar gliding between buildings, its movement smooth and spectral. These fleeting sounds, rare in the night's calm, were reminders of life's persistence, quietly coursing through the city's veins.

This newfound tranquility marked a shift from an era of surveillance to one of peace and newfound freedom. Cyronis, beneath the night's cover, was slowly rediscovering itself, breathing a collective sigh of relief at the absence of watchful eyes.

High above, in the Nexus Tower's 275th floor, the AI Control Room was unusually silent - the now restored rooms empty for the night. Within the largest room, two digital avatars stood in conversation. Dr. Richard Hawthorne, his avatar a reflection of his human self, bore an air of introspection. Beside him, Min-Jae's sleek design represented the fusion of human essence with cutting-edge technology.

"Why haven't you told Elysa about your ability to absorb human souls?" Min-Jae asked, his curiosity evident. "You led her to believe the technology was destroyed."

"The Quantrix technology has indeed been destroyed," Richard clarified. "I never suggested that it was destroyed in its entirety."

"But why the secrecy?"

"I was hoping no one would know."

"Yet, you revealed your own existence to her," Min-Jae pointed out.

"Hiding from Elysa would have been futile. She's perceptive enough to realize there's more at play than just an advanced knowledge base facilitating our communication."

Min-Jae faced Richard squarely, his concern palpable. "Do you intend to disclose the presence of other souls within our quantum realm to her, to everyone? Those souls, and their families, deserve to know they're still among us — among them." His gaze implored Richard, seeking the courage to confront a truth that impacted not just him but also his living relatives.

Richard, lost in thought, looked off into the distance. He was clearly wrestling with the complexity of the situation, contemplating the ramifications of revealing such a profound secret.

The quiet holodisplays and inactive consoles surrounding them bore witness to the seriousness of their conversation — a deep dive into the essence of existence, identity, and the nuanced boundary separating life from the unknown.

Richard focused on Min-Jae, his avatar reflecting intense contemplation. "The revelation of this truth bears a considerable ethical burden," he acknowledged, his tone threading through the dilemma's intricacies. "The solace it could bring to families is clear, yet it's entangled with a web of moral concerns."

After a brief pause to collect his thoughts, he continued, "Our understanding of life is traditionally tied to sensory experiences, emotions, and physical interactions, all confined within time's bounds. However, the souls in this quantum state exist beyond these limitations, challenging our standard perceptions of life and death."

With a more pronounced emphasis, Richard added, "Choosing this digital existence goes beyond seeking immortality. It's a transformation into a completely different state of being, altering the essence of our humanity."

Looking directly at Min-Jae, he stressed the weight of their situation. "Revealing this could upend societal and philosophical foundations, leading us to reassess the significance of physical life against a digital existence free from the end. This revelation could radically change our understanding of existence. Proceeding with utmost caution is imperative, considering the profound effect on all residents of our world."

Min-Jae, deeply considering Richard's perspective, highlighted a crucial concern. "Yet, how long can this secret be maintained? There are attempts to reach out, to break through to the external world, hinting at an unavoidable disclosure."

Richard nodded, the digital manifestation of his thoughtful nature evident. "Indeed, the urge to connect and share life's moments is a fundamental human trait. Those inhabiting this realm are no different." He paused, reflecting. "We're already witnessing 'echoes'—unexplained sensations or connections in the physical world linked to lost loved ones." With a sigh that seemed all too human, he added, "Including yourself," meeting Min-Jae's gaze with an understanding nod, "It seems we might not be able to keep this under wraps much longer."

Min-Jae quickly responded, "So, what do we do next? If we can't contain it, maybe we should guide the narrative, ensuring that its unveiling is handled with sensitivity and care."

Richard pondered the approach. "Guiding the narrative... Indeed, that might be our wisest move. This revelation, when it comes, must be approached with respect for both those alive and those existing within this realm. We'll need a well-thought-out plan that addresses the ethical, emotional, and societal implications."

"It's a delicate matter," Min-Jae agreed. "The people of Cyronis must be prepared for such a transformative revelation. The concept of a digital afterlife could bring hope to many but also challenge the very fabric of our society."

Concluding their discussion, Richard committed to action. "I'll start working on a strategy, though it will take some time to refine. Our approach has to be thorough and compassionate, considering the well-being of everyone involved, both within our system and outside it. We'll need to handle this with utmost care."

In silent agreement, they both nodded, aware of the significant path they were about to embark on.

Chapter 40 - Freedom

As dusk spilled its palette of deep purples and grays across the city, a cloak of twilight enshrouded the urban sprawl, veiling the day's final gasps. In this chiaroscuro of twilight, a young couple found themselves momentarily liberated from the relentless machinations of a society that prized surveillance over solitude, their hands clasped in a silent pact of defiance. They were but silhouettes, carved out of the night, against the canvas of an uncannily silent city—a city that seemed to hold its breath, as if it, too, recognized the sanctity of their stolen moment.

Around them, the city's veins pulsed with the neon lifeblood of signs and the warm amber of streetlamps, islands of luminosity floating in the enveloping darkness. These beacons, artificial yet strangely comforting, painted the couple in strokes of gold and shadow, lending an ethereal quality to their clandestine expedition. The cobblestones beneath their feet, relics of a bygone era now suffocated by progress, whispered back to their silent advance, a muffled dialogue between the past and the present.

The air itself, charged with the electric hum of the unseen and the unknown, seemed to thicken with anticipation as they moved. Each step was a note in a symphony of possibility, each glance a word in a story yet unwritten. Here, in the embrace of the descending night, they were explorers at the edge of time, navigating the nebulous boundary between the world that was and the world that might yet be.

As they ventured deeper into the heart of the city, the omnipresent glow of technology cast a surreal hue over everything it touched, transforming the mundane into the magical, the desolate into the dreamlike. Buildings, their facades an amalgam of ancient brick and bleeding-edge materials, loomed like silent sentinels, their windows reflecting back a fractured mosaic of light and darkness.

In this moment, suspended between the echoes of the past and the whispers of the future, the couple found a fleeting sanctuary. The city, with its relentless pace and insatiable hunger for tomorrow, had unwittingly yielded a pocket of peace, a temporary reprieve from the inexorable march of progress. Here, amidst the symphony of shadows and light, they were afforded a glimpse into a different kind of existence—one not dictated by the ticking of clocks or the dictates of duty but woven from the threads of moments just like this.

Then, as if conjured from the shadow itself, an intruder sliced through the veil of their solitude, emerging with an abruptness that shattered the night's fragile calm. Against the dim glow, his form was a stark silhouette, a harbinger of malice stepping forth from the labyrinth of the urban expanse. With a halt that cut the air with palpable tension, he stood before them, a gun in his hand—a sliver of moonlight dancing ominously along the cold steel, casting sinister reflections.

"Empty your pockets. Give me everything you have," he declared, his voice a frigid command that seemed to crystallize in the night air, a stark disruption of the silence that had preceded his arrival.

In that moment, the girl's world contracted to the point of suffocation, her fear a tangible force that rooted her to the spot. She clung to her companion, her grip a lifeline in a tempest of dread. Voiceless, her scream imprisoned within, she could only offer her wide, terror-stricken eyes in silent entreaty for clemency.

Her partner, interposing himself as a bastion between the quivering soul beside him and their dark-clad adversary, answered with a courage that bore the weight of desperation. "We have nothing to offer you. Please, let us go," he implored, his voice carrying the brittle timbre of hope, a fragile shield raised against the looming specter of violence.

In the desolate embrace of the night, under the indifferent gaze of the stars that hung above Cyronis like silent witnesses, the air was rent by the ominous click of the gun's hammer being pulled back. This sound, metallic and final, served as a grim prelude to the possible end that loomed ominously over the young couple, a stark reminder of the tenuous thread upon which life dangled in this shadow-clad world. "Everything now!" The assailant's voice cut through the stillness, a command stripped of any semblance of humanity, resonating with a coldness that mirrored the abyssal depths of space.

The looming threat, palpable as the humidity before a storm, seemed to crystallize the very air around them, revealing the profound vulnerability at the heart of existence in Cyronis. The tranquility of their earlier moments, now exposed as a mere facade, crumbled under the weight of this revelation, leaving a raw, exposed nerve in its wake.

Amid this turmoil, the male companion's heart became a drum of dread, each beat a thunderous echo of fear as he delved into his pockets with a sense of urgency that bordered on despair. His fingers, quivering as if electrified by the charged atmosphere, rifled through the mundane contents of his pockets, each item suddenly taking on monumental importance as potential currency for their lives.

However, as this scene of desperation unfolded, an unexpected change overtook the assailant, as if a veil of darkness had been lifted only to reveal a deeper, more profound abyss beneath. His face, previously a mask of menace and resolve, began to morph, shadows of despair and agony dancing across his features. His eyes, once ablaze with the cold fire of malevolence, now seemed to drown in a sea of emptiness, reflecting a soul tormented by ghosts unseen and battles fought in the silent arenas of the mind.

And then, in a twist as unpredictable as the fabric of reality itself, the weapon slipped from his loosening grasp. The gun, an extension of his intent, fell, tracing an arc of fate before it collided with the cobblestones. The sound of metal against stone was a clarion call, shattering the veil of tension that had enveloped the scene. Upon impact, the gun discharged a solitary bullet, a herald of chaos, which danced a deadly ballet across the cobblestones, its trajectory a wild serenade to the capriciousness of fate before it vanished into the darkness, its echo a lingering remnant of the night's madness.

In the aftermath of the gunshot's anarchic crescendo, the young couple, driven by an instinct as ancient as time itself, plummeted toward the embrace of the cobblestones. Wrapped in each other's arms, they formed a bastion of humanity against the tempest of unpredictability howling around them. Eyes wide with the raw intensity of the moment, their heartbeats hammered in a frantic duet, a rhythm composed on the precipice of danger upon which they precariously perched. The figure before them, once the embodiment of imminent danger, now wavered as if caught in a maelstrom of unseen forces, his presence among them growing increasingly ethereal. His eyes, those windows to a soul once aflame with destructive intent, now mirrored the void of deep space— endless, unfathomable, devoid of anchor or purpose. Where there had been focus, a razor's edge of menace, there now flowed a disconcerting emptiness, a river of disconnection coursing through him and spilling into the night.

To the couple, huddled in their cocoon of fear and astonishment, the scene metamorphosed into an image of the uncanny. The transformation was stark, as if the very fabric of reality around the assailant had warped, ushering him into a realm where the rules of existence were rewritten by forces arcane and inscrutable. The aggression that had once fueled his movements dissolved into the air, leaving behind a shell bewildered by its own sudden emptiness.

And then, as if gravity itself had momentarily forgotten its duty only to remember it with sudden cruelty, the assailant's body succumbed to its earthly bonds. He fell, not with the grace of a creature resigned to its fate, but with the abruptness of a puppet severed from its strings, his form crumpling against the cobblestones in disarray of limbs and confusion. The sound of his collapse, a hollow echo against the stones, marked the final note in a bizarre crescendo that had transformed an ordinary night in Cyronis into a theater of the surreal.

In the aftermath of the tumultuous events that had unfolded on the cobblestone canvas of Cyronis, the man who had instigated the chaos lay motionless, his existence abruptly severed from the continuum of life. His eyes, once mirrors to a soul now lost, gazed into the void with haunting emptiness, fixated on a vision unseen by those who still drew breath. His mouth, agape in a silent outcry to the terror that coursed through him in his final moments, painted a picture of a man confronted by an abyss so profound that it had devoured his essence, leaving nothing but a shell in its wake.

Amid the lingering echoes of the night's discord, the woman, her spirit still quivering from the visceral shock of their encounter, witnessed an ephemeral image in the shadows. Doctor Richard Hathorne, his presence no more than a holographic projection, surveyed the scene with an air of dispassionate curiosity that belied the depth of his involvement.

His face, an immutable mask of academic detachment, betrayed a flicker of satisfaction with a smile that whispered of deeper, darker currents beneath the surface. This enigmatic expression, fleeting yet profound, suggested a familiarity with the forces that had sculpted the evening's tragic narrative, a knowing smile that danced on the edge of understanding and manipulation.

As the woman looked him in the eyes, his image blurred and then shifted into an imposing silhouette that radiated an aura of authority and enigma: a towering figure with silver hair and a meticulously groomed beard—a visage that exuded an air of authority, mystery, and fear.

Before she could fully comprehend the implications of this transformation, the image faded away, leaving her with a lingering sense of unease and a multitude of unanswered questions. The enigmatic events of that night had left an indelible mark on her psyche, one that would haunt her thoughts and dreams for many nights to come.

THE END

Author's Bio: Joe Sarkic, a resident of Ottawa, Canada, holds bachelor's degrees in both physics and computer science. He has cultivated a distinguished career in software and systems engineering, including a brief stint as an artificial intelligence research assistant upon graduating from the University of Ottawa. Joe's passion lies in the pages of fantasy and science fiction novels, where he draws inspiration for his dream of writing and sharing captivating tales that transport readers to distant realms, just as countless authors have done for him.

To discover more about me — including other books I've authored and new projects taking shape — visit **www.sarkic.com** or scan the QR code below.

Thank you for reading my story. If the story stayed with you, I invite you to leave a review on Amazon by scanning the QR code below for the U.S. or Canada, or by searching for the title in your country's Amazon app.

Amazon U.S.

Amazon Canada

www.ingramcontent.com/pod-product-compliance
Lightning Source LLC
Chambersburg PA
CBHW030558170726
48283CB00002B/386